PRAISE FOR
CHARLIE N. HOLMBERG

THE PAPER MAGICIAN

"Charlie is a vibrant writer with an excellent voice and great world building. I thoroughly enjoyed *The Paper Magician*."
—Brandon Sanderson, author of *Mistborn* and *The Way of Kings*

"Harry Potter fans will likely enjoy this story for its glimpses of another structured magical world, and fans of Erin Morgenstern's *The Night Circus* will enjoy the whimsical romance element . . . So if you're looking for a story with some unique magic, romantic gestures, and the inherent darkness that accompanies power all steeped in a yet to be fully explored magical world, then this could be your next read."
—Amanda Lowery, *Thinking Out Loud*

THE GLASS MAGICIAN

"I absolutely loved *The Glass Magician*. It exceeded my expectations, and I was very impressed with the level of conflict and complexity within each character. I will now sit twiddling my thumbs until the next one comes out."
—*The Figmentist*

"*The Glass Magician* will charm readers young and old alike."
—Radioactive Book Reviews

THE MASTER MAGICIAN

A Wall Street Journal *Bestseller*

"Utah author Charlie Holmberg delivers ... thrilling action and delicious romance in *The Master Magician*."

—*Deseret News*

THE PLASTIC MAGICIAN

"The everyday setting with just a touch of magical steampunk technology proves to readers what an incredible job Holmberg does with her world-building. Fans of previous Paper Magician books will love this addition to the world, and readers new to it will quickly fall in love with the magic-wielding characters."

—*Booklist*

THE FIFTH DOLL

Winner of the 2017 Whitney Award for Speculative Fiction

"*The Fifth Doll* is told in a charming, folklore-ish voice that's reminiscent of a good old-fashioned tale spun in front of the fireplace on a cold winter night. I particularly enjoyed the contrast of the small-town village atmosphere—full of simple townspeople with simple dreams and worries—set against the complex and eerie backdrop of the village that's not what it seems. The fact that there are motivations and forces shaping the lives of the villagers on a daily basis that they're completely unaware of adds layers and textures to the story and makes it a very interesting read."

—*San Francisco Book Review*

SMOKE &
SUMMONS

ALSO BY CHARLIE N. HOLMBERG

The Paper Magician Series

The Paper Magician

The Glass Magician

The Master Magician

The Plastic Magician

Other Novels

The Fifth Doll

Magic Bitter, Magic Sweet

Followed by Frost

SMOKE & SUMMONS

THE NUMINA SERIES

CHARLIE N. HOLMBERG

47NORTH

Text copyright © 2019 by Charlie N Holmberg LLC
All rights reserved.

Published by 47North, Seattle

www.apub.com

Amazon, the Amazon logo, and 47North are trademarks of Amazon.com, Inc., or its affiliates.

ISBN-13: 9781503905436 (hardcover)
ISBN-10: 1503905438 (hardcover)
ISBN-13: 9781503902435 (paperback)
ISBN-10: 1503902439 (paperback)

Cover design by Ellen Gould
Cover illustration by Marina Muun

Printed in the United States of America
First edition

*To my mom, who fostered both my creativity
and my craziness.*

Chapter 1

Sandis had several reasons for staying.

The food was good. Better than what her meager income had once afforded, and far better than anything she might scrounge off the streets. Better even than what she'd had back home, when her parents were still alive. The roof never leaked. The constant *drip, drip, drip* in the slavers' bunker had nearly driven her mad. She never had to do her own laundry, or her own mending. She got plenty of sleep, as factory shifts had long since been cut from her routine. Her bathwater was always warm.

There were other reasons, of course. If she was caught, she'd be punished, and Kazen's punishments were memorable. If she wasn't caught—and that was a big *if*—she'd probably starve on the streets until her corpse was thrown into one of the city's numerous trash heaps. Any work she was qualified to do wouldn't pay enough for her to get housing *and* food. She and Anon had always barely scraped by, and that was with them both pulling overnight shifts.

Sandis tried to focus on the first set of reasons as she poked at the broiled pig flank, cubed potatoes, and pickled apples on her plate. The food *was* better. *Focus on the food.*

Ignoring her own advice, she glanced at the pale ceiling above her and imagined the earth, cobblestone, and abandoned buildings above it. Sandis wasn't exactly sure how far down she was, only that it would take a long time to dig herself out, if she ever tried. Ever since she was brought here four years ago, the rest of the world had felt very far away.

"Sandis?"

The small voice came from Alys, who sat across from her. Fifteen years old, just a year older than Sandis had been when she met Kazen. Her brown eyes were Kolin, but her blonde hair didn't match that of any of the other vessels or the numerous grafters who lurked about Kazen's lair. Sandis wondered if she had a mixed heritage, but had not yet asked.

She put her finger to her lips, urging Alys to be quiet. Kazen liked his slaves to be quiet. Alys replied with a nearly imperceptible nod and returned to her food. *Good girl,* Sandis thought. Alys was already blending in nicely. She hadn't even gotten solitary yet. Sandis would make sure she never did.

The clunking of wood on wood drew her attention as Heath sat down beside her. He didn't look at her, simply set his plate in front of him and sat heavily on their shared bench. Wielding fork and knife, he cut his food with slow, deliberate movements. Unlike Alys, Heath looked like a true Kolin—dark eyes, dark hair, just like Sandis. Just like his brother, who sat at the end of the table, eating silently and staring straight ahead . . . except for when his eyes shifted to Kaili, beside him. Sandis wished they wouldn't sit together. Kazen hated any form of friendship among his vessels. Rist's eyes gave him away.

Beside her, Heath jolted. Peering through the curtain of her hair, cropped an inch above her shoulders, Sandis studied him, taking in the slight wrinkles between his eyebrows, his flared nostrils, the tautness of his shoulders. Something was bothering him, more so than usual. He was upset and trying not to look it.

Something dropped in the next room over. Heath flinched. Despite having been here longer than Sandis, he was always jumpy. He refocused on his meal, his brow and hand twitching as he speared a piece of pork.

He wanted to leave, too. Sandis was sure of it. Most of the vessels—Rist, Dar, Kaili—were complacent in their roles. Like they had forgotten their lives before their brands. Like they really did focus only on the food. But Heath . . . Could something have triggered that unspoken need for freedom? She couldn't ask, not here. Especially not with Zelna, rotund and covered in wrinkles, standing in the corner, washing dishes.

Then again, even *if* Sandis didn't have her reasons to stay . . . what would she go home to? A muted pang echoed in her chest at the thought of her younger brother. Four years since he'd vanished, and it still hurt like an open wound. She'd been searching for him when the slavers grabbed her. The day she'd learned the worst—that he was dead, not just missing—she'd become complacent, too.

Almost.

The door to the small dining hall opened. Sandis jumped. She hated it when she didn't hear him coming.

Setting down her utensils, she looked up at the man in the doorway—tall and lean, with a large hooked nose and a black hat drawn down over his forehead. Kazen wore that hat far more often than he didn't, and he always donned dark colors to match. All the grafters did. The vessels' beige garments seemed bright in comparison.

The brands on her back itched. She didn't scratch them.

The others held their breath. No one chewed; no one looked away. Heath trembled—he'd been doing that a lot more lately—and Sandis pinched his thigh beneath the table. Not hard enough to hurt, but enough to steady him. Alys was attentive. Good.

Kazen's eyes, a rare blue, scanned the vessels before landing on Sandis. Her skin prickled in memory of burning and ripping, of being swallowed whole by otherworldly beings. Of being made a weapon.

A warm pressure built under her skull—a presence she wasn't supposed to feel, and one she could never tell another soul about, ever.

Vessels weren't supposed to be *aware* of their numina, even those they were bound to.

3

She didn't want Kazen to know she was special. It didn't take a scholar to determine that being special was dangerous.

"Sandis."

Her toes curled in her slippers, but she stood the moment he said her name, straight and erect and as perfectly as she could muster. Things with Kazen always went smoother when she was perfect. She felt the others' eyes on her, but her eyes stayed on her master.

He gestured her forward with the crook of a single bony finger protruding from his aged hand.

Leaving her food half-eaten, she came.

In the fourth hour of the night, in a drafty basement room filled with men, Sandis was a threat. That was why Kazen had brought her there—why he ever brought her anywhere. Why, despite the chill, she wore a loose tunic with a wide-open back, exposing the ancient Noscon script branded with gold leaf down the length of her spine.

That had been one of her least painful experiences in her time among the grafters.

Sandis herself was nothing to fear. She was no stronger than the average eighteen-year-old female, and she had no particular skills outside of what she'd learned working on an assembly line as a child. She wasn't particularly muscular or overly tall. She didn't even have a scarred face to instill terror. She was unarmed.

And yet the men here—bankers, accountants, and a few Skeets from the local mob summoned by Kazen—knew what she could become. With a few whispered words from her master, she would cease being Sandis, slave, and would become a creature that didn't even exist on the mortal plane. A creature whose name was tattooed in mixed blood above the impressions of golden writing burned down her back. A creature that would be completely under the control of his summoner.

Ireth.

"I assure you that everything is in order," said one of the bankers. Sandis knew he was a banker by the way he was dressed—simple and clean-cut. She also knew he was afraid. Not because he trembled, but because he couldn't meet anyone's eyes, and because sweat glistened on his upper lip. He stood with two others on the opposite side of the table, farthest from the door.

A mistake.

"I'm sure it is." Kazen's voice was smooth and unhitched despite his age. He'd never disclosed the number to Sandis, but she guessed him to be in his midsixties. He loomed above the banker—above her, and above nearly everyone, save the broad-shouldered Skeet in the back. The mobsmen were not so different from the grafters, save that they didn't delve into the occult to fight their battles. They didn't make humans like Sandis into heathenish weapons. In general, they stayed clear of the grafters. But Kazen had recently done business with the Skeets, and money made for easy alliances . . . as did common enemies, which these bankers appeared to be.

Still, the Skeets kept to themselves as Kazen challenged the bankers. Few knew the rituals necessary to dip into the ethereal plane, and even fewer had the courage to try. If the bloodwork wasn't right, a numen could go wild and attack its summoner. If the police discovered *any* involvement in the occult, the summoner *and* his vessel would go straight to Gerech Prison, which was, perhaps, the one place in Kolingrad more frightening than Kazen's lair. It was also heresy—not that Kazen cared for religion.

Sandis did. Or had. But that didn't matter anymore.

The brim of Kazen's hat cast a shadow across his long face. A shadow that concealed the glimmer of his eyes—a glimmer that, if read properly, would reveal his intentions before his words did. Sandis had become fluent in the language of Kazen's eyes. He was unaware of that fact, or so she hoped. She had few advantages when it came to her master. She liked to think the language of the glimmer was one of them.

"My request to see the ledgers should not be of any particular consequence," Kazen insisted.

Did the banker hear the threat in his words? They raised gooseflesh on Sandis's arms. A simple request, but nothing Kazen ever did or said was simple. In all the years she'd spent with him, Sandis had never once heard the man raise his voice, barter, or plead. He'd never needed to. Every person in this room—in this city—was a game piece, and he was a champion player.

The banker nodded and turned back to his two associates. They whispered something under their breath—one of the three Skeets leaned in to listen. Kazen stood erect save for the slight tilt of his head. Both of his large, spidery hands clasped the silver top of his cane. He did not look at her.

For the most part, Sandis kept her face forward. Kazen did not like his vessels participating in his business, and so she never did, even with her expressions. But her eyes dipped as the banker brought out a locked box and set it on the sterile table before him, fidgeting with the key until he had it open.

"I don't think *they* are necessary." The banker glanced at the mobsmen.

Kazen took the first ledger, looked it over, and set it aside. He picked up the second, read the cover, and flipped it open. A ledger with last month's expense reports, judging by the date. Sandis made sure to avert her eyes once she'd read it. Vessels weren't allowed to read. Kazen believed she couldn't. Another small advantage she had, and one she would *not* give up.

"Your shortcomings affect my business with them. They are quite necessary." Kazen flipped through another page, and another. One of the Skeets met her eyes, but he quickly looked away.

Alliances aside, he had every right to fear her, though she could do no harm without Kazen. She rarely remembered what he used her for. That was another secret she kept from her master. A vessel was *never* supposed to remember what happened when she was possessed.

Ireth. The name sounded so loudly in her mind that for a terrifying second, she thought she had spoken it. But the proceedings continued on as normal, with her as a forgotten amenity. Carefully, she glanced around the room, trying to read faces, trying to ignore the smells of sweat, kerosene, and fear that these dark, solid walls seemed to amplify. There were two safes in the farthest corner of the room. No windows. All the lamps but two had been moved to hang over the table where Kazen flipped through pages with painstaking care.

One of the bankers, a younger, thinner man, looked ready to faint. His face was white, his eyes rimmed purple. Sandis didn't linger on him long—she didn't want to make him feel worse by setting her attention on him.

A stretch of corkboard pinned with various papers and notes lined the wall to her left. More ledgers, binders, and papers sat stacked on the cabinets beneath it. Her gaze moved slowly over the lettering—she could read, but she'd never had a classroom in which to practice. It took a moment to piece things together.

Donations, that's what it said. And next to it, *Gold Exchange*.

Kazen muttered something, but as Sandis moved her gaze back to the bankers, her eyes caught a word that she read instantaneously—a word she knew well, for it was her own last name: *Gwenwig*.

Her breath caught, and as soon as it did, she forced herself to look forward until it returned to an ordinary pattern.

"That is how banks work, Kazen." This time the third banker spoke—not the wet-lipped one or the overly pale one, but the oldest one. Wrinkles crimped his forehead into a tangle of lines. "There is always borrowing and lending."

Sandis glanced back at the ledger and found the name once more. *Gwenwig.* It was not a beautiful name, and it was not a common one. She knew only three other people with that name, and they were all dead.

"Oh, but, Mr. Bahn," Kazen said, the silkiness of his voice making Sandis shudder, "I have a special deal with your corporation. That is not how *my* funds work."

Gwenwig. She dared to tilt her head a little more to read the full entry: *Talbur Gwenwig.* A male name. Not her father's or brother's. She'd never heard it before.

Breathe, Sandis. She swallowed and willed her heart to steady. Kazen noticed everything, even when it seemed he did not. She moved her eyes forward again, but upon seeing the terror on the three bankers' faces, she let her gaze fall to the floor.

Gwenwig. Gwenwig. Gwenwig.

Could she have family somewhere in Dresberg?

Did she have *family*?

Her mouth went dry. The discussion in the room dribbled to a buzz in her ears. Her parents had died when she and Anon were still young. Her brother had perished shortly before Kazen bought her. She had no one left. No one but the grafters, and Ireth.

But . . . *Gwenwig.* Could her salvation be sitting a few feet to her left?

Kazen's cold hand landed on her shoulder, his long fingers curling around it. Sandis lifted her eyes but did not meet his. What had she missed? Something terrible, if her master was paying her attention. He only did so in public for one reason.

The three bankers watched her with stark fear. Two of the three Skeets left the room.

"Kazen," the oldest banker said too loudly, perhaps trying to push authority into his voice. "This is unnecessary!"

"I don't believe so." Kazen turned Sandis toward him, away from the ledger she desperately wanted to read. If she turned back, he would know, so she looked at the floor and closed her eyes, waiting, her blood running faster in anticipation of the summoning. Kazen hesitated for a brief moment—was he looking over her shoulder?—but then his palm pressed into her hair, and she forced herself not to cringe. He must be eager to act; he usually made her undress first, so as not to waste clothing.

It never got easier. No matter how many times Kazen summoned a numen into her, it never got easier. Neither did the fear it instilled into Kazen's victims, nor the pure, unrelenting pain possession wreaked upon her body.

Her stomach tensed, but she opened her mind, welcoming Ireth. Acceptance made the transition more bearable.

Ireth didn't mean to hurt her.

The old, fluid words flowed from Kazen's tongue with an evil sort of reverence. Four lines, but they felt like four syllables. Sandis breathed and missed them.

White-hot fury descended upon her. Sirens screamed in her ears. Her body was a thousand threads pulled apart, breaking, snapping. Iron and bile, acid and *ripping, tearing, twisting*—

Sandis awoke with a start. The familiar checkered brown pattern on the ceiling of the vessels' quarters greeted her. A chill prickled the skin of her arms, but beneath her forehead was a residual heat, and when she closed her eyes again, she felt the impression of fire. Of need. Of . . .

It was gone.

She sat up slowly, knowing quick movements would rattle the headache already beginning to surface behind her temples. She breathed deeply, slowly, staring past her gray bedcovers, trying to remember . . .

but there were no memories this time. Only fleeting impressions. She tried to grab on to them, mull over them. *Fire.* Ireth always left the impression of fire. *Need.* That had been a frequent one, too.

For three and a half years, Sandis had awoken from possession with nothing more than black gaps in her mind. Not even dreams had filled that void.

These flashes had started six months ago. The memory of a face, a scream, the sound of Kazen's voice giving an order she never could or would have completed in her mortal human form.

Ireth was reaching out to her. Sandis had told no one. She was an enigma, she knew that, and the puzzle of what the fire horse *needed* remained largely unsolved. The numen could not speak to her directly, or at least, he had not done so yet.

Blinking rapidly, Sandis allowed herself to come fully back to reality. She winced at a headache. Wasn't surprised to see herself in a new shirt and slacks—Ireth would have destroyed the ones she wore to the bank. When she reached for the water on her side table, her muscles whined of an overuse she could not recall. She downed the liquid in the wooden cup in three swallows, grit and all. The medicine had settled on the bottom. She'd been unconscious longer than usual.

Her stomach growled. She scanned the room, relieved to find some cold meat and an apple set on a tray near the door. She was a slave, yes, but Kazen kept her and the others well fed. Summoning into a broken vessel rarely ended well.

As Sandis carefully stood on still-shaky legs, she heard a muted, choking sound from the corner of the room. She turned and scanned the narrow beds. Six, including her own. All property of Kazen. Her gaze settled on the quivering lump on Heath's mattress.

She glanced back at the meat. Sighed. "Heath?"

The lump flinched.

Were it any of the others—Alys, Kaili, Dar, even Rist—Sandis would be more concerned. But Heath was often unwell. His moods changed quicker than a shift at the firearms factory. He wore his fear like a heavy cloak.

Sandis stepped toward him slowly until she knew dizziness would not claim her. "Heath, what's wrong?"

He rolled over, his dingy long brown hair peeking out from his blanket cocoon. His eyes were bloodshot—Sandis's probably were, too. It happened, with possession. She'd likely have more gray hairs as well.

"I'm next," he whispered, sounding more like a child than a man two years Sandis's senior. "I'm next, I'm next."

"Kazen probably won't need us again just yet." Sandis inched toward Rist's bed and perched at the edge of it. "Are you hungry? I'll share."

"Don't pretend you didn't hear the screams this morning."

Prickles cascaded down Sandis's neck. She lifted her hand to rub the skin beneath her dark hair but winced at a prick of pain. A small red dot on the inside of her elbow told her Kazen had taken a syringe to her while she'd been out. She frowned, but it was expected. Kazen needed her blood to control Ireth.

Refocusing on Heath, she said, "I was dead."

Not literally, of course.

Heath shook his head. Shot up suddenly and clasped both sides of his head with his large hands. "There was screaming. Last week, too."

The prickling returned. Sandis had woken in the middle of the night to *that* screaming. She'd covered her ears and rolled over, singing a lullaby to herself until it went away. She hadn't investigated. Kazen didn't like them coming out of their rooms at night, and Sandis followed his rules to perfection.

Screaming wasn't uncommon, down here.

Heath circled his arms around his knees and rocked back and forth. "He's experimenting again."

Her shoulders tensed. "Again?"

"He's doing something. Summoning . . . something new. I don't know. I'm next, though."

Sandis glanced at the door, ignoring the waiting food there. "Why are you next?" Her voice had less strength with that question. She cleared her throat. One had to be assertive when talking to Heath during one of his episodes.

Heath shook his head. Rocked. "I'm next. He hates me, I know it. And I'm not bound."

Bound, like Sandis was. She reached back, tracing Ireth's name at the base of her neck. Being bound to a specific numen made summoning it much faster. Ireth was a strong numen—a seven on the scale of ten. Kazen used him frequently. Dar and Rist were bound as well.

"Being bound isn't a privilege." And yet she'd started to feel a strange closeness to Ireth, a creature she'd never met. A creature she *couldn't* meet. She knew Dar and Rist did not have similar feelings. She could tell by the way they talked, by the way they answered—or avoided—her careful questions.

Sandis watched Heath's rocking long enough to grow nauseated. He said, "He wouldn't use a bound vessel to summon that thing. He'd use his spares."

Sandis straightened. "Summon *what* thing?"

No, this wasn't good. She was feeding Heath's worries. He'd lose it, and then Rist would blame her for riling him up.

She swallowed. "You're valuable, Heath. You know that." Not just anyone could be a vessel. There were requirements. The first was good health. No sickness, sturdy bones, the basics. Scars and piercings had to be minimal for higher-level numina. Vessels also had to have what Kazen called an "open" spirit, which was either something a person was born with or something he or she obtained through a great amount of meditation. They had all cost Kazen a fortune—a fortune Sandis suspected he'd earned back quickly.

Kazen had been a vessel, once. Only those who had been possessed at some point in their lives could become summoners. There was no doubt, however, that Kazen had since destroyed his brands so he'd never again have to feel the pain he so readily inflicted on others.

"Not like you. You're his favorite. He'd never use you."

She tried another tactic. "Alys and Kaili aren't bound, either, and you're stronger than they are. Kazen wants you to be . . . flexible." Heath could summon a seven or less, like herself.

When was the last time Kazen had used him?

But Heath whimpered and buried his face against his knees. Rocking, rocking . . .

"He's right."

The new voice startled her. Rist stood at the door, his arms folded across his chest. His dark hair flopped lazily over his eyes.

Heath mewled.

"Not about you." Rist sounded annoyed. He lost patience with Heath more quickly than anyone else did, which Sandis had always found odd. They were *family*.

Moving away from the door, Rist murmured, "Kazen's had a lot of slavers by lately."

Sandis's stomach tightened. "You've seen them?"

"Kaili has. And I saw one of their stamps on a paper in his office."

Gooseflesh pricked Sandis's arms. Her ensuing whisper was almost a hiss. "You can't go through his things again, Rist. Last time he was lenient."

Kazen would never have his vessels beaten enough to cause them permanent harm, but he had other methods of tormenting them. Last time Rist had been caught snooping around, he was locked in solitary for nearly a week . . . and Rist couldn't even read. The isolation had nearly broken him. Sometimes food or water would be denied or changed, or Kazen would sic Galt on one of the other vessels and make the offender watch. Sandis hated that one. Often, however, Kazen got creative. Not knowing what to expect was the worse punishment to

Sandis. That was why she tried so hard to never break any rules. Why she tried so hard to be, as Heath put it, the "favorite."

All she had ever wanted was to be *good*.

Rist pressed his lips together for a moment before saying, "Regardless, I think he's doing experiments at night, when he has someone to practice on. Maybe potential vessels he can easily discard. Hosts he can get for cheap."

"But they're so hard to find," Sandis countered.

Rist shrugged. "Here, maybe. Not across the border."

Heath covered his ears. Sandis put her hand on his shoulder. "It won't be you. Any of us. We'll be fine."

She didn't like the uneasy look on Rist's face, so she turned away from it. But that only brought her attention to the other cots. Alys, Dar, and Kaili were elsewhere. Maybe one was being briefed on an upcoming job, or doing a chore for Zelna, or being punished for something Sandis didn't yet know about. She tried not to think about where they were; the worry could be maddening.

Her gaze lingered on Alys's bed. She was still so new to this, and the weakest of Kazen's vessels. If these slavers didn't deliver, would Kazen decide she was expendable?

No. She's safe, Sandis told herself. *You've taught her everything she needs to know. She keeps her eyes down, stays quiet, follows all the rules, just like you. She'll be safe.* Sandis would make sure of it.

Yet uneasiness bloomed in her gut like a rancid flower. Telling herself it was merely hunger, Sandis left Heath's bedside for the food tray.

She forced down every bite.

Chapter 2

The best way to travel in Dresberg, Rone had discovered, was above it.

The air wasn't any cleaner—smoke rose, after all—but there was a lot less traffic, fewer people, and a much smaller chance of him stepping in a puddle of unknown refuse. A person never got used to that.

One might say that jumping from building to building—occasionally using ropes, boards, and other creative measures—wasn't safe. And yet Rone was certain his chances of not getting mugged, stabbed, or spat on were better five stories up than down on the cobblestone pathways.

And if he fell, well, he had his special trinket for that.

The overly orange sun had dropped behind the city's massive wall a few minutes ago—a wall one could compare to the hefty mountains separating Kolingrad from all other civilization. A wall that reminded him this place was a cage where people had shat in the corner so long they couldn't remember what clean air smelled like. Up here, Rone could see *over* the wall. If he kept his eyes up, he could almost pretend it wasn't there. That it was simply him, wide roads, and general nothingness for miles.

He'd also fall to his potential death, so he kept his eyes down, sprinted, and *jumped*.

Dresberg was a cesspool of people and factories and work, work, work. Disease flourished in its densest parts, and yet the people kept trying to cram more things into them. Taller buildings. Narrower rooms.

Children to stuff into every nook and cranny. But at least the lack of space made Rone's job easier. His legs were long enough to hop alleyways, and sometimes the buildings leaned up against each other so tightly that jumping them was like a twilight stroll.

That was the best way to start a burglary. Strolling.

This wasn't a burglary per se. The item had been paid for. The money just went to Rone and not to the item's owner. Regardless, tonight's quarry was an ancient Noscon headpiece, so really, the true owner had died a thousand or something years ago. It was a thousand, right? Rone had never been a great student. Then again, his absent father hadn't tried very hard to teach him foreign history.

Rone paused on top of . . . the library, he thought, to catch his breath and gain his bearings. The wealthiest city denizens lived closest to the wall, as far from the smoke ring—and the poor people who dwelled there—as they could get. Again, why anyone with a steady and enormous income would *choose* to live in Dresberg was beyond him, save for the worthless politicians holed up in the Innerchord, making pointless laws and eating baby animals. Rich people always ate tiny meat.

Rone was rich at that moment, but tiny meat was expensive, and so was his rent.

City lights flickered on drowsily beneath him as he took the long way around the police hub and, begrudgingly, dropped down to a two-story building with a sturdy drainpipe and then slid the rest of the way to the ground. His gray clothes helped him blend in. The nice cut of his collar would hopefully do the same if he was caught snooping around one of the finer flats in the area.

He rechecked the address he'd written down. District Two, a neighborhood on the northeast side of the capital. He turned down one street, hopped the gate on another. Oh, not a flat. A *house*. No shared walls or anything. It was even *white*. Leave it to the fanciest people to paint their houses white in a city where the constant spew of factory smoke turned rainfall into sludge. Some lucky orphan had a good job cleaning up for these folks.

No, Rone wasn't going to feel bad about this at all.

There weren't many people in the streets here—the residents were the sort who didn't have to work long shifts or late hours. It was past bedtime by now, and so Rone, on feet that had been lashed by his old master until they could walk without sound, approached his target.

The use of tiny quartz chunks in the slender yard was annoying—Rone had to walk on the concrete border or risk his steps crunching. At least Ernst Renad—this was *his* house, supposedly—had enough sense not to keep a garden. Plants didn't grow in Dresberg. Not outdoors, anyway. Everything the people ate was shipped in from the farms in the north, away from the smog.

He reached the southwest corner of the house and utilized the brick chimney and white cornices to haul himself up to the third story. Dear Ernst had been kind enough to offer him a small balcony. He settled onto its railing, checking his pocket for the small golden trinket that had saved his life too many times to count. Unlikely he would need the amarinth for this—the robbing of ancient artifacts from one of Dresberg's richest denizens was actually one of his safer jobs—but he preferred to be cautious.

His employer had given a detailed explanation of where Ernst Renad kept the headpiece in question, as well as what it looked like, but Rone had never worked with the man before and didn't know whether he could fully trust him. Some factory owner or the like, based on what Rone had gathered from their short in-person meeting. Rone was a freelancer, so his clients varied.

Rone slipped down to the balcony floor. Only problem with robbing the wealthy was if you were caught, they could push money down the throats of jailers and politicians alike to ensure your sentence far outweighed your crime. There were laws, lawyers, and judges, but when it came down to the final ink on the paper, Dresberg operated on money. The whole country did. Rone's trinket couldn't save him from corruption.

He wiped a hand down his face, calluses catching on stubble. Now or never.

He pulled a shiv from his back pocket and jimmied open the white-washed door that led into the house. Held his breath, stepped into the room, and dropped into a crouch. The bed was bigger than most people's flats. Two lumps lay in it. Rone slipped by, willing his eyes to adjust to the new darkness. The bedroom door was open. He passed through. Ernst Renad had two children, both grown and possibly out of the house. Rone wasn't sure. He kept his guard up as he moved.

A rail followed the hallway and guarded passersby from dropping down two stories to the first floor. The architecture featured a huge square cut out of the second- and third-story floors so one could see all the way up to the highest ceiling upon entering the home. What a waste of space. Rone crept around the corner and counted doors. That one should be the sitting room—nope, that was a linen closet. This door . . . yes, this was it.

Rone stepped in and shut the door behind him, turning the knob hard to the right so it wouldn't click when it latched. Even with all the shadows and darkness—only the smoke-covered moon illuminated the space—the room made his stomach turn. He could work every hour of every day of his entire life and not be able to afford half of this room's furnishings. Gilded mirrors—he looked a little scruffy—framed paintings, and weird egg-shaped things with maybe-real, maybe-not-real jewels in them. Fine carpets and end tables with intricately carved legs, holding up board games with intricately carved pieces. And was that a *harp*? Rone rolled his eyes.

His quarry was in the corner, behind a thick, droopy rope that was meant to tell the entitled, *Look, but don't touch.* Purely ornamental. He stepped over it and approached the wire dummy wearing an incomplete Noscon armor set. The breastplate had a chunk missing, and the edges were eroded. A millennium or so stuck under another's city would do that. The original settlers of Kolingrad hadn't even cleared out all the ruins before building on top of them. Rone settled his hand over his pocket. Then again, he should be thanking them for that.

A muscle in his shoulder tightened and stabbed him with a pain that said, *Hurry up.*

Rone lifted his eyes from the armor to the headpiece settled on top of the dummy's head. A sort of gold-braided crown, beaded with jade. A triangle-shaped bluish gemstone marked the front, meant to rest against the forehead. Worth a fortune, of course—not because it had any magical properties like the amarinth, but because it was old. Why his employer wanted this specifically, Rone hadn't asked. It wasn't his job to ask.

It was his job to do what others thought impossible. This wasn't a great example, but sometimes he did achieve awe-inspiring feats.

Rone swiped the headpiece with little grace and marched to the nearest window, unlatched it, and dropped down to a chipped cornice.

He scaled the side of the house carefully before dropping to the ground on the balls of his feet, but that damnable quartz wrapped all the way around the house, and it crunched audibly under his six-foot frame. Slipping the artifact into his coat, Rone did not go out the way he'd come in—he jumped the fence and crossed the neighbor's yard to the next street.

Why did everyone in this neighborhood use crunchy rocks in their landscaping?

Rone shoved his hands into his pockets and kept his head low, striding with purpose down the lane. He was almost out.

The moment lamplight crossed his path, he sighed.

"You there." A policeman in a deep-scarlet uniform hurried toward him from the north. Two others followed behind. Yes, three scarlets to patrol the wealthy neighborhood. Someone was probably being beaten up for a crust of bread in the smoke ring right now.

Rone lifted his head and smiled. His mom had always told him he had a nice smile. So had a number of other, very pretty, women.

"Is there a problem?" He shielded his eyes from the lamp.

"Odd time to be out for a jaunt," the policeman said, looking him up and down. His gaze lingered on the tailored collar, a style favored by the rich. "Do you live here?"

"Just up ahead." Rone pointed.

"Someone turned on their panic light. Said they saw a shadow."

Rone raised an eyebrow and put on the most incredulous expression he could muster. "A shadow? At *night*? I can count two dozen from where I'm standing, you being one of them."

The scarlet knit his brow. Glanced back at Rone's collar. Hand still in his pocket, Rone pinched the edge of his amarinth. If he couldn't blandish his way out of this, he'd have to run, and then he'd have three guns pointed at his back. The amarinth would give him sixty seconds to outpace them. Glancing past the accusing policeman, Rone sized up his companions. He could do it.

The officer lowered his lamp. "Just up ahead?"

Rone gestured with a tip of his head. "The one with the light on."

There were two houses matching that description.

"Go on, then." The officer seemed disappointed. If Rone really were fancy, he'd be offended. "Keep indoors at night, son. You waste our time, frolicking out here."

And you waste taxpayer money, strutting around these villas, answering the calls of anyone who lights a red lamp. God knew he hated Kolingrad. Then again, he also hated God.

He tipped his head in good nature toward the police officer and continued on his way, matching the pace he had kept before.

The minute the lamplight turned from his back, he cut across another yard, lifted a manhole cover in the street, and dropped into the sewer.

Chapter 3

Fire.

Need.

Sandis started awake with an odd pressure in her skull—like she'd dived too deep into a canal. Her eyes were dry. Each breath burned her sinuses. She reached for her water and fumbled to get the last swallows from her pitcher to her cup to her mouth.

The pressure and impressions gradually eased away. Sandis rolled her neck, hearing it crack multiple times. Her hair, falling just past her chin so as not to cover her script, masked either side of her face. Her bowels churned with nerves. Looking around the room and seeing only darkness, save where dim light highlighted the edges of the door, she calmed herself with the thought *Not tonight. He doesn't need you tonight.*

A vessel never got used to the agony of summoning. At least she didn't.

Sandis lay back down, listening to the even breathing of the others, punctuated by a muffled scream winding its way through the hallway.

The hairs on her arms stood on end. Pressing her face into her pillow, she thought, *It's just the wind.* Never mind that she was two stories underground. Never mind Heath's talking about the screams.

She closed her eyes and tried to sleep, but those sensations—which she was still convinced came from Ireth—nagged at her mind and drove sleep away. What time was it? There was no clock in this room. No lamps or candles.

Fire. Need.

It had been a man's scream.

Sandis lifted her head off her pillow, squinting through the darkness. Their beds formed a sort of horseshoe, close together without being side by side. Everyone was head to toe, with Sandis being nearest the door. Alys's still form slumbered ahead of her, and then Kaili, Heath, Rist, and Dar.

She squinted harder. Gritting her teeth, she slipped off her bed, lowering herself onto her hands and knees on the floor. Crept forward, her clothes gently swishing. The vessels slept in their day clothes—simple pants and, for the women, those baggy, high-necked shirts that hung open in the back. A draft cruised up the length of her golden scars.

Sandis paused. Licked her lips.

Heath's bed was empty.

He could easily be out with Kazen, though it usually woke Sandis when Kazen and his nasty little sidekick Galt opened the door to summon one or more of them.

Heath's fear-fed words from earlier rattled in her ears.

"I'm next. He hates me. Summon that thing . . ."

Sandis crept back to the side of her bed. Sat on her heels. Stared at the door.

Vessels weren't allowed to leave their room at night unescorted, even to eliminate. The bucket in the corner was for that.

The second, distant scream, despite being quieter this time, made Sandis jump.

"You're his favorite."

Sandis hoped that would play in her favor if she got caught wandering. The heavy door sang her disobedience as she pulled it open and slipped through.

The hallways were empty. They usually were, even during the day. Grafters kept to themselves in their little colonies, only merging together when it was time to storm another's nest. But Sandis didn't need to go far. She knew where Kazen would be, if he was experimenting again.

The ceiling in the corridor was low, the walls close together, making the passageway narrow enough that two grown men passing each other would brush shoulders. It curved slightly, like a sickle. Yellow light flowed feebly from beneath two of the closed doorways—one to her left and one at the end.

Sandis hugged the wall, avoiding that light as though it were red-hot iron. She paused as she passed the first lit doorway, Kazen's office. Zelna muttered to herself inside. Whisking past on slippered feet, Sandis tiptoed to the door at the end of the corridor, the one that led to the summoning room.

Pressure built under her skull. *Ireth?* But of course the numen couldn't answer. Never once had the fire horse spoken to her directly.

She touched the knob, turned it as quietly as she could, and inched the door open to a crack. The room beyond was the largest in the lair, roughly the size of a small warehouse. She saw Galt first; he was probably in and out, fetching whatever Kazen needed like a good little dog. Likely why the door wasn't locked. Galt was a stocky man, perhaps in his late thirties. Might have been attractive if he weren't hopped up on brain dust every evening, and if his soul weren't both blacker and slicker than spent oil.

"He's ready." Kazen's voice was low and soft, yet pierced through the air like lightning. Sandis flinched from it and, one finger at a time, removed her hand from the door. Ready to flee in an instant. Or make an excuse. She wasn't known as a rule breaker—a good excuse might be believed. Maybe. If she acted sleepy, pretended she thought Kazen had summoned her . . .

The click of horse hooves brought her attention back to the crack. Galt had vanished from view, but he returned a moment later, tugging a rope lead on a well-muscled horse. A mare, Sandis guessed. She'd never known much of horseflesh, though her mother had loved the creatures. They passed out of her line of sight again and didn't return.

Sandis bit her lip. They were going to kill the poor thing, weren't they? Sacrifice was necessary for an unbound summons, but to her knowledge, Kazen had never killed something as large as a horse before. Sandis wanted to cover her ears, but it would prevent her from hearing them if they came close to the door . . . and she couldn't bring herself to leave.

She thanked the Celestial when the horse only made a small noise as its throat was slit. The floor shuddered when its body hit.

The light wavered. Sandis dared inch the door open, just a little more, with her toe. She choked down a gasp.

Heath. Kneeling, not standing, in the growing crimson puddle beside the fallen animal. He looked out of sorts, like he was drugged or . . . like he'd given up. Kazen had written Noscon script all over Heath's limbs. Sandis couldn't decipher it, but she knew it wasn't part of a usual summoning.

The pressure returned to her skull. She pressed her cheek to the doorjamb, straining to see.

Kazen stepped into the blood and pressed his palm to Heath's head. As he pulled back, he chanted familiar words that still lanced cold into Sandis's core.

> *Vre en nestu a carnath*
> *Ii mem entre I amar*
> *Vre en nestu a carnath*
> *Kolosos epsi gradenid*

She mouthed the unfamiliar name Kolosos just before a burst of red light blinded her.

She stumbled back from the door, hand rushing up to her tearing eyes on instinct. She rubbed them, smearing the salt water. Opened her eyes to spots, and tried to blink them away. All the while, she thought, *No, it should be white light. It's always* white *light.*

The sound that poured from that crack was unlike anything she'd ever heard before. A mix of soggy boots squelching, leather tearing. A throat choking on water without any air. A bug crushed underfoot.

Though a few spots lingered in her sight, Sandis leaned toward the door, nearly gagging on the smell of meat.

The pool of blood was twice as large now, and—

Bile rushed up her throat. Afraid that her retching would give her away, Sandis rushed from the door on the balls of her feet. Biting her tongue and swallowing to keep half-digested food in her stomach.

The blood. The *meat.* That was Heath.

Had been Heath.

She paused near the vessels' room, pressing her moist forehead to the cold wall outside the door. She breathed hard, too agitated to worry about the sound. Stared into nothing.

Heath.

Vessels had died in summonings before. She'd witnessed it happen. Either someone was consecrated for it who didn't meet all the requirements or a master summoned too strong a creature into too weak a vessel. There was always a flash of light, and then the body crumpled, dead. Sometimes blood leaked from the lips, nose, or eyes. That was it.

Heath . . . Heath had turned *inside out.*

She'd seen so much evil, so much darkness, since coming into Kazen's acquaintance. But never this. Never *this.* What was he planning? Why would he attempt to summon such a thing?

She swallowed, her stomach protesting. The pressure in her skull grew until she thought her head would split. Did Ireth build it, or her own horror?

Kolosos. Sandis mouthed the long, low syllables. *Kolosos.* That was the name of the creature Kazen had attempted to summon into Heath. Heath, who could hold a numen with the power of seven, like Sandis.

25

That could have been her.

Sandis's mind turned over, her decision made as swiftly as the striking of a firing pin. She had to leave. *Now.* If she didn't act immediately, it wouldn't happen. She'd lose her courage, or she wouldn't succeed. But she'd have to do it alone, with no money in her pockets, no roof over her head, no guarantees—

A sound echoed down the hallway. Without turning, Sandis slipped into the darkness of the sleeping chamber. Held her breath long enough to listen for sounds of wakefulness among her peers. They slept on.

Maybe, hope whispered to her. *Maybe you're not as alone as you think.*

Talbur Gwenwig. She'd seen his name at the bank. Anyone with that surname *had* to be related to her, one way or another. But would he take her in? If she hid the truth about what she'd become, if she pleaded with him and followed all the rules . . .

She bit down on her first knuckle, the smell of Heath and his failed summoning still clinging to her nostrils, encouraging her to run.

The sound had faded from the hallway. *Now. It has to happen now.* She could take nothing with her. No extra clothes, no provisions, no weapons. Kazen's men would suspect her if she tried. But should she warn the other vessels? Part of her felt a duty to do so, but they might not believe her. Might not wake in time. And they couldn't *all* walk out without raising suspicion. No, Sandis couldn't take anything with her, even her comrades.

The thought pressed thorns into her heart. She looked up at the sleeping forms. She had to tell them. They wouldn't say anything, would they? Or would someone give her away, getting her caught before she had a chance to run? Maybe Kazen would beat the information out of them . . . or simply beat them out of frustration.

No, she assured herself. Kazen wouldn't hurt them without Sandis there to watch. So long as she didn't come back, they couldn't be tormented on her behalf.

Her gaze dwelled too long on Alys, on her hair that seemed to shine even in the darkness. Sandis had taught the girl everything she knew, hadn't she? Alys would be fine. Kaili would take care of her in Sandis's absence, just as she had once taken care of Sandis. The thought tore at her heart. *Go. Go now.*

She might never see them again.

But *family*. She had *family*, somewhere in the city. Her staying wouldn't stop Kazen's experiments. Her obedience hadn't protected Heath, only herself.

Gritting her teeth until her jaw ached, Sandis turned her back on the other vessels and slipped into the hallway. Every step she took broke a thread carefully woven between her and them, bits stitched under tables and in the dark, where Kazen and his men couldn't catch them fraternizing. *Snap. Snap. Snap.*

She walked away from Kazen and his workroom with a calm, even stride. Head up, with purpose. Like Kazen walked beside her, one hand on her shoulder, permitting her to leave her confines. She moved onward, silently, passing through shadows. *Snap. Snap.* Staps, another grafter, leaned his large body against the wall in the hallway, picking at his nail, his corded hair falling over his shoulders. Sandis did not look at his face. She held her head high as she passed, feeling his eyes on her—but Sandis was the perfect slave. Kazen's favorite. Staps didn't bother her. No one wanted to risk Kazen's wrath. *Snap.*

I'm sorry.

She prayed for each person she passed—at least the ones she knew by name. They didn't know they'd already invoked Kazen's rage.

Up the stairs. Through a door. Past a group of men gambling, then two prostitutes chatting in an alcove while they counted their money. One began to speak to Sandis, but her companion grabbed her arm and shook her head in warning. Sandis could feel their eyes on her back. She needed to hide her script before she left the lair. Any connection to the occult, even against her will, would sentence her to the noose.

Though sin was branded into her with flair and expense, the Celestial blessed her on her last, shaky stretch toward the city—a jacket lay on the floor outside the laundry room. The patches on the elbows told her it belonged to Kazen's lackey Ravis, and while he was a thin man, the garment was too large for her. Still, it hid what it needed to hide.

A beefy man she knew as a guard stopped her at the door. His name was . . . Marek? "Where's Kazen?" he asked, eyeing her jacket.

Sandis met his eyes, hoping fear didn't glint in her own. She said the most terrifying thing she could think of. "Ireth is coming."

If this man knew the details of summoning, he would know the emptiness of her words. But he had been hired for his size, not his study. His eyes widened, and he stepped back, pressing into the wall as if Sandis were some sort of snake. Glancing down the way she had come, he opened the door.

The cold dark night of Dresberg, carrying the familiar scent of smoke, engulfed her.

Chapter 4

Rone's energy waned with the night; he liked to get his jobs done quickly and efficiently, so he'd already wrapped the headpiece in nondescript garbage and left it at the designated drop-off location. His payment had been waiting there for him, and it now sat happily and heavily in his coat pocket, opposite his amarinth. The sluggish sun had dragged itself over the horizon, obscured by Dresberg's sludge-stained wall. While Rone's own flat sang to him from across the city, he decided to make one more stop.

Knowing his mother, she'd already be up. Just in case, however, Rone used his key instead of knocking.

The door swung open to a nice, if simple, flat, nearly twice the size of his own. A living space stretched off to the right, and a kitchen with a small dining space—all the nice flats had *dining spaces*—sat to his left. A small bookcase stretched just inside the door was filled with foreign titles purchased at high prices from southern merchants. His mother's room, privy, and storage space wrapped around the back of the apartment.

Rone kicked the door shut loudly to announce his approach.

A warm but stern voice called from the bedroom, "That had better be you and not an overzealous salesman, Rone."

Rone smiled. "What if I'm selling cash?"

"You realize the absurdity of that statement, yes? One moment. I'm dressing."

Rone pulled out a dining-table chair with his toe and plopped down on it, dropping his head back and closing his eyes. Sleep stirred in dull colors behind his eyelids. Maybe he'd pass out on the couch for a bit before heading home. He wasn't in the mood for more jumping, or wasting money on a cab.

His mother came out a moment later, brushing her hair. She wore a smart but simple cotton blazer and skirt.

"You working today?" His mother took a shift three times a week for a lobbying firm near the Innerchord, where all the government's lackeys congregated to act important. She filed papers.

"Yes, so I don't need your charity."

Rone reached into his pocket and grabbed half his stack of cash, then plopped it on the table. "Too bad."

She set down the hairbrush and planted her hands on her hips. "Rone, I mean it."

"You know I'll just stuff the landlord's pockets if you don't take it."

Adalia Comf sniffed and rolled her eyes. "Take half of it."

"That is half of it."

"Then divide it again. Why did I spend all that money on private education if you're not going to use it?"

Rone snorted and divided the stack, splitting it too high to the top. He shoved the smaller "half" into his pocket, crinkling the bills. He splayed the rest in his fingers like a magician presenting the end of his trick.

His mother leaned forward and took the money. Wrinkling her nose, she said, "You stink."

Taking his collar in his hand, Rone sniffed it. "Sorry."

Adalia frowned and pulled out the chair beside him. Sat. Apparently he didn't stink badly enough to drive her away. Her dark eyes stared squarely into his. "Do you want to explain to me why you're gallivant-ing in the sewers again?"

He shrugged. "Work?"

"Mm-hm. And what exactly did you do all night? Don't try to feed me a tale that you got up especially early to barge in here at the crack of dawn as a surprise."

Rone grinned and spread his arms. "Surprise!"

His mother sighed. "I worry about you."

"I'm whole and hale, Mom."

"For now. Thank you for looking out for me, but be careful what you get involved in. There are dark corners in this city, waiting to eat up a nice boy like you."

Rone barked a laugh at that. He couldn't help it. His mother still liked to think well of him.

His mother pinched his arm.

"Ow!" He drew back. "It's fine. Nothing scandalous or dangerous." This last job was on the easy side of the spectrum, so he wasn't lying.

"And that's why you're so open about it?" Shaking her head, she added, "What would your father say?"

His mirth died. "He's not my father."

"Biology, Rone." Before he could retort, she held up both hands. "I'm sorry. I shouldn't have brought it up. But families are permanent. Remember that."

Rone sucked in a deep breath and expelled it all at once, pushing his rising anger out with it. "Yeah, I know." He stood, leaned over, and kissed his mother's forehead.

"Ugh." Adalia waved her hand in front of her nose. "Use the bath before you leave. You smell like an armpit."

Rone smirked. "Then I'll fit right in with the rest of the city."

Sandis's desperate need to fit in kept her from gawking as she walked the streets of Dresberg. She'd been taken outside by Kazen often enough, but being aboveground by herself, *in the daytime,* was near dreamlike. Like the whole thing was a rumor she'd suddenly discovered to be true. A feeling not unlike nostalgia brimmed her thoughts. Nostalgia, and urgency.

Kazen would have found her missing by now. She didn't have much time to disappear.

Little had changed in Dresberg since Sandis was fourteen, but she found herself getting turned around anyway. Her attention kept focusing on people rather than places. She didn't want to find any familiar faces. A familiar face would mean a grafter. It would mean they'd already caught up with her.

She pulled the hood of her stolen coat tighter around her head and paused under an eave as a wagon driver whipped his horse and shouted at passersby to get out of his way. Many shouted back—one even threw a broken cobble at him. It went wide. Sandis filled her lungs with a deep breath and looked up, attempting to gain her bearings. She vaguely remembered which bank Kazen had taken her to less than a day ago. Her life depended on finding it.

Checking the street—the faces—one more time, Sandis hurried across the road, feeling the mortar between each cobble through her thin shoes. An older woman made eye contact with her; Sandis looked away. There—she recognized that key shop. She knew where she was. She could do this.

She wiped clammy hands on her pants as she wound around the block, crossed another street, and took a shortcut down an alley—only to find it closed off at the end, a new building shoved into the space. She retraced her steps. The bank was on the eastern edge of the city in District Two, so she at least knew which direction to travel. She hiked up a hill, staying close to the storefronts, weaving through people milling about between their factory shifts. Everyone in Dresberg worked in factories. Sandis and her brother had, too, before Kazen. The poor manned the lines, the middle class managed the poor, and the rich owned the lot of them.

The sun peeked between clouds, its color a mustardy yellow from the smoke. Brighter than usual. Sandis stared at it a long moment, until her eyes burned and watered. She so seldom came outside during the day. She'd always loved the sun. No matter how hard things got, the sun was a bright constant against the city's smoke and fear.

She blinked her eyes clear and saw a tip of bronze over the high wall that surrounded the city. It belonged to the Lily Tower, where the head of the Celesians, the Angelic, lived. It was the only structure that rivaled the size of the Degrata, the building at the center of the Innerchord. The government tower was rumored to be the tallest building in the country. Perhaps that was why the Lily Tower sat outside the city walls. To forbid contest. Alys had said a person could take refuge there, even if the scarlets wanted them for a crime. It was a right granted to the Angelic on behalf of God—the Celestial—one not even the triumvirate dared take away. Could Sandis hide there? Would they hurt her if they discovered she was a vessel, or simply kick her out?

The tolling of a clock-tower bell startled her forward. It was warm outside, but Sandis clutched the coat around her, feet moving as quickly as the crowds allowed. By the time the clock rang the next hour, she'd found the bank. She stretched her sore calves before heading in.

The first thing Sandis did was search every face inside the building. She wasn't sure what Kazen had done to the bankers two nights ago . . . and she'd rather not dwell on it . . . but she did need to ensure no one here recognized her.

All were strangers. She pulled down her hood and smoothed her hair before approaching the first teller. She kept her chin up and shoulders back. Tried to emanate the quiet confidence that simmered around Kazen like heavy perfume.

"Pardon me," she said to the woman. She looked tired but well kept. Possibly the same way Sandis looked, for she hadn't slept since her escape. "I made an exchange of gold here last week, and my records don't match my receipt." Sandis had practiced this story all night long and into the morning. Practiced a more Kazen-like dialect so she'd sound like someone who went around making exchanges in gold. "Might I see the record?"

The teller looked her over. Sandis wished she could hear her thoughts. "What is the name on the account?"

"Talbur Gwenwig." It was the first time she'd said the name aloud. Chills ran down her arms. When the teller looked up again, Sandis added, "He's my uncle."

He very well could be. Though as far as Sandis knew, her parents had no living siblings. Her heart beat quicker.

"One moment." The teller rose from her chair and disappeared through a door in the wall behind her. Sandis licked her lips. Heard another person enter through the heavy front door and glanced behind her—a stranger. Relief engulfed her in a cold embrace. She faced forward. Tapped her toe on the gray-tiled floor, caught herself, and stopped. Wrung her hands together. Glanced around again. The shadowed stairs in the corner were the same ones she and Kazen had taken to the earlier "meeting." Part of her wished Ireth had allotted her memories of it . . . but perhaps it was better if she didn't know. Some of the things she'd seen, things she suspected . . .

Don't think about that now.

The teller returned, carrying the very book in which Sandis had seen the name. She wanted to jump across that desk and grab that book, flip through its pages until she found it . . . but she clenched her hands at her sides and forced herself to remain calm. As calm as she could be, at least. Any information, *anything*, would help her find—

"There's no exchange for Talbur Gwenwig in here." The woman flipped a page, then another. "You said it was last week?"

Blood drained from her face. "Y-Yes, last week."

She'd *seen* the name. Talbur Gwenwig. She was sure that was it. The writing was burned into her memory like a brand.

The teller shook her head. "I . . . oh. Hmm."

Sandis grabbed the edge of the desk and leaned in. "What? What is it?"

The teller set the book down. "There's a page missing." She fingered the tiniest nub, almost too small to notice, at the bottom of the book. The remnants of a page torn out.

Sandis stared at that nub for too long. Missing? How could it be missing? It had been there two nights ago—

Her blood turned cold. *Kazen* hadn't taken it out, had he? But why would he have? She'd been so careful not to stare, and he still thought she couldn't read . . . didn't he?

Yes, she was being paranoid, surely. He'd come here on business related to his accounts, not the gold exchange.

But one often had to be paranoid, with Kazen.

The teller began opening drawers full of files. She searched through one twice. "I don't see an account here under Gwenwig." She clucked her tongue. "Let me ask my supervisor." She stood and disappeared behind that door again.

Sandis grabbed the book and turned it toward her, scanning the pages, searching for her surname. It wasn't there. She touched the nub. Nothing.

Had Kazen expected her to come here looking for Talbur Gwenwig?

A hard beat of terror pulsed in her chest. Sandis dropped the book as though it were hot iron and backed away from the desk. Turned around, scanned faces. She thought she felt Kazen's cold fingers on her neck and jumped.

The need to leave pressed in on her.

She ran out the door, back into the city. Searched for him—her master. Spotted the dark-scarlet uniform of a police officer instead.

A reminder that it was illegal to be involved in the *occult*, as the Celesians called it. Illegal to be what she had been forced to become.

Sandis turned the other way and jerked up the hood of her coat. Bumped into someone as she hurried away, but her apology caught in her throat. Where would she go? Where else could she find the name?

What if it didn't exist?

No. Don't think that. She knew what she'd seen. This unknown relative had to exist, or else she had no one to turn to. Nowhere to go. She certainly couldn't go back, not without severe punishment for both herself and the others.

She had no hope. She needed hope.

The library? Could she search for the name there? Unless Talbur Gwenwig was a politician or mentioned in a newspaper, the library wouldn't help, but it was a start, wasn't it?

Her stomach tightened and growled. She kneaded a knuckle into it. She'd have to steal food to eat. She had no money. She had nothing. She checked the pockets of the coat, but they were empty save for a slender pocketknife and a charcoal pencil.

She glanced up and ventured down a less crowded street. How would she do it? Go to the market and palm an apple? If she was caught, she'd have no space to run—the market was always crowded. Maybe no one would notice her stealing in the thick of the throng . . . or they would, and they'd grab her and see the script, and then the scarlets would arrest her or a grafter spy would report her . . . She'd either have her neck in a noose or between Kazen's hands.

She swallowed, and her belly protested at the emptiness of it. It might be better to go to prison, where they could only hurt her body, than back to Kazen. He knew how to hurt her outside *and* inside. Like when Kaili had angered him that day three years ago—Sandis still didn't know what she'd done—and he'd forced her to watch while Galt shoved some sort of awful poison down Rist's throat, making him vomit over and over until blood spattered his lips. Sandis hadn't seen it, but Heath had. Kaili hadn't spoken to any of them for nearly a month after that.

Kazen would never have their bones broken or skin torn. That would lower his vessels' ability to summon high-level numina, or leave them unable to host at all. But anything that didn't leave a mark was fair game. Galt often leered at her and the other women. Kazen would never let him ravish any of them; being virginal was another vessel requirement. But maybe, in his anger, Kazen would permit other things . . .

Sandis shook her head. Sidestepped to avoid a boy leading a skinny goat by a rope. *Stop thinking about it.*

The library. She could try the library. And food . . . Could she go to a restaurant, order something, and then flee before she paid? Or would she be asked to pay first? She'd never been to one. Perhaps she could try it, and if she had to pay first, she could claim she'd left her wallet at home and leave before anyone suspected her.

Yes, that. She would do that. Repay the establishment someday, if she could. But she had to eat. Just this one time, until she could find Talbur Gwenwig and explain herself. He'd take her in, surely. Even as a servant . . . She would work for free, for his favor. Anything to keep her from sleeping on the streets. Anything to protect her from Kazen and—

She stepped into a tavern, and the smell of goat cooking on a spit immediately reminded her of Heath. She bit her lip to keep her empty stomach from heaving. Her appetite nearly left her . . . but she needed the energy. Weakness would make her slow. She'd be caught for sure.

She scanned the room. There were few people there at this early hour—taverns made their money on the nightlife. Wooden booths lined two of the walls, and small round tables featuring an array of cards and gambling games took up the center of the floor. The far wall had a small bar with an overweight, bald man standing behind it, picking at a sliver on a shelf holding glasses. The slack in his forehead told Sandis he was disinterested in his work, and the shadows beneath his eyes whispered he hadn't slept much the night before, either. A small nook behind him led to the kitchen, where the smell of Heath wafted into the room.

Kolosos.

Sandis swallowed. Eat first. Think later.

She studied the two other guests—a young man, perhaps midtwenties, counted money in a booth. A steaming mug sat beside him. His posture was relaxed, his knees apart. Confident, especially since he was counting bills in plain sight, though the droop of his shoulders said he also lacked sleep. An older gentleman with a long mustache sat two booths behind him, holding a newspaper in one hand and a roast chicken leg in the other. The ferocity with which his teeth dug into the flesh, paired with his too-tight hold on the paper, whispered he was frustrated about something, perhaps angry. Sandis needed to keep her distance from him, but her focus returned to his food.

Her mouth watered.

"Hey, you."

Sandis jumped and clutched her coat to herself. She turned toward the voice. The first man had stowed away his money and was staring at her with frank interest. She didn't recognize him from her life *before*, and it was obvious he wasn't a grafter. No physical signs of being a mobsman, at least not for the Riggers, Skeets, or Aces.

To her surprise, he smiled. "Skittish, are we?" He tilted his head toward the bench across from him. When she didn't move, he held up his hands and said, "If you want to sit by yourself, by all means . . ."

Sandis shouldn't talk to him. Shouldn't connect him to her. Yet in a moment of panic—or perhaps desperate need for kindness—she hurried to the bench and sat. Let out a breath. "Sorry."

The man glanced at her hand—checking for a ring? Oh. She touched her hair, tucked it behind her ear. She wasn't used to *that* kind of interest, minus the leering looks Galt often cast her.

"Little early for a drink, isn't it?" he asked. He was trying to be funny. If not for the crinkles on the sides of his eyes, Sandis might not have picked up on it.

She glanced at his mug. "You're the one drinking."

He smiled again and tilted the mug toward her so she could see its dark contents. "Cider, I swear. What's your excuse?"

Sandis fiddled with the button of her coat. Was someone supposed to come by to take her food order? "I'm just getting a bite to eat before my shift."

"Where at?"

"The firearms factory." It would be easiest to answer his questions as if she were still fourteen and normal. Better for keeping track of what she said.

"Which one?"

"Helderschmidt's."

The man folded his hands and leaned his chin on them. "Isn't that District Four? That's a ways away."

Sandis stiffened. Did he not believe her? But he didn't look at her in an accusing way. He looked at her the way Rist looks at Kaili.

Did he think she was pretty?

Her cheeks warmed. "Um. This is where we found space to live, I guess." *Not "I guess." Sound sure.*

"We?"

She swallowed. "My brother and I."

The brother she had been desperately searching for when the slavers picked her up. At the time, she hadn't yet accepted she was looking for a dead boy. The heat in her face instantly iced over.

She cleared her throat. That must have been the way to summon service, for a girl no older than twelve hurried over and asked what she'd like. Guilt ate at Sandis nearly as much as the hunger did. She was stealing from a child.

She asked for chicken and cider. The girl bobbed her head and retreated.

The man across from her was fairly handsome—dark eyes and dark hair with a bit of a curl to it. He needed a shave, but his collar was nice.

"What's your name?" he asked.

"Sandis." She winced internally. Should she have used a fake name?

"Rone."

"Hm?"

He pointed at his nose. "Rone. My name. There. We can be friendly now."

Was she not being friendly? Maybe she was focusing so much on his expressions she'd forgotten to check her own. She cleared her throat a second time.

Rone slid his cider toward her.

Thanking him with a nod, Sandis took it, forcing herself to drink slowly. The cider was spicy and sweet, with a hint of cinnamon.

Rone shifted in his seat so the side of his foot touched the side of hers. He was flirting with her, she was certain, but she didn't know how to respond. She'd never flirted before. Kazen didn't let anyone touch his vessels, and he didn't let them touch each other, either. That was why Rist and Kaili exchanged *looks* and nothing more.

"So, firearms. That's exciting." His eyes searched her face.

Sandis forced herself not to turn away. *He's not suspicious. Act . . . pretty.* She managed a smile, which apparently was the right thing to do, for Rone matched it and leaned in closer. She said, "I suppose it's better than cotton."

"Why? Cotton is so . . . soft." His toe rubbed against her ankle.

Sandis shook her head. "In the factories, little bits of it flutter everywhere. People breathe them in. It collects in their lungs, makes them sick." Her father had always had a nasty cough from working at the cotton mill.

"Oh. Um, sorry." He rubbed the back of his neck.

She shrugged. "It's not your fault."

"Figure of speech."

Sandis turned the empty mug over in her hands. "So . . . do you work at a factory?"

He grinned again. "Not exactly. I'm more of a—"

The door to the tavern flung open and smashed into the wall behind it. Without turning around, Sandis knew. Somehow, she knew.

That pressure began building in her skull again. Spinning around, she saw Galt and four other grafter lackeys push their way into the quiet establishment: Marek, the heavy door guard. Ravis, whose coat she wore. Another two she couldn't name. Her heart sped until her vision swam. She desperately looked around—window, kitchen?—for somewhere to run.

"What's the meaning of this?" The bald man from behind the bar marched out, hands on his hips.

Sandis's breathing accelerated. Could she hide under the table? They must have followed her from the bank and seen her come in here—

Rone's fingers touched her wrist, and she jumped. His brows knit together. "You all right?"

She swallowed. Searched for words. Shook her head.

Rone glanced at the men, who were already shoving the barkeeper aside. "They're after you?"

She nodded.

He grinned. *Grinned.* Sandis pulled her wrist back.

"Don't worry." He cracked his knuckles. "I'll take care of them. We'll discuss payment later."

Did he glance at her lips? He definitely winked.

Sandis was incredibly confused. Then Galt saw her and pulled out a knife, and confusion turned to cold stone.

Rone's hands disappeared under the table for a moment, and Sandis thought she heard a brief whir. Then he stood and launched himself at all five men.

That dreamlike sensation came back to her for a moment as she stared, still frozen in place, her blood pounding through her veins. Rone soared toward Galt and moved like water away from his knife. Grabbed his wrist and brought it up and over his head, disarming him—

One of the unnamed charged at him, throwing a fist. Rone easily ducked it and dragged Galt down with him—

But there were *three more*. Marek pulled a knife. Sandis screamed when it thrust under Rone's arm and deep into his ribs.

Rone barely flinched.

He *barely flinched* . . . and turned around to slam his knuckles into Marek's cheek. The man fell back, ripping the knife out as he did.

No blood.

There was no blood. No wound. Nothing but a hole in Rone's shirt.

Sandis's mouth fell open. *But . . . how?*

The grafters were skilled—they moved quickly, and Sandis had a hard time keeping track of them. But Rone moved quicker. He twisted limbs. Slammed elbows into noses, feet into guts. Another knife stabbed into his collar, but it left no more of a wound than the first one had. Marek went down, followed by Ravis. Rone was fighting the two unknown grafters when that faint whirring attracted Sandis's attention again.

Daring to take her eyes off the scene, she lay down on the bench and looked under the table.

She gasped.

There, spinning in the air as though held up by invisible string, was a golden ornament about the size of her fist. It was made entirely of gold bent to form a loopy kind of star around a spinning center—the source of the whirring sound.

An *amarinth*. Kazen had sketches of similar objects. He'd talked about them before at length. They were incredibly rare artifacts of Noscon make that granted their owners immortality. Brief immortality.

What were the rules again? A minute of life for every twenty-four hours of the day?

Sandis had thought it a legend—perhaps a test of her gullibility—but there was no denying what she'd seen. The grafters' knives had come out clean, and this golden thing hung in the air before her. How long had it been spinning? Thirty seconds? Forty?

She dared not touch it, lest she stop its spinning and get Rone killed.

She looked up as Galt hit the floor, cradling a bloody mouth.

Rone had an amarinth. The grafters couldn't hurt him.

If she took it, they wouldn't be able to hurt *her* . . .

Sandis's gaze flicked between the amarinth, Rone, and the grafters. Time was nearly up. The grafters were almost incapacitated. She had to choose.

For the second time that morning, her mind made itself up like a firing pin depressed.

The second the last grafter fell, Sandis grabbed the amarinth and bolted for the door, losing herself in the crowd before Rone could catch his breath.

Chapter 5

Introduce yourself to the pretty girl, he'd thought. *Impress her with your protective abilities,* he'd thought.

Now he was chasing her through Dresberg at the busiest hour of the day, and she *had his amarinth.*

Idiot. He ran, bulldozing through two children holding hands. They'd get over any scraped knees, but he had to get that amarinth back, or life as he knew it was over.

That relic was *his,* damn it!

"Thief!" he tried, turning heads even as he pushed through them.

Men, women, and children alike packed the streets and sidewalks. Lunch hour at the factory was the absolute worst time to chase someone. Those who heard him turned about, looking for the accused, but they didn't know whom to look at, let alone apprehend. Rone was moving as fast as he could, yet barely covering any ground.

This was *exactly* why he preferred rooftops.

He struggled to keep track of the woman who'd shared his cider and then stolen his most treasured possession. He stepped on a lot of feet and was battered by a lot of curses, but he couldn't take his eyes off her. She pulled up the hood of her coat, which helped her blend in. She wasn't short, but there were plenty of tall workers in the crowd, and every time she ducked around one, Rone panicked a little more.

"Thief!" he yelled again. He didn't have time to contemplate the irony of the accusation.

Rone growled and crossed his arms in front of his chest as a shield, picking up speed and plowing through the crowd. He burst out onto a new street, where there was an extra finger's breadth or two between people. He pushed through. Got cussed at. A woman hit him with her bag as he passed. He didn't care. He had to reach Sandis. He *had* to reach her.

How the hell was she moving so much faster than he was?

Someone shouted a protest far to Rone's right—he dared to glance over, only to see two of the men from the tavern shoving their way through the crowd just as he had. The stocky man he'd punched in the mouth, the ringleader, and another one of the thugs.

Good. Whatever trouble she's in, I hope they catch her! He shook his head and gritted his teeth, barking at two chatting men to move. *No, I don't. If they get her, they'll get the amarinth.*

He was the stupidest person he knew. Stupid, stupid. Thinking with his pants instead of his head. *Idiot, idiot, idiot—*

He blew through the crowd, stumbling onto a bit of street not completely overflowing with people. He was near the end of the exodus. He sprinted as fast as he could. A little farther, and—

No. Rone stopped. Spun around. Rushed back to the crowd. Weaved through the street. Slipped into one alleyway, then another. *No, no, no, no, no!*

She was gone.

Sandis ran until she couldn't run anymore. Until her lungs were fraying sacks, her legs rubber bands with no more give, her skin a sweaty mess beneath the coat she dared not take off. She limped down a narrow road packed with narrow flats, not unlike the one she'd grown up in. The smell of the overflowing garbage bin in her path burned her nostrils, but she leaned on the brick wall beside it, out of sight. She closed her eyes, ignoring the looping pieces of hair glued to her forehead with perspiration, and wheezed, trying to catch her breath. After a moment, she slid down the bricks to sit on the road. This one was packed dirt and gravel, no cobblestones.

Her stomach growled. Leaning forward, Sandis pulled off one of her shoes. The thin sole was filthy, and the fabric stitched to it had started to tear. Her foot was covered in red spots, some raised and filling with fluid. Everything else was bruises. She pulled off her other shoe and gave her aching feet a moment to rest. All she could do now was breathe.

And pry her fingers off the gold trinket clutched in them. She had to use her other hand to do it—she'd been gripping the amarinth so hard, and for so long, her joints had stiffened and locked. Sandis made a protective wall with her knees and massaged her hand until the artifact dropped out of it.

She studied its thin, looping bands of gold and the pale, glimmering orb suspended in the center without anything to hold it up. The gold alone would fetch a good price, keep her fed for a month at least, surely. But the actual amarinth . . . it was priceless. Of course, if anyone found out she had it, they'd probably take it from her without a penny passing between them. That, she didn't doubt.

She turned the amarinth over, trying to figure it out. Taking hold of one of the gold loops, she spun it. The device made that gentle whirring sound as the loops rotated around each other. Sandis released it, and it fell against her stomach, lifeless. It had suspended itself midair at the tavern. Its magic must have been spent. Yes, that was what Kazen had said. One minute, once a day.

She grasped the treasure and shoved it into an interior pocket in her coat. She had to stay out of Kazen's grasp for another twenty-four hours before the amarinth would work for her. And then what? What could she accomplish in a single minute? She couldn't move the way Rone had. She had no training in martial arts.

Frowning, Sandis slouched against the wall, stomach grumbling once more. Rone had been nice to her. Helped her. She'd be back in Kazen's grasp by now if he hadn't risked himself to protect her. And what had she done? Taken his amarinth. She pressed her palms against her eyes and took a deep breath, then another. She didn't have the energy—or the water—to cry.

She was terrible, wasn't she? But she needed some way to protect herself until she found her relative. Talbur Gwenwig had gold, if he was doing the gold exchange. Sandis would bet he'd have the resources to find Rone again. And Sandis would apologize and give the amarinth back. Get a job at a factory and pay some interest, if she could. But for now, she needed the relic more than he did. He was so confident and so strong . . . She was sure she needed it more.

Someone tapped her shoulder.

Sandis jumped, ready to run, but it was only a boy. Seven or eight years of age, she guessed, and in need of a bath. His clothes were thin, and his pants had holes over both knees. He didn't wear shoes.

He held out a heel of bread to her.

Sandis stared at it, then at the boy.

"My mom says you look like you're in trouble." He glanced behind him, to where a woman of about forty years scrubbed clothes in an old washbasin in front of one of the narrow flats. The woman nodded at the boy—or, perhaps, at Sandis—and the boy turned back and continued, "She said she used to be in trouble, too, and we need to support each other."

He offered the heel of bread again. With shaky fingers, Sandis took it. A tear burned her eye. "Thank you," she whispered.

The boy smiled—he was missing several teeth—and ran back to his mother's side. Sandis waited for the woman to look up once more; then she nodded her thanks and dug into the heel. It was delicious. It became hard to chew after a few bites—her mouth was too dry and the bread was old—but Sandis kept working on it until the entire thing lumped in her stomach. Then, gathering her courage, Sandis put her shoes back on and limped over to the woman and her son.

Without speaking, she knelt down and got the next piece of dirty laundry and dunked it into the basin, working out the stains one by one.

Sandis spent the night on the small family's porch—it was warm enough to do so. The step was hard and uncomfortable, but Sandis was so tired that for the majority of the night, she honestly didn't mind. She hadn't dared accept their invitation to sleep inside. She knew how Kazen's men worked. When they wanted someone, they hunted down their entire network. It narrowed where the quarry could hide . . . and usually motivated the person to stop running.

Perhaps it would be better, then, for her to wait for Kazen to give up before trying to find Talbur Gwenwig. To protect him. But if he was rich—and the presence of his name in the gold-exchange record whispered that he would be—maybe *he* could protect *her*. Celestial bless it to be so.

Until she found the man who shared her surname, Sandis fortunately didn't have a network. It didn't *feel* fortunate, but she reminded herself that it was better to keep these kind people—any people—at a distance. They would be safer, and she would be harder to find. Kazen would never *want* to give up, but even he had to run out of resources eventually, right?

It would be different if Alys had been the one to run. She had a low summoning level. Sandis didn't. For one reason or another, her body could tolerate the possession of a strong numen. Though she had never tried, she suspected she could probably go up to an eight on the scale. That made her nearly irreplaceable.

Of the six vessels Kazen had owned yesterday, three had been capable of hosting a level seven—she, Heath, and Dar. Now he only had one. Heath had died beneath the weight of this Kolosos, and Sandis had run away. Alys and Kaili never hosted anything stronger than a five, whereas Rist had peaked at level six. There was a chance Kazen would never allow her to get away, regardless of the resources it cost him. If that was the case, she may have made a terrible mistake.

Sandis pondered this as she moved through the city at dawn, the first bells for factory shifts ringing. She crossed through the smoke ring, where most of the factories lay, and coughed her way toward the library.

The answer was to try to leave Kolingrad. She'd likely starve to death before she got to the coast, and even if she did survive the journey, she'd have to find a way of crossing without alerting the border guard. The ocean in the north was frigid, and no one would dare smuggle a vessel. She could steal a boat, but she didn't know how to sail. To the south, the mountains were nearly as high as the heavens, and the passes were guarded. From what Sandis had heard, a person needed expensive and rare documents to get past the guards, and a lot of bribe money on top of that.

Not to mention that by leaving Kolingrad, she'd be leaving the others for good. Alys, Kaili, Rist, Dar. But how would she ever rescue them? She was struggling to rescue herself.

The triumvirate did not like people leaving the country any more than Kazen liked his vessels leaving the lair.

She fingered the amarinth as she approached the library. When did it open? Would they let her in? Her clothes were decently clean. She combed her fingers through her hair. She'd only been to the library twice before, both times when her parents and Anon were still alive. Her father had been eager for her and her brother to learn how to read.

Sandis missed him dearly.

The library was closed, and so Sandis, hood up, snooped until she found a garbage bin with half an apple in it. She forced herself to eat it, for she had to keep up her energy. She walked the perimeter of the library, searching the road for dropped coins. She did find a penny, but nothing cost so little in Dresberg. She pocketed it anyway and thought of Rone's amarinth. If things got desperate enough, would she sell it? Surviving Kazen's men would do her little good if she starved to death . . .

When the doors opened, Sandis entered without issue. She was unaccustomed to approaching people—Kazen had always kept her in a passive role—but she found a custodian who looked friendly enough and asked if there was a catalog of names.

If Talbur Gwenwig were an author, it would have been easy to find him. However, he was not.

Despite her doubts, Sandis searched authors, politicians, and people of note, but her surname was nowhere to be found. She began searching periodicals, but quickly realized it would be fruitless to continue the search. For a moment she was tempted to look for the paper that had written about her father's death, but she didn't want to relive that experience. She needed to stay positive. Hopeful.

To her relief and guilt, she found a stairway that led to a private area for the librarians. One person had left his lunch in there. Sandis had meant only to eat the nuts, but hunger drove her to consume the entire meal. She apologized to the empty box and hurried from the library as the second-shift bells tolled.

She could check another bank. But would Kazen have spies posted at those places? Sandis would need to act soon, before the city's grime stained her clothes and skin. Before she looked homeless. Beggars were seldom treated with kindness, and were never allowed in prestigious places like banks and libraries.

What had Sandis gotten herself into? At least the amarinth should have reset by now, though at the moment, it seemed wholly unimportant.

She needed to get a job. But a job would make her stationary. They would find her if she got a job. If she even could.

The hot, wet smell of Heath burned in her memories. She hugged herself as the sun began to set.

Ireth, are you there? What should I do?

The numen did not reply. Sandis stared up at the heavens, imagining she peered into the ethereal plane. No knowledge filtered down to her.

She needed to find a safe place to sleep.

Would the grafters look for her in the wealthier neighborhoods? Perhaps not, but some do-gooder would probably turn her in to the scarlets, which would be just as bad. She couldn't hide the gold-leaf branding on her back. She'd be thrown in prison and bumped to the top of the list for execution, surely. She shivered.

Talbur Gwenwig, where are you? Who *are* you? He might reside in one of the wealthy neighborhoods. Maybe if she asked someone, they would know him. The likelihood was slight, but Sandis only had hope to sustain her. She'd feed it as much as she could.

Quickening her pace, Sandis changed direction and headed north, where the wall was closest. All the wealthiest people lived in proximity to the wall—as far as possible from the smoke ring. She'd need to start asking around before the sun went down. Before she would be condemned as a beggar on sight.

She passed another clock tower, a factory that made railway parts, a linens shop. A man at the edge of the market tried to hawk fruit to her, so she must have still looked decent. Decent enough to afford fruit. Her mouth watered. She kept going.

Her shoulder bumped into someone, and she muttered an apology. Paused. The faintest smell wafted toward her. Burned brain dust. Galt always reeked of the drug. A lot of the grafters did.

She looked up. Not Galt, but she *knew* him, and fear coursed down her spine like lightning. He had the sallow skin of a grafter, dark clothes, knotted cords of hair. Staps. One of Kazen's men. The one who hadn't questioned her the night she walked out of the lair.

The smell of the drugs made her eyes water. Pushed her pulse faster. Made her want to scream. Recognition dawned on his face.

She bolted, nearly twisting her ankle when she turned back the way she had come. Staps cursed and ran after her, his calloused fingers brushing her elbow as he tried to grab her.

Sandis pushed her legs as fast as they would go and barreled into a nearby crowd of people, hoping to lose herself among them. Hoping her smaller body would navigate the throng faster than his larger one, like it had with Rone.

A shrill whistle sounded behind her. Not a police whistle. She knew that sound. A cry rippled up her throat and caught on her heavy breath.

Staps wasn't alone. He wasn't alone.

Celestial, save me!

But God didn't listen to sinners.

She ran, battering her swollen feet against the cobblestones until they numbered. A stitch bit her side, then another. Fear bubbled and boiled inside her gut, powering her like a steam engine.

But she wasn't fast. Not as fast as she used to be. There wasn't any space to run in Kazen's lair. She would have to hide.

Sandis's gaze darted about, anywhere but behind her. People, stands, garbage bins, the linens shop.

She veered for the linens shop, down its side to its back door. Locked. She ran down the next street, nearly barreling into a waiting horse. The thumping of two—three?—sets of feet followed behind her. The sun dipped behind the city wall.

She rushed for the clock tower. Tried its door. Unlocked, bless the Celestial! She ripped it open and ran inside, only to find a small, closed-off room, empty save for a set of stairs.

She took the stairs two at a time. The door slammed open behind her just as she hit the first landing and turned to ascend the next set.

A cry escaped her, tearing up her throat as it expelled from her huffing lungs. A door, a door. Please, a door! She hit the fourth flight and grabbed the railing, trying to pull herself up faster, faster. They were almost close enough to grab her. She could hear their breathing over her breathing—

Fifth flight, and a *door*. She grabbed it, and for a split second thought it was locked. But the old knob gave way under her sweating hands. She shoved the door open.

Cool, smoky air hit her face.

It was all ledge—a winding balcony below the clock face. Meant for maintenance.

Staps and the other two grafters erupted from the door. Sandis ran the length of the platform, searching for another door, another set of stairs. There was no way down. Thudding feet thundered behind her. She grabbed the rail.

Her mind formed the decision in a trice. She stepped over the rail. A gust of air rushed past her, cooling her perspiration. Her teeth chattered. The city was six stories down. A sliver of sun sparkled off her eyelashes.

Her pursuers paused.

The one with a shaved head, Ravis, stepped forward. He eyed her—and his jacket—and put his hands up in mock surrender. "Sandis Gwenwig. Let's return you home. This is nonsensical."

Sandis looked away from him, then let go of the rail and fell.

She'd never fallen so far in her life. It was strange. Her stomach rose into her throat, and time moved both too quickly and too slowly. Her mind couldn't compute the city rising up to meet her. She couldn't distinguish people, shapes, or sounds. Only that weightless sensation and the beating of her own heart.

Gold pinched her hand. The amarinth didn't seem to mind the fall, or the wind rushing up at them. She spun it.

Then she hit.

It didn't hurt. Jumping from a clock tower onto hard cobblestones *should* hurt, but it didn't. Her skull didn't fracture into a thousand pieces. Her bones didn't break. Her skin didn't tear. She hit with a heavy sort of pressure, like she was a flying bug and the street was an open hand. Though she held on to the amarinth, the gold loops that weren't pinned by her fingers continued to spin.

She stared at it. One minute. She had most of it left.

She was *alive*.

She felt the weight of dozens of eyes and lifted her head. People all around stared at her, gaping, hands pressed to mouths and chests. She hid the amarinth in her coat. Looked up at three grafters staring at her from beneath the clock face of the six-story tower.

A long, deep breath filled her lungs.

Thank you.

Finding her feet, Sandis ran.

Forty seconds later, the amarinth stopped spinning.

Chapter 6

Rone was going to bald early if he didn't stop trying to pull out his hair.

He'd searched everywhere. Scoured. Even followed the men from the tavern, but they'd led him on a wild-goose chase. Where had she gone? Where had his *amarinth* gone?

God's tower, if she sold it . . . he didn't know what he'd do. Other than pull out his hair.

And the city, thanks to its utter lack of courtesy, went about its usual business. As if he hadn't just lost the most precious thing he'd ever owned and his employment alongside it.

His shoulder ached, as if saying, *Good one. Too bad you can't get rid of me, too.*

Rone grumbled and massaged the tight muscles there as he trudged up to the property manager's office. His means of living was, *temporarily*, lost, but the rent was still due on both of the flats he paid for—his and his mother's. At least he still had money in his pockets. More than most. Just not enough to get him and his mother across the border.

He'd figure this out. One way or another, he'd figure this out.

Dropping his hand from his shoulder, he rolled his neck, wincing when it pulled on his old injury. He stepped up to the window and fetched his wallet from his pocket, counting bills.

"Hello, Rone," the old man inside the window said. He turned away for a moment, then looked back so quickly his head might have flown off his neck. "Rone? What are you doing here?"

Rone looked up. Blew a wavy bit of hair off his forehead. "Check your calendar, Tus."

"I know it's the end of the month. But are you sure you want to keep an empty flat? I don't double up on leases."

Rone's hand paused midway to his money stack, the next bill wrinkling between his fingers. The blood drained from his face and neck. "Tus. What do you mean, an *empty* flat?"

He'd visited his mother two days ago.

Tus's face fell. "You haven't heard."

"Tell me."

He frowned. "I thought you would have. Unlike her, really. She was carted off to Gerech a couple days ago."

Rone's eyes widened. The bills dropped from his hand, and his fingers shot out to grab Tus's collar. Rone leaned in as close as the windowsill would let him. "What the hell do you mean, *Gerech*? Who told you? Why?"

Gerech. Also known as Dresberg Prison. Also known as the jail with the highest rollover rate in the country, thanks to too many criminals and not enough cells. That didn't mean the jailers let people go, of course. Most of them left in coffins.

"Sh-She was accused of theft," Tus said, shaking, and Rone forced his fingers to open. Tus swallowed and rubbed his collar. "Stole a Noscon headpiece right from the Renad household."

Rone's body turned to stone. *"What?"*

Tus kept going as if he hadn't heard. "I don't know how she managed to do it. Security up there is pretty good, I hear. But Ernst isn't a forgiving man, and . . . well, you know how it goes with rich folk. They'll spend a fortune to make someone suffer for stealing a penny—"

"A Noscon headpiece," Rone whispered.

"That's what I said. Makes no sense. She must have known she wouldn't be able to sell it without the theft being traced back to her."

They had blamed his *mother*. Arrested her right after his visit, if Tus's timeline was right.

Damn the Celestial to fiery hell. He'd been two-timed. But why? And why had they set up his *mother*? The blasted woman felt guilt over killing *spiders*. No one should even know about her connection to him. He'd always been so careful.

Rone slammed a short stack of bills on the sill. "Keep it open. I'll be back."

He needed to find the bastard who'd hired him. Didn't matter that he didn't have the amarinth. The man responsible for this was going to wish he'd never set eyes on him. Rone clung to that anger, that push to fight. Because if he didn't, the guilt would devour him alive.

Marald Helg. That was the name of the man who'd hired him to steal the headpiece. It was very possibly a fake name, but then again, Rone used an alias as well. All his past and future employers knew and would know him as Engel Verlad. His true surname, Comf, was far too telling.

But this Helg guy had figured it out. How else would he have known who his mother was?

The more Rone thought about it, the more he realized he should have detected something was wrong. The ease of the mission. The lack of motivation for wanting the headpiece. The client's home—though it was a large flat with two floors, which denoted wealth, it had been nearly empty. There were marks on the walls where pictures or other ornamentation had once hung. A lack of furniture. Was he moving, or had he sold his belongings? Rone hoped for the latter. He might not find the man if he had moved.

Now that he thought about it, there'd been something off about the client. The glint in Helg's eye. His tone of voice. He'd looked at Rone differently than others. Like he hated having to hire him.

Rone gritted his teeth until they squeaked from the pressure. He was going to fix this. One way or another, he was going to fix this. His mother was a strong woman. If anyone could make it there . . .

Gerech. His stomach rolled, and not because he'd just leapt a six-foot gap between roofs. Rone had a feeling Gerech Prison wouldn't take an exchange, even if Rone offered up himself. The guilt hardened into a leaden ball in his stomach. A leaden ball with teeth.

The buildings began to distance themselves from one another, so Rone picked his way down to the street. Hitched a ride on a passing cart. If he found the flat empty, he would figure out a way to get his man. Engel Verlad was known for doing the impossible. Or the near impossible, anyway. And when he found Marald Helg, he would hang him off the clock tower until the man sang for mercy and turned himself in as the true thief.

Even that might not be enough to free his mother.

To make matters worse, it started to rain.

Rone cursed and dropped from the cart, then crossed the street to the nearest eave, as did many others. Bodies pressed up against one another to get out of the downpour, while other, more prepared denizens pulled out umbrellas or newspapers to shield themselves. It was one thing to get wet; it was another to get wet within the first ten minutes of a storm. The drops passed through layer after layer of smoke and pollution before hitting the ground, turning into falling sludge. The only bright side was that after a hearty rainstorm, the air had a semblance of freshness for a day or two. If the rainstorm wasn't hearty, everything just got dirtier.

Rone groaned and rested his head against the wall behind him. The building was a small laundry for those who could actually afford to pay others to launder their clothes. Rone had come by a few times during his busier months. His mom didn't like him "wasting" money on such things. *"I can do it if you're too busy. I don't mind."*

Rone muttered every curse word he knew as the ball in his gut began shredding his intestines.

The folks huddled around him chattered about nothing. A few hurried out, pulling their collars up as high as they could. They talked about how long the rain would last. About being late for their shifts. About the stains on their skirts. Oh, to have such problems. Rone sighed and looked out over their heads, watching the gray rain pelting the gray cobbles. Another, smaller crowd had formed beneath a mobile fish stand—he didn't envy them. Even if they avoided the rain, they'd stink of fish when they got to wherever they were going. Someone stepped out from around the corner, hawking pieces of scrap metal and cardboard anything wide and flat enough to keep off the sludge. A few darted across the street to make a purchase.

Rone blinked at the lingering group. Rubbed his eyes. Squinted.

God's tower, that was her. That was *her*. Sandis. The thief who'd lifted his amarinth while he saved her neck.

He pushed past some of the huddlers to get a better view, and they happily took his prime spot against the wall. Yes, it *was* her. Her clothes were the same from before, except they looked dirtier now. She had the hood of her coat pulled up, but kept looking up and down the street, searching for something. Giving Rone a good shot of her face again and again.

Sludgy precipitation forgotten, Rone charged toward her.

Sandis turned too soon and spotted him. Eyes wide, she bolted into the slick street, her dainty shoes slapping against the wet cobbles as she ran.

He was faster. He gained on her, slowly and surely.

She dashed behind another shop, then down a road packed with flats. Took another sharp turn, and another, buying herself a few extra steps of distance that Rone closed within seconds. They barreled past more people taking refuge beneath eaves. A drop of brownish water hit Rone in the eye. He wiped it off, never slowing. He reached out, and—

His hand snagged her upper arm. She jerked, and they both fell to the road—a packed-dirt one, which meant a mouthful, face full, and everything full of mud. Sandis grunted and twisted in his grip, trying to land a kick. Rone grabbed her ankle.

Her fist hit his face. Which wouldn't have been so bad, had she not jabbed her knuckle right into his eyeball.

"Damn it!" Rone shouted, letting her go. She scurried to her feet, and he ran after her. They both made it a few paces before he seized her again.

"Let me go!" She twisted her arm out of his grasp. Wily thing.

"Give me back what you took, and maybe I will," Rone spat. He reached for one of her pockets. She danced out of the way. He really, really didn't want to hit a woman to get his amarinth back, but this had *not* been a good day.

"You!" shouted a bystander crouched under the eaves of a nearby flat. "If she says no, she means it! Let her go!"

Rone did not. "It's not like that. She's a thief."

The man and his large friend took a step out from under the eaves.

Rone put his hands up in surrender. Sandis sprinted away.

Rone went the other way, around a flat, and ran across a narrow road to intercept her head-on. He grabbed her shoulders, fingertips digging into her coat.

She struggled. "Please, go away. You can't be seen with me!"

"Give it back!" He checked another pocket. She tried to elbow him in the face, but he easily moved out of the way.

"I will! I will . . . later." Her voice went hoarse with desperation. "Please, you have to leave."

A horse and carriage came galloping down the road, forcing Rone to drag Sandis out of the way before they became trampled meat.

Jerking out of his grip the moment he completed the move, she ran in the direction the carriage had come.

Rone dashed after her. Before he caught up, she spun around, dirty rain whipping from her hair. Her hood fell back.

"Please." She was begging now. "I need it more than you. You don't understand." She backed up, searching the road again.

"I severely doubt that." He seized her wrist. Enough of this.

"You can't be seen with me!"

He spun her around, pinning her back to his chest. She tried to stomp on his foot. He shifted, and she missed. He checked another pocket, then stuck his hand inside her coat. Felt a familiar lump. *Finally.* He pulled the golden trinket free.

A gun hammer clicked alarmingly close to his head.

Rone and Sandis both froze. His grip on her loosened. She took a single step forward, then stopped as a second gunman emerged from behind a squat building, holding a fancy-looking pistol in his hands. Rone recognized him from the tavern.

The muzzle of the first gun pressed into the back of his head.

Yeah, he was pretty positive *he* needed the amarinth the most right now.

"They followed you," Sandis whispered, sending chills up Rone's arms. "Please tell me you have a gun."

He didn't; guns were too clunky and too loud for his line of work. He didn't bother explaining.

"You again," the second gunman said, appraising Rone before his gaze darted back to Sandis. Why were they after her? What was so special about her?

"What's your name?" the first gunman asked.

"I'll give you a hint," he said, trying to measure where the man behind him stood. "It rhymes with Muck Kerself."

They didn't laugh. Sandis looked at him with eyes as wide as a hungry puppy's. She visibly trembled. She was terrified.

61

The second gunman trained his pistol on her.

She whispered, "Kazen won't let you put a hole in me."

What in the Celestial's name was going on?

Rone spun the amarinth—relief rushing through him when it responded—and chucked it toward the gutter.

He ducked and threw his elbow behind him, hitting the first gunman in the rib. The guy shot, and his bullet grazed Rone's bad shoulder, barely missing the girl. The second gunman lifted his pistol from Sandis to Rone. Rone launched forward and grabbed the muzzle, shoving it against his neck just as the man fired.

The bullet didn't hurt, only felt like pressure. Like his throat was going the wrong direction and he'd swallowed a huge chunk of meat.

It passed through his neck and went right into the face of the man standing behind him.

Sandis screamed.

Rone pushed the pistol away and slammed his fist into the second gunman.

Sandis spun in the pelting rain. "They're coming," she croaked.

Rone shoved a knee into his assailant's groin and let him fall to the ground. "Who?"

She hesitated a moment. Perhaps she didn't want to tell him. She met his gaze; rain dripped from her eyelashes. "The grafters."

Rone's skin became almost too heavy to hold up. *"What?"*

Grafters? These men were *grafters*?

He swore.

Sandis moved for the still-spinning amarinth and swiped it. Rone grabbed her wrist. Cursed again.

This was a very, very bad day.

He dragged her across the street, but Sandis took *his* wrist in her free hand and pulled him back the way they had come. "This way!"

He didn't have time to question her. He ran, towing Sandis behind him, though she kept up moderately well. He should have ripped the amarinth from her fingers and ditched her, but the terror in her eyes—

And bloody *grafters*. He wouldn't leave anyone to those nightmare-worshipping scumsacks if he could help it, even a thief.

His eyes searched for a sewer lid. He didn't see one, but the alleyways between the flats up ahead were narrow and winding. Changing direction as suddenly as Sandis had before, he wound through the maze. His own place wasn't far from here.

He crossed a road, turned toward a factory—

Sandis pulled back on his hand, forcing him to stop.

She bent over, wheezing. "They're . . . gone."

"How the hell do you know?"

She looked up at him, disheveled and gaunt. But the fear had receded from her eyes. Now she just looked angry.

She didn't answer him.

God's tower, she looked like a wet, beaten dog. He glanced at her other hand. No amarinth. Was it stowed in her coat, or had she chucked it somewhere?

He tensed.

"I . . . have . . . it," she huffed.

Rone set his jaw. Growled.

"Come on." He tugged her down the road, not as quickly as before, but she stumbled at the pace anyway.

Looked like Rone was taking her home after all. Just not in the way he'd originally hoped.

Chapter 7

She'd sensed a numen. Which one, she wasn't sure. Maybe Kuracean, the level-six numen bound to Rist, Heath's brother. Or perhaps it had been Alys or Kaili with Isepia. That numen was more humanoid in appearance. Kazen would want to use one of the less obvious ones. That he'd come for her himself, and in daylight, told her how angry he must be. And while part of Sandis yearned to see one of the other vessels again, she knew what getting too close would mean. Pain for them and pain for her. Sandis didn't think she could bear it.

Did Rist know how his brother had died? Did he mourn? Had he been allowed to?

Sandis pushed that thought away. Regardless, she had sensed a numen nearby, and Ireth had pressed fire into her mind. What strange comfort that small act had given her. If only the fire horse weren't trapped on the ethereal plane, far from Sandis's reach.

She couldn't tell Rone.

He knelt across from her in a moderately sized flat, furnished simply but with sturdy chairs and tables. It even had a second room and a small hallway, which she assumed led to a toilet. *His* hallway and toilet. *His* flat. He'd taken her, a thief, out of harm's way and to temporary safety.

She'd painted a target on his back.

Rone groaned. "Take off the coat. It's soaking wet."

Sandis pulled the itchy, sodden garment closer around her instead. The brand on her back seemed to sizzle against it.

Rone leaned back on his hands. He sat on the floor, his legs loosely crossed, giving her a decent-sized berth.

He wiped a hand down his face. "I can't believe I said 'muck kerself' to a grafter."

Several expletives followed the statement.

Sandis bowed her head. "I'm sorry." Her neck itched where it was coated in sludgy rain. She didn't scratch it.

Another realization surfaced. *Kazen* was looking for her himself . . . and he'd taken a fresh sample of blood from her the day she'd run. How long would it take for her blood to leave his system? She frantically began counting . . . three days. It had been three days. Kazen usually refreshed himself every week or two, depending on how often he had to use Ireth. But was that to prevent any lapse of control, or did his system clear her blood out that quickly? If he found her before that time was up . . .

"What are you thinking?"

Sandis's head snapped up. She must have worn quite an expression, for surprise passed over Rone's features and he held his hands up in mock surrender. "Just asking. Your breathing quickened all of a sudden."

Sandis breathed deeply to calm herself. "Nothing."

Rone frowned. "You're a grafter, aren't you?"

The brand burned anew beneath her coat. Better that he should suspect her of being a grafter, associated with the occult, than of being a direct part of it.

Rone tipped his head back and stared at the ceiling for a long moment. Closed his eyes. His lungs inflated, deflated. Judging from his tight forehead and slack spine, he wasn't angry, just . . . exasperated. Or simply exhausted. He muttered something about Godobia, the country immediately south of Kolingrad. A few more seconds passed before he asked, "And why are you in trouble?"

There were all sorts of reasons a grafter could be in trouble with another grafter. Sandis could think of three valid ones off the top of her head: She owed someone money. She'd killed a useful colleague. She'd traded insider secrets.

It felt wrong to lie to Rone, so she simply said nothing.

A growl echoed in his throat. He stood and ran a hand back through his hair, only to pull it free with a scowl—his fingers were covered with lingering rain sludge. He tromped toward the door.

"Stop."

Rone paused and looked at her.

Sandis swallowed. "You can't go out there. They want you, too, now."

He shook his head. "They don't know who I am."

"They do. Or they will." She looked back at the hardwood floor beneath her. It was old and stained. She picked at a crack between planks. "It's not hard for them to find the information they need. If you're connected to me . . . they'll do whatever they can to bring you down, too. They move like shadows."

"Is that how you knew they were coming?" he asked, sarcasm weighing down his words. "You saw 'shadows'?"

She narrowed her eyes. "I saved your life."

"It wouldn't have needed saving if you hadn't stolen my amarinth. *Speaking* of which." He strode toward her with his hand outstretched.

Sandis scooted backward until her shoulder hit a chair.

Rone groaned. "I'd rather not force it from you, but I need it."

"It's dead for twenty-three hours," she countered.

Rone grabbed another dirty fistful of his hair. "You are *incredibly* frustrating. It doesn't matter. I want it. It's mine." Another growl. "I don't have time for this—any of this. I have to find someone sooner, not later, and—"

Sandis perked. "You're looking for someone?"

Rone's forehead wrinkled. "Yeah, and now I'll have to do it discreetly because your scumsack posse is probably infesting the whole damn neighborhood." He moved toward the door and punched it, then shook out his hand.

"I'm sorry," she offered.

He glanced at her.

Sandis steeled herself. "I know I haven't exactly earned your favor, but please, hear me out."

He waited.

She stood. It felt appropriate to stand. Her wet clothes itched with grit and rain. "I need help."

"I don't get involved with grafters." Rone folded his arms.

"I'm not a grafter."

Rone spoke over her. "I did once, and I swore it would be the last time. No offense, but they're nasty sons of whores who will skin you alive if you so much as look at them wrong."

"I'm aware." The words were flat and without feeling. Rone frowned.

She took a deep breath. "I'm looking for someone, too. A family member. His name is Talbur Gwenwig." She waited for recognition to pass Rone's face, but it didn't, and her hope dwindled. If only it could be that easy. "The grafters are after me because I ran away from them. I saw this man's name in a bank record, and I thought he might be related to me."

"Sandis Gwenwig?" he asked.

She nodded. "I . . . I don't have any other family. I've never run before, because while the grafters are horrible—" A lump formed in her throat as dozens of memories churned through her mind. Most of them didn't even involve her, outside of as a witness. She swallowed. "—horrible people, they fed and clothed me. I had . . . friends . . . there. I told myself it was better than living and dying on the street. But I thought, if I could just find Talbur Gwenwig . . . I'm sure he's related to me. It's not a common surname. If I could just find him, maybe he would take me in and help me. Hide me. Pay Kazen off." *But maybe I would bring the grafters down on him, too.* Unless they couldn't find him, either.

Rone dropped his arms. "You're a slave." It wasn't a question.

"I didn't choose to be."

Rone turned away. Grabbed the back of his neck with both hands. Turned back. "Ah hell."

"I'm sorry," she tried again. "I'll give it back. Here." She plucked the amarinth from the back of her waistband and held it out to him. "I didn't *plan* on taking it . . . I just thought it could help me. And it has. I should thank you for not finding me sooner."

Rone stared at the amarinth. "Helped you how?"

"I jumped off the clock tower."

He looked impressed.

She continued holding out her hand to him. "Please, take it. Just help me find Talbur Gwenwig."

Rone stepped forward and snatched the amarinth from her palm. His countenance instantly relaxed. But he shook his head. "I don't get involved with grafters."

"I'm not a grafter."

"Close enough."

Her hope sputtered to an ember. She sat down in the chair behind her. Stared at the floor. Rubbed her eyes.

She felt the impression of fire beneath her fingertips. *You can do this.* The words were hers, not Ireth's, but it wasn't difficult to imagine the numen encouraging her.

Rone walked toward the other room.

"Kazen is the leader of that group of grafters," she said, her voice quieter. As far as she knew, his group was the largest in the city. "I left because he started these . . . experiments. He hurts people." The name Kolosos echoed in her thoughts, and the warmth she'd felt from Ireth instantly chilled. Were the others still all right? Would Kazen unbind

Dar and use him next? "I think he has bigger plans, ones that might be a danger to all of us, but I don't know what they are. He killed one of my friends."

Heath had been so scared . . .

"He's gone," Sandis continued, "but Talbur Gwenwig is out there somewhere, and he's . . . permanent."

Rone paused. "What?"

"Families are permanent." She looked up. "Something my parents used to say."

The hardest curse Sandis knew exited Rone's mouth. He ran a hand down his face. "Fine. *Fine.*" His brow was wrinkled with annoyance, and his voice was heavy with it. "God's tower, could you be any more pathetic?"

Sandis frowned.

Now he wiped both hands down his face. "Yes. I'll help you find this guy. But *only* if you get the grafters off my case and *only* after I get my crap done first. Understand?"

She didn't think she could do the first, but she nodded. Tears burned her eyes. "Thank you."

Rone shook his head. "There's a washbasin back there and a hose in the wall. Cold water, but it's better than nothing. Go clean up." He vanished for a moment, then returned with a gray button-up shirt, which he chucked at her. "Just . . . go."

Sandis fingered the clean cotton and jumped to her feet, smiling despite herself. "Thank you, thank you, thank you."

Rone turned away and gestured toward the hall.

Sandis hurried to oblige, but paused halfway to her destination. "It doesn't stop spinning once it starts, right?"

Rone glanced at the amarinth. "So you've noticed."

"Why not pocket it when you fight, instead of leaving it under the table?"

Rone rolled his eyes. "Do you want to fight with a magical lump of gold shaking and floating in *your* pocket? It gets in the way and draws unwanted attention." He mumbled something.

"What?"

"It gets *linty*," he said, exasperated. He pointed again toward the privy. "Black ashes, woman, just *go*."

She smiled and danced away.

Cold water had never felt so warm.

The light wasn't bright, and yet it was blinding. Liquid flame. Reddish orange and swirling. Split by black cracks. It pressed all around her. Built up the pressure in her head.

She closed her eyes, but the light permeated her eyelids. It surrounded her. *Fire,* the sweltering air whispered. *Need.*

Ireth?

A bone-shaking groan sounded low in the earth—deep and rich. Sandis tried to turn to see it, but her world was full of fiery light and black cracks. She pressed the heels of her hands to her forehead. The pressure began to hurt.

Fear. Ireth was *afraid*.

The cracks shifted at once, pushed by an unfelt wind. They gathered together into a smoking wall, then split apart to form a pointed oval that shifted toward her.

No. That was an *eye*.

Sandis started awake, staring down at her knees. When had she sat up? Her hairline was cold with sweat. The room was dark, yet colored spots marred her vision, as if she'd just stared into the light of a lamp. She breathed hard, the impressions of *fire* and *need* slowly receding from her aching head. Her pulse fired in every direction.

Footsteps. The urge to run struck her, then faded when she elbowed the thin cushion on the couch. She stared at it, memory trickling back to her.

Couch. Rone's flat. She was here. She was safe. For now.

She mouthed Ireth's name.

The footsteps paused. "Sandis?"

She blinked away the spots, straining to remember images from the dream. *What? What was that?*

Perhaps it was Sandis's own mind playing tricks on her, but she felt a single name form on her tongue, one she didn't dare speak.

Kolosos.

Was Ireth trying to show her Kolosos?

Was that burning, watching *thing* what had ripped Heath apart?

She shivered.

"Sandis."

Rone's voice ripped her from her thoughts. He stood two paces from her, his hair mussed, his nightshirt untucked.

"S-Sorry," she whispered. "Nightmare."

Rone let out a long breath. "Isn't it, though?"

He didn't explain, merely turned back for the second room. Sandis heard his body plop onto the narrow bed within.

Rising, Sandis poked about the small kitchen area until she found a cup to fill with water. She drank slowly. The pressure had receded from her head, along with the pain, but the red, orange, and black images stayed fresh.

Kolosos.

No wonder Heath had been so afraid. Yet what frightened Sandis was not so much the glimpse of hell Ireth had shown her, but the knowledge that Kazen wanted such a monster under *his* control.

"You're going to leave?"

There was a subtle note of fear in her question. Rone glanced over at Sandis, who had wedged herself into one corner of the sofa, as if trying to take up as little space as possible. She'd cleaned her pants and paired them with his shirt. He couldn't blame her—hers was odd. Good material, but heavy and with a wide-open back. He'd never before seen that fashion in Dresberg, and most would consider it scandalous.

He wouldn't complain if she donned it again.

"I told you, I have to find someone."

She glanced toward the single window. "But it's still dark."

"I know my way around."

"The grafters will still be looking." Her voice was quieter.

Rone let a half smile pull at his lips. "Not where we're going."

"We?"

"I take it you don't want to sit here twiddling your thumbs. Besides, I don't trust you with my stuff."

She studied him a moment, then stood without further comment. At least she wasn't overly chatty. And she looked slightly less pathetic this morning.

He tried not to shudder at the thought of what he'd gotten himself into.

They slipped out the door, leaving the flat dark. Rone massaged his shoulder as he walked toward the back of the three-story building. He lived on the second floor. Dawn would be breaking soon—blue already edged some of the clouds. From his experience, most people were home at this hour.

Sandis followed, up the ladder and onto the roof, without complaint. Once Rone got his higher vantage point, he studied the city. There were always people out, but the streets were fairly empty. In another hour, the first-shift workers would pool onto the cobblestones.

His gaze lingered on the shifting shadows. Had the grafters already found them? God's tower, he'd rather deal with one of the mobs. At least they were honest, when threatened. Threats didn't work on grafters. He knew—he'd forfeited half his pay for a delivery he'd made to them two years ago. The creepy grafter who'd swindled him had worn an eye patch and two gold teeth. Rone had threatened plenty to no avail, and he'd left as the scared one.

"You're going to jump the roofs?"

Smart one. "Yeah. Hope you're athletic."

Sandis clasped her hands under her chin and crept to the edge of the building. Searched. Pointed west. "That one isn't too far."

Rone nodded. "Should keep us out of the grafters' line of sight. I doubt they look up much."

He'd meant it as a religious pun. Sandis simply nodded.

He jumped to the next roof, another building of flats, trying to be light on his feet so as not to disturb the tenants. While he didn't particularly care if he roused them from sleep, he didn't want anyone investigating. He turned right and rushed for the next edge, this one no more than a three-foot jump. Another residential building. Engineers knew how to wedge them in.

Sandis landed softly behind him, impressing him with her silence. His old teacher, Arnae Kurtz, would have liked her.

He wanted speed, but slowed down to keep Sandis behind him. She stumbled a few times in those worthless shoes of hers. He took a more looping path southwest, trying to make the jumps easier, and, whenever possible, led Sandis to the roofs where he'd previously stowed boards to ease his journey. So far only the storms had tried to stall their journey. The one nice thing about the wall surrounding the city was it choked out most of the wind.

Black ashes, he hated this place. He and his mother would have left the country a long time ago if the emigration papers didn't cost a man's lifetime salary.

They touched down to the street once, then climbed back up a four-story building that obviously made Sandis nervous. Why, Rone didn't know. Was a grafter, of all people, afraid of heights? The things their kind did . . . But then again, Sandis had been a slave, right? He wondered what sort of slave, then snuffed the line of thought when it got too miserable. Regardless, she was at the bottom of the food chain. He had to remember that.

Ugh. He hated feeling pity. It made him *nice*.

The tip of the sun inched over the horizon by the time Rone got to where he was going—a large apartment building just inside the smoke ring. Large, because the people who lived here had some money, not because the landlord shoved in as many tenants as the space would allow, as was common with most residential buildings in the area.

Marald Helg's flat was on the top floor. If he hadn't moved.

"Stay here." He pointed at Sandis like she was a dog in training. She glanced around. Sat near the part of the roof that sloped. She'd have to wash those pants again.

Rone withheld a sigh. He checked for his amarinth, despite knowing its magic had not yet refreshed, then lowered himself off the lip of the roof and swung around its eaves to a large window. Kicked in the glass. He didn't care to be quiet. He was here to make an impression.

"Helg!" he barked, striding through the guest room and into the sitting room, which was empty save for a tweed chair. He marched down the stairs, heading toward the office where he'd made his disastrous deal with Helg. "Wake up, you filthy bastard!"

He heard a low chuckle that made his skin light up like coals. He whirled toward the bedroom and kicked open the door.

Marald Helg sat up in bed, his thinning hair mussed from sleep. Dreary dawn light poured in through a window masked by sheer curtains. The sole other piece of furniture in the room was a three-legged side table. Cheap. There were marks on the wall from where furniture used to be.

Marald Helg coughed, covering his mouth with one hand. When he finished, he licked spittle from his bottom lip.

Rone marched toward him, entertaining a million thoughts about how he'd like to kill him. He'd never killed a man, not directly, but that was a record worth tarnishing.

He raised his hand—

"I've been waiting for you, boy."

The words caught him off guard for a moment. Recovering quickly, Rone grabbed Helg by the collar of his night-robe and lifted the smaller man from his sheets. He threw him onto the floor. Helg had a gauntness to his face that hadn't been there before. He looked older. His hair was whiter. Rone didn't care.

"I don't know how you know her," Rone spat, stepping toward him like a wolf stalking its prey, "but I'm going to make Gerech look like a resort by the time I'm finished with you."

Helg laughed. *Laughed.* Rone bristled and grabbed Helg's collar again, slamming the man against the wall.

Helg winced, coughed. That made Rone feel minutely better.

"You . . . deserve it," he choked.

"You deserve *this*," Rone countered, and pulled back his fist—

"You want the story, don't you?"

Rone hesitated.

Helg smiled, which was all the invitation Rone needed to slam his fist into Helg's mouth. The feeling of teeth ripping from their gums made the sting across his knuckles pleasant. He let Helg fall to the ground and took a step back.

"Why, yes," Rone sneered. "I'd love a story."

Helg cradled his mouth. Pushed off the floor so he could sit upright. There was a slight hump in his back. "Do you know . . . who I am?" The man spat out a tooth.

"A backstabber?"

"Marald Steffen." He moved his hand from his mouth. Blood smeared across his cheek. He waited. For what, Rone didn't know.

Helg—Steffen—scowled. "You don't remember me."

"Obviously."

Steffen took a deep breath. "Do you recall Fran Errick, then?"

That name rang a bell. Rone mulled for a moment, never changing his stance or his expression. A previous client, he was sure.

"Let me jog your memory, foolish boy." Steffen licked his lip, which only spread the blood farther. "Fran Errick owns the Errick, Fritz, and Helderschmidt firearm factories. I owned the Graybrick. He hired you to steal plans for a new musket from my property."

Rone's eyes narrowed. He remembered this. It had happened about eight months ago.

"You," Steffen grunted as he clasped at the wall to stand. "You ruined me."

The words dripped from him like venom.

"I spent every last penny I had to hire you, *Engel*." He turned, looking even frailer and older than before, and glared at Rone. The rising sun highlighted his dark eyes. That hard ball of guilt began to churn in Rone's belly again. "Sent you to the most privileged man in Dresberg. I had you followed, you son of a whore."

Rone launched forward without thinking to. His hand clasped around Steffen's neck. Pinned him again to the wall.

Steffen didn't seem to notice. "I found out who you were. But you're a sly cur, Rone *Comf*. Oh, wouldn't Daddy be proud to learn about you . . . Or does he even care?"

Rone growled. His hand tightened around Steffen's throat.

The older man wheezed as he spoke. "A sly cur. You'd get away too easily. So I went for her. So simple. I hope"—he tried to swallow—"they kill her."

Rone slammed his fist into the old man's eye. He released his throat and then delivered a second punch to his cheekbone. Another to his nose, breaking it. Then his mouth again. Marald Steffen fell to his knees, and Rone spun and landed a hard kick to the side of the man's head, knocking him over.

Steffen groaned, his eyes closed. His chest still rose and fell.

Rone moved toward him. Pressed the toe of his shoe to Steffen's throat. A little pressure was all it would take. The bastard deserved it for making business personal. For attacking an innocent rather than Rone himself.

Anger made his arms tremble. Ignited new pain in his bad shoulder. Pain that radiated up his neck and into his skull.

Rone's sore hands formed fists, which he slammed into the wall after pulling his foot back from the unconscious factory owner.

Damn it. Damn him and all of them to hell.

And yet . . . he couldn't escape the thought that *he* was the one who'd done this.

It was his fault. He should have kept records. Should have watched his back. Should have hidden his identity better. Should have, should have, should have.

He needed to get his mother out of Gerech, and this bankrupt bastard wasn't the way to do it.

Rone dragged himself back up the stairs. Punched another wall and winced at the shock of it. He massaged his knuckles. Pressed his forehead against the same wall.

Damn it. Damn it. Damn it.

"I'm sorry."

He jumped and turned. Sandis stood at the edge of the hallway. The window behind her was open, and a soft breeze stirred her hair.

Rone let out a single dry chuckle. "You heard that, huh?"

"Part of it."

Rone rubbed his face. Shook out his raw hands. "Whatever. Let's figure out your mess."

"I'm sorry."

He glared at her. "So you said."

He climbed his way back to the roof. Hopped to the next one. Started for the third, then forced himself to stop so Sandis could catch up.

He'd said he'd assist her. For now. *This* side of his problems wasn't her fault. Just the other side.

He fingered the amarinth. He'd figure this out.

Somehow.

Chapter 8

Rone tossed her an apple and a stale oat bar. She felt guilty, taking so much without giving back. She had nothing to give now, but she'd find a way to repay him after she found Talbur.

The air inside his flat felt like the air before a winter storm. Cold, stiff, impending. It all emanated from Rone, who leaned in the corner closest to the door, eating an apple of his own. He stared at nothing, his eyes unfocused. Sandis worried her lip, watching him from her perch on the couch.

She took a deep breath. "Who?"

Rone's dark gaze moved to her.

She swallowed. "Who was he talking about? The man we . . . visited."

Had Rone been Kazen, that man would not be alive. Kazen would have used one of the numina to kill him, probably Ireth, his weapon of choice.

A memory—one of Ireth's—surfaced in her mind. Black walls still burning, the shadows of corpses on the ground, and Kazen, so much shorter than he was to Sandis's eyes, lovingly scratching under a charcoal muzzle—

Rone took a loud bite of his apple, snapping Sandis away from the image. He took his time chewing and swallowing. "My mother."

"What happened?"

A shake of his head dismissed her. "If you want to find this guy of yours, we need to track him down. Banks, libraries—"

"I've checked banks and libraries."

"—and citizen records."

Sandis perked up in her seat on the couch. "Citizen records?"

Rone nodded. "Citizen and historical records are kept in a building in the Innerchord. Everyone ever born in Kolingrad has records there. Immigrants, too." He laughed like that was a joke. Then again, Sandis supposed not many immigrated to Kolingrad, since so few people were allowed to leave its borders.

The Innerchord, where the triumvirate and other government officials congregated. Sandis had never been to the center of the city, but its looming buildings could be seen from any roof in Dresberg, so long as another building didn't block the view. The Degrata looked similar to the Lily Tower, but the Lily Tower's tiers were narrower and more cake-like, and its stone had the color of water-diluted rust.

She nodded. "All right. Let's—"

"That will be the first place they look for you." Rone took another bite of apple.

She shook her head. "But they don't know I'm looking for . . ." She paused. *Do they?* She couldn't be sure the grafters had stolen that page from the bank record, but they'd found her so soon afterward.

Did that mean Kazen knew she could read? Her hands tightened to fists, fingernails digging into her palms. She hated not knowing. She couldn't plan ahead if she didn't know.

The thump of Rone tossing his apple core into the garbage bin drew her attention away from her thoughts. He scratched his stubble-coated chin. "I'll think about it. I need to go somewhere first. Alone."

Sandis glanced at the window. Were the grafters good and gone? Would Rone take to the rooftops, even in the light of day? "Where?"

He paused, searching her face. "Gerech Prison. Alone. I'll be quick."

He said nothing more, merely opened the door and let himself back into the city.

Gerech Prison was west of the Innerchord, right outside the giant moat that surrounded it, in District Two. It was a huge building, comparable in size to the Degrata—if someone were to slice the enormous tower into stories and lay them out. Gerech was a single story, aboveground, anyway, though its massive front gate reached two. If one could call it a gate. It was a gargantuan construction made of two cylinders bound together by a massive black door. Every window, vertical and horizontal alike, was barred with iron. The lamps were always lit, even on days when the sky was clear and the sun beamed through the city's haze. Rone imagined it was because everything was dark inside, so the warden always wanted a ready source of light.

The walls were an odd color, like moldy cheese. Rone didn't know what stone they were made from—something pebbly, textured, and impossible to scale. Armed guards were everywhere, boasting heavy-looking breastplates adorned with symbols of a sail-less boat, an homage to their ancestors and to the triumvirate. At least it wasn't a lily.

Every guard's gaze followed Rone as he walked toward the prison, to the barred window where the clerk sat. *Every* eye. He felt them like jagged icicles pressing against his skin. He acted like he didn't notice. Stood in line. Gerech held thousands of people, so there was always a line of visitors. Rone saw someone get turned away, and the ball in his gut doubled in size. But he'd gotten the paperwork and filled it out; legally, he couldn't be rejected. Legally, he got one visit.

Unfortunately, it wouldn't be to his mother.

Hands shoved into his pockets, Rone fiddled with the amarinth with his right and a wad of cash with his left. Just about everything he had left. He needed work, but this was higher priority.

The clerk, an overweight, middle-aged man with saggy bags under his eyes, sat in an old booth surrounded by twisted cast-iron bars. He looked exhausted. Rone didn't care.

Rone approached, retrieved his papers, and slammed them down on the desk.

"I want to see the warden."

The clerk didn't even look at him, merely brought the paperwork up close to his eyes and sighed, ignoring the spectacles pushed to the top of his balding head. He flipped to the second paper and read. "You can't see the warden *and* the prisoner."

"I'm aware."

Frowning, the clerk shuffled the papers back into order and fumbled for a stamp beneath his little desk. He dipped it in blue ink and stamped the bottom of the first page, then signed below it. He then signaled for one of the guards near the booth. The large man walked up, the sword at his hip clanking against his polished greaves. The clerk handed him the papers.

"Warden. Fifteen minutes," the clerk mumbled. "Next!"

The guard said nothing, merely jerked his head in the direction he wanted Rone to go. Rone fell in step behind him, trying not to listen to the crying of the woman who approached the clerk next.

If the triumvirate employed as many policemen in the city as they did guards at Gerech, crime would disappear. There were so *many* of them. Every five feet of wall had its own guard, ranging from Sandis's age to his mother's. Many were broad-shouldered, bulky men. Well fed. How much were they paid? What percentage of citizens' taxes went toward the food in their bellies and the metal on their persons?

Every single one had a sword and a gun. Every. Single. One. Rone could stuff his pockets and pants full of amarinths and still not have enough immortality to make it past these walls, let alone back out of them.

The guard led him to a smaller door at the end of a long alcove crammed with more guards, all of whom were wide awake and focused. It was eerily silent in that alcove. No talking, no shifting. These men didn't even seem to breathe.

Another armored man opened the door. Rone stepped through with his chaperone, only to be confronted by a second door that had to be unlocked, and then a third. The moment that third door opened, the wrongness of the place assaulted him like smoke.

The smell was something he'd never before encountered, and he used to clean sewers for a living. The subtle scent of mildew, but . . . soured. The distant aroma of human feces, mixed with acid and . . . snow. A hint of iron, a pinch of body odor. Even that had its own distinct tinge—like the people here sweated vinegar instead of water.

There were no prisoners this close to freedom. Three dark halls stretched before him, one in front and one to either side. All appeared to be unending tunnels, disappearing into a black void.

He imagined the one in front of him—the one that led deeper into the prison—led to the first rows of prisoners. Was his mother there, or deeper down? Was her cell beneath his feet?

The ball in his gut expanded until Rone had to lean over to compensate for its weight. He struggled to breathe. Perspiration pebbled his skin, and his teeth chattered from the coldness of it. The guard pulled a lamp from the wall beside him.

There were no lights down these corridors. Surely that meant they each ended in some sort of sealed door, something obscuring the light from within. Surely his mother wasn't sitting in utter darkness, wondering what she'd done to deserve her place in this dank hell.

Rone swallowed. A headache twisted behind his eyes. "Do they hurt the prisoners here?"

The guard regarded him with dark eyes. "This way," he said, leading him down the corridor to his left. After a few steps, he said, "Not the quiet ones."

Rone's hands shook, so he stuck them in his pockets, finding some solace in the amarinth and the wad of cash. His mother would be fine. She followed the rules. She wasn't the type to scream her head off if wrongfully incarcerated.

She had been utterly silent the day his father left.

The guard's lamp illuminated walls covered in metal sheeting; Rone could see the blurs of his reflection in them as they walked. The corridor turned. They approached another door. The guard knocked, and a slit opened, exposing a set of eyes. It closed, a bolt shifted, and the door opened.

More light, Rone thought as he passed into the small room lit with half a dozen lamps, their smoke mingling before lifting through an air vent in the ceiling. *Thank the damnable god for that.*

He finally got some air into his lungs. His chaperone muttered something to one of the other guards in the area—there were three—and showed him the papers. They reviewed them together. Nodded. His chaperone passed the documents to the new guard, who said, "This way. The warden's last appointment just left."

This would never happen in Godobia. Or Ysben. Or even Serrana. While he'd never been to any of those places, their traders and merchants infiltrated Kolingrad often, especially during the summers. That, and his mother liked collecting foreign books. They all might have been fiction, but they painted the picture of the southern countries well enough.

Rone nodded and cleared his throat. He didn't want to sound afraid when it was finally his turn to talk.

The new guard took a key ring off his belt and opened another door. They passed through another hallway, through another guarded door, around various twists and turns, and then came to a stop in front of yet another door, where the guard with Rone's papers finally knocked.

Rone had a fantastic sense of direction, but he wasn't sure he could find his way back out of this place without help. How intricate did the labyrinth become, deeper in, where the lamps didn't shine?

A voice called out to them from inside. The guard cracked open the door and, reading off the papers, said, "Rone Comf to see you, order of visitor rights. Son of Prisoner 084467, Adalia Comf, imprisoned thirty-six hours for grand theft."

Sweat traced down Rone's spine. *She didn't do it!*

He wanted to shout, to scream, to object. To turn himself in.

He said nothing.

"Let him in," the voice within said. The guard pushed it open and gestured for Rone to enter.

He tried to hide his surprise that the person behind the large desk was a woman.

"Sit down, Mr. Comf," she said. She didn't tilt her head or gesture to the single chair across from her, but Rone sat in it regardless. He pressed his fists against his thighs and stared at the warden. She was in her late forties, he guessed, and overweight like the clerk. Her skin was horribly pale, likely from sitting inside this awful place day after day. Her dark hair was pulled tightly back from her forehead and knotted behind her head. She had sad, tilted eyes and a too-wide mouth. Her voice was low and unfeeling.

So was Rone's.

"I believe my mother is being unjustly punished. Her persecutor's name is Ernst Renad—"

"Yes, I know Renad." She glanced at a ledger on her desk, uninterested.

Rone's pulse thumped in his right temple. "Are you neighbors, or is he just a financial contributor to this institution?" He swallowed the venom leaking into the polite accusation.

The warden looked back, her wide lips twitching. Did she find this *funny*? "He's a financial contributor. I always ensure our contributors are well taken care of, Mr. Comf. Now, is there a purpose to your visit here? You're aware you will not be allowed into the cells after this." She leaned back in her chair. "But you look like someone who's read the charter, hm?"

Rone scowled. "I'm hoping to take over Renad's payments." He pulled the cash out of his pocket and set it on the desk. "I'm hoping to *convince* you to actually follow the law."

The warden dropped her gaze to the money and laughed. *Laughed.* "A sweet attempt, my boy, but you're a guppy playing with sharks." She reached out long-nailed fingers and pushed the money back toward him. "Increase it by a dozenfold, and maybe I'll listen to your complaints. Of course, you've already used up your visitor rights, haven't you?"

Fire lit inside him. His hand slammed down on the cash, and he leaned forward. "You're right. I've read the charter. I've studied the whole damn constitution. I can recite verbatim every law you're breaking, and if you think I won't—"

Her laughter cut him short. It echoed off the walls like the cries of a whipped cat, high pitched and raw.

His fingers crumpled the money into a tight wad against his palm.

Once the warden caught her breath, she said, "So can I. So can I. Oh, dearie, do you know how many sweet young men and women—cute, educated ones like yourself—have tried to use threats to bow this establishment to their will? Do you think the scarlets *care* what happens within these walls? They keep our cells full so there won't be any vacant spots left for *them*. Do you think the triumvirate *cares* who did what, or what the consequences are? I take care of the riffraff so they don't have to. So they can keep the country running smoothly and live their dreamy little lives."

She folded her hands on the desk and leaned in close. "As far as they're concerned, you and your dear mother—all these prisoners and all these families—don't exist. You're all cockroaches to them, don't you see? Every last one. Why would they bat an eye at which ones get stepped on?

"But *I* care, darling. I care about the big ones. Bugs like Ernst Renad, who soothes his ego by throwing around more money than your small mind could ever dream of." She smiled. "Try again if you gather the means."

Rone's fingers reached for the amarinth, tightening on its coils. Sixty seconds. Sixty seconds to put her in her place, to wipe that smirk off her mouth, to show her—

"I did it."

She cocked an eyebrow.

Rone licked his lips, finding a crack in them. His muscles tensed. He thought he could hear the darkness from the hollow chambers beneath his feet beckoning to him.

His mother was down there.

"I did it," he repeated. The ribbons of the amarinth threatened to cut into his fingers. "It wasn't my mother. I'm the one who broke into Ernst Renad's home and stole the headpiece."

She smiled. "Isn't that sweet?"

Rone only managed to half swallow his replying growl. "You think I'm trying to cover for her? I'll tell you the exact route I took. The layout of his house. Which walls his gilded mirrors hang on, and the color of the wood stain on his harp."

His heart paused its beating for a moment, making him feel stiff and cold. Was he really doing this? Condemning himself to rot and die in Gerech?

But this was his fault. His mother deserved freedom. And Sandis . . . she would have to fend for herself.

The warden shrugged. "Whether you did or you didn't, the quota is full, and it would be a headache to re-sort the paperwork for this."

The fire inside him snuffed out, drenched and wet and cold. The residual smoke pushed against his skin, seeking for an escape he couldn't give it.

"You're not going to take me in her place." He sounded like a little boy.

She offered him a lopsided, cynical smile. "Like I said, Mr. Comf. Contact me when you have the money." She waved a hand toward the guard behind Rone, who opened the door leading back to the world of the living. It took a long moment before Rone found the strength to pry himself from that chair, his fingers still pressed hard into the amarinth. The only means he *might* have to get his mother out, if he wasn't swindled then, too.

He felt the warden grin at his back.

Rone wasn't finished with her yet.

Sandis went through all of Rone's cupboards, hoping she could cook something for him—did she remember how to cook?—but the man lived like a true bachelor. He didn't have much in there—not for baking, at least. He seemed to be decently well off. He'd never told her what he did for work, had he?

Where had he learned to fight like that, anyway?

Giving up that venture, Sandis decided to clean instead. The flat was tidy, but there was dirt in the edges where floor met wall, spiderwebs in the window, and a ring in the tiny tin tub they'd both used yesterday. She found only vinegar to clean with, but it worked. She cracked a window, leaving the curtains closed, to air out the smell.

After that, she dared to step out of the flat. She scoured the street below, pulling her shirt collar over her nose to hide her face. She didn't see anything out of the ordinary. She climbed onto the roof and looked again. Maybe they hadn't been followed this time. Maybe Sandis had truly gotten away.

Five stories up. Sandis's heart quickened as she remembered the fall from the clock tower. Could that be the secret to losing the grafters once and for all? Faking her death? It would have to be believable. Kazen's men had seen her survive that fall, so they knew something was keeping her safe.

Did Kazen suspect she had an amarinth?

Sandis shuddered. If he did, he'd want her even more. Want Rone, too.

She'd tried to warn Rone to stay away. She was glad he hadn't listened, but she couldn't allow any harm to come to him on her behalf.

She'd have to make her death believable for the grafters, which would mean concealing her body from their eyes. But how? A fire? Water? She could do it in one of the canals that sectioned off the city's districts . . . but no, she couldn't go there. Not anymore. Not after what happened to Anon.

A *thud* startled her, and she turned to see Rone behind her. He must have leapt from the southwest building. His face was long and tired and looked older than his years, which she guessed to be around twenty-five. On closer inspection, his eyelids were heavy and his cheeks sallow. He hunched like he'd been whipped.

He looked like someone who'd had a nightmare and was still waking up.

"What happened?" she tried, her voice tiny.

Rone paced a moment. Sighed. "I think I can get into the records building, but we'll have to wait until tonight. Can you write? More specifically, spell?"

Sandis studied him. His stance, his inability to look her in her eyes—all of it told her he was angry. Hurt. She'd seen it with the other vessels, the men especially. Something terrible had happened in his visit.

It was evident from his evasion that Rone didn't want to talk about it. She didn't have the right to press, so she simply nodded.

"Good. I'll need you to write down the exact spelling of the guy you want to look up, as well as any pertinent relations—"

"I'm coming."

Rone crooked an eyebrow. "No, you're not."

Sandis didn't want to hurt him more, but she couldn't stand to remain in one spot while the grafters lurked close by. Taking a step toward him, she implored, "Please, Rone, let me come. I can help if I'm there in person. The name wasn't always Gwenwig." She tugged at her memories of her father. He'd told her about the name change late one night after a shift at the cotton factory. "I think it was originally Gwender?"

Rone rubbed a crease from his forehead. "I don't think it's a good idea—"

"I don't want to be alone."

The words rushed out of her unbidden, spoken so quietly she wouldn't have thought Rone had heard them had he not paused. He studied her for a moment before his shoulders slackened. "Fine. *Fine.*"

Sandis smiled, but the joy of her success receded as reality pushed into her thoughts. "We should go soon. It's safer from the grafters during the day, when the police are out and there are witnesses."

"Trust me." He looked at her pointedly. "It will be better to go at night. It will be harder for them to follow us."

Sandis skewed her brow. "How?"

A slightly sadistic smile touched Rone's lips. "You might want to bring a change of clothes."

***

Sandis didn't have a change of clothes, since she refused to wear her old shirt. From the jerky movements and muted grunts Rone made as he packed extras of *his* clothes in an oiled waterproof canvas bag, she could tell he was annoyed.

"We're not . . . going in the canal, are we?" Sandis asked. Her voice quavered.

"No." He pulled the strings on the sack tight and glanced at her. "You *can* swim, right?"

She nodded. "Well enough."

Rone slung the bag over his shoulder and blew out the candle. Shadows engulfed the flat. Again, he led her up to the rooftop. They took a different route, hopping buildings for maybe a tenth of a mile before Rone descended to the street.

They were nowhere near the Innerchord.

Rone paused for a moment, looking around—or, more so, looking down, like the cobblestones held some secret Sandis could not determine. He back-stepped and glanced down an alley. "This way."

Sandis held her breath as Rone led her down a narrow road constricted by brick buildings. It looked eerily similar to the one the slavers had driven her down four years ago.

The alley ended at an iron fence. Despite the darkness—only the last indigo wisps of twilight glimmered through the polluted clouds—flies were active. Their buzzing jumbled in Sandis's ears. She smelled the overflowing garbage bin before she spotted it. No trash carrier had been down here for a long time.

The scraping of metal and stone drew her attention back to Rone. He crouched, moving something—a manhole cover.

The faint smell of feces wafted up from the slow-flowing water beneath. He felt around under the cover, then cursed.

"What are you doing?" she whispered, checking over her shoulder.

"It's a drop-off point. Where those in the know can leave me tips for jobs." He set the manhole cover aside instead of replacing it. "Might as well start here."

Sandis eyed the manhole, then the sack with the extra clothes.

"You're joking," she whispered.

"Once upon a time, it was my job to clean these suckers," he explained. "There's a whole network underground that very few know about—including policemen and, I assume, grafters."

Sandis inched closer. Squinted to see better.

"How well do you know your history?"

She swallowed. "Decently."

"This whole place is built on abandoned Noscon ruins. They built their colonies with the earth, while Kolins forced the earth to comply with their architecture."

Sandis's stomach turned as she took a step back from the manhole. "I don't understand your point."

"Everything up here is flat. Everything down there is not."

"And?"

"Closer to the newer areas of the city, it's a tight squeeze. Move away from the wall and toward the Innerchord, and the sewers open up. They cover the entire city, even the poorest parts. Do you want to find this guy's record or not?"

Sandis listened to the flowing water. She was getting used to the smell, at least. She glanced at Rone's bag. Nodded.

"It's dark down there, so you'll need to follow me. This part and the last stretch will be the easiest, but the water gets high in the middle." He grimaced. "At least it's not spring. It's really high then. And cold."

She stared at Rone. Then the manhole. Told herself the grafters couldn't find them this way and the longer they squatted here talking, the more likely Kazen would track her down.

Talbur Gwenwig. Her best hope had always been to find him.

Rone dropped into the hole. Sandis expected to hear a splash, but there was only the soft landing of his shoes on something hard.

"I'll catch you," he called.

Swallowing, Sandis lowered herself into the manhole until the muscles in her arms started to burn. She let go, and for a split second, nothingness surrounded her. Then two hands grabbed her waist, and she ungracefully landed half on a cement slab and half on Rone, nearly knocking him over.

Easing her aside, Rone grabbed a long stick from the wall and used it to pull the manhole cover back into place. Darkness surrounded them, save for a muted glow of moon and street light through the holes in the manhole cover. Rone replaced the staff in its brackets. "This way."

The platform narrowed to a passage barely wide enough for a person to walk on. Worse, it slanted toward the water. The cold, foul water lapped at Sandis's toes as she turned herself sideways, following after Rone. How deep was the water? What would happen if she slipped?

She silently thanked her father for teaching her how to swim as she continued sidestepping through the darkness. It went pitch-black for a moment, and Sandis's heart began to race, but she followed the sound of Rone's movements, and gradually new wisps of light lit up another chamber of the sewers, identical to the last.

When the sewer branched ahead, Rone led them to the right. "This part will be less pleasant. Watch your step. You don't want this in your mouth. Or eyes. Or other holes."

Sandis cringed, thinking of what *other holes* the wastewater might contaminate.

"Don't worry—this is the cleaner stuff," Rone said, voice low, but it sounded like he was laughing. "Chances of us getting some horrible disease are much lower than in the west sewers. Higher elevation here. The wastewater hasn't been sitting for as long."

Sandis slicked her hair back from her face. "How much farther?"

Rone sighed and looked ahead. "A ways."

The tunnel narrowed, and the walkway vanished. Sandis stepped into the water, following Rone's movements exactly, cringing when something solid brushed by her leg. The water started at her ankles, then moved up to her calves, her knees, her thighs, her hips . . .

She could barely make out an archway up ahead, its crest only a foot above the water. Rone pushed off the wall of the sewer and swam toward it, his chin grazing the water's surface as he sliced through it.

Pinching her mouth firmly shut, Sandis followed. The water slowly receded after that, and they were able to walk on a concrete platform for half a mile before the ceiling got painfully low. Sandis hunched with her face inches from Rone's backside—or so she imagined, for the dim light came and went. Rone lifted her into a dry but rank tube—"It's for winter overflow"—and she crawled on knees and elbows until the skin on both was raw and threatened to tear. Then they swam through another underground canal, walked, swam, walked, crawled. Rone checked a couple of covers on the way. When he finally climbed up a rusted ladder to another and said, "We're here," Sandis could have kissed him. He dropped back down to another platform, barely large enough to fit both of them, and opened his bag.

"Can't do much for the smell, but you won't leave a water trail this way." He handed her a change of clothes from the sack.

Sandis waited for him to turn before getting dressed. It was dark, yes, and Kazen often undressed her before summoning Ireth. But she still had some semblance of modesty. More importantly, she couldn't let Rone see her script.

She quickly dressed, keeping her back away from him and out of the light trickling through the manhole cover. Because of that, she caught him when he started to turn his head to peek. She grunted her protest, and he whipped his face forward as if nothing had happened.

The tips of her hair were still dripping when she climbed the ladder and crawled out of the sewer. The first thing she noticed was that the cobblestones here were much wider and paler than they were elsewhere in the city. Lamps, bright and burning, illuminated the courtyard with tawny light. The buildings around them stood clean and tall, their architecture much more aesthetically pleasing than the factories and flats that crowded the smoke ring. Eaves were thick and long and angular, fences with fancy balusters wrapped around well-maintained walkways, and the windows had geometric panes and were rounded on the top. There was even a fountain nearby, though its water was stale.

Sandis crept toward it and washed her hands and face as best she could.

"This way." Rone moved into the shadows of a long white single-story building. There was a tablet above its front door, but it was too dark for Sandis to read. They didn't go far—their destination was next door, a three-story structure much less glamorous than its neighbors. In the light, it looked rectangular and brown, with fewer windows and no special design.

Two men entered the courtyard, walking and chatting. Scarlet uniforms. Policemen. Sandis pressed herself against the stone wall.

Rone pulled out a shiv of some sort and crammed it between the door and its frame. It opened with a soft creak.

Sandis guessed this was the back of the building, for the door was unremarkable and somewhat small. She slipped inside the moment Rone opened it, and he followed, carefully closing the door behind him.

"Security should be light in here, if not nonexistent. Few people care about stealing genealogy." They were in a stairwell. He paused for a moment before climbing up. "Come on, hurry."

"Thank you," she whispered after him.

"Just hurry."

Rone assessed the first floor they reached, then led her up to the next, changed his mind, and hastened her back to the first. He paused in the stairwell as footsteps sounded nearby. Sandis held her breath, waiting for them to fade.

Silence descended upon them like heavy snow.

Rone reached for the door handle.

"Rone."

He paused, glanced back at her.

She hesitated a moment, then asked, "Why did you go to Gerech?"

It was dark, but she saw his lips press into a thin line. He pulled the door open an inch, then eased it closed again. His voice was so low and hushed she could barely pick out his words. "My mother is there."

Shock prickled outward from Sandis's chest and into her shoulders. His mother, his *family*, was in that horrible place? When Sandis was a child, her parents had used two frightening stories to encourage her and Anon to behave: one about misshapen demons—numina—hiding beneath the city and the other about scarlets carting bad children away to Gerech.

"I made a mistake, and she's paying for it," he added, not meeting her eyes. He eased the door open. "Let's go."

Rone got several steps ahead of her before Sandis found the strength to urge her own legs forward. *Gerech.* What would she do if her mother were in that terrible place? Sandis had been bitter for a long time after her mother's selfish passing, but living with the grafters—losing Anon—had broken her hard feelings into dust. Were her mother alive, Sandis would stop at nothing to free her, even if that was an impossible goal.

Bright white light exploded to her right, and she winced, eyes tearing. The scent of kerosene filled her nostrils.

Her heart quickened before she realized it was just a lamp.

"This way." Rone moved forward with the newly lit lamp, which he'd taken from the wall.

Once Sandis cleared her vision of spots, she saw Rone had brought her somewhere that looked very much like a library—rows of shelves and drawers, trees of information spotting mostly bare brick walls. She noted words on the end of each aisle—last names, sometimes solitary letters. Her heart quickened as she read them. *L*s, *K*s, *J*s . . . *G*s.

She hurried ahead of Rone and began picking through the bins that filled the shelves. Scanning them, she paused at the second-to-bottom shelf. Gwenwig should be in this one. She knelt down and pulled the entire bin from its place on the wall. "Bring the light closer," she whispered.

Light dusted the records. Near the back, she found the first Gwenwig.

A small sound like an airy squeal eked from her throat. She pulled the file out. *Santos Gwenwig.* That was her paternal great-grandfather. She pulled out another, then another. She found her father's record—it was outdated, listing that he only had a daughter. It included her mother's name and the date they were married.

The next name jumped out at her like a fish out of water. *Talbur Gwenwig.*

Her breath caught.

"You found it?" Rone crouched beside her.

Sandis pulled the file from the bin and arranged the papers in the direct light of the lamp. She wasn't practiced enough to read speedily, but she pushed herself over the words.

Though she had no memory of Talbur—or his name—the family tree in the file indicated he was her father's uncle, the half brother of her grandfather. So there was still blood connecting them. Sandis smiled.

She pressed her finger to the information, dragging it down as she read. Birthdate . . . he was sixty-eight years old. No death date listed, but of course he'd still be alive if he recently traded at the bank. Male, of course. No marriage record or children, and—

Her finger stopped. *Oh no.*

"What?" Rone pressed his shoulder to hers, trying to see better, but it blocked out the light. Sandis pushed him back.

"It says he lives in Thaughtez."

Rone glanced at her. "That's about two hundred miles out."

Sandis shook her head. "He can't. He wouldn't travel clear from Thaughtez to make a gold exchange at a bank in Dresberg. The record is outdated." Just like her father's.

She sat back on her heels.

"You're sure?" Rone took the record and read it himself. "Hmm, yeah. This stamp says the last entry was seventeen years ago. Whoever keeps these needs to be fired."

A dead end. Hope dribbled out of her body and puddled on the floor.

She sucked some of it back in. At least she knew who the mystery Gwenwig was—her great-uncle. At least she had that. She opened her grandfather's record and skimmed over the family tree—there was Talbur's name, written a few lines below her father's.

She glanced back at the bin. Fingered through it. Frowned. Opened her father's record.

"What is it?"

She shook her head. "When do they start records for citizens?"

"When they're born. Why?"

She searched one more time. "I don't have one."

Rone paused, brows skewed. "Please don't tell me you're under seventeen."

"I'm eighteen. I'm on this record, here." She pointed to her name on her father's record. "But I don't have my own file."

Rone looked over the record himself, then searched those in the bin. "Huh, yeah. I bet it was stolen."

"Stolen?"

Rone shrugged. "You're Kolin, yeah? Kolin citizens can't be sold as slaves. I wonder if your master or whoever had it taken so you couldn't be traced."

Sandis's lips parted. She'd never considered the idea. Did the government think she was dead? Did they know she existed?

Did they care?

Sandis closed the records she'd opened and carefully returned them to their cradle, then shoved the bin back onto the shelf. What would she do next? Where else could she look?

Rone stood. "We should go."

She nodded and followed his light. As she passed the shelves, something caught her eye.

She moved toward it as if mesmerized. Rone groaned and hurried after her. Yes, it was a Noscon symbol, painted on a book spine—what it said, she couldn't be sure, but she recognized the art of it. As Rone neared, his light illuminated a few more ledgers beside it, crammed together inside a small bin, which bore a Kolin label. Sandis sounded the words out in her head: *Noscon records.*

"We need to go," Rone whispered.

Sandis nodded, but let her fingertips touch the ancient script.

Her eyes exploded with fire.

Hot air pressed in on her from all sides, crushing her until she couldn't breathe. Need. Hurry. Need. *Emotions that weren't hers crawled along her skin like centipedes. The pressure increased, then built in her skull, pushing outward. She grabbed her head.*

Ireth, stop it. Stop it!

The pressure built until Sandis felt she would crumple like old paper. A single pulse of fire blazed from her crown to her toes. Fear.

Sandis turned around and saw two slitted eyes like hot iron bearing down on her. Hot darkness engulfed her. Living shadow. The smell of burning flesh filled her senses—the smell of Heath.

An earth-shattering roar pierced her ears and rent her to pieces.

Sandis screamed.

Chapter 9

Her scream echoed between shelves and walls, threatening to shatter glass.

"Sandis!" Rone hissed as she fell backward. He grabbed her by the shoulders, then yanked his hands back, palms burning. Sandis collided with the floor. She stared upward, unblinking like a corpse.

Her hair steamed.

Rone's stomach dropped to his knees. Cursing, he crouched at her side. "Sandis? Sandis?" He carefully touched her arm—the heat had receded, but it was still unnatural. He took her face in his hands and gently shook it. "Sandis? The hell? Sandis!"

She blinked, her eyes coming into focus, then rolled over and coughed as though her lungs were full of tar.

Sweat broke out along her skin. Her entire body trembled.

This was no sewer disease.

He slapped her back a few times. Once she caught her breath, he grabbed her shoulders. "Are you all right? What happened?" He glanced at the records. But no, it couldn't have been those.

What had those grafters done to her?

She pressed her palms to the floor and pushed herself onto her knees. Breathed heavily. On the fourth exhale, she muttered, "Kolosos."

Nonsense. "What?"

She shook her head. Sat up and pressed her fingers to her forehead. "I . . . I'm sorry. I'm . . . fine."

Rone flexed his hands, pulling the burned skin tight. He stared at her. How . . . ?

He heard footsteps on the floor below. God's tower, anyone in the courtyard would have heard her.

"We need to go." *And figure out what the hell just happened later.* "Come on."

He took her elbow and hefted her to her feet. Was she always this light? His own fear was probably fueling his muscles. He reached for his amarinth, hoping he wouldn't need to use it.

They went back the way they'd come—the way Rone had already mapped. He didn't like going into things without some knowledge of what he was doing. Sandis faltered once on the stairs, but otherwise kept the pace.

"Come on. Hurry." He opened the door. Peeked out. Sprinted for the manhole cover. Lifted it and ushered Sandis down the ladder.

He scanned the area one last time before jumping in. A shadow moved by the science building. The glint of eyes, then the man turned away and vanished.

Rone stiffened. A witness. And if he was moving away instead of coming toward them, it wasn't security or police. But how could the grafters have followed them here? Even if they'd found his flat, they couldn't have tracked them through the sewers.

Unless they knew Sandis was searching for her great-uncle. Then they might plant a solitary lookout. One who would have heard her scream.

They had to hurry.

He could ditch her after this, right?

The question spun in his mind as he pushed himself through knee-high water, trying not to splash Sandis as he went. He'd done his part.

He'd gotten her to the records. It wasn't his fault the information had been lacking. It was very much *her* fault that the rats of the city may or may not have been pursuing them.

Had he been overconfident? Could the grafters know the literal underground so well? It was a big city, and a lot of people were employed in sewage. One of them could easily be a grafter, or sympathetic to one. Or enslaved by one.

But if this Kazen guy was so interested in recapturing Sandis, why would he have let her out of his sight in the first place?

He didn't have time for this.

There were no streetlights over the nearest manhole, only cloud-filtered moonlight. Running his hand along the wall to feel for a ladder, Rone trudged toward it, frowning when his fingers found nothing but slick concrete and mold. The manhole wasn't terribly high; if he jumped, he could dislodge the cover.

"What are you doing?" Sandis asked behind him.

"Can't go back the way we came. There was a lurker in the courtyard. If we're lucky, it was a thief."

He didn't bother to say, *If we're not,* for the small gasp Sandis made told him she understood completely.

Good. They had no time to talk about that. Or about Sandis's maybe stroke. Rone launched himself up and pushed both hands into the manhole cover, knocking it askew. Jumping again, he got his fingers over the lip of the manhole and pulled himself up.

Apparently it had rained only enough to tar the cobblestones with sludge. Not that Rone wasn't covered in something similar. He checked for his amarinth, wrung out his sodden clothes as best he could without taking them off, then lay on his stomach and lowered his hands into the sewer.

Sandis's fingers slid down his as she tried to get a solid grip. Water splashed up when she fell back down. *Come on, come on.* He couldn't ditch her in the sewer. Even he wasn't that despicable.

He thought of his mother and felt sick.

Sandis's hands found his, and he grabbed them tightly enough to cut off blood flow. With a grunt, he hauled Sandis up until she got an elbow onto the street and could pull herself out the rest of the way. She slicked hair back from her face.

"Wring out, hurry." Where would they go? He thought of a few places, including a tavern he'd holed up in a couple of times when jobs got too intense. He didn't have his wallet on him, though. Would they take credit?

Sandis stood, her wet clothes sticking to her and making her look like a drowned mouse. Rone put a hand on the back of her shoulders and pushed her down a nearby street. He reached the end of it before realizing he'd forgotten to close the manhole cover.

He turned down another street, but Sandis grabbed his shirt and stopped him, shaking her head.

Rone stifled a groan. "There's a guy I know who—"

"That leads right into Grim Rig's territory. He hates beggars, and we don't look much better."

The name rang a bell—one of the local mob bosses. Rone nodded and chose a different way—a curving street with no rhyme or reason and a lot of foul-smelling garbage bins. There had to be a butcher nearby. Rotting meat had a very distinct and stomach-churning smell.

Rone guided them down another road, his footsteps slowing when he neared the end of it. He didn't know this area very well, and the darkness made it that much worse. Lack of lamps, lack of homeless . . . this wasn't a good sign.

Footfalls sounded somewhere ahead of them. Rone grabbed Sandis's arm, guiding her back the way they'd come. She didn't protest, which meant she didn't know the area that well, either.

They got to an intersection. The sound of a clicking gun hammer filled the empty space.

Sandis turned around first and choked. Rone followed her lead.

Seven men stood gathered behind them, all in black, all large in stature except for the one in front. He was tall but lean, pole-like. He wore a black hat too elegant for the circumstances, and it was pulled down to shadow his eyes. Moonlight illuminated a long nose, wide mouth, and pointed chin, as well as the column of gold buttons trailing down his vest and silver ones trailing down his trench coat.

He was the only one without a visible firearm.

Sandis shook like an overheated boiler next to Rone. She mustn't have exaggerated her importance to the grafters. He'd never heard of so many men being sent after one person.

Their network was extraordinary.

"I think this nonsense has gone on for long enough," the man in the hat said. His form was unmoving, save for his mouth. Rone inched his hand toward his amarinth. "The sewers? Really, Sandis? I rescued you from those slavers, brought you into my home, and this is how you've chosen to repay me? And Mr. Rone Comf. Or should I say, Engel Verlad?"

Rone stiffened. They'd found him out so easily? *A very good network.* They likely knew his address as well. Possibly his history. And if they knew his history, they'd know he knew the sewers . . .

He and Sandis had never had a chance.

Rone could have been standing there naked and felt less exposed.

"We have to move." Sandis's voice was so muted and strained he barely heard it. "We have to go *now*."

"Obviously," Rone muttered. Two guns were trained on him.

Sandis grabbed his arm with both hands. She shook hard enough to make his teeth rattle. "That's Kazen in front."

The big bad. Great.

"Rone, if Kazen touches me, he'll control me. *We can't let him touch me.*"

"What?" Rone asked, a little too loudly.

Kazen shifted enough that Rone could see the bottom of one eye from beneath the brim of the hat. "I don't appreciate being interrupted."

"Yeah, well . . ." Rone squeezed the amarinth. Seven of them, at least six armed. How would he fight his way out of this? "I don't like your hat."

Sandis squeaked.

Kazen frowned, then took a step back. Behind him stood a petite, pale girl who could be no older than fifteen. There was a childish roundness to her face. Her blonde hair was cut in the same style as Sandis's—straight across, about an inch above her shoulders.

Sandis gasped. "Alys." Her nails dug into his arms.

He ignored the sting. "Who?"

He saw her throat bob as she swallowed. Her lips moved, but little more than air passed through them.

Rone didn't understand, and he didn't have time to sort out her fears. He didn't know what to expect. He hated not knowing what to expect.

Kazen pushed the blonde girl forward. It was hard to be scared of someone Rone knew he could snap like rotted wood, but Sandis was stiff as steel next to him, her nails digging, digging—

"Wait." Sandis's small voice seemed to shout in the tense space around them.

All eyes turned to her.

"I'll come willingly."

Rone hadn't figured out a way to save them yet, but at the very least, he could spin the amarinth, pick up Sandis, and run . . . *somewhere*. "Sandis," he hissed. What had she said to the grafters last time? That Kazen wouldn't want holes in her?

They wouldn't shoot her, for whatever reason. Maybe, if they split up—

Kazen settled a limp hand on Alys's shoulders and a smug look on his face. "Excellent. We'll discuss how you and Mr. Verlad will be punished later."

"Let Rone go, please. I . . . forced him to help me. H-He doesn't have anything you want." She took a step forward, then another, her head tilting slightly as her eyes peered across the street. Rone tried to see what had caught her attention past the shadows.

They stood next to a metalwork factory—had he been paying attention to his senses instead of the men ready to shoot him full of lead, he might have noticed the smell. No doors—they were probably at the back of the thing. A pipe about two feet across snaked up the outer wall, bending once just above a valve—

A steam valve.

On a very large pipe.

Rone's eyes darted back to the guns carried by the men in black as Sandis took trembling fourth and fifth steps. Four pistols, two rifles. The long barrel on the rifles meant slower draw but better aim. If Rone were to run, those were the guns he'd worry about. The pistols were more likely to miss, especially if he didn't run in a straight line.

There were only two rifles.

Sandis moved forward again. Kazen twitched—she was testing his patience. Did she want Rone to get to the valve? But the gunmen were too close, pistols or not.

It had to be her. Rone prayed she'd been right about Kazen's men.

"It's all right, Sandis," he prompted her. "They won't shoot you."

She glanced back at him.

"*Now*, Sandis," Kazen snapped.

Understanding flashed across her eyes.

Inside his wet trouser pocket, Rone grabbed his amarinth.

Sandis bolted to the right.

"Stop her!" Kazen launched after Sandis and jerked the blonde girl with him.

Rone spun the amarinth and chucked it into the shadows, out of sight.

He ran straight into the grafters.

He landed a fist across one face and a kick into a stomach before two bullets rammed into him almost simultaneously—one in his kidney, the other in his heart. He felt only mild pressure as they dug into him and then, slowly, began to retreat from his skin.

A loud creak sounded to his right, and hot steam engulfed him and the men Kazen had left behind.

Men screamed. Steam clouded his vision. Rone's skin tingled pleasantly as the scalding water sprayed over it.

A glimmer of gold sparkled near the valve. Pushing away from the grafters, he grabbed the amarinth by a single loop, so its spinning wouldn't fight his grip, and bolted toward the factory. He wouldn't be able to stop the other loops from spinning—it was always one minute, all at once, or nothing.

Kazen, the blonde girl, and another lackey ran down the street, fast in pursuit of Sandis.

"If Kazen touches me, he'll control me."

What the hell had she meant by that?

Rone growled and ran, but not before he picked up one of the grafters' fallen pistols. He shook the thing next to his ear. A few more shots, at least. He wasn't an arms man, but he pointed the thing forward and shot anyway.

He missed, but the threat of gunfire sent Kazen's flunky hurtling down an alley. Sandis darted hard to the left, Kazen and the girl following after her. Or rather, Kazen dragged the girl by her hair. They disappeared around the building.

Moments later, a loud, birdlike shriek pulsed through the neighborhood like the snap of a whip. For a moment Rone slowed, his heartbeat pounding in his neck.

But he didn't have time to sort it out, especially if any of the other grafters had survived. They'd be on his tail any second now if they had. Rone took an early left instead of trailing Kazen, hoping the roads would connect. He didn't have time to climb to the rooftops.

His amaranth would stop spinning any moment now.

He knocked over a garbage bin as he ran and jumped a short fence, landing in a puddle of sludgy rainwater. The passageway stretched into the distance, but he took his first right—

Sandis slammed into him, nearly knocking him over. The pistol ripped from his hands and slid somewhere into the shadows.

"Hell, San—"

"Go, *go*!" she cried. "If he touches me—"

That shriek sounded again, louder, chilling his blood. He looked past Sandis, down the dark road—

At the woman hovering above it.

For half a second, Rone was sure it was a trick of the shadows, but she levitated even as she flew toward them on a single crooked wing. Black hair cascaded over her shoulders and bare chest, and her hands, clawed like a falcon's feet, reached toward them.

Black ashes and hellfire.

He'd never seen one before in real life, but he'd heard enough scriptural condemnation and bedtime stories to piece together what it was.

A *numen*.

Rone's skin seized as though he'd touched a hot stove. He turned and bolted down that long passageway after all. Sandis followed him, too slowly. He grabbed her wrist and pulled her, urging speed into her legs.

"What the *hell*?"

"Run!" Sandis cried. *"Run!"*

He did, as fast as his legs would take him. Over a garbage bin and a wall built too short. The landing shocked his ankles, especially when Sandis practically fell on top of him. He bolted forward, dragging her with him. Took a corner, then another. That she-beast cried out again, but it sounded farther away.

"How will," he panted, "Kazen . . . control you . . . if he . . ."

"Not me, *Ireth*!" she sputtered. "And then he'll kill you!"

A sharp pain exploded in his lower-left side. Rone stumbled, slamming his shoulder into a sludge-slick wall. Sandis urged him forward, and he forced his legs to keep sprinting.

He knew this tearing, hot feeling. He hadn't even heard the gun. Curses flooded his mind as he struggled to focus on the path ahead and pocketed the immobile amarinth.

Lamplight gleamed off puddles at the next intersection—he and Sandis rushed toward it. A main street; it'd be harder for the grafters to chase them there, where there were more people out and about. A large chance of scarlets and people milling about as they made their way to and from night shifts. Surely this Kazen guy wouldn't follow them into the open, where he and his highly illegal numen would be seen. If any scarlets were nearby, the grafters would be shot the moment their identity was known. Didn't matter whose pockets Kazen had lined—the powers that be wouldn't stand for such an open display of lawlessness.

Forget the law. They'd shoot them out of pure fear.

They reached the road. Rone turned toward the brightest lights, still running, gritting his teeth against the radiating agony above his hip. Was his pace slowing, or was Sandis's? Either way, they couldn't afford it. If the grafters caught up to them, he didn't have any defense short of his own fists.

He looked around. Startled a horse tied outside a noisy tavern. He knew this place. His old teacher lived not far from here. Surely Rone and Sandis could find refuge there, and perhaps some extra help.

"This way." He jerked Sandis to the left. She stumbled; he stumbled.

People were approaching to his right. He shoved Sandis down an alleyway, behind a garbage bin, and crouched beside her. Tried to slow his breathing, but his lungs pumped desperately for air. He leaned on his right leg, trying to take pressure off his left side. His damp clothes made him shiver. Everything was cold except for the warmth dripping into his waistband.

The men passed, talking low. Gold earrings dangled from their lobes. Just the mafia.

Just the mafia? God's tower, what had he gotten himself in—

He paused. Looked at Sandis, who had both hands pressed over her mouth to stifle her breathing. Until now, he hadn't had a spare second to register any of it. The girl. The one-winged woman above the alleyway. The number of grafters.

He'll control me.

Not me, Ireth.

Then he'll kill you.

Lectures from his father spun through his mind. The occult. The Noscon records. Her unwillingness to take off her coat or reveal her back. The fact that they wouldn't shoot her.

The name *Ireth*.

Rone fell onto his backside and stared, his fingers cold, his lungs suddenly void of the air they craved.

"You're a vessel."

Cold lanced his skin as the words left his mouth. Sandis dropped her hands from her face, her eyes round as marbles.

Holy hell in the pits of despair. No wonder the grafters wanted to kill him.

He was protecting one of the most powerful blasphemies in existence.

Chapter 10

Rone's stare was as relentless as it was hard to read. Shock, yes, but Sandis couldn't detect any disgust or awe. Just pure, simple surprise.

Another gunshot went off. Sandis winced. But no—that had been elsewhere, in the distance behind them. Not the grafters. Some other brawl involving neither them nor the scarlets. She couldn't hear Isepia anymore, either. Had Alys been hurt? Distracted? Dismissed? To summon her so quickly . . . Kazen *must* have bound Alys sometime after Sandis left. Maybe Heath had been right, and that would protect her from Kazen's experiments. Sandis prayed it did.

And now Rone knew the truth.

Her stomach squirmed.

Rone finally tore his eyes from her. "We need . . . we need to go." He leaned against the brick wall next to them to stand, then winced, breath hissing through his clenched teeth. Sandis stood and grabbed his elbow.

His left side was dark and warm.

"Celestial, you're bleeding," she whispered. She touched the darkest spot, and Rone flinched.

She let him lean against the wall and checked her belongings, hoping there was something she could use to help him, but of course she had nothing but sodden clothes. Rone's clothes. She didn't want to make a bandage out of any of the potentially disease-ridden cloth, but she didn't want Rone to bleed out, either.

Her mind whirred through the medical tricks she'd learned during her time with Kazen. Nothing pertinent came to mind.

At least Rone's shirts were long, so she wouldn't expose her script by tearing off the bottom of the one she wore. She used her teeth to get it started, then spat, not wanting any sewage water to linger on her tongue. She tore a wide strip.

"Hey," Rone complained.

"We're both in trouble if you pass out," she said, and looped the thin bandage around his hip. He groaned loudly in his throat when she tightened it. It was a pathetic attempt at care, but it was the best she could do for the moment.

"Tell me where we're going." She put one of his arms over her shoulders.

He pulled it back. "I'm fine." He straightened, then leaned back on her. Grumbled. "Ahead. Just help me walk. It's not too far."

Sandis pulled him along as quickly as she could. They needed to get off the streets. Kazen wouldn't give up so easily, but at least she'd proven she could outrun him.

She added that to the small list of advantages she had over him. Of course, Galt could outrun her, and nearly had.

Rone's weight increased on her with every block. Sandis's limbs were aching and tired from lack of sleep and the long trek through the sewers. Her legs shook with every step. But she had to get Rone help. They had to find sanctuary. She'd even risk the Lily Tower, if it weren't so far away.

"Right." Rone's voice was low and strained. Sandis tried to push her steps faster. Her muscles refused, but at least they remained steady.

Rone guided her a little farther before a measured sigh passed through his lips and ruffled Sandis's hair. "Here."

"There's no door—"

He leaned to his left, groaning, forcing Sandis to move or let him fall. She moved. Rone reached for a handle hidden underneath a brick and pushed it down. A narrow door swung inward.

It was dark inside and smelled of cigar smoke. Sandis hurried them in. The way wasn't wide enough for both of them, so she tried to ease Rone in first. But he was too big, too heavy, and her body was little more than rags. After pushing him in through the door, she promptly fell atop him.

A groan-smeared curse erupted from Rone's mouth.

Sandis rolled off him and kicked the door shut with her feet. Hidden. Well hidden—she would never have found that door, even in the daylight. Trying not to step on Rone, she stood, feeling around for a lamp, a match, anything.

"Rone?"

He didn't reply.

"Rone, answer me."

"Go to hell."

She let out a long breath. Still alive. Light, light—

A kerosene lamp burned to life ahead of her, illuminating a long, narrow hallway lined with shelves and hooks. At the end stood an older Kolin man, maybe Kazen's age, though he looked healthier. He was stocky and wide, with thick gray hair cut short and slicked back from his forehead. His eyes were sharp and equally gray.

"That is a very special entrance, young lady," he said. His voice was not accusatory, nor was it friendly. He had bags under his eyes. From lack of sleep or from age, she didn't know.

His eyes fell to Rone.

"He's hurt," she said, pleading with every syllable. "He led me here, said—"

The man put down the lamp at once and took two long strides toward Rone. "Rone Comf. So this is how you finally pay me a visit?"

Rone made a strangled sound in reply.

The man met Sandis's gaze. "All right, young lady. You get his feet, and I'll get his shoulders." He looked her over. "If you can manage."

Sandis imagined she was a sight to behold, but relief at this stranger's kindness drove back her fatigue. She nodded and stepped back to the door, grabbing Rone's feet.

They lifted him up. Sandis said, "He's been shot . . . his hip, I think."

The man merely nodded and turned at the end of the hallway, bringing Rone into a dimly lit room without windows. Several sacks and jars lined one wall, and an alarming number of weapons lined another, everything from knives to chains to firearms. Sandis recognized seven of the eight displayed.

"Set him down," the stranger instructed, and Sandis obeyed. He then left through another door, one that led into what looked like an ordinary flat. He came back with a bedroll and set it right next to where Rone lay.

Together, Sandis and the stranger hoisted their patient onto the roll. Sandis cringed at the bloodstain he'd left on the hardwood.

The man left again, then came back with an assortment of medical supplies, some Sandis had never seen. "Bullet's probably still in there. Stupid kid. Here, roll him onto his other side and keep him from moving."

Rone mumbled something unintelligible.

Sandis bit her lip, looking between Rone's pained face and the stranger's sure one. "Will it hurt?"

The man laughed. "Of course it will hurt! No more than he deserves."

Another groan. Sandis squeezed Rone's bicep.

The stranger pulled out a long pair of tweezers.

Sandis looked away.

Sandis awoke feeling groggy and stiff—both in body and in clothing. She had no idea how long she'd slept, thanks to the lack of windows in the too-warm space. The first thing that caught her eye after blinking clear her bleary vision was the candle, burned down to a quarter wick. Was this the first candle the man, who'd introduced himself as Arnae, had lit, or had he replaced it with a second? Sandis was sure she'd slept at least half a day. She felt like she'd been possessed again.

Ireth. She swallowed and pushed herself onto sore knees. She'd never before had a *vision* like the one that had assaulted her in that records room. It was the same horrific being she'd seen in her dream, but she'd never experienced such a thing while awake.

Kolosos. She felt it in her bones. That was Kolosos.

Ireth was afraid of him, and he was trying to send her a message.

She closed her eyes. *Ireth, what should I do?*

The fire horse didn't answer.

A moan drew her attention to the other side of the room, to Rone's bedroll. Forgetting her sore muscles, Sandis hurried to his side. Felt his forehead. No fever. Thank the Celestial—Arnae had said it would portent badly for him if he developed a fever.

"Rone?" she tried. A line appeared between his eyebrows, and she rubbed it smooth with her finger.

He cracked one eyelid. Took a deep breath. "You're still here?"

Sandis flicked his temple.

He waved her away.

"How do you feel?"

"Like I got shot." He tried to roll over, winced, and gave up. "What time is it?"

"I don't know."

Rone fumbled with his hands until he pulled the amarinth out of his pocket. He spun it. The gold coils fell lifeless to his stomach.

Sandis gaped. "You're going to check the time with *that*? Isn't it a waste?"

Rone pocketed the artifact. "When it resets, I can spin it and become immortal again. Mortal wounds cannot exist on an immortal body."

Sandis sat back on her haunches. Tingles crawled up her arms. "It heals."

He nodded.

Sandis rolled her lips together. "Rone."

He winced like her voice annoyed him. She hoped it didn't. Maybe he had a headache. "What?"

"You could save lives with that."

He groaned.

"Rone." She inched closer until her knees pressed into his arm. "Can you imagine? Going to a hospital, to a sickbed . . . Someone with no chance for life could *live* again—"

"And then everyone would know about it." He winced, but from his injury or the thought of giving up the amarinth, she wasn't sure.

Sandis pressed her lips together. Yes, in the wrong hands, the Noscon charm could be used for wrong. But in the *right* hands . . .

People could live. Sickness, dissolved. Injuries, swept away. Suffering, eliminated. Surely there was some way—

She looked at the golden loops clutched in Rone's hands and pulled herself back to reality. Without the amarinth, they'd both be dead. Or waking up in Kazen's lair.

Sandis swallowed. "If the grafters didn't know about the amarinth before, they do now."

He looked at her.

She readjusted herself to a more comfortable position. "It's something Kazen would want. He's talked of them before."

"It's something *anyone* would want." He looked at her pointedly, as if reminding her that if she hadn't stolen the thing in the first place, he wouldn't be lying on the floor with stitches in his hip.

Sandis glanced at the door. "Who is Arnae?" He had seemed so familiar with Rone, mocking him in such a familial way. He'd asked after Rone's mother. Sandis had given him the unfortunate news.

Rone snorted. "He must like you to have given you his first name."

That made Sandis smile.

"Arnae Kurtz. He's my old teacher."

"What did he teach?"

"How to throw a punch."

Sandis blinked. "Oh."

Rone sighed. "When I was a kid, I worked sewers and cleanup in this area. Kurtz offered to tell me stories if I would clean the sludge off his flat. I thought it was a pretty stupid trade, but I did it anyway. He got sick for a while, but I kept doing it because I liked wasting my time."

"Because you were being *nice*?"

Rone rolled his eyes. "Anyway, apparently it impressed him. After he recovered, he offered to teach me seugrat—the old form of martial arts used by Kolin nomads. I was here almost every day until I found . . ."

He didn't finish, but Sandis guessed he meant to say, *the amarinth.* The relic's power had allowed him to become this Engel Verlad figure.

"He's nice," she said.

Rone massaged his forehead. "He's all right."

"He saved you."

He grunted.

Sandis watched the candle flicker for a moment. "What do you do? As Engel?"

Rone lowered his hand. "I think the more important question is, What the hell, Sandis?"

Her breath caught somewhere above her heart.

Rone tried to push himself up on one elbow, winced, and fell back onto the bedroll with a sound of frustration. "I'm right, aren't I?

Everyone knows grafters are all about the occult, and you've got dozens of them after you. You're a vessel."

She shifted her focus back to the candle. "Keep your voice down."

He cursed. Was silent for a moment. "You know that's illegal."

She glared at him. Rone's activities weren't exactly legal, either. She'd seen him break and enter and beat up that man. She was half tempted to say as much.

Silence filled the room instead.

She swallowed. "I didn't choose it."

Rone rubbed the scruff on his jaw. "I suppose this Kazen guy did."

She licked the back of her teeth. "When I was fourteen . . . I lost my brother. I went looking for him, and two slavers grabbed me."

"In Dresberg?"

She nodded.

"Doesn't sound right."

She shrugged. "They did, and Kazen found and bought me a little while later. Said I was special. Turned me into . . . this."

"A vessel."

She nodded. "Not anyone can be one. There are requirements—good health, no piercings, virginal—"

Rone grunted.

"—an open spirit—"

"A what?"

"Open spirit," she repeated, though she knew he had heard her clearly. She didn't look at him while she spoke—she'd never talked about this to anyone before. For years, her sole companions had been the other vessels, and they all knew as much, or as little, as she did. "It's . . . I don't know how to explain it, but it makes you receptive to the ethereal plane."

"And the demons."

"The *numina*, yes." That vivid image of Kolosos crossed her mind. "Kazen has a special sort of insight. A way of seeing things about you that you fail to see in yourself. Part of me is glad he took me; the slavers weren't . . . kind. Kazen is at least decent, if you follow his rules."

Rone pressed his lips together. Looked away.

"But he is also evil. Not the way the slavers were . . . a darker, more manipulative way. It's an evil that reaches out and draws you in. He made us a part of what he was doing. But it was easy to pretend, you know? Pretend it was all right. Most of the time. But after . . . I always knew it, but after . . ." Her throat constricted, choking off her words.

"After what?"

She steeled herself. "He wanted to—wants to—summon a numen called Kolosos. Something powerful. Something . . . awful. I've seen glimpses of him." She shook her head. "The night I ran away, he tried to summon Kolosos into another vessel named Heath. It killed Heath. Violently."

A curse soft as a feather flowed from Rone's lips.

"I know Kazen," she continued, "and I know he hasn't given up. But I don't know how to stop him. For one man to have so much power, especially a man like him . . ." As an afterthought, she added, "I'm one of his strongest vessels."

Once again, she found herself thinking that it could have been her in that room, not Heath, standing in that blood. Had she not been so meticulous in following the rules, at being the *favorite*—

"What happened with those records?" Rone interrupted her grisly thought. "The ones you . . . touched?"

Sandis swallowed. How much to tell him? How much did she even know? But she didn't have anyone else to advise her. And didn't Rone deserve to know the truth? He'd taken a bullet for her.

She knit and unknit her fingers together. "I had a vision. From Ireth."

"You mentioned that name before."

She nodded. "Ireth the fire horse. Strength-seven numen. I'm bound to him. In order for Kazen to control a numen he summons, he has to have the blood of the vessel in his veins. He took mine the same day I left. I don't know if it's still there . . . If it is, then Kazen could still use me to summon and control Ireth."

Rone had that look again, that shocked expression that did nothing to tell Sandis what he was thinking. "And he has to touch you."

"My head, yes."

"And you can't . . . control it?"

She shook her head. Picked at the wood grain in the floor. "I cease to exist when Ireth takes over my body. Except . . ."

"Except *what?*"

She took another moment to think before meeting that still-shocked gaze. "Except that, sometimes, I remember. Kazen doesn't know. I'm not supposed to. Ireth . . . Ireth has been communicating with me. Or trying to."

Now Rone's expression was incredulous. "You talk to a fire horse from hell."

"He's from the ethereal plane." A tiny bit of venom laced the statement. "It's not his fault Kazen makes him do terrible things."

"But you talk to it."

"I . . . no. Ireth can't . . . talk. Or he hasn't. I just . . ." This sounded loony, didn't it? Especially to someone who hadn't experienced it. "I feel it. Him. What he's trying so say."

Rone took his time mulling over that. After what felt like forever, he said, "And what, exactly, is Ireth trying to say?"

"That Kolosos is dangerous. Ireth is afraid of him. He needs . . . something, but I'm not sure what."

Rone shook his head, smiling a strange smile, and stared at the ceiling. "This is farcical."

Sandis's brows knit together. "This is true."

"This is a dream. You're a *vessel*. When I was younger, I honestly thought the occult wasn't real, that my father spoke about it to scare us—"

Sandis perked. "Your father?"

He dismissed the inquiry with a wave of his hand. "And this guy picked you, of all people, to summon a slagging *fire horse* into."

"There are five . . . four others. You saw one of them yesterday."

Rone whistled. "This is insane." He paused. "And this is why Kazen wants you? Because you're some special thing that can summon this Ireth?"

She nodded. "I'm bound to him. So long as I am, no other vessel can host him. And few meet the criteria for vessels. We're . . . rare." As far as Sandis knew, there were far more numina than there were vessels. Hundreds of them, though Kazen had his favorites.

"And can you *unbind* yourself?"

She paused. "I . . . yes."

That apparently piqued his interest. "How?"

"Break a qualification, I suppose." Give herself a permanent injury. Lose her virginity. "Breaking my script would be the easiest. But I can't."

"Your script? What? And why not?"

She shook her head. Leaned away from him. Rone wouldn't understand, but she felt the need to clarify. "Because I'll lose Ireth. I'll never learn what he's been trying to tell me."

"But Kazen wouldn't want you anymore."

She breathed in deeply, held the air until it hurt, then released it all at once. Perhaps Kazen wouldn't, save for revenge. He was not a man who relished being cheated.

"Maybe. But I can't. Ireth." She paused. "I have to know what he wants. I have to learn everything I can about Kolosos. I have to . . . stop it."

Her own words surprised her. *Stop Kolosos? Stop Kazen?* Even if she could control the fire horse, Ireth was no match for Kazen's monster. Sandis had felt Ireth's fear. And she was certainly no match for her former master.

Maybe Kazen wouldn't succeed. Maybe he'd try over and over again until he had no vessels left and he gave up on the venture. Maybe Sandis wouldn't have to do anything.

Her muscles felt too tight.

"This . . . thing you summon is that important, huh?" Rone's voice had an edge to it, but she couldn't tell if it was an edge of wonder or judgment.

She nodded. "Ireth is . . ." *A messenger. A guardian. A friend?* "He's like . . . family."

Sandis knew the declaration was absurd, and yet it didn't feel far from the truth. Ireth was not human, and certainly not related to her. She'd never, technically, *met* him. But she had a growing affection for him similar to what she'd felt toward her brother. He was a burning presence in her breast. He felt like . . . missing someone. And he cared about her. Unselfishly. He needed her.

She had so little of that in her life, especially now that she was separated from the other vessels.

"Can you fake it?"

The question broke Sandis from her thoughts. "What?"

"Fake it. I mean"—he gave her a wolfish smile—"how does he *know* you haven't broken a qualification? You know, with me?" Sandis's cheeks heated, and Rone let her stew in the flush for a moment before adding, "Or done one of the other things."

Sandis considered. Her mind traveled back to her old room in Kazen's lair, to the horseshoe ring of empty cots.

"The others."

The space between Rone's eyebrows crinkled.

"The other vessels. We're not all bound. Kazen would try to summon Ireth into one of them. If he failed, he'd know I still have him."

Rone was quiet again, this time for longer. Sandis stood and looked over the shelves. Her stomach growled; she ignored it.

"What script?"

She turned back to Rone, who had successfully propped himself onto his elbow. His eyes watched her, dark and oddly genuine. Not accusatory. Not disgusted. It kindled an odd kind of strength in her.

She touched the base of her neck, her fingertips lingering just above where Ireth's name was tattooed in their mingled blood—blood taken from her before the summoning, and him after. "All vessels have a script on their backs; it allows the numina to possess them. Noscon magic. I don't understand it."

"That's why you wouldn't take off your coat."

She nodded.

Rone paused a moment. "Can I . . . see it?"

She hesitated. Glanced at the closed door Arnae had disappeared through some hours ago. Licked her lips. Her heart beat faster, but she turned away from Rone and began undoing the buttons of his torn shirt.

She let the dirty, stiff material fall off her shoulders and heard Rone gasp. She could perfectly envision what he saw, for she'd seen it in the mirror and imprinted in the skin of other vessels. A long brand of Noscon writing that stemmed from the top of her spine to the small of her back, the width of a grown man's hand. Gold leaf burned into the characters. Above it, a black bar of smaller Noscon letters spelling out Ireth's name.

She pulled the shirt back up and fastened the buttons.

When Rone spoke again, his voice was softer, without its interrogative edge. "Does it . . . hurt?"

She turned back to him, studying his pale, shocked, and concerned face.

No one had ever asked her that before.

The door opened. Sandis jumped. Arnae Kurtz stood in the doorway. His hard gaze focused on Sandis, and for a moment she was sure he would berate her, grab her, throw her into the street and summon the scarlets, or perhaps the Angelic himself.

His focus switched to Rone. "This is grave, Comf."

Rone grumbled. "Did I mention," he said, without breaking eye contact with his teacher, "that my master is a terrible eavesdropper?"

Sandis's heart sank into her stomach. She took a step back, then another. Telling Rone was one thing; telling this stranger was . . . dangerous.

Arnae held up a hand, stilling her. "I won't hurt you, Sandis." Then, to Rone, "The occult is not all the Celesians make it out to be, but it *is* real, and it *is* a threat, especially if what your friend is saying is true."

"You have such a way with words." Rone lowered himself onto his back and hissed as he did so.

"Don't jest with me, Rone."

Sandis squeaked, "You believe me?"

Arnae raised a gray eyebrow. "I am a spinner of stories, young lady, and even I could not fashion one as great as yours. I think you've done well in your choice of allies."

Her heart bounced back to its proper place. "You'll help us?"

But the old man shook his head. "Not me. Rone."

She glanced at the injured man on the floor.

Arnae followed her gaze. "Take her to the Lily Tower. Today."

Sandis's pulse raced. "But—"

Arnae held up a hand. "Do not fear, Sandis. You have done nothing wrong."

Rone snorted. "The Celesians won't see it that way. The Lily Tower is the last place she should be."

"I think we can all think of worse places."

Sandis hugged herself. All three of them sat in heavy silence for several seconds. Celesia was the prominent religion in Kolingrad. Technically, *Sandis* was Celesian, though she'd rarely worshipped at the cathedral. She prayed to the Celestial from time to time, despite being a horror in its sight.

"You have a responsibility." Arnae's finger pointed at Rone. "The Celesians denounce the occult, but they understand it, and you have a better chance than anyone of getting their help."

Rone growled. "Don't just assume—"

"If nothing else, Rone, he can help your mother."

Rone's face blanked. Sandis's gaze switched between him and Arnae so quickly she made herself dizzy. *He?* Who was *he?* It occurred to her belatedly that she'd forgotten to mention that she'd told Arnae about Rone's mother.

She longed to ask them to explain, but it would have felt . . . irreverent.

Rone glanced at Sandis before pressing the heels of his hands into his eyes. "You're a son of a whore, Kurtz."

"Do you find power in stating the obvious, *Engel?*"

Rone groaned. "Of course you know."

"I know a lot of things." Arnae turned back for the door. "Sandis, clean up, and you can help me with lunch. Rone can lie here until his little secret resets."

Sandis's mouth formed an *O*, but she nodded and hurried after Arnae, eager to take advantage of his kindness.

Rone cursed the both of them.

Chapter 11

Rone didn't sleep well. Could have been because he'd been shot. Could have been because he'd been lying on his back all day in the hidden room in the rear of Kurtz's flat, staring at the same wood slatting of the ceiling for hour after damnable hour. Could have been the pain in his hip and the weird drugs his old master kept forcing down his throat, or the worry that he had a rather large number of enemies roaming the streets of Dresberg.

The insomnia also could have been due to Sandis's revelations and the knowledge that his mother was sitting in a dark, rank cell, alone.

His inability to move gave him far too much time to think, and his thoughts flopped back and forth like a dying fish. The vision of Sandis's bare back lingered behind his eyelids. Her . . . God's tower, those were *brands*. Very large, deep brands, with *gold* melted into them. She'd been, what, fourteen? What had they used to draw them? Iron? Forged gold? A hot poker? How did a person, let alone a child, survive something like that?

He cringed and spun the amarinth, which teetered depressingly in his fingers. Rone knew the history of the occult; it'd been drilled into him as part of his religious education, along with all the other jokes about God and faith and what have you. His roving ancestors had sailed the Arctic Ribbon and stumbled upon what was now Kolingrad, a vast and relatively fertile land previously inhabited by the Noscons, who, for some unknown reason, had abandoned all of their colonies and cities. No one knew what had become of them, but bounteous lore and tall tales revolved around their fate. Many thought they'd taken to the ocean, just as the Kolins once had.

The Noscons had left behind evidence of one aspect of their culture: they were heathens. There were few surviving texts, but scholars had uncovered tablets that focused on the ethereal plane and numina and what was now considered the "occult." Historians had continued to study the Noscons until one of their self-righteous contemporaries went off about how there was one true god and the worship or study of anything else was blasphemy. That scholar talked his way into all the fancy religious power he wanted and became the first Angelic. The Kolins then plowed over the Noscon ruins to build their cities, and anyone who still cared an ounce about the twisted Noscon magic was declared a heathen, subject to imprisonment and execution, thanks to the sway the Angelic had over the government. That sway had lessened over time, but old habits died hard.

For most of his life, Rone had thought vessels and numina and summoning were all fairy stories. After he found the amarinth and began working his way through the darker layers of the city, he'd heard a rumor here or a story there. That was it. Now a vessel to some powerful, otherworldly equine demon was sleeping ten feet away from him.

He spun the amarinth. It continued to resist him. He watched candle shadows dance across the monotonous ceiling. Did his mother have enough light to see shadows, or was her world entirely dark?

If they hurt her, Rone would . . . what? *What* on this damnable earth could he *do*? Gerech was an impenetrable fortress. Even caring nothing for his own life and armed with the amarinth, he'd never get past the first wall. He'd used his one visit. He'd need to bribe his way past the guards, bribe the warden . . . *Money, money, money.* Where would he find a buyer who understood the worth of the amarinth but would be honest enough to offer a fair trade? Grafters would covet it, certainly, but they'd sooner shank Rone's kidney than fork over their life savings with a smile.

His thoughts turned darker yet. Did Gerech torture its prisoners? Starvation? Whips? Boiling water? Molten iron?

Brands. The loops of ancient golden writing on Sandis's back seemed to draw themselves on the rafters overhead. What was it like, to be possessed? Sandis said she didn't remember details, that it was all pain and then waking up. But she also claimed there was some kind of communication between her and this Ireth. Rone closed his eyes, trying to imagine another being taking over his body. *Becoming* his body.

There was no way that didn't hurt.

Did those brands hurt even when she *wasn't* possessed?

He turned his head toward her. She wore a simple dress—why Kurtz owned a dress Rone didn't know and didn't *want* to know—and lay facing away from him, her single blanket pooling at the dip of her waist, highlighting the curve of her hip.

If she'd been ugly, he never would have gotten involved in this. And now Kurtz was rooting for her and wanted him to bring her to the Lily Tower, of all places. God's tower. He hadn't been there since he was thirteen, and he'd vowed never to go back.

He thought of his mother. Guilt squirmed through his gut like hunger. Any moment now, the amarinth would reset, and he'd be able to get up and leave this place, even if there were grafters hunting him. Meanwhile she was locked in a cell, persecuted for a crime *he* had committed.

Leave this place. And go where? Check his other drop-off spots, he supposed. See if he'd found work. He needed money to make this right.

A thought surfaced. Why wait for someone to hire him?

Chewing on the inside of his lip, Rone let his mind pursue the idea. He did odd jobs for the city's elite, whatever it was they wanted. He didn't care who hired him, so long as they had enough money.

How much sweeter would it be if the cash came with a side of revenge?

Ernst Renad obviously had plenty of money . . .

Rone's body began to tingle with alertness, eagerness, the need to *get up* and *get moving*. He had never stolen for himself before. Theft could be such a gray area that way. But this was his *mother*.

He spun the amarinth; it twirled lazily, useless.

He knew exactly where the guy lived. Not terribly far—Rone could get there while it was still dark. He also knew the layout of his house. Knew where he kept valuables that could be sold for enough cash to appease the twisted warden.

He'd be able to save his mother.

He'd be able to keep his vow to never return to the Lily Tower.

Rone spun the amarinth again. It responded with its blessed whirl and floated a few inches above his navel. Rone let out a sigh as pain receded from his side and the heat in his hip cooled. His muscles relaxed, then tensed again as his intentions—*get up, get moving, and get the money*—pulsed through his veins. Pushing the still-spinning amarinth aside, Rone sat up and cracked his neck. Stretched his arms. Rolled his shoulders, feeling the familiar tug in his left shoulder. The amarinth was a miracle, but it only healed life-threatening injuries, not the purely annoying ones.

Standing, careful not to wake Sandis, Rone grabbed his things and readied himself to leave. The amarinth was spent, but he hadn't needed it last time, had he? This was a simple burglary, no magic required.

The amarinth's loops slowed and stopped, and the artifact fell. Rone caught it before it hit the ground. Pocketed it.

Now or never, he thought, picking his way through the darkness to the alley-facing door.

He inched it open and slipped into the night.

Kas Kirstin had taught him how to pick locks.

Rone was fifteen years old when he met Kas. The older boy had apparently worked some unsavory jobs before getting caught and fined, so when a job opened up in Rone's sector for sewage, he had been shoved there without a second thought. By that time, Rone had already picked up an enthusiastic street dialect and disregard for adults in general. He'd worked really hard to be all the things his father hated.

His father would have *hated* Kas.

Rone didn't pick the lock on the gate that sectioned off Ernst Renad's neighborhood; he scaled it in the same place he'd used five days ago, where the road naturally bumped to give him a lift. The route had been proven once before; why change it now?

Rone tried to remember everything he'd seen in the sitting room where he'd lifted the Noscon headpiece. Armor, but that was too heavy to carry. He wanted small, light, valuable pieces. There had been some egg things on the mantle. If the jewels in them were real, a couple in his pockets might be enough to persuade the warden to actually listen to the law.

He'd snap the strings on the harp while he was at it.

As he reached the intersection for Renad's road, a light crossed his path, forcing him to backpedal or be spotted. The warden's claim about the scarlets keeping Gerech's cells full so they themselves wouldn't occupy them ran through his mind.

They were corrupt, all of them. The police, the triumvirate, even the Celesians with their precious Angelic. They were no better than the mobs and grafters.

Black ashes and slag, he hated this place.

Retracing his steps, Rone hugged the edge of the narrow road between fancy three-story houses and stuck his hands in his pockets. He fiddled absently with his amarinth. Cut through someone's backyard to circumvent the scarlets. His pulse was starting to pick up in anticipation of meeting the bastard responsible for his mother's suffering. He ought to throw Renad out the window.

A moving chain to his right. Rone turned in time to see two glowing eyes charging toward him. The dog barked, and Rone backed up two steps. The dog's chain yanked the animal back a foot from where Rone stood.

The moment the light hit the back of his head, he realized he wasn't wearing his fancy collar. That, in fact, he still smelled alarmingly of sewage.

Groaning inwardly, Rone turned and held his hand up to block the light from his face. *Not tonight, Renad. But soon.* He'd have to blandish his way out of this one and hope the bloodstains on his shirt from his now-healed gunshot wound weren't terribly noticeable.

"Can I help you, sir?" asked a large man in his fifties. He wore a gray mustache and a tightly buttoned scarlet uniform. "This your home?" He appraised Rone's clothing skeptically.

"No, I'm down that way." He randomly gestured to his left. "Thought I saw someone creeping around over here, but turned out the Fensteins moved their dog's post. After what happened to Ernst, you can't be too careful."

A second officer came up beside the first, holding a lamp of his own. "That's why we told everyone to stay inside after dusk."

Whoops. "Like I said, I thought I saw—"

The first scarlet elbowed the second and gestured toward Rone with a tilt of his head. Rone didn't like that tilt. He backed up, only to have the mutt behind him try to take a bite out of his thigh.

The second officer asked, "What's your name, sir?"

Stay calm. You've done nothing wrong. Yet. "Peter Aves. I'm sorry for the trouble. I can head back home." He stepped away from the dog.

Officer number one held up a hand. "I'd like you to come with us for a moment."

Rone took another step away. "Why's that?"

Both scarlets stared at his face like they'd never seen another human before. The second held up his light. He muttered something to the first that sounded alarmingly like "That's him."

The pieces clicked together.

They knew who he was. They knew what he looked like.

"They'll do whatever they can to bring you down," Sandis had said.

Wanted sketches. Had to be. Nothing swayed the Kolin justice system like money, and Kazen was no doubt loaded.

Rone ran.

"Stop!" the first officer bellowed after him, but Rone bolted down the street, cutting through the first property without a high fence. Keeping anything—houses, brush, trees—between himself and the scarlets. He needed to gain as much distance as he could before they called their friends.

Their whistles tore through the night as he leapt a fence, landing hard in the darkness on the other side.

***

"Put this on."

Rone handed Sandis a strip of cloth he'd procured from the gray shirt he'd worn into the sewer—the one that had been festering inside his canvas bag while he lay on the floor with a gunshot wound. After losing the scarlets and making it back to Kurtz's home, he'd scrubbed the shirt until the woven fibers threatened to pull apart, then cut it into two wide strips. His old master had kindly painted a four-petaled lily on the center of each one. Though Kurtz had not commented on Rone's absence, he seemed to know about it nevertheless. The man always knew everything.

Sandis turned it over. "What is it?"

Rone rubbed wakefulness into his eyes. "A pilgrimage band for your left arm. How is it you've lived in Dresberg your whole life and you haven't worn one of these, or at least seen someone else . . ."

He swallowed his words. *Oh yeah, because you were poor. Also a slave. Good one, Rone.*

Sandis merely blinked at him. He covered for himself by helping her tie the sash around her arm. There was a certain way to do the knot.

She smelled good. Like lavender and sugar. Had she always smelled like that? Rone fumbled his knot and started over. Sandis reached her hand around and pressed it into the center of his work to hold it in place.

"It's a joke, really." He stepped back and scrubbed weariness from his face, though the sweet scents of lavender and sugar lingered. He tied his own with the use of his teeth as his master entered the room and fiddled with some dishes. "From here it's, what, a six-mile pilgrimage? Some show of faith that is."

Rone thought he saw the slightest smile on his old master's mouth before the man slopped overnight porridge into two bowls and set them down on the table. He gestured for them to sit. This morning, Rone was more than happy to oblige.

"Go out the front door"—Kurtz handed out spoons—"but not until the clock tower strikes and the shift changes. I don't want any lurking grafters to spy you coming out of my house." He focused on Sandis. "I don't mean offense, young lady, but they are not the kind of folk I want to be associated with."

Sandis nodded, but Rone didn't miss the glimmer of light that died in her eyes. First Rone's flat, now Kurtz's. One safe house after another was turning them out. The Lily Tower would be next . . . he knew it. For all their preaching for righteousness and charity, the Celesian priests were some of the coldest people he knew.

After last night, he didn't know if he had any other options left. How widely was his picture being circulated? Maybe there wasn't a sketch at all. Maybe he was overthinking this.

Sandis stirred her porridge with her spoon. She looked toward the shuttered window near the flat's door. She'd been doing that a lot this morning. "Are we sure they won't see us?"

"No," Rone said, "but it's dawn, and there's already a crowd outside—"

"That won't stop them." Sandis paused. "Not necessarily."

"As good a deterrent as any," Kurtz chimed in. "I'd cut through Grim Rig's territory and loop around the courthouse. Both of those places should be safe enough from the grafters."

Sandis shook her head. "Grim Rig has eight fingers because Kazen took two of them."

Both men turned to her. "What?" asked Rone.

Sandis swallowed a mouse-sized bite of porridge. "I don't know what happened. That was one of Heath's missions . . ." She glanced at the window again. Blinked. "Isn't the courthouse west of here?"

"The daily pilgrimage meets at the cathedral at noon, then they walk to the tower together." Rone took a bite of porridge. It was surprisingly well seasoned.

"They walk all that way?"

"It's a requirement, to show humility." Satire laced his words. "They literally check your hems at the door. If they're too clean, you have to walk around the city wall as penance."

"That's not true." Kurtz hesitated and rubbed his chin. "Is it?"

Rone gave him a blank stare.

His old master shrugged. "Hurry up." He tossed a razor Rone's way. "If you have time, clean up."

Rone frowned but pocketed the razor regardless. He glanced at Sandis, but she was timidly asking Kurtz about his guns.

He had a feeling today was going to be a bad day.

Rone nicked his chin when the clock tower chimed, dropped the razor into Kurtz's old sink, and grabbed his washed clothes and canvas bag before pushing his way outside. He'd forgotten how dim Kurtz kept his flat—the sunlight blinded him. The smell was pretty terrible, too. Whoever had taken Rone's old job had not been tempted to excellency by Kurtz's stories.

Sandis was silent as a rock as they took the path through the Riggers' territory and pushed their way into the crowded streets of the smoke ring. Nobody looked at their pilgrimage ties twice, if they noticed them at all. Most shuffled forward with their eyes on the cobblestones or the back of the person in front of them. A glum bunch, but Rone couldn't blame them. There was little to be happy about in this part of Dresberg.

The crowds were thicker than usual, which Rone normally would have hated, but each melancholy factory worker acted as a shield against watching eyes. Rone pushed his way toward the center of the road, letting the people herd around him. He and Sandis blended right—

Sandis.

Rone cursed and stopped, earning a similar curse from the person behind him. He weaved against the crowd, which meant he was barely moving at all. To his relief, Sandis appeared only seconds after he realized he'd lost her.

"Keep up!" he called.

"What?" she asked.

Rone opened his mouth, then thought better of it. Shaking his head, he grabbed her hand and held on tight as they slowly navigated the narrow road. It might have occurred to him that, despite having known several women intimately, he had never actually walked about holding one's hand. But the day's mission pressed too hard on his thoughts for him to notice. Much.

Many roads near the center of the city had been widened over the years to accommodate the growing population, but engineers and laborers couldn't move buildings, so the girth of streets could only expand so much. People had to leave before the sun rose if they wanted to get anywhere without pressing bodies with strangers, and in the smoke ring, wagons were hopeless. There wasn't space, at least not during shift changes.

Smoke towers spewed rolling gray clouds into the sky, which occasionally mixed with the steady spit of steam vents. Despite an earlier bath, Rone felt dirty by the time he reached the edge of the smoke ring. The crowds began to thin, but he still took the busiest roads toward the cathedral, constantly searching intersections for grafters—those he had met, and those he hadn't.

Sandis squeezed his hand, even when there was little chance of them separating.

Once upon a time, Rone had thought the cathedral beautiful. It was likely still the most aesthetic building in Dresberg, if one didn't count the Lily Tower itself. While so many buildings adhered to utility—making roof hopping all the easier—the cathedral broke the mold, standing out amid its surroundings. The Central Cathedral of the Celestial was mostly a giant tapering tower that came to a point, from which jutted a solid gold pole reaching toward heaven . . . wherever it lay beyond the polluted sky. The base of the tower folded out into a long, flattish structure, like a lying dog with its tail in the air. Two small wings flared out from either side of that. The cathedral wasn't whitewashed—someone had used their brain when building it—but its exterior was patterned with dark river stone. In the late-morning light, its windows looked like sapphire.

Apparently the cathedral also used to have well-kept grounds, but the city had eaten those up as it demanded more and more space for industry and the Angelic lost more and more rapport with the government. But the building itself still stood, and its halls were still filled with worshippers, priests, and pilgrims, so that had to mean something.

It means these people are gullible suckers, Rone thought as he trudged toward the building's front doors.

A white-garbed priest stood outside the doors greeting people. When he saw Rone's and Sandis's pilgrimage ties, he nodded and directed them inside. "Just down this hall, my friends. You'll see a small atrium filled with other pilgrims. Have you come far?"

Sandis glanced at him.

Rone bowed. "Aye."

The priest seemed pleased. Rone pushed past him with Sandis in tow. He released her hand halfway down the corridor, trying not to be annoyed with her slow pace as she took in their surroundings. Several paintings of past Angelics hung on the walls, along with embroidered scripture spewed out by the man who'd started it all. Panels of four-petaled lilies, designed to look geometric, were interspersed with the other decorations. That was how the Celestial was portrayed—either as a lily or an androgynous, overweight person with white skin and white clothes. The Celestial had no gender.

The atrium Rone and Sandis entered—one that brought up a cluster of half memories Rone immediately shoved back down—was centered around a statue of the latter portrayal of the Celestial. Every aspect of it was round and glistening. A window in the ceiling shone light down onto its marble head. About a dozen pilgrims stood around it, half of whom actually did look like they'd traveled far. Despite the throngs and industry within Dresberg, the land surrounding the capital was pretty barren. Dry in the summer, buried in snow in the winter. A few towns and trading posts dotted it here and there. The next-biggest cities were populated by fishermen on the northern coast, and from what Rone understood, they were small compared to Dresberg. The farmland and ranches lay farther south, where the rain was decent and the cold not so severe. Judging by the pilgrims' clothes, he guessed two-thirds of them were farmers, the rest tradesmen.

One of the former leaned toward his pregnant wife and said, "Soon, darling. Soon." A rather pretty woman, Rone noted.

He turned his back to them and shoved his hands into his pockets.

Sandis approached him, with eyes wide, taking in their surroundings until finally settling on him. She blinked. "What's wrong?"

He straightened and pulled his hands out of his pockets. "Nothing. Just have to wait until noon." He glanced at her worn shoes. "Maybe they'll have something that fits you in the donation box."

Sandis looked at her feet. Wiggled her toes. "These are all right."

Rone rolled his eyes, broke away from her, and headed back the way they'd come. Was it this way, or . . . Ah, there. He turned right and found a short hallway lined with crates of donations for the poor. People who could actually afford to do so brought in their used goods, food, and sometimes money to be distributed among the believers, for what good it did. Rone used to think of them as "guilt boxes," since priests had to guilt the sinful rich into donating anything of real use.

He found a crate half-full of shoes and sorted through them. There was a pair of beaded heels in there. Who would have use for those? They'd been wedged between several worn pairs of kids' shoes and some work boots ready to fall apart.

He pulled out some sturdy-enough boy's shoes that looked like they might fit her. On his return trip to the atrium, he noticed a boy talking to Sandis—he was probably three or four years her junior and two inches shorter. Sandis didn't protest the company, but Rone walked faster, anyway.

"Here," he said, tossing the shoes at Sandis's feet. "Try these."

The boy looked at Rone and instantly turned around, scurrying back toward the cathedral's entrance.

"Who was he?" he asked.

Sandis shrugged. "I don't know. Came over as soon as you left, asking me where I was from."

Rone frowned, peering down the way the boy had left. He hadn't worn a pilgrim's sash, had he? "Did you tell him your name?"

She shook her head and reached for the shoes.

He waited for her to remark on their wear, or on the poor fashion, or even on the fact that they were designed for a teenaged boy, not unlike the one who'd just left, and not for a woman. But she said nothing as she slipped off the dainty things she had on and pushed her feet into the new ones.

She smiled. "They're a little big, but better for running, I think. Thank you."

Her gratitude scurried up his neck like the wings of a moth. Rone shrugged. Looked for a clock. Still some time to go. He sighed and shoved his hands into his pockets again. Fingered the amarinth.

"Thank you, Rone."

"I heard you."

"No." Her hand touched his forearm, drawing his attention back to her. She met his eyes for a moment before looking away, though her warm touch lingered. "Thank you. For everything else. For helping me. I . . . don't know what I would have done, had you not come along."

The muscles in Rone's back tensed in a weird, shivery sort of way. He lifted his hand—Sandis dropped hers—and rubbed the back of his neck. "I didn't exactly volunteer."

"I know. But thank you, anyway."

"Uh, yeah. You're welcome."

She smiled at him. Despite everything, he sort of smiled back.

A small gong rang at the head of the room. Rone glanced at the clock. There was still half an hour until—

Celestial on a stick, they're going to preach to us. He barely stifled a groan.

A high priest garbed in white and a tall hat motioned the pilgrims forward. Sandis seemed interested. Good. That meant only one of them had to fake it.

They loitered near the back, Sandis lifting herself onto her toes to see better as a few stragglers entered the atrium, Rone counting tiles on the floor. The high priest mumbled something about charity and cleanliness and whatever else would make the pilgrims, even the locals, feel good about themselves. Finally, after what felt like an eternity, the high priest stepped aside and let two lower priests come to the front of the group. They organized the pilgrims into two columns, and Rone shouldered his way forward so he and Sandis wouldn't be at the tail end. Harder to be picked off that way.

"Pull up your hood when we're out there," he mumbled to Sandis. Her expression instantly changed to that of pale fear. It was then that Rone realized she'd been . . . what, *happy*? Did she eat this stuff up like everyone else? Despite what she'd been forced to become?

He sighed and faced forward. She'd know the truth soon enough.

To Rone's relief, the trek to the Lily Tower, though long, was uneventful. No grafters, no policemen, not even a rudimentary check of his identification. Though outside Dresberg's walls, the Lily Tower was still considered part of the capital, and thus citizens could go to and from it without being harassed by guards. Leaving the city in any other direction required a review of papers. The walk made Rone's feet hurt, but his hems would be soiled enough to appease even the sternest of gateway priests.

He rubbed his stomach as they approached the Lily Tower—a seven-story structure made of granite and quartz piled atop one another like a layer cake. The tower was cylindrical, though the topmost floor was smaller in diameter than the rest. Enough circle-top windows had been cut into the thing that the stone resembled lace. Somewhere inside, a woman was singing.

Rone's neck felt too tight, like his vertebrae were fusing together. He kept his face forward. Forced his tense shoulders down.

Sandis noticed. "Rone?"

He simply shook his head.

They reached the door. It happened just like before. No one paid him any particular notice, save for a sweeping glance that ended at the hem of his trousers. A priestess murmured something soft and kind to the pilgrims as they passed. Rone didn't hear what she said to him.

Inside, everything was so blasted white. He didn't think he would remember it this well, but he did. He remembered all of it. He remembered having to take his shoes off like he was now. Remembered the texture of the carpeting under his feet. He swore he could even remember that giant fern growing in the middle of the round sitting room they passed through, though it was bigger now. To his chagrin, he found himself gaping like Sandis did, like all the other pilgrims did.

They entered a small space with pillows scattered on the floor. Everyone sat on one. Rone followed suit, hovering in the back with Sandis. Yes, he remembered this, too. Someone was going to come talk to them about the importance of the pilgrimage and how it first started. A story he'd heard time and time again. He tugged at his old memories as a high priest chattered away. They'd have to separate themselves from the rest of the group, but not too soon. Not if they wanted to talk to the Angelic personally, and without an audience . . .

"Rone?" Sandis whispered.

He didn't look at her. "Just stay close."

When the sermon was over, the priests directed the pilgrims to rise and—yes, Rone remembered these stairs. He thought he recalled blue carpet on them, but they were solid marble. Had they been renovated, or was Rone's memory faulty?

A headache began to build at the base of his skull. More sermons. Maybe one for each floor? The Angelic would be at the top. It symbolized walking toward God, or at least to the Celestial's mouthpiece. Yes, that was—

Sandis jumped beside him. Rone instantly went on alert, but there were no apparent threats around them, nothing but paintings and flowers and a passing priest. The priest lifted a brow at Sandis's reaction, but then nodded at Rone and went on his way.

Sandis stepped so close to him he nearly tripped over her. They passed a room of worshipping women, and Sandis shied away from it, nearly running into a marble column.

Rone was about to ask what her problem was when it hit him like a mallet. He'd only found out the truth about her *yesterday*, and already he'd forgotten how high the stakes were for her. She was a godforsaken *vessel*. A walking sin. If any of these people discovered the markings on her back . . .

She was terrified, and he hadn't thought twice about it.

That constant, gnawing guilt in his belly doubled over. He stifled a wince.

They turned the corner, and Rone put his arm around her shoulders. "Breathe," he whispered as quietly as he could manage. "They don't know. They won't. Nothing will happen to compromise you. I promise."

She took in a deep breath and nodded. Another priest passed. She watched him go, but this time she didn't startle.

The pilgrims gathered into a second room, then a third, listening to stories of their predecessors and the glory of the Celestial. Rone's churning thoughts and broken plans made the time pass surprisingly quickly. By the time they moved toward the stairs again, hunger and guilt had rolled into a dull ache against his spine, hardening his resolve.

He made sure he and Sandis lingered at the back of the group as they ascended the tower. He glanced behind to ensure no disciples followed them. As they reached the seventh-floor landing, the pilgrims fell into a reverent silence. Not helpful. The priest leading the group began to chant. This was Rone's cue to act.

He found a pillar and pushed Sandis toward it, behind it. Spotted a privacy wall. Moved toward that. Sandis silently followed him. He pushed aside a curtain so they could see, but lingered to the side, where they would not yet be seen.

He stood at the front of the room. The Angelic. The mouthpiece of the Celestial. He looked different—but of course he did. He was older, and a little heavier in his face. He wore long white-and-silver robes and a hat with a thick linen veil hiding the sides and back of his head. A lily marked its front, as well as the breast of his robe.

The pilgrims approached him with awe, some with tears. They knelt before him in a perfect line. The Celestial opened his arms to each of them in turn. Rone's insides turned to lead.

"My children, my friends," the Angelic said. "Welcome to the Lily Tower. Welcome to the home of the Celestial."

Rone winced—his hand had been forming a fist. He forced his fingers open. A small amount of blood welled up from three crescent-shaped cuts at the base of his palm.

Sandis touched his elbow. He held a finger to his lips, urging her to be silent.

The Angelic addressed the group of pilgrims just as the priests before him had, congratulating them on their journey and speaking of his god. Then he talked to each person individually, his words too soft for Rone to hear. The pilgrims thanked him, blessed him, cried against the backs of his hands. It took a long time—the Angelic did not rush, even as he reached the last of the pilgrims. The priest who'd guided them in looked around at one point, perhaps realizing two people were missing from the group. But he did not interrupt the ceremony to go searching for them.

Rone's skin itched more and more with each passing minute, but he didn't scratch. He barely breathed. Sandis leaned close to him. He almost wanted to brush her away. He almost wanted to hold her hand, if only to remind himself that he wasn't doing this alone. Not like last time.

Finally, *finally*, they finished. The pilgrims rose, bowed to the Angelic, and were guided back down the stairs. They would all be fed, and those who had come from afar would be granted board for one night. The Angelic watched with a warm smile as the pilgrims left. Once the last one disappeared from sight, he turned back for the curtained hallway behind him to retreat to his quarters or study or whatever lay beyond this space.

Rone pushed his way into the room. He didn't try to mask the sounds of his footsteps. The Angelic turned around, his white brows pulling together in confusion. He opened his mouth to say something, but Rone spoke first.

"Hey, Pops," he said in his most jovial, sarcastic tone. "Miss me?"

Chapter 12

A slight widening of the eyes. That was it. The only reaction his father gave him.

Rone's fingernails dug back into the crescent cuts on his palms. "I know what you're going to say." He tried to make the words light-hearted, but each passed his lips like the tip of a razor. "Oh, Rone, you're taller. Puberty's been good to you. Yes, well, thank you for that."

Sandis touched his wrist—a featherlight touch that was barely there—and looked between him and the Angelic. "Your . . . *father*?"

The Angelic squared his shoulders. "All men are my children, my friend. I am sorry if you traveled here with the other pilgrims and lost your way. If you entreat the priests, they will give you a room, and you may return here to worship on the morrow."

The enamel on Rone's teeth threatened to chip, he ground his molars so hard. "Not here for the Celestial, *Pops*. Here to talk to you."

The Angelic shook his head. "Dear child, my schedule is very full. Please, seek out one of the priests."

He turned away.

He *turned away*.

Sandis's touch tightened. She stepped in front of Rone, as if to go after the Angelic, but stopped at the length of her arm, unwilling to let go. "I don't understand," she whispered.

"Oh, don't you know?" Rone's eyes pierced his father's back, and he spoke louder than was necessary. His voice had a slight echo in the spacious room. "Once a high priest accepts the election for Angelic, he becomes . . . what did you call it? 'Father to all.' He disowns his real family for the glory of the tower."

It was just like before. Why would Rone think anything had changed? Though his father had been elected to the position, he'd *chosen* to accept it, despite the fact that doing so would cut him off from his real family. From his wife of thirteen years. From his twelve-year-old son. They were left without a father and a husband, and his abandonment had been financial as well as emotional. They'd gone from being comfortable to having no income.

Rone had taken the best-paying job available: cleaning the sewers. Still, he and his mother had moved out of their small house and into a grubby apartment in the smoke ring after selling everything of worth they had to pay the rent. And his father hadn't come back. Hadn't sent money. Hadn't done *anything*.

Rone hadn't believed it at first, of course. His father had always been a stern man, but he was his father. He wouldn't just leave them as if they were nothing. So when Rone was thirteen, he made a "pilgrimage" to the Lily Tower against his mother's wishes. To see his father. To have the reassurance that, though God had claimed Adellion Comf, the Angelic still loved his own flesh and blood.

Rone had been little better than ignored. Cast away when he grabbed his father's robes in tears. Chastised by the other priests. He'd left both his hopes for his family and his faith in the Lily Tower that day.

The Angelic didn't pause at Rone's truthful accusation. He pulled the curtain aside and stepped down, almost gone—

Anger like lava bubbled up Rone's throat. "Mom's in Gerech."

The Angelic stopped. It was a strange sort of relief. Maybe Kurtz's suggestion that they come here hadn't been completely insane.

Slowly, Adellion Comf turned back around. Glanced at Sandis before settling a weary gaze on Rone. "What has she done?"

His voice sounded like that of a man burdened with the weight of another's sin. A small rivulet of warm blood ran down Rone's palm.

He forced his hands to relax.

"*She* hasn't done anything, other than survive when the man who swore *to the Celestial* to protect her abandoned her for his career."

A vein pulsed in the Angelic's forehead. Good. His soul wasn't completely dead.

"Rone," Sandis murmured.

He ignored her. "She's been framed." He'd leave out the fact that she was being framed for *his* crime. "Theft. From one of the wealthiest families in Dresberg, so of course they're paying off anyone with power to ensure she's punished to the highest degree."

The Angelic closed his eyes for a moment, and in that brief span of time, he looked twenty years older. Like if Rone touched him, he'd turn to pale ash inside that white-and-silver robe of his. Then some other priest would take the position, abandoning his family just as Adellion Comf had abandoned his.

The Angelic opened his eyes. Straightened. "There is nothing I can do for her."

Rone lunged forward, breaking Sandis's hold on his wrist. "That is pig fodder, and you know it!"

His father's eyes hardened. "Do not raise your voice in this holy place, my friend."

"I am your *son*, not your *friend*." Rone jutted a finger toward the Angelic's chest. "Are you really going to stand here and tell me you don't care? That you'll let her rot half to death, until a noose finishes the job? You *know* that's what they do in Gerech! *You* have power. You can intervene. Grant her sanctuary. Pay them off. Do *something*, damn it!"

Rone knew the answer before the Angelic even spoke. He saw it in the coldness of his expression. The stiffness of his lip and shoulders. The tightening of his breath.

He would do absolutely nothing.

Mom was going to die.

Rone stepped back and plunged both hands into his hair, pulling on the curls until it hurt. His bad shoulder protested the angle. "Damn you. Damn you and your Celestial."

The Angelic turned away.

"S-Sir."

Rone spun around. He'd forgotten Sandis was there. He expected his father to ignore her, to storm off in his righteous indignation, but he didn't. The coldness remained on his face, but he stopped to listen.

Sandis eyed Rone. Walked silently to close the gap between her and the leader of the Celesians. "Sir, if you do not . . . care for . . . that"—she swallowed and glanced at Rone guiltily—"then perhaps you might listen to another matter."

The Angelic sighed. "Quickly, child."

"The occult underground is spiraling out of control."

His countenance slacked. "The occult?" That obviously was not what he'd expected to hear.

Rone released a long breath. Tried to refocus himself. Tried to bury the pain and panic rising in his chest. "The grafters have vessels."

"I know this." The Angelic's voice was curt. "That's what makes them grafters, I believe."

"One of their leaders, a man named Kazen," Rone continued, his shoulders tense as iron rods, "is trying to summon a numen supposedly greater than all others." He looked at Sandis, who nodded confirmation. "He's already killed innocent people to do it."

"Kolosos," Sandis whispered.

The Angelic jerked as if stabbed by a knife. "What did you say?"

Sandis spoke louder. "Kolosos, sir. That's the numen's name."

The Angelic shook his head. Paused. "And how do you know this?" His eyes narrowed at Sandis.

Rone took a step forward, putting one shoulder between Sandis and his father. "They thought she was the daughter of someone who owed them money. Captured her. Turned her loose when they realized the mistake." He inwardly winced—the grafters would never turn a prisoner loose, mistake or not. Hopefully the Angelic didn't realize that. "But she saw things when she was down there. Heard things."

"Please," Sandis said, gently easing Rone back. "We have no voice with the government. No power. Surely you can . . . do something."

But the Angelic shook his head, denying them again. Rone was sure his skin would melt from the amount of heat brewing inside him.

"Do not fear, child," the Angelic said. "He will not succeed. You speak of a depth of the occult that is incapable of being summoned into our world. No vessel would survive that amount of evil."

Sandis blinked, and Rone noticed a tear on the rim of her eyelashes. "But, sir—"

The Angelic dismissed both of them with a wave of his hand. "Leave now. I do not want to force you to depart, but I will call upon the priests' arms if need be." He focused on Rone. "Do not come here again."

And just like that, he vanished into the curtained hallway. The sound of a door opening and closing echoed around them, followed by the clicking of a lock.

Rone almost chased him down. Almost kicked in that door and grabbed the selfish, godly man by his collar. How good it would feel to throw a fist into his father's wrinkled face . . .

But he didn't. For a long time, he didn't move, trying to garner some sort of control over himself. Because otherwise, he'd kill the Angelic right there in the Lily Tower, and then he'd be in Gerech, too.

"Rone."

Rone growled.

Sandis grabbed his arm and tugged. *"Rone,"* she whispered. "Someone is coming."

He blinked. Turned toward the stairs. Of course no one would leave the Angelic alone for so long. Rone couldn't possibly be the only person who wanted him dead.

He ushered Sandis back the way they had come, behind the privacy wall and the sheer curtains surrounding it. A priestess came up with a broom to clean the already-immaculate space. When her back was turned, they quietly snuck down the stairs. A small priest asked them if they were lost, but Rone plowed past him without a word, Sandis scrambling to keep up. He wanted out of this place.

He descended the next set of stairs, then the next, feeling eyes on him. He ripped off his pilgrim sash.

His mother. What was he going to do about his mother?

As much as he hated to admit it, he'd held on to a sliver of hope that his father would help them. That his heart would soften for the family he'd forsaken.

Now what would Rone do? He needed money. But he'd never make more than Ernst Renad. He'd never be able to out-bribe the briber.

She'll be all right. She's strong, he reminded himself.

He reached their shoes; about half the pairs left by the pilgrims had been taken, their owners already en route back into the city. Rone paused.

The city. They had nowhere to go. Kurtz's home was out of the question. So was Rone's flat. Could they go to his mother's? Maybe, but if the grafters knew who he was, they could easily figure out her residence.

He cursed under his breath.

"I'm sorry, Rone."

Her words sounded like winter.

He closed his eyes. Rubbed at the headache at the base of his skull. Pilgrims were granted one night in the Lily Tower before venturing back home. One night to figure out what the hell they were doing next.

Even if he left Sandis, they'd still come after him.

Besides, he didn't want to leave her. Not yet.

He sighed. "Come on." He led her away from the shoes, away from the stairs, until two white-garbed priestesses with lilies embroidered on their robes greeted them and asked if they were hungry. Rone lied about their backstory, and they were granted a room. He doubted his father would intervene, if he even heard Rone had lingered. He wouldn't care. As far as he was concerned, Rone was a ghost.

At least his belly would be full.

His story had named Sandis his wife, so one of the two priestesses took them to a room with a bed barely large enough for two. Half the far wall was eaten up by a circle-top window that let in bright sunlight dimmed by only a portion of the main city's pollution. Sandis hurried to it and put her hands on the sill, looking out at the sky with something like wonder. Rone crumpled into a chair by the door and put his forehead in his hands, wincing when the scabbing cuts on his palm met the salt of his skin.

"It's so pretty," she said, pressing her nose to the glass. "The sky looks blue."

Rone grunted a response.

He heard her pull away from the window and settle on the edge of the bed. "I'm sorry . . . about your father."

Rone lifted his head and snorted. "Don't be. As far as I'm concerned, he's not."

Sandis frowned.

It irritated him. It shouldn't have, but it did. "What?" he snapped.

She leaned back as if the word had physical force. "I . . ." She looked away. "I think it's sad. To be alone, even when you have living family."

Rone growled. "He *chose* to leave. When the Angelic dies, the high priests petition together for his replacement. The man they select can choose whether to take the position or not; it isn't an absolute." He pushed his head against the stone wall behind the chair and folded his arms across his chest. "He *chose* to leave."

Sandis's eyes glistened. God's tower, was she going to *cry*? This was his life, not hers.

"I'm sorry."

"So you've said. Twice."

She was quiet a moment, tracing a ray of muted sunlight on the bedspread. "At least you still have your mother."

He glared at her. "My mother is in the pits of the worst prison in Kolingrad."

She nodded. "But she's alive. And she still loves you, doesn't she?"

The ball of guilt rolled around stupidly in his stomach. Those damn scars on Sandis's back resurfaced in his mind. Slave. Her record taken. No one had come to look for her, had they? From what she'd said, the sole family she had left was a distant uncle she couldn't find.

"Maybe you can talk to him." Her words were barely louder than a whisper.

Rone gritted his teeth. "He obviously doesn't want to listen."

"Not your father." She scooted along the edge of the mattress to get closer to him. "The man accusing your mother."

"Ernst Renad? Ha!"

"It's worth a try, isn't it?" She thought for a moment. "Talbur has, or had, a sizeable bank account, I'm guessing. If we can find him, maybe he can help."

"Maybe." Rone nearly dismissed the dreamlike possibility, but Sandis's suggestion gave him pause. "You found his name on a gold-exchange record?"

She nodded. Studied his face.

He turned away and rubbed the scruff growing on his jaw. What if Sandis was *right*? Only wealthy men dealt in gold. Maybe this relative of Sandis's *could* help him. What Rone needed was money . . . money he could preferably get without risking being thrown into Gerech himself. If Sandis pleaded on his behalf . . . *maybe*, depending on how much the guy was worth . . .

And who wouldn't want to reward a man handsomely for returning his long-lost niece? And if Talbur didn't turn out to be the charitable type, Rone could take it.

It wasn't an idea he relished, but the city had taken so much from him over his twenty-five years. Maybe it was time to start taking back.

The city. "You're sure he's in the city?"

Sandis nodded, still watching him. He wondered what his face betrayed. But he wasn't *using* her; he had planned to help her regardless, more or less. He already had, hadn't he?

Then he remembered. "All the pilgrims sign a book before they leave. Maybe one of the priests will let you sort through the names." It was worth a shot.

Sandis lit up like a candle. "Really?" She bit her lip, and Rone could see thoughts swirling behind her eyes. "Everyone makes a pilgrimage once in their life, surely. Maybe he's there. Maybe he came recently!"

She grinned. Was it so easy to make her happy, even after everything she'd endured? Rone almost mirrored the smile. Almost.

"No one will question you if you keep your shirt on and watch what you say." He gestured toward the door with his head. "Go. They'll kick us out in the morning."

Sandis jumped to her feet. "Thank you, Rone."

The sincerity in her words eased the cramping in Rone's middle. He nodded, and Sandis danced into the hallway, leaving him to his tangled misery.

Chapter 13

Sandis's fatigue evaporated the moment her eyes found his name.

It was in the eighth book she'd tried, two-thirds of the way through. They were not small volumes. An acolyte no older than fourteen had brought her candles and helped her look through the well-kept records; he looked over when she gasped.

"You found it?" The boy set down the volume sprawled open in his lap.

Sandis licked her lips and nodded. Blinked tired eyes to make sure she had read it right. *Talbur Gwenwig.* He'd come to the Lily Tower over six years ago on his own pilgrimage. The entry didn't list his sins or the like, but he had indicated his place of residence was *District Three.*

It wasn't a true address, but it confirmed that Talbur Gwenwig most likely resided within Dresberg. This was the first true lead she had on her great-uncle. She'd narrowed down his location by seventy-five percent! Her eyes stung with a few rogue tears.

The acolyte leaned close. "Are you all right?"

Sandis nodded and wiped the back of her hand across her eyes. "Yes, yes, I'm fantastic." She scanned the entry again, ensuring she hadn't missed anything. She even memorized the date and the jagged edges of his penmanship.

She closed the book and walked back to the shelves in the tiny room, where the pilgrimage records were kept.

"Get some sleep, miss," the acolyte said. "It will only take me a few minutes to clean up."

Sandis smiled. "Thank you." She offered a bow—she'd seen several priestesses exchange greetings as such—and hurried from the room, taking a candle with her so she could find her way up the stairs. The higher she climbed, however, the further her success seemed to diminish.

Rone had looked so . . . miserable earlier, when he'd confronted the Angelic. *His father.* She could hardly imagine how much it must hurt to be swept away like that. To have family, and yet *not* have family. Like her mother before . . . but that had only been for a brief time.

A hollow pocket in her chest opened, and it ached for him.

She neared a room of priests chatting and sped up, shielding her light. Rone had assured her she'd be fine inside the Lily Tower, but she didn't want to draw attention. Didn't want to be asked questions, for fear of slipping up.

She pushed open the heavy door to the room. Rone stood at the window, his arms folded, looking out at the darkened sky. She had assumed he'd be asleep by now. Was he still thinking of his father?

He glanced back at her. Silent.

Setting the candle down, Sandis offered him her happy news, hoping it would help. "I found him. He lives in District Three!"

Rone straightened. "He does? Where?"

"I . . . that's all the record said. He didn't write an address." Only about a third of the entries had one.

Rone frowned, an expression that looked deeper and longer in the flickering candlelight. "That's not much."

"But it's *something*." She smiled, wishing he would smile, too. "I feel so much closer. I'll knock on every door in District Three until I find him."

"That will get you caught in no time." He looked back out the window. Specks of silver caught Sandis's eye. Excitement built at the base of her throat, and she hurried over to the window, straining to see as far up as its large panes would allow.

"Oh, wow," she whispered.

"What?"

She pointed. "Look at all the stars! I can see . . . seven of them!"

Rone snorted. "If you left Dresberg, you'd see a lot more."

Pulling back from the cool glass, Sandis said, "Truly? How many more? My father once said that in the country there's whole clusters of them, and they make shapes."

He raised an eyebrow at her. "You're like a kid."

She rolled her eyes and looked back at the dusty black sky. "What's wrong with loving stars? They're so rare . . . but so bright. Even when you don't see them, you know they're there. And to think there's more we can't see . . . it's like the Celestial is keeping them secret, and it makes you wonder why."

Rone chuckled.

She looked at him. "Have you never lain back to look at the stars?" Sometimes, after a good rain, Sandis had been able to see a few stars from her old home. Never with the grafters. There, she'd been too far underground most of the time to even see the sky.

Rone pulled away from the window. "Come on."

She turned. "What?"

"Just come."

She followed him out of the room and back up the staircase. It wasn't the same one that had led them to the Angelic—the steps were narrower and simpler. Unadorned. A servants' staircase, perhaps. They reached a landing with two opposing doors. Rone hesitated before opening the one on the right, which led to a shorter flight of stairs. At the top of the dark passageway was a flat door, like the kind leading to a cellar. He unlatched something and shoved his shoulder into it to open it.

Cool air rushed down and tousled Sandis's hair. Rone stepped out, then offered her a hand.

They were on top of the Lily Tower.

Sandis gaped, looking down at the roads and wide space behind the tower, the distant light of a town shining up behind a small hill in the distance. She turned back for the city. It was a dark bangle, an obsidian bowl filled with spots of light. She could barely see over the wall.

"That way, Sandis." Rone pointed skyward.

Sandis dipped her head back. "Oh."

There were so many stars speckling the black. A cloud of gray smoke swept by them, but the wind carried it away, letting the bluish lights shine through. Sandis counted quietly to herself. Thirty-seven! She'd never seen so many stars in her life.

Refusing to take her gaze from the sky, she carefully sat down, then lay back against the rough shingles atop the tower. She stared at the stars, absorbing the sight with reverence, trying to find shapes within them. A few clustered together looked like the head of a horse. She thought of Ireth and thought she felt a warm recognition from him in return.

Surely Kazen had lost her blood by now, right?

"What?" Rone asked.

He stood over her. She glanced up at him in question.

He shrugged. "You looked so happy for a moment; then . . . you didn't."

She offered him a small smile. "I am. Thank you, for bringing me here." She let her vision drift back toward the horse head. "I was thinking about Kazen."

Rone sighed. "Yeah. I've got to figure that out."

"We will."

"Hmm." He sat down next to her and leaned back on his hands. "They're all right. The stars, I mean."

She smiled again. "They're all right."

If only she could stay atop the Lily Tower forever with the stars, and with Rone. Sandis knew such things were not meant to be, so she let herself absorb the moment until she brimmed with it. Carved the memory into her mind so she could lean on it if . . . when . . . things got bad again.

She had a feeling it wouldn't be long before they did.

***

She dreamed of the astral sphere.

Kazen kept a model in his office. It was a globe about a foot and a half tall, made of ten rows of disks etched with rounded Noscon letters. Kazen used it to navigate the ethereal plane so he could summon new numina.

But in this dream—somehow, Sandis knew it was a dream—the globe looked different. It spun clockwise, faster and faster until the letters blurred together. It reminded her of the center of Rone's amarinth. When Sandis reached for it, the globe slowed, and under her fingers she found one of the few Noscon words she could read.

Ireth.

When she woke, it was with the residual impression of *fire*. Not the hot, breath-stealing fire she'd experienced when she touched the Noscon writing in the citizen-records building, but a gentler, softer fire. A well-tended blaze that could easily be stoked to destruction.

What can I do for you? Her mind reached out even as it crawled toward consciousness. *What do you need?*

She shivered for the lack of a blanket. Rone had insisted she take the bed, though she would have gladly shared it. She'd given him all of the blankets for a pallet on the floor. Truth be told, she would have preferred the spot by the door. If she'd lain there all night, she wouldn't have awoken to this awful, sinking sensation. She wouldn't be wondering whether Rone had left in the night. Whether he'd changed his mind about helping her after his own father turned him away.

Holding her breath, Sandis quietly, carefully rolled away from the blue morning light streaming in through the window and studied the shadows on the floor. There was the mound of blankets, and—

She sighed. Rone was still there, one arm behind his head, his face slightly tilted toward her. He hadn't left. She had a lead on Talbur Gwenwig's location, and Rone hadn't left. He had a boyish way of sleeping, his lips slightly parted, his dark eyelashes splayed against his skin. The large curls of his hair were mussed on one side, giving Sandis the urge to smooth her fingers through them to correct their shape.

She smiled.

They didn't have many things, but Sandis gathered them together anyway and used Rone's unconscious state as an opportunity to change back into one of his shirts and her loose slacks. He still hadn't stirred, so she decided to find her way to the kitchen to get them both breakfast. There was just enough space for her to open the door without disturbing him. When she reached the kitchen, two priestesses, dressed in white and silver, were handing out bowls of oatmeal with cinnamon. Sandis thanked them profusely and took two—one for her and one for Rone to eat when he woke.

Breathing in the spicy steam, Sandis searched for a quiet spot to sit and eat her breakfast. The room was large enough to accommodate daily visitors, and double doors opened on either end of it. She heard a male choir singing in the distance and strained to hear, wondering if she could recognize the song.

As she moved toward the music, however, she glimpsed a familiar face passing the far exit. The wide-set eyes, the shaved head. He wore a gray pilgrim's sash on his arm.

Sandis immediately turned away, cold bumps rising up along her arms and down her neck. Her heart knocked against her ribs.

She headed straight for the entrance and back the way she'd come, spilling oatmeal on the stairs and elbowing a priestess as she went.

Ravis. That had been Ravis; she was sure of it. She'd had no more than a split second to look . . . but she was *sure*. But how could he have found her? How?

The boy. The one from the cathedral. He'd lurked a ways off and hadn't approached her until Rone left. Though she'd thought it odd that he'd asked so many questions, she hadn't lingered on it. It now occurred to her that he hadn't come to the tower with the other pilgrims.

Had he been paid off to watch the cathedral? Had Kazen guessed she might try to find refuge there?

Sandis was running by the time she reached the room, and her hands burned from gripping the too-hot ceramic bowls of oatmeal. She couldn't turn the doorknob with her hands full, so she kicked the door ruthlessly with her toe—

It opened, and Rone, disheveled and holding up his unfastened trousers, said, "What—"

"They're here." Panic choked Sandis's voice, and she shoved a bowl of oatmeal at Rone as she hurried inside and slammed the door shut. She checked for a lock, but there was none. "Ravis is here."

"Ravis?"

She nodded, her short hair falling over her cheeks. "One of Kazen's grafters."

Rone stared at her for half a second before cursing. "Black ashes," he spat. "Just him?"

"He's all I saw."

Rone set down the oatmeal and fastened his pants. "Did he see you?"

The spoon in Sandis's bowl rattled against the ceramic.

Reaching forward, Rone put his hands over hers, steadying them. Looking into her eyes, he asked, "Did he see you?"

She looked back, at the ring of lighter brown that separated Rone's irises from his pupils. "I don't think so."

He offered her a strange sort of smile, a half smile that managed to be sympathetic and incredulous at the same time. "All right. That's good. We can work with that."

She set the bowl down. "How?"

He grabbed the bag she'd packed earlier.

"Most of the pilgrims who stay the night at the tower have come from far away. Maybe some of them are heading west, circumventing the city. If we go with them, we could leave and then reenter the city through the west gate. Might be a good way to lose your friends."

Sandis's hope rekindled. "Let's hurry."

They rushed down the stairs, nabbed their shoes, and asked after the departing pilgrims. A priest pointed them out back and offered them a scripture, which neither of them lingered to hear.

Sandis stayed close to Rone as they exited the tower. A breeze swept by, carrying bits of dust. It felt warmer than Sandis had expected, but it gave her goose bumps anyway.

She recognized the men packing up a trio of wagons—their families had already been worshipping at the cathedral when Sandis and Rone arrived yesterday. Their clothes were looser, with broader sleeves, than what people wore inside the city. She wondered how far they had traveled. Were they farmers? Merchants? Could they see all the stars wherever they were going?

Maybe, after Sandis found Talbur, she could go someplace like that, too.

Rone approached the older of the two men and paid his respects with a brief bow. For some reason, seeing Rone bow was odd. He seemed the sort who could stand in the middle of a winter storm and refuse to move to the ice and wind.

Rone gestured back to Sandis, who approached trying to look as innocent as possible.

"If you could take us as far as Ieva, we would be incredibly grateful."

The man glanced at Sandis, considered, then nodded. That gesture made Sandis's body feel incredibly light. "It is not far, and not out of our way. You'll have to sit in the back of the first cart. It won't be comfortable."

Rone nodded. "We'll take it. Thank you."

The man escorted them to the first wagon, which was filled to the brim with supplies—supplies purchased in Dresberg, most likely. They were held back with lengths of rope, but there was a little space between the rope and the edge of the wagon for Sandis and Rone to sit. After giving her a hand up, Rone mumbled something about helping their new friends pack to earn their favor. Sandis pulled her knees up to her chest and pressed her back against the rope and the keg of ale behind it, making herself small, letting the shadow of the wagon wall hide her.

She breathed slowly, listening, trying to stretch her hearing beyond the caravans. Was Ravis still in the tower? Would the priests discover him? Would he hurt these kind people?

Had she made a mistake in coming here?

It took another twenty minutes for the pilgrims to finish loading the third wagon and settle into the second. Rone returned to her, sweat glistening below his hairline. He sat on the back of the wagon and leaned his head against a sack of something—maybe flour or sugar—and took a few deep breaths.

"They're crazy," he whispered, wiping his sleeve first across his eyes, then across his forehead. "They bought a statue of the freaking Celestial. A *heavy* one. But as soon as the guard passes through, we'll be off."

A jolt passed through Sandis. "Rone?"

He sighed. "Yeah?"

"Is . . . the guard checking for papers?"

His eyes came into focus. He looked at her for several seconds before saying, "You don't have any."

She shook her head and tried to keep her voice level. "Not anymore." She couldn't remember if she'd left them at the flat when she'd gone searching, again, for Anon, or if they'd been on her person and the slavers had taken them. Vanished, just like her records.

Like she didn't exist.

Rone swore and looked behind him. The wagon was packed. Sandis started pressing against the odds and ends, hoping one would give or that she'd find a space she could crawl into to hide—

She heard voices approach. The guards?

Rone grabbed her wrist and yanked her down. "Pretend like you're asleep," he hissed. Opening his bag, he grabbed a set of his undergarments and shoved them at her. "Put this under your shirt. Head on my lap. Hurry."

She didn't question him. Her shaking hands did as told. She wadded the clothing against her stomach and lay down with her head on Rone's thigh, bending her knees to fit the space. She faced away from the wagon opening and closed her eyes. She clenched her jaw, then forced it to relax. *Sleeping, sleeping, sleeping.*

Rone smelled like rain.

"Name?" a low, masculine voice asked seconds later.

"Rone Comf." Rone took his time rustling through his bag. Sandis heard the stir of papers.

A pause. "Comf?" Another pause. "Related?"

Sandis thought she felt Rone shrug before rummaging through his bag again. "Hold on—I swear I saw her put them in here. My wife, she's been sick ever since we left the farm. Hoping the travel doesn't jostle her too bad."

His hand brushed her shoulder. Sandis dutifully played the ill, pregnant wife. It wasn't the first time she'd pretended to be asleep to avoid unwanted attention.

The guard grunted. Papers shuffled—he must be handing them back to Rone. His steps faded away.

Rone said nothing. They held still for a long time, until the voice of the older traveler who had granted them passage said, "One of the priests is riding with us as far as the west side of the city to ensure we're not bothered by bandits."

Shortly afterward, the wagon lurched forward. Rone squeezed Sandis's shoulder, and she sat up slowly. Rone met her eyes for a moment—the bright sun turning his irises a dark topaz. She had meant to say something, but she couldn't remember her words right then.

Rone looked away first. "Glad that worked."

"Thank you." She pulled his clothes free and handed them back to him.

Rone's mouth twisted. "Why is a priest riding with us? What's he going to do, pray the grafters away?"

Sandis pursed her lips at the jab. Outside of the Angelic, the priests had been kind. They'd offered them board and food. They'd treated her like a real person, unaware of the sin that scarred her back with gold.

Despite all the weight pressing it down, the wagon rocked and shook, yet Sandis found the ride calming. The risen sun warmed the air and calmed her further. She didn't see any grafters or suspicious people lurking around the Lily Tower once they came around it, following the great wall of the city west, so she let her legs dangle over the side of the wagon and watched puffs of dust spit up from the back wheels.

"If only it were so easy," Rone said, more to himself than to her. He had one knee up, his elbow resting on it, and his brown eyes watched the distancing wall.

"What?"

"Leaving." Rone scratched the side of his nose. "That's what it feels like, doesn't it? Like we're just walking away from it all."

Sandis furrowed her brow. "We *are* leaving, Rone."

He shook his head. "Not the Lily Tower. Dresberg. Kolingrad. All of it."

Ah, that was it. "You don't like it here."

His dark gaze dropped to her. "Do you?"

She shrugged. She'd like it more if life could return to how it used to be. If her family were still . . . If Kazen and the grafters didn't exist. Family was what mattered, not place.

"You're right." He leaned his head against the rocking wall. "I hate it. I've looked into leaving before, but even my best jobs can't get me past the border guard."

Sandis frowned. Looked at the wagon behind them. The floor bucked beneath her as the wagon pulled onto the paved road leading out of the city. While everything was industry and cobblestones in Dresberg, there was so much *space* outside the city walls. The land stretched open and vast before them. Empty, or very nearly. Sandis marveled at it for a moment, fighting the urge to slip off the wagon and run ahead of the train. She hadn't experienced such lack of confinement for a long time, if ever.

Her thoughts pulled back to Rone. Though it made her feel heavy to suggest it, Sandis said, "Maybe you could stay with them."

Rone laughed. "With who?"

She cocked her head toward the second wagon. "With them. Wherever they're going."

Rone rolled his eyes. "If I'm going to be trapped in Kolingrad, I might as well find my work in Dresberg. I'm used to a certain lifestyle." His countenance fell. "Besides, I wouldn't leave my mother."

Sandis pinched her lips together, considering the situation with Rone's family. She could see how it pained him to be unwanted by one parent and fearful for the other. Sandis's family—outside of Talbur Gwenwig—was dead, but at least they'd wanted her when they were alive.

"We'll figure it out." Sandis wasn't sure if Rone heard her over the tumult of the wagons, so she gingerly placed her hand on his knee. He looked at her hand for a moment before shaking his head.

"Because this uncle of yours will magically be the savior we need." His tone was sour and dark.

"I hope so."

He glanced at her, a single eyebrow raised. "I don't know if I should admire you for your hope, Sandis, or hate you for your naïveté."

A loud *snap* sounded somewhere behind the second wagon, followed by a few shouts. The driver of the second wagon pulled his oxen to a halt, and within moments the driver of their wagon followed suit. The ale keg behind Sandis pressed against the ropes and against her, but the bindings held.

Rone stood immediately in the wagon bed, grabbing the wagon's roof and looking over it. "What's wrong?"

The driver passed by them, shaking his head in confusion. Voices began to sound one over another; Sandis couldn't decipher them.

The driver came back. "Wheel on the rear wagon broke." He kicked the road. "Damn. We have a spare, but we'll be delayed."

Sandis brushed dust from her face. "Do you need help?"

The driver waved her inquiry away and disappeared around the second wagon.

"Wonderful," Rone grumbled.

Sandis peered toward the wall. They'd come decently far—she couldn't see the Lily Tower anymore. They were somewhere along the northeastern portion of the great wall. The road branched off ahead of them, leading to one of the many tunnels that burrowed through the wall, granting entrance to the city.

It wasn't hard to enter or leave Dresberg. Just the country itself.

Rone sat on the edge of the wagon bed and shook out the front of his shirt. "Might as well take a nap."

Sandis slid from the wagon and tested her new shoes against the road. She peered toward the rear wagon. Nearly all the adults in the group had huddled around its back wheel, arguing with each other and shooing away children. Their driver, the one who'd allowed them passage, stood by with the replacement wheel, drumming his fingers against it. The priest who'd accompanied them waited to one side. A soft breeze blew at the white flaps of his hat, giving Sandis a glimpse of his face. He was a stout man, perhaps a few years shy of forty. He leaned back, watching, and—

Sandis gasped and ducked behind the second car, her heart tumbling in her chest, her stomach squeezing, threatening to lose its meager contents. Cool sweat dappled her skin.

A trap. It was a trap. It was—

"Sandis?" Rone pushed himself off the wagon lip. "What's wrong?"

She grabbed the front of his shirt and pushed him around to the opposite corner of the second wagon, the one farthest from the families. "The priest." The word choked in her dry throat. "It's Galt."

"Who?"

"Galt," she hissed. She hadn't realized her fingernails were digging into Rone's chest until he winced and wrestled out of her hold. Sandis hugged herself, shivering, trying to think. But Rone . . . Rone would know what to do. "Kazen's right-hand man. He was there, with the steam . . ."

Understanding dawned on Rone's face, and he spat out two curses, one harder than the other. He rubbed a hand down his face, turned around, then turned back and tried to peek around the wagon—

Sandis grabbed his arm and yanked him back. "Don't! He'll see!"

"He obviously knows we're here," he snapped back. Curses danced around him like moths. "Just him?"

She nodded. "The wheel . . . He was on the rear wagon. He must have broken it—"

"—so the others would have time to catch up," Rone finished for her. He paled. "Smart sons of whores."

"Rone," she pleaded.

He bit his lip. Grabbed his hair and looked around.

Sandis danced from foot to foot. "We could hide behind . . . No, they'll search everything. And they'll hurt these people. We have to run for the city."

They were still close to the wall. It wouldn't be too far to the tunnels. One didn't need papers to get *in*, just to get out. The guards wouldn't stop them.

Rone snapped his fingers. "There are horses on this wagon. We can take one and get a head start."

Sandis's heart lodged in her throat. "We can't steal their horse!" The rushed whisper escaped her like pressurized steam.

Rone looked at her like she was insane. "Do you want to die instead?"

"We'll strand them—"

"They can dump a few things and make it back fine. They'll be in more danger if we stay. Let's *go*, while they're distracted! Before the grafters come!"

Sandis shushed him, though his voice was no louder than hers had been. She gritted her teeth. She felt sick. She was going to throw up . . .

"Fine. Are any saddled?"

Rone glanced back at the third wagon before heading around the opposite side of the first one. "No. We'll manage."

"Can you ride?"

Rone blinked. "No . . . and I'm guessing you can't, either."

Sandis's heart inched toward her navel. *Oh Celestial, we're going to die. I'm so sorry for entering your tower. I won't do it again. Please save us. Please, please—*

"Sandis!" Rone waved his hand in front of her face, demanding her attention.

She shook her head. "We have to run. *Now.*"

He retreated to the back of the wagon and peered toward the wall. "If they've been following us . . . if they have horses . . ."

Tears burned her eyes. "*Now*, Rone!"

His hands formed fists. He growled deep in his throat. Nodded. "Keep up."

He offered his hand. Sandis took it.

The moment their fingers touched, Rone jerked her toward the wall.

Chapter 14

Dresberg had become a maze.

Panic distorted everything. Turned buildings into walls, shadows into monsters. Nothing was familiar. Sandis didn't see people, only obstacles. Each hard footfall radiated up into her skull.

It was sheer luck they had gotten this far.

She didn't look behind her—she never looked behind her—but Rone did, and his foul words told Sandis all she needed to know. Their mad sprint for the city hadn't gone unnoticed. The grafters were too fast—though they would have needed to ditch their mounts outside the wall. The ways were too narrow and the crowds too thick for a man on horseback to keep up with someone on foot during the day.

A clock tower rang the hour, the echoing chimes pressing against Sandis's skin like dull needles. Sweat threatened to break the grip she had on Rone's hand.

A bullet whizzed by her forehead before it exploded against the brick corner of the bookstore behind her.

Rone jerked her down a skinny space between buildings. "Are you *sure* they don't want to shoot you?"

Sandis's breaths burned up and down her throat. She pushed herself faster through the maze. Had that bullet been meant for her? Did this mean Kazen had determined she was disposable, and only sought to take back Ireth?

Sandis hadn't simply run away. She'd stolen from one of the most powerful men in Kolingrad.

Ireth was worth more than gold.

They reached a busier street. Rone jerked to a stop before barreling into a cart full of potatoes. Sandis turned around, but two people were running toward them, and there was nowhere else to go. She pushed Rone into the mass.

He didn't complain. He simply tightened his grip on her fingers as they pushed through people, earning inquisitive looks and hard words as they went. "They'll bring the police down on all of us at this rate." Rone's voice was hoarse and broken by heavy breaths. The race to the wall had not been a short one.

The police. They were just as dangerous to Sandis as the priests.

She'd take either of them over the grafters.

Shouts sounded behind them, angry and confused. The grafters pushed through the crowd. Marek using his bulk to knock down men and women alike. Staps toting a pistol in either hand. Another gunshot went off, and the crowd scattered. Rone jerked Sandis down a winding sideway crammed between a shuttle station and a metalworks. The heat from the working bellows steamed the tears from her eyes.

"Can you . . . fight them?" Sandis pushed the words out between labored breaths. "The . . . amarinth—"

"No." They ducked under a clothesline and darted to the left. Sandis thought she heard a police whistle in the background, but she wasn't sure. "You have to wait"—sharp turn to the right—"for the critical moment. Only one spin. I have"—he huffed—"a sense for this."

He glanced up, perhaps trying to determine if they could get up onto the roofs before the grafters caught them. Shaking his head, he instead pulled them to a main street.

Sandis had been wrong. The grafters hadn't entirely given up on horses.

A steed black as coal—an animal Sandis recognized immediately—pulled up in front of them, its nostrils wide and panting, its rider garbed darkly, albeit without his usual hat.

Sandis's legs became dead weight as she and Rone skidded to a stop on slick cobblestones. Kazen. And behind him, Rist.

The sight of Rist slammed into her like winter wind. It felt as if years had passed since their last encounter instead of days. Her gut rolled with the knowledge of what he could be. A weapon. *Kuracean.*

Did Rist want to fight her? Did he hate her for leaving? She tried to read his wide eyes, but found no answers.

Kazen wouldn't summon in the city in the middle of the afternoon, would he? With so many people nearby? Isepia he could hide, but Kuracean—

Rone was already pulling her back. Sandis nearly rolled her ankles as she stumbled after him. Another police whistle ripped through the air, closer.

Kazen pulled a gun from a holster at his hip. "Enough of this," Sandis thought she heard him say, his tone bored but laced with that subtle anger it had taken her years to pick up on. And his eyes . . . his eyes burned like two smog-choked suns.

Rone jerked Sandis's arm, forcing her face forward. Why she felt the need to say it, she didn't know. Rist could no more control the numen chained to him than she could summon Ireth at will. Still, she cried out, "He killed Heath! He *killed* him!"

Her friend's name ripped from her throat like the cry of a dying animal.

Then they ran. Ran. Ran. The buildings grew darker and closer together. The air became colder as they jumped a fence and wove through flats. Sandis's chest and legs felt like they were being eaten by acid by the time she realized this particular cluster of flats was abandoned.

She pulled back on Rone's hand, though it merely slowed him. Sweat ran down the sides of his face like rain. "Rone, stop!" she croaked.

Oh Celestial, that's why Kazen didn't chase us, just blocked us—

She dug her heels into the broken cobbles of the ill-kept street.

Rone stopped and whipped around, his eyes mad, the amarinth clenched in his fingers. "Sandis! We have to—"

"They're *corralling* us!" New tears burned in the corners of her eyes. "We're so close . . . God's tower, we're so close, Rone . . ."

She spun around, searching. Pulled him down a passageway barely wide enough for him.

"Close to *what*?"

"The grafters." The words came out on a whisper. They reached a dead end. Sandis spun, frantic. Jerked Rone in another direction. "This is their territory. We're practically walking over it."

Her entire body was cold. Her joints felt rusted. Her muscles ran on embers.

Footsteps thundered behind them.

Rone yanked Sandis down another path, one she didn't recognize. "Look for a ladder," he sputtered. "A rain pipe. Anything. We need to get *up*."

They rounded a corner and faced another dead end. Turned back.

Three grafters, including Galt in his white-and-silver priest's robes and Ravis in all black, blocked the way out.

Rone's hand, the one holding the amarinth, snaked behind him as he stepped in front of Sandis. Her entire body went numb, save for her desperate, starving lungs, but she retreated when he did. Her foot landed in something foul and sticky; her back hit brick.

Nowhere else to go. No fence to climb, door to open, crevice to hide in. They stood at the end of a brick box. Even sunlight couldn't worm its way in.

"I can take them," Rone whispered, readying his amarinth even as three separate firearms trained on him. Sandis believed him—she'd seen him take out five people at the tavern. But as Rone went to spin the golden loops of the artifact, four more people appeared behind the original three. Marek and three men Sandis didn't recognize, short of the neckerchief poking up from one man's collar. She knew those colors.

Straight Ace's mobsmen. Kazen had a mob searching for her now. What bribery had he used to earn their cooperation? How many more did he have under his sleeve? At least he hadn't allied with one of the other grafter gangs. At least they didn't have an army of numina—

The base of her skull tingled until ice shot down her script. She felt the color drain from her skin. Her fingers trembled. She was not reacting to the mob, however, but to the numen coming toward them.

"Kuracean," she whispered, hairs standing on end. "He's summoned him."

Rone glanced back at her, still clutching the amarinth. It wouldn't be enough. One minute wouldn't be nearly enough . . . and it would only protect him, not her. She didn't even have a garbage bin to hide behind! Where were the police? The border patrol? Had they not seen the chase? Had Kazen paid them off?

Did they even care?

She heard the heavy *click*, *drag* of armor against cobbles before the numen's bulbous head hovered over the seven men poised to attack her and Rone. Though it crouched to fit in the small space, it was still nine feet tall. Half of Kuracean's head was a toothless mouth, but Sandis had seen it take off heads in a single chomp. Just once, when a mob that no longer existed had made a foolish attempt to take over Kazen's territory. Kuracean's massive front legs, ending in great pincers, one larger than the other, slid behind the mobsmen. The rest of its spidery body was hidden by the crumbling building that acted as half of Sandis's cage.

Rone didn't even swear when he saw it. He almost dropped the amarinth, but it dangled from his index finger by a single golden loop. He looked like a ghost beneath his dark hair. Sandis could see the blue veins in his neck.

Trapped. They were trapped.

Kazen, now with his hat firmly tipped over his forehead, walked out from beneath Kuracean as though the great monster were merely a startling sculpture. The numen growled softly in its armored throat but didn't move. Not without its master's order.

"Look what you've made me do, Sandis." Kazen's voice was that of a tired mother. He held his arms out, gesturing to his armed men and his mighty monster, so much stronger than Isepia. His face was unreadable, like always, but his hat could not hide the glimmer in his eyes. It was a subtle, swirling shine that raised gooseflesh on her arms.

She'd never seen him so angry.

"I have such a mess to clean up," he continued. "You've riled the city folk this time. Their little police force won't be happy."

Rone shook his head. "I can't . . . ," he whispered.

Sandis tried to swallow but found she couldn't.

"And you." Kazen's silvery gaze fell upon Rone. "I think we need to have a nice long *chat*. After I see what you're hiding behind your back." He smiled. "Foolish boy. You have no idea what trouble you've gotten yourself into."

They were going to kill Rone. Maybe kill her . . . but no, that would be too easy for Kazen, wouldn't it? Sandis's mind couldn't even fathom what would happen after this. Her imagination didn't stretch that wide.

Her eyes shifted to Kuracean's turtle-like face. To that hard, pointed lip. She still remembered the sound the mobsman's neck had made when Kuracean severed his head from his body. Still remembered the spurting fountain of blood. It was the last thing she'd seen before Kazen had summoned Ireth to join the battle.

Ireth.

She felt pressure in her head even as she thought the name. She couldn't fight these men. Rone couldn't fight these men, even with the amarinth. They especially didn't stand a chance against Kuracean. But Ireth could. Surely Ireth could.

But Ireth needed to be brought into the world by a summoner. Sandis was only the vessel . . . and Rone couldn't summon him. He didn't know how, for one, and he didn't meet the qualifications of a summoner. He didn't even come close.

Kazen gestured to Marek and two of the bulky Aces behind him and sent them forward. "Knock out the man, but keep him alive for now. Don't hurt the girl. I need her restrained." Kazen pulled from his pocket a needle, tube, and vial. So the power of her blood had faded, and he needed to renew his control.

Twenty feet separated Sandis and Rone from the mobsmen. Nineteen, eighteen—

"Come, Sandis. I'll give you a chance to explain, once you're home." Kazen's voice was so soothing. Hushed, yet it carried over the distance. If Sandis hadn't spent the last four years of her life with him . . . if she hadn't seen him turn on friends as frequently as he did enemies, she might have been fooled into thinking that he cared about her. That he wanted the best for her. That he provided safety, home, *family*.

Sandis's family was dead. All except one. One she still had to find. She shook her head.

The slightest twitch of Kazen's eye betrayed his rage.

Rone backed into her, pressing her to the brick wall. "I'm sorry," he whispered, not looking at her. His wide eyes focused on the approaching men. Marek's eyes narrowed in his wide face, his stride sure. "I can try . . . maybe you can escape . . ."

She needed Ireth.

She needed Ireth *now*.

It struck her like cold rain. Every summoner had to serve as a vessel at least once. That meant she met the qualifications of a summoner, didn't it? The ones she knew . . . and she thought she knew them all.

Seventeen feet. Sixteen. Fifteen.

But a vessel couldn't summon into herself!

And yet Sandis knew she wasn't an ordinary vessel. Ireth had tried to communicate with her on multiple occasions. She'd *felt* his presence. Could swear she felt it even now. She remembered things she shouldn't. And then there was her strange reaction to the Noscon writing at the records center . . .

Had Ireth been urging her to take matters into her own hands? To act? And if she was wrong, what would it cost her? Embarrassment? What a small price to pay.

Fourteen feet. Thirteen. Twelve.

She knew this. She *knew* this.

Fear curled around her limbs like smoke.

Kazen's men continued their approach, Kuracean and Kazen's small army looming behind them. Kazen was so sure. Sandis was so unsure.

Eleven. Ten.

Keeping her eyes on Kazen, Sandis pressed her palm against her head. Muttered under her breath, *"Vre en nestu a carnath."* Words she'd heard so many times. Words she didn't understand. *"Ii mem entre I amar."* Her hand grew hot. Burning.

Rone turned toward her. "What?"

Nine feet. Eight. Seven.

"Vre en nestu a carnath." Pressure flooded from her head into her limbs, straining on the border of tearing. Readying her for the excruciating pain that came with possession.

Kazen tilted his head. "Sandis, what are you mumbling?"

She hooked her foot around Rone's and jerked it back, sending him to the ground. Leveling her gaze with Kazen's, she finished, *"Ireth epsi gradenid."*

Her body exploded.

The light was blinding, searing, *burning*. Fire engorged her chest and cut off her air; hot coals raked down her back and breasts. Her body contorted, twisted, wrenched—

And stopped.

It stopped there, at the height of agony. Sandis blinked flames even as they seemed to flay the charred skin from her body.

She saw Kazen. The Aces. Kuracean.

She was on *fire*.

She was going to die.

And yet the moment she thought it, she felt his presence. Ireth. His essence braided into her own in a way it never had before, filling her nostrils with the scent of molten iron, her skin with ripe agony, her heart with . . . a strange sort of pressure. Like an embrace. Like being wrapped in the arms of her parents, shielded from the rest of the world.

Despite the sensations of her body tearing in two, her blood boiling beneath her skin, and her bones warping and snapping, Sandis smiled.

Forward. Fight. Destroy.

She understood.

Sandis threw the pain and the tremors and the burning forward, engulfing the alleyway in white fire.

Chapter 15

The amarinth wheezed as it spun. Tears from the blinding light poured rivers down Rone's face. A great, low bellow filled his ears—the cry of Kazen's monster, punctuated by the screams of burning men.

He pressed himself into the ground, his face inches from Sandis's ankles. Ankles that were on fire. She was *on fire*. Everything was.

The amarinth spun, its gold tines reflecting bursts of red and white. The hairs in Rone's nose singed, as did the threads of his shirt. While instinct told him to cower, he looked up.

Her body radiated impossible light, blinding him from the surrounding world. She was still Sandis, but a halo of white fire surrounded her, and her eyes—her eyes were blacker than coal.

He gawked, feeling heat that should have flayed him, but the magic of the amarinth spun around him, carrying its soft, protecting song.

For a fleeting moment, Rone forgot to breathe. Then, like the snapping of fingers, the fire snuffed out and cast him into absolute darkness.

A body thudded down beside him.

Rone blinked wet eyes. Rubbed them. Darkness turned to colored spots. To bits of light. He lifted his head. Blinked. Ash filled the alleyway.

The monster was gone. And Sandis—

He turned. She lay on the broken cobbles—unconscious and completely naked.

For a moment, Rone simply stared at her. Not at her nudity, but in utter awe. *How?*

The amarinth stopped spinning. In the silence that followed its magic, Rone came to himself.

This wasn't over. This was far from over.

They had to *run*. Now.

He grabbed Sandis, shoving one arm under her knees and the other around her shoulders. His bad shoulder shot a spike of pain up his neck, but he couldn't exactly take a break and massage it. He hooked his pinky around the amarinth almost as an afterthought. He sprinted down the alleyway, kicking up ash as he went. One of the men moaned close to the junction near the road, trying to drag his devastated body to help.

Sandis couldn't have killed all of them—there wasn't enough ash, and the stretch of burned brick didn't reach far enough. Kazen, where was Kazen? And his monster? There was no enormous pile of embers to mark the incineration of the numen, and both it and Kazen had been far back in the alleyway. Had they run?

His vision swirled with black splotches. He was still in their territory—but he wouldn't be able to get far. Not in daylight. Not with a naked, unconscious woman in his arms. He had to hide. Hide.

He started down a wider road, purposefully leaving an obvious trail of ashy footprints, then turned around and retraced his steps, walking as close to the wall of a decrepit building as he could. Pushed himself down alleys that were not meant to be traveled. Found a warped door and kicked it in, then quietly pressed it back into place with his shoulder.

It was dark inside, save for a few glimmers of light from windows on the second and third stories that shone through the holes in the roof above him—a floor that could likely come crashing down on them at any moment. They couldn't stay in this abandoned place. They couldn't leave.

Rone checked for debris with his foot before laying Sandis down. He took her face in his hands. "Sandis," he whispered. She felt warm under his fingers. Not fire warm, but fever warm.

Had she summoned Ireth on her own? She hadn't brought forth the numen, however. Only his fire.

He shook his head. Patted her cheeks. "Sandis. Sandis. God's tower, please wake up." His heart sped. Sweat traced trails down his forehead. She breathed steady and slow, like someone in a deep slumber.

Rone checked himself. He didn't feel any burns—thank the amarinth for that—but the back of his shirt was charred and threadbare. Even as he pulled it off, he felt ash fall into his hair. Whatever. He could afford a new shirt. He laid the ruined article of clothing over Sandis. His eyes were starting to adjust, and he didn't trust himself not to look.

She'd saved his life. The least he could do was not ogle her while she was unconscious.

Rone sat next to her and wiped a filthy hand down his face. First the one-winged, claw-handed woman, then that . . . pincer monster. The more he saw of the occult, the more it *scared* him.

He glanced at Sandis's supine form as he shoved the amarinth into his trouser pocket. This Kazen wanted her back. Badly.

Exactly *what* sort of hellish creature had possessed her?

***

Rone didn't want to explore much, for fear of the building falling on top of him, not to mention worry that any noise would bring both grafters and numina upon him. But he looked around, searching for anything that might be of use. He found a lot of old nails and other debris. Mice, dead and alive. That was pleasant. No food, but if he had found food, he wouldn't have eaten it.

He did locate a curtain. It was yellowed and ugly, but it was intact fabric, so it would do.

He settled it over Sandis and waited. When the light outside began to draw a purplish tint, she finally stirred.

He was at her side in an instant, surprised by the extent of his relief. "Sandis? Sandis?"

She groaned. Lifted a hand from under his shirt and the curtain and pressed it to her forehead. Her eyes fluttered open and shifted back and forth in obvious confusion. They finally settled on Rone's face.

She stared for a moment. "We're alive."

Rone grinned. "Hell yes, we are. But keep your voice down. Just in case."

She blinked. Examined their surroundings. Sat up, grabbing the fabric and holding it to her. For some reason, being naked didn't surprise her. Did her clothing spontaneously incinerate *often*?

Though he'd expected the decision to become Engel Verlad would bring him adventure and danger, he'd never fathomed getting tangled up in something like this.

Her shoulders tensed. "We're still here."

Rone sat back. "Yeah. I don't know how many of them survived, but at least one person has walked by in the last six hours. I couldn't get far with a naked woman in my arms."

She glanced back to him. "Six hours?" No comment on the nudity. Maybe he should accept nothing scandalous was going to come out of that.

He nodded.

She frowned. Looked at her palm in the dimming light. Opened and closed her fist. "I'm usually out for longer than that."

"Longer?"

She nodded. Studied one arm and then the other. "But this wasn't the same."

"The summoning?"

She licked her lips. Cleared her throat. "Water?"

Rone frowned and shook his head.

She accepted it with a nod of her head. "I don't know. I've never done that before. But that was . . . Ireth. Part of him."

Rone ran fingers back through his hair. "So you mutter something in . . . what, ancient Noscon? And you get fire powers?"

She hugged her knees to her chest. "It felt like a summoning. The heat, the pain—"

"So it does hurt." There was a hitch in his voice, and he cleared his throat.

She met his eyes. "Like nothing I can describe. Like . . ." She thought for a moment. "Like every fiber of your body is being torn apart. Like it's burning up, but the fuel never runs out. Like you're twisting into something else."

Rone's stomach tensed. He tried to imagine it . . . but all he felt was a nauseous shiver that made him grateful their roles weren't reversed. "That . . . sounds awful."

She simply nodded. It was all so ordinary to her. How could something like that be anything but horribly spectacular? "It happens all at once, and then you wake up the next day. But this . . . this wasn't like that."

Setting his elbows on his knees, Rone shook his head. She talked about pain like it was a bad storm that had happened last week. Talking about possession like she would a case of the sniffles. He let out a short, heavy breath. "You're incredible. You just . . . lit up like a torch and destroyed them. There was ash everywhere . . ."

The smile faded. She hesitated before saying, "I suppose that's for the best."

"You *suppose*?"

She shrugged. "I . . . no one ever tells me what I do as Ireth. Usually I don't remember enough to put the pieces together. Though I suppose I wasn't entirely Ireth this time. I was conscious."

"How?" Rone asked, meeting her eyes. "How did you do it if it hurt that badly? If you were . . . half-possessed, unable to fall into the bliss of unconsciousness?"

The smile returned. And with the utmost sincerity, she answered, "Because I felt Ireth's love for me."

That was not the reply Rone had been expecting. He tried to speak, choked on a few possible responses, and settled on, ". . . the fire horse." One of the hell demons cursed in scripture and preached against by any and every person who donned the four-petaled lily. One of the deranged beasts used to bribe children into eating their dinners and brushing their teeth. A weapon used by the lowest and darkest scum in the city.

She shrugged. Black ashes, a slagging fire demon *loved* her, and she shrugged. "I felt it. I connected with him like I never have before. It . . . I don't know. I can't explain it." She looked up, peering at the darkening windows through the wide holes in the floors above them. "We can't stay here."

Rone ran a hand down his scruff-lined cheeks. She was so . . . different. And it bothered him that that *didn't* bother him. "No. But I'm positive there are grafters and mobsmen crawling all over this place. Maybe police farther out. The moment we leave, someone will be tailing us."

Sandis considered this for a moment. "If we wait a little longer, we could go to Helderschmidt's."

"The firearms factory? Did you really used to work there?"

She nodded. "Before the slavers took me. It's closed at night, except for custodial work, so it will be mostly empty. I know how to get in. We could arm ourselves and hide, at least for the night."

Rone licked his lips, considering it. They weren't terribly close to Helderschmidt's, but they also weren't far. If they could get on a roof, it would be better.

"All right. Here, I'll rip armholes in this curtain. You can put the shirt on backward underneath. It's . . . something. I'll try to snatch from a clothesline on the way." He stood.

Sandis handed him the curtain. "I don't want to take from anyone—"

"Then you're going to get a lot of attention." He looked knowingly at her bare legs. His shirt only covered to the tops of her thighs.

He looked for a little too long.

Sandis frowned, but whether it was at him or their situation, she didn't specify. Merely nodded.

After Rone measured the curtain as best he could with his eyes, he used his teeth to start a hole for one arm, then the other. They were more or less even. He held it up to the fading light. "I should have gone into fashion design."

Sandis chuckled.

He handed the overly long curtain vest to Sandis, whose eyes fell to his chest, his stomach.

Feeling oddly self-conscious, he asked, "What?"

She shook her head and took the curtain. "Nothing. Thank you."

He turned around so she could assemble her pathetic outfit. When he turned back, she'd tied the bottom of the curtain together around her legs in the semblance of an ill-fitting diaper.

"Nice." He tried not to laugh. Laughing was loud, and they needed to keep a low profile.

Sandis shrugged. "The amarinth?"

"Spent. Otherwise I'd be crispy in that alley, too."

She blanched. "Oh God, Rone. I didn't even think—" Her voice jumped nearly an octave as it choked up her throat. "I could have killed you. I'm so sorry."

Taking a step forward, she reached out her hand, then awkwardly dropped it. She looked like she was going to throw up.

Rone blinked at her. The grafters, the fire horse, the nudity . . . none of it had garnered much of a reaction from her. But him nearly dying? *That's* what got to her?

Something twanged in his chest. He couldn't tell exactly what, but it hurt and excited him at the same time. Dissolved, for a moment, the constant pain of that ball of guilt in his stomach.

She cared about him. His own father didn't care about him. But she—

Clearing his throat, Rone glanced away. "It's fine. If I hadn't spun the damn thing, I probably could have jumped behind you. Either way, it's nothing to fuss about."

She swallowed so hard he could see it through the muscles of her neck. Her stomach rumbled. She pushed a fist into it.

"Are you able to run?" She had no shoes, and he could only imagine summoning a fire-beast into oneself was exhausting.

She took a deep breath. "I think so." She didn't sound sure. But it would have to do. Their options were too few and far between.

"All right," Rone said, scanning the rafters. "Let's figure out a way *up*."

There was no exhilaration in jumping from roof to roof this time. No sense of freedom. His heart pounded harder than it usually did. Perhaps because he knew they were being followed. Perhaps because the amarinth was spent. Perhaps because Sandis was slow and achingly pale. That bizarre half summoning of hers had saved their lives, but it had obviously taken a toll on her, and Rone couldn't do anything about it.

He could at least see her dressed. The first clothesline he found, he confiscated a dress and threw it to her. She put it on without complaint, looking more thankful for the chance to rest than the fashion upgrade.

They dropped back down to the city near the smoke ring. Factories were not the easiest buildings to jump around on, especially if they had smoke towers or steam vents. Except the cotton ones. Cotton factories were nice, long boxes with barely a slant to their roofs.

Unfortunately, they also operated all hours of the day. Sandis and Rone wouldn't get far into a cotton factory's packed looms before someone threw them out or called the police. With his mother already imprisoned and his father an unfeeling bastard, Rone didn't have anyone to save him if he had a mishap with local authorities.

That ball of guilt rolled in his gut again as he pushed Sandis across an intersection. His mother. She was still there, rotting away. Because of him.

I'm coming, I promise. Rone glanced over his shoulder, searching for pursuers. He knew they were there. He sensed them like the beetles beneath an overturned cobblestone. His bad shoulder throbbed all the way to his neck from all the looking and lifting and fleeing for his life he'd been doing. It usually didn't get this bad in the summer.

Sandis's breaths were heavy, her voice raspy and dry. "Over here," she said as they approached the firearms factory. The late hour meant few people walked the streets. Near Helderschmidt's, there was only a beggar and two kids with their heads pressed together, reading a grubby book of some sort.

Rone didn't know if Sandis planned to pick the lock—the large man standing guard made that unlikely—find a key hidden under a mat, or access some sort of secret tunnel. As far as Rone knew, none of the sewer entrances that went into the building were large enough to fit a person.

Sandis wrapped around the building to the narrow four-foot-wide alley separating it from its counterpart. A network of pipes ran up the brick. Sandis squeezed past several feet of them before reaching a water meter. She hoisted herself on top of it, arms shaking, and began to climb.

"Sandis?" Rone whispered after her. She didn't answer, so he followed. Twice, the climb became precarious—he had to reach across an expanse of no pipe to grab a broken brick or window ledge to pull himself up. Sandis's foot slipped at one point, but she found purchase. They made their way up to a dirty glass window. Sandis pressed against the pane, straining, and it creaked open.

Her sigh of relief was loud and sweet. She climbed in. Rone followed after her and found himself in some sort of smelly rest facility.

"Anon broke the latch in here years ago and was too scared to tell anybody." She eased the pane shut. "Security is heaviest downstairs."

She ran to a water pump in the corner. Rone almost stopped her, telling her the noise might attract someone, but her thirst was written across her skin, so he helped her instead.

She drank more than should fit into a person's stomach, then took over the pumping so Rone could drink, too. The water was stale and metallic. He didn't care.

Something *clunked* nearby.

Sandis froze. "We should move," she whispered. "Not too far . . . but we should go."

Rone agreed with a nod and let Sandis lead the way. The halls were lit just enough for a security guard to pass through. She checked the path, then hurried down the hall to a stairwell. Waited. Rone thought he heard footsteps above them. Sandis must have heard them, too, because she forwent the stairs and continued down the hall, testing one door—locked—and then a set of two—open.

They stepped onto scaffolding that surrounded scads of expensive-looking machinery. Large machinery. On the ground beneath them, assembly stations stretched between the various machines.

Sandis grabbed the precarious railing at the edge of the scaffolding, and for a moment, Rone thought she was going to jump. But she merely peered into the darkness beneath them, searching. A few heartbeats later, she stumbled back, spinning around until her eyes landed on his waist.

She rushed toward him and grabbed the belt cinched over his trousers.

"I'm not necessarily complaining—" He grinned. Yeah, they were running for their lives, *still*, but he couldn't help it. "—but this isn't exactly how I thought this would play out."

Thoroughly ignoring Rone's half-honest joke, she undid the buckle and yanked the belt out of his trouser loops fast enough to hurt. Then she rushed to the door, crouched, and knotted the leather between the handles.

Speeding for the stairs, Sandis waved for Rone to follow her. He should have nabbed her a darker dress. The light color of the linen she wore shone like a beacon against the shadows, but at least it made her easy to follow in this unknown territory.

They slunk down to the main floor. Tiptoed around the assembly lines and workstations. Sandis reached for a table and pulled it toward her. The legs screeched against the floor, and they both froze, worried the sound had carried. Rone allowed himself two breaths before grabbing the table opposite her and hefting it up, testing its weight. "We'll have to pick it up," he whispered. "Where do you want it?"

She gestured with her head to a corner behind a large, bulbous machine, similar to a furnace. It sat near the dark wall at the back of the room, a ways below a high window. A good place to hole up, though not the most comfortable to sleep.

Rone lifted the table up until two of its legs were off the ground. Sandis got her shoulder under her side of the table and did the same. As quietly as they could, they moved it to the spot she'd chosen, gingerly setting it on its side, forming a short wall in the shadows. Sandis leapt over the thing and went to retrieve another table, which Rone helped her move beside the first.

Grabbing his arm, Sandis said, "There's a shallow bin over there, against the far wall." She pointed. "It holds half-assembled rifles. Bring me some."

Rone glanced in that direction, a question forming on his tongue, but the sound of footsteps overhead made him swallow it. Nodding, he jumped the tables and hurried toward the bin, careful not to knock anything over. His heart started to pulse in the thick artery of his neck. He had to cross the entire floor, but he got there without incident. Inside were a handful of rifles, though it looked like someone had sawed them in half. Stocks, bolts, levers. He grabbed two, one in each hand, and hurried back.

A thump, again from above, but farther . . . what, north? Like a body dropping. A security guard? Had they been found already? Maybe they'd been watched the whole time, and the scout had simply waited for reinforcements to strike.

Rone jumped the tables again, and for an alarming second, he didn't see Sandis. She emerged from the narrow pass near the wall, her skirt folded against her waist. She knelt and let its contents spill—a bunch of metal that Rone slowly recognized as various firearm pieces. The assembled bits of a firing mechanism, minus the trigger guard. A barrel and chamber. A magazine.

She grabbed one of the half rifles from his hand and began assembling it like it was a children's puzzle. Her hands moved like birds, piece after piece snapping expertly into place.

"This is why you kept asking about guns," he whispered.

She nodded. "I worked here for a long time. Including at the end of the line."

"End of the line?"

She raised a completed rifle to her shoulder and peered over it. It lacked a scope. "Testing."

Rone almost whistled, then remembered himself and stopped. He'd never actually fired a gun before meeting Sandis. He didn't own any. His father hadn't believed in them, of course, and he didn't use them in his own business because they were too bulky, too loud.

Sandis moved faster on the second firearm, though one of the parts got stuck and she had to disassemble and reassemble it. Finished, she handed it to Rone.

More footsteps, far away. One story up. Rone doubted the guard had suddenly multiplied. They'd been followed, which probably meant Kazen hadn't been killed in the alley. He and Sandis either needed to find a door out and hope it wasn't being manned or stay very, very quiet.

Sandis bit her lip. Stood.

Rone grabbed her wrist.

"I need ammunition," she whispered. "I'll be right back."

She sounded confident, so he let her go, and she danced away into the shadows. Rone strained to listen to the footsteps. They came and went, sometimes closer, sometimes farther. Sweat licked his palms.

Sandis returned with a box, and Rone tried not to let his sigh of relief be audible. As she knelt on the ground and began loading the rifles, a new question came to mind.

"Sandis," he whispered, despite knowing that, for now, they were alone. "Who's Anon?"

She glanced at him, confused.

He pointed toward the scaffolding. "You said Anon broke the lock."

Her eyes saddened. "He's my brother. Was."

The one she'd been looking for when the slavers had found her. That story still sounded so odd to him. Random slavers in Dresberg, kidnapping citizens in alleys . . . He pushed the skepticism away. Sandis wouldn't lie about that. He hadn't known her long, but he was sure of her honesty.

"You never found him," he tried.

She shook her head. "No, but he's dead." Her body wilted under the statement. "Drowned in a canal."

"You saw him?"

"Kazen told me."

"And we trust him now."

She lifted her head. Swiped hair from her face. "He's gone, Rone."

"But how—"

"He hadn't come home for three days . . . That's why I was looking for him when . . ." Her throat tightened around the words, and she shook her head. "I know Anon. He would have come after me. Even if it was a lie . . . if my brother came looking for me, Kazen wouldn't have liked it, you know?"

Rone nodded. Either way, a dead brother.

He bent his knees and rested his arms on them. For a moment, he thought he heard footsteps in the room . . . but no, those came from above.

"My father worked in cotton," Sandis continued. She'd set the guns aside and cleaned her thumbnail with her other thumbnail. "I'm not sure what happened. Someone smoking inside, maybe. But the place lit up. He died in the fire. When I was branded . . . I wondered if his death felt something like that."

Rone's shoulders drooped, and something pinched deep inside him. She had a way of messing with his insides. "Oh, Sandis."

"My mother gave up living after that," she went on. "Just . . . stopped going to work. Stopped eating. Stopped drinking. Lay in our flat until she died. Anon got a job here first." She scanned the shadows. "We managed to keep everything afloat for a few years. Then he went missing . . . You know the rest."

He frowned. Yes, he knew the rest. "How old were you, when they died?"

"I was eleven. Anon was nine."

Rone rubbed his hands together. He wasn't cold, but it gave him something to do. It was no wonder she wanted to find this Talbur guy so badly.

Sandis knew a little about his mother, and she'd gotten to see in person what a winning father he had. That ball of guilt moved back and forth inside him. The story of his mother would have the same depressing notes if he didn't get her out of Gerech soon.

"Three years ago, when I was twenty-two . . ." Already the story sounded awkward. He'd never told it before. "I was still working in the sewers. Still cleaning Kurtz's street." He chuckled. It wasn't funny, really, but he couldn't help it. "I was picking garbage out of one of the sewer tunnels. When the collection is slow to pick up people's trash, they like to throw it down the manholes. Real generous of them."

Sandis smiled.

"Anyway. I was scooping something out of the water when the tunnel collapsed."

She stiffened. Waited.

"I obviously made it out all right," he said, "though a big chunk of something hit me in the back. Messed up my shoulder." Thinking about it made the muscles ache anew, and he reached back to massage a knot at the base of his neck. "I clawed my way out of the rubble. The concrete had crumbled all the way to the street. Some sunlight came through the wreckage, and it glinted off something. Even though I couldn't move my arm and I was bleeding from my head, I dived for it. No one around here turns down gold."

He pulled his fingers from his sore shoulder and pulled the amarinth from his pocket. Tossed it up, caught it. "Found this sucker. The first Kolins, they leveled everything out when they came here, but they didn't clear it all. I assume there was some sort of crypt over that tunnel. Not sure—never searched for bodies. I was going to sell this, but some bastard went bat crazy trying to steal it from me. If not for Kurtz, he would have gotten it."

"Kurtz saved you?" she asked.

Rone laughed. "I saved myself. Second time I ever got to use what he taught me, you know? Anyway, it took me a while, but I figured out what it was." He let out a long breath and stuffed the artifact back into his pocket. "From there I conjured Engel Verlad, quit my job, and started making more money."

Sandis nodded, slowly. "And what does *Engel* do?"

Rone shrugged, the action tugging unpleasantly on his shoulder. "I do what others are too scared to do. Steal things, spy, deliver one person to another."

She pulled back from him. "Assassination?"

Rone shrugged a second time, then resumed rubbing that knot. "I don't know what they do with them. I don't ask. I won't kill anyone myself, though. Those jobs I turn down." He wasn't a killer. Maybe Kurtz's philosophies had stuck more than he'd like to admit. Maybe his father had drilled morality into his brain too solidly, before he left. It was why he didn't work for mobsters or grafters, if he could avoid it. Their jobs got too dirty. Too political.

He let the amarinth dangle from his finger. "It was a job I did . . . the one with Marald Steffen—"

"The old man you beat up."

His lip twitched. "Yeah. Sorry about that."

Sandis shrugged.

"It was a job I did for him that got twisted and put my mother in Gerech. I tried to pay off the warden and turn myself in, but . . ." He shook his head. "God's tower, I hate this place."

They were both quiet for a moment. Rone didn't have anything more to say. Sandis was probably judging him. Here she was, running for her life to find family she didn't even know, and he'd let his innocent mother get thrown into prison. He knew what she'd ask next. *Why not sell the amarinth, Rone? Wouldn't that be enough money?* But she wouldn't understand, wouldn't—

Sandis pushed herself onto her knees and pulled Rone's hand from his neck.

"What—" he started, but Sandis gently eased his head over and prodded the area.

"This side?"

His injured shoulder? "Uh, yeah." She pushed a tender spot, and he started.

"Turn around."

Rone wasn't sure what was happening, but the footsteps above quieted, so he did as he was told, putting his back to her.

Her fingers followed his shoulder blade, then his spine. "The grafters don't employ doctors," she said, her voice close to his ear. "But Kazen makes sure his vessels are in good health. We don't work as well otherwise."

"You talk like you're a thing."

"To him, I am." Her touch crept up to his neck. "I'm glad you don't think so."

"Why would I—"

She shoved the heel of her hand into his neck and wrapped her other arm under his shoulder, pulling it in the opposite direction. A sharp *pop* sounded in Rone's bones, and he barely had the forethought to stifle his scream. He ripped himself from Sandis's grip.

"The hell, Sandis?" he asked, rubbing his shoulder . . .

It felt better.

Rone paused. Felt for the knot he'd been working. Couldn't find it. "The hell, Sandis?" he asked again.

She sat on her heels. "Better?"

Rone rolled back his shoulders. "Yeah. What did you do?"

"We have to learn a lot of self-care, with the grafters," she said as he settled back down. She looked away before adding, in a softer tone, "They fight back sometimes. The people Kazen sends us to punish. They can't hurt the numina, but they can hurt us. We learn how to fix it when they do." She hesitated. "I've only seen one other vessel die, right after I met Kazen. That was the angriest I've ever seen him."

"Even in the streets? Chasing you? Us?"

She nodded.

Rone shook his head. "That guy is psychotic."

They fell silent again. A police whistle sounded somewhere beyond the factory's thick walls. Rone held his breath and listened. It didn't sound again.

Maybe the scarlets had found the grafters and were going to do something about them. Now *that* deserved a chuckle.

Without the distraction of conversation, each passing minute put him more on edge. Where were the grafters? When would they strike? His eyelids felt thick, but he was too anxious to sleep. His nose itched, then his leg, then his hand. The more he thought about it, the more he itched.

He pulled out his amarinth again, fiddled with it. Rolled the loops around themselves.

Sandis gasped and clawed at her heart.

Rone straightened. "What?" He looked around, searching for a grafter.

"I . . ." She shook her head. Pulling his focus from the machinery, Rone noticed she was staring at his amarinth. "I . . . felt something. I was watching it, and . . ."

"And what?"

Her eyes met his, dark and endless and frightened. "It was like . . . burning copper. It hurt—"

Her words cut short as the door to the scaffolding—the same one they had come in through—shook. Something rammed into it, but the belt held.

Sandis grabbed her rifle. Her right ring finger trembled.

She didn't want to kill anyone, either.

Reaching for the other rifle, Rone watched her crank the lever on her weapon, never taking her eyes off the door. She put the butt to her shoulder mechanically, like she was making a conscious effort *not* to tremble.

He put a hand on her shoulder. Her dark eyes met his, and for a split second, he forgot there were grafters at the door. Forgot she was a vessel. Forgot that this night might end with them both dying.

Maybe he should kiss her. A last hurrah before mortality failed him. But if they lived . . . how mad would she be that he'd taken such a liberty?

The door shook. Sandis stiffened, her gaze shooting back over his head.

A knife blade thrust between the doors and sawed at the leather belt holding them closed.

Chapter 16

Sandis struggled to clear the sensations the amarinth had left in her mind as she readied the Helderschmidt lever-action sixty. It hadn't been a vision, exactly, but an impression of something like . . . metal. This heat had not felt like Ireth's familiar heat—it had hurt, like nails digging around her heart. And the smell that had accompanied the impression . . .

It smelled like Heath.

Nausea assaulted her stomach. The grafters finished cutting through the belt and crept onto the scaffolding like spiders, searching. The lighting was poor, but Sandis had no trouble identifying them. Guards always carried lamps.

Maybe if she and Rone stayed quiet enough, the men would give up and leave. But she didn't believe the thought even as it flitted through her head.

Rone was so still she couldn't even hear him breathe. His face was turned away from her, watching the shadows on the scaffolding. Sandis held very still, palms sweating around the rifle. She tried to focus on the warmth funneling from Rone's calloused hand into her shoulder. It was a safe sort of warm. It kept her calm, even when the hunters were so close.

Rone leaned in, his nose almost brushing her cheek. She shivered from the nearness and from his breath touching her ear. "Numina?"

She shook her head. None had been summoned, at least. She could only sense a numen that was summoned and near, not unoccupied vessels. But it made her hopeful nonetheless.

A grafter ventured down the stairs while another lit a lamp. The burst of light reflected off Ravis's shaved head, and his narrow body created a shadow like a crooked tree across the far wall of the workroom. Staps was directly behind him, followed by several mobsmen with Straight Ace's colors.

Rone shifted onto the balls of his feet, ready to fight, but he had no amarinth, and every one of these men was armed. A bead of sweat trickled down the back of Sandis's neck. For a moment, she considered calling Ireth . . . but her energy was too low. Even if she succeeded, another half summoning might knock her out before she could tap into Ireth's fire. She'd be unconscious for another six hours. She couldn't leave herself so vulnerable. She couldn't put the burden of their combined safety on Rone alone. Besides, this was a *firearms* factory. Dabbling with uncontrolled flame was too dangerous.

Though she couldn't do so now, she *had* summoned him, partially. She had brought a level-seven numen into her body and *held on*. She was stronger than she thought.

She was strong enough for this.

The lamplight only reached so far, and the machine they'd chosen as their hideout shaded them from its glow. Ravis and Staps whispered to each other; Ravis turned around and went back the way he'd come. Six men had been left behind.

She wondered what they'd done to the security guards. Clenching her teeth, she readied her gun.

"You have to wait for the critical moment," Rone's voice whispered.

Swallowing, she glanced back at Rone, only to find empty shadows.

Her heart leapt into her throat. Where had he gone? She frantically searched the shadows for his form.

Something clamored near the back of the workroom.

"We know you're in here, Sandis. Engel." The gruff voice was Staps's. Sandis's fingers shook. She hunkered behind the table and set her barrel atop it. Flexed her fingers. *The critical moment.*

Please, Celestial, forgive me for hurting them.

And please, don't let me shoot Rone by mistake.

The lamplight moved away from her and toward the sound, though one grafter still stood atop the scaffolding, surveying.

"You!" another man shouted, but it was followed by a choking sound and something metal striking something soft. Sandis winced. The surveying grafter fired his gun. The bullet ricocheted off a machine—she saw the spark.

"Two o'clock!" the surveyor shouted.

Warmth pressed against Sandis's forehead. Ireth . . . but she couldn't use him this time. She closed her eyes, sharpening her focus and intent, even as grafter footsteps thundered toward the surveyor's destination. Toward Rone.

Opening her eyes, Sandis pointed her rifle's front sight toward the surveyor and fired.

She cranked her lever. Heard someone shout her name, nine o'clock. Two more gunshots echoed through the space.

She fired again, the rifle's kick burning her shoulder.

One of the lamps dropped and extinguished.

She cranked her lever.

A hand grabbed the back of her dress and yanked her down just as a return bullet whizzed past her hair.

"You're amazing," Rone whispered, grabbing the other rifle. "Ahead!"

Sandis popped back over the table. A shadow moved.

She fired, and it dropped. Another shadow; Sandis shifted to the left and fired again, but missed. These rifles only held four shots, so she took Rone's and cranked the lever, hearing the double click as the bullet entered its chamber.

It had been four years, but she still knew these firearms like she did her own script.

Rone swept away again to punch, kick, whatever he did with the lingering grafters. Three of them were down, though Ravis could come back at any time.

A window broke somewhere, the shattering glass piercing her ears like a scream. Something hit the closest machine and made it ring like a heavy gong.

Then Rone was there, grabbing her shoulders. "Run, run, run." He pulled her onto her feet and dragged her toward the newly shattered window. An exit. He must have remembered she had no shoes, since he scooped her up into his arms before pushing through the frame. A triangle of glass caught on his shirt and tore it.

Sandis gripped her rifle as she became weightless. Her body jerked with Rone's when he hit the street. He grunted and ran to the end of the factory before setting her down.

A police whistle blew. As far as the oncoming scarlets were concerned, Sandis and Rone were just as guilty as the mobsmen and grafters.

Sticking his fingers into a dip in the cobbles, Rone opened a manhole.

"Hold your breath," he said.

Sandis gripped the gun in her hands. She finally had one, with three shots left. The water would ruin it.

"Sandis!"

Gripping the barrel, Sandis jumped into the darkness.

She lost the rifle in the current.

Chapter 17

Rone set a tray of bread, cheese, and apples on the small table in the room he'd rented that morning. It was a pricier establishment, unlike the holes he typically chose—when meeting a woman *didn't* escalate into running for his life—but he figured grafters would be less likely to look for them here. With luck, they were still reeling from Rone's thorough beatings and the holes Sandis had put in them.

Rone dropped into the sole chair in the room—it was a single room, which made it cheaper and all around easier to protect. Sandis popped over to the food and smelled the bread like it was ecstasy in loaf form. Despite her obvious hunger, when she tore off the heel, she offered it first to him.

Rone waved it away.

She frowned. "You're hungry. Eat it."

He frowned back, looking at the food clutched in Sandis's thin, almost elegant fingers. She had a weirdly hopeful look on her face, like a refusal would break her heart. He snatched the bread, still warm from the oven, and took a too-large bite that pressed against his windpipe when he swallowed.

The vast space around the bread in his belly made him realize how long it'd been since he'd eaten, so he took another bite, then a third. The chewing started a headache, though the pain was more likely from lack of sleep than anything else. Rone was used to sleeping in, not snoozing on the run.

After he swallowed again, he said, "I'm going to Gerech today."

Sandis perked up, half an apple slice sticking out of her mouth. She crunched down, shoved it against her cheek, and said, "Your mother? Will they let you visit?"

No. "Maybe. I've got to see what I can do. Figure out who's in charge of visitors and what he takes for bribes." He leaned forward and turned the bread over in his hands. "And get another job. I'm almost out on the money front. This isn't helping."

Sandis's hand paused on the way to a cheese curd.

He shook his head. "Eat. We both need the energy."

She hesitantly picked up the morsel. Pinched it between her fingers. "Can I help? Can I . . . do . . . something?"

"You can stay here. I'm faster on my own. You'll be safe." He stood and moved to the window, peering out from behind its yellow curtains. This was a very yellow establishment, he noticed. A poor attempt at cheer in the cesspool that was Dresberg. "They won't attack a place of this size. Not in the day, especially. And it should take Kazen a while to regroup his men."

"He doesn't need men."

Rone dropped the curtain and looked at her. She still had that cheese in her hands. But she looked up and smiled. It didn't reach her eyes, but at least it was a smile.

"All right," she said. "I'll stay here. I'll . . . make the bed. And fold the laundry."

The laundry was already folded and on the edge of bed, thanks to the in-house maid who gracefully hadn't asked why it all smelled like fecal water or why Rone had paid her to find them new clothes. Popping the cheese into her mouth, Sandis walked to the bed and pushed the laundry onto the floor. "Yes, I'll fold it."

Rone smiled. He couldn't help it. He tore another piece from the diminishing loaf on the table. "I'll go now. The sooner I leave, the sooner I'll be back. We'll figure out something."

"Thank you."

Through a mouthful of bread, he said, "Stop thanking me."

She smiled. A sincere one this time. With that smile and the light coming in through the pleated curtains, she looked like something ethereal. A strong reminder of why Rone had ever approached her in the first place. His thoughts started to turn—they were presently alone and safe, and her skin looked so soft. And she cared about him. She'd said as much, after the mess in the alley. She was an enigma. So different from the occasional woman who warmed his bed only to disappear from his life the next morning. Different, too, from old colleagues and friends like Kurtz. Different from his mother. *Very* different from his mother.

And while you're thinking all this, your mother is slowly rotting in prison.

That thought snapped his mind into order. He shook his head, shaking off his desires and questions like dust. Now wasn't the time. Now was just . . . temporary.

He grabbed his wallet from his bag and slipped out the door without saying goodbye.

It took a long time to get to Gerech Prison. Maybe because it was far away, and this wasteland city was enormous. Maybe because Rone was tired, and his joints felt like they'd aged fifty years overnight. Maybe because, deep down, he knew this mission was going to be fruitless.

He reached the iron bars that caged in the prison clerk. Different from the one he'd spoken to before.

"Paying a visit" was all he said.

The clerk, an older man with a long face, flipped open a heavy book. Rone tried not to notice how many entries had been blacked out in it. "Name?"

"Adalia Comf."

He turned the sticky pages with aggravating slowness. Dragged the tip of his index finger down one until it settled on his mother's entry. "She is"—he paused—"oh. Not seeing visitors. Her visit was expended on the warden."

Rone growled and pulled out his paperwork. "I'm her son. I need to see her."

Legally, he knew he had no grounds. One visit had been allowed, and he had used it on his meeting with the warden.

The clerk looked over his paperwork. "I'm sorry, but the rights for this prisoner have expired. Where did you get these?"

From a filing clerk who takes low bribes. Rone countered with a question of his own. "How much will it cost to make them viable?"

The clerk pressed his lips together, considering. Ultimately, he shook his head. "Good day, sir." He closed the book. "Next."

It wasn't a surprise, but Rone's muscles quivered with restrained rage as he stepped away from the window—but not away from the prison. No, he followed the wall under the watch of all those eyes until he almost got to the door. *Almost.* He didn't dare bribe guards who were trusted with the actual door.

He stood in front of two men with rifles strung to their belts on one side, sabers on the other, and a thin club in the front. One raised his eyebrow. The other folded his arms.

They were both about Rone's age. For all he knew, he'd gone to church with them.

Keeping his back to the city, he pulled out his dwindling wad of cash and started counting bills. "Adalia Comf is in sector G for thievery. Getting additional punishment from a rich man. I'd like to see her treated well."

The first guard narrowed his eyes. The second reached out his hand. Rone stuck half the wad in it. Seeing his companion being paid, the first gave in and took his share.

With nothing left to say, Rone turned for the street.

"Hey."

He looked back. The second guard had spoken.

His face looked grim. "I have a shift in sector G. I know her. Nice lady."

Rone's pulse sped.

The guard shook his head. "It's not going well for her, but we'll do what we can."

His heart nearly stopped. He forced his stiff neck to nod his head. Found some reserve of strength to move his legs. He half limped toward the main road. Remembered to breathe at some point, and the air burned his throat on its way in.

He couldn't keep entertaining Sandis's fantasies about finding a benevolent, rich uncle who'd help them both. A job. He needed another job. He'd take *anything*, even if it went against his rules. He'd kill a triumvirate member if it meant getting his mother out of prison. Not like the politicians were doing anything to improve this hellish place.

His hand clutched the amarinth until his fingers bruised, but he felt utterly powerless.

Rone's first stop was his mother's flat. The one he was still paying rent on. The one he'd get her back into somehow. His mother was a frugal woman; she might have something stowed away. If nothing else, there were the trinkets Rone always got her on her birthday. Those would fetch a few kol.

He knew something was wrong before he reached the door. The window was broken.

Cursing, he hurried inside, noting that the door was unlocked and the door frame had seen better days. Inside, the place was a mess. Ransacked.

"Damn your god to hell!" he shouted, running through the first room to the bedroom. His mother's jewelry, gone. That stupid glass lily, gone. The silverware, gone. Nothing left to sell.

"You were supposed to take care of her!" He picked up a chair in the kitchen and threw it across the room. "You preach love and charity, yet your own vows mean nothing to you! *We* mean *nothing*!"

He grabbed another chair and hurled it, cracking a window and snapping off one of the chair's legs in the process. He grabbed fistfuls of hair and fell over the counter, the wooden countertop biting his elbows. Breathing hard, Rone shut his eyes, trying to temper the black hate gagging him. Hate for his father, and hate for himself.

He nearly ripped out his hair when he stood. Marched for the door. Slammed it shut. Locked it.

It was a good thing Sandis was the one who could summon Ireth. If he could set fire to all of Dresberg, he would.

He usually checked his "hire sites" at night, when he was less likely to be seen. But every extra hour his mother spent in that prison brought her closer to death.

At least it's not winter, he told himself as he headed for Goldstone's Bank. *At least the guard seemed sympathetic. He'll help her. He'll help her.*

The broken lantern behind the bank was just that—a broken lantern. No note, no coordinates for a meeting. No signs.

He turned right around and caught the back of a wagon carrying leathers. Rode it directly to his next spot—another manhole lid. He picked it up, ignoring the endless people walking around him. Nothing had been fastened underneath.

Engel Verlad only advertised through word of mouth. The city's best criminals and wealthy elite had all heard of him by now, but there were six different drop-off sites he used. Six different places potential clients could leave a message to request his services. There were four more he could check. They were not close.

Rone slammed the manhole cover back into place and pushed through the crowd, oblivious and uncaring of whose toes he stepped on or whose balance he threw off. He jogged until he found a building with a fire ladder he could climb to its roof.

On to District Three.

The sun was threatening to set when he made it to location four. Nothing. Absolutely nothing. Rone had slow periods, yes, but individual jobs paid so well it usually didn't affect him. Before now, he'd never needed exorbitant amounts of money.

He crouched in an alley—a surprisingly clean one—and hung his head, struggling to think. His brain was cobwebs and black ashes. His whole body hurt and begged for sleep. He was going to be very, very sore tomorrow.

And he was hungry, which reminded him of how little he had at the moment.

Groaning, Rone stood and counted the small amount of cash he'd reserved for himself. And Sandis. They needed supplies if they were going to stay on the run. Rone needed to ask around for flats for rent; they could bum off the empty spaces for free until a payer came along. It would keep them moving, and keep the grafters guessing.

Or you can walk away and not look back. Hedge his bets and sell the amarinth, bribe or threaten the warden to get his mother out of Gerech, and vanish. Maybe he should follow Sandis's advice and hitch a ride on a wagon headed out into the country. Sleep in some farmer's barn at night and pick his corn during the day. Live a poor, boring, *safe* life, taking care of his mother until her time came.

"You have a responsibility," Kurtz had said. But hadn't he satisfied his responsibility by bringing Sandis to the Lily Tower? He had become one of Kazen's targets, too, but he didn't *have* to be. A man couldn't hit a target he couldn't find. And the guy was old. Rone could go out to the country for a decade or so, then come back to the city, and . . .

Shut up. Just . . . shut up. He shoved his hands into his pockets and began walking to the closest store before it closed. He could leave, yes. He would . . . eventually. But not now. Not when Sandis said "thank you" in that way she did. Not when she was waiting for him.

The time would come when they'd go their separate ways.

But it hadn't come yet.

Chapter 18

Gerech was some ways away, wasn't it? Rone hadn't said how long he'd be gone. It might be all day. All night. He hadn't told her how long they were going to stay at this inn.

Sandis began to fret as the sun started its descent. What if the grafters had followed them here and were simply waiting for nightfall? What if they'd gone after Rone? Kazen hadn't been at the factory. He would still be out looking for them. She had a hard time believing their chase had ended at Helderschmidt's.

She worried her lip as she stared out the window. Surely she'd see Rone's silhouette bounding over the rooftops at any moment. He'd jump down this way and scare her. She leaned closer to the window in anticipation, but of course he didn't come. Frowning, she glanced at the door. It had only opened once since Rone left, and that was the maid coming by to ask for lunch requests. Sandis had asked for simple bread and butter. She hated costing Rone money. She didn't wish to be a burden. Someday, soon, she wouldn't be.

Contrary to her thoughts, she smiled. Rone was so kind to her. She couldn't have asked for a better ally. She hadn't expected to have one, especially not someone like—

Heat crept into her ears. She pressed her fingertips into them until the skin cooled. The sensation made her wonder, what would have happened had she not stolen his amarinth that day? What sort of *payment* had he had in mind?

She shook her head. Regardless, if not for Rone, Kazen would have grabbed her a long time ago.

A shiver coursed through her at the thought of the grafters' underground lair. She wondered what the other vessels thought of Kazen's hunt for her. Especially Alys and Rist, who had seen her since. Rist didn't usually care much about anything, but Alys did. Did she feel betrayed? Had Kaili taken care of her, as Sandis had hoped? Relief that Alys hadn't been hurt by the bursting steam valve still pricked cool tingles on the underside of her skin. Sandis would never have forgiven herself if she'd caused the young girl such pain.

Her stomach rumbled. The maid hadn't been by again for a dinner order. Perhaps she was late. Perhaps people here ate late. Perhaps Sandis should have ordered a bigger lunch. She'd get a bigger dinner, one she could share with Rone when he got back.

Pressing her forehead to the windowpane, she peered at the street five stories below her. It wasn't *as* crowded in this part of the city, and there were more horses and carriages in the streets than near the smoke ring, but the roads still bore a decent-sized crowd between the buildings' growing shadows. She searched for Rone among the various shoppers and workers, but from up here, everyone looked like Rone, minus the ones with hats. He never wore a hat. And he shouldn't—she liked his hair.

Forcing herself away from the window, Sandis plopped atop the bed, running her fingers over the striped pattern of its comforter. She'd taken a nap already today and couldn't convince her body to sleep anymore. She'd paced a great deal, and thought a great deal more, though she avoided lingering on the events at Helderschmidt's, or in that alleyway. She didn't feel *guilty*, exactly, but she did feel . . . No, she wouldn't think about it.

The priests would hate her now, wouldn't they? Even if they forgave the gold symbols embedded into her back. Was it all right to kill in self-defense, or if the person was a *really bad* person? She couldn't remember. Before her parents died, she'd only gone to the cathedral once a year. After they died, she and Anon had never had time. One of them was always working, and the other didn't want to go alone.

Stop thinking about it. Rone would know. She didn't think it would bother him if she asked a doctrinal question. If he was in a good mood.

He'd been gone so long . . . Instinct told Sandis he might not be in a good mood. But that was all right. She'd insist he have the bed, and she'd have dinner waiting for him . . . That would cheer him up, wouldn't it?

Standing, she leaned toward the window again. Searched the rooftops. Still no sign of him.

He's fine. His amarinth had reset, so he had ample protection. She'd seen him knock out five grafters before, including Galt.

Her stomach rumbled again.

Sighing, Sandis moved toward the door and looked out into an empty and carpeted hallway. Glad for something to do, she made her way toward the stairs. A tenant she passed on the second floor smiled at her. She smiled back, her hope garnering strength. There were still so many good people in Dresberg. So many. Perhaps Talbur Gwenwig was one of them. And maybe, after Rone got back, they could go to District Three and start searching. If the grafters were reeling the way Rone thought they were, then they needn't rush.

For the hundredth time, Sandis wondered what her great-uncle was like. Was he in good health or no? She wouldn't mind being his nurse. It would give him a good reason to keep her. To claim her.

As she started for the main floor, she smiled to herself. Perhaps he knew stories of her father, ones she'd never heard before. What if she'd met him as a child? He might even remember her. He could welcome her. She could have *family* again—

A middle-aged couple stood at the clerk's desk on the main floor; she watched them as she took the stairs down. She wasn't sure where the kitchen was. Should she ask the clerk? She didn't see the harm in it.

"Yes, for Jeris," the woman said. Her hair was especially light for a Kolin. Her husband was balding, and . . .

Sandis frowned as she reached the last steps. The man was balding, but he had terrible burn scars over the side of his face. They reached into his receding hairline and down into his collar. Recent ones, too, judging by the redness of them—

The man turned at the sound of her approach. Their eyes met.

Sandis froze.

The banker. The banker from before . . . from the last time Kazen had summoned Ireth. She recognized him. Her blood turned to ice.

She'd done that to him.

He recognized her, too, by the way his eyes widened.

Hunger forgotten, Sandis quickly turned around and raced back up the steps, hoping she'd misjudged his expression. Hoping he'd doubt himself. One of his eyes was nearly swollen shut . . . Perhaps he couldn't see very well. Perhaps he'd only stared because he was trying to clear his vision.

Oh Celestial . . . *she* had done that to him.

Her hands were shaking by the time she threw her shoulder into the door of Rone's room. She slammed it behind her. Pressed her back into it. Threw the small bar above the handle to lock it. Her dress caught on a fine splinter as she sank to the floor.

Though Sandis had some memories from housing Ireth, they were more like fleeting impressions. Feelings. Rooms, fire, sometimes screaming. Sometimes blood. Always sadness. She hated the sorrow more than anything else. But until now, she'd never confronted the realities of what Ireth was forced—through her—to do. Never before had she seen one of the people again in everyday life. Of course, until now, her everyday life had been spent underground.

Her heart pounded in her neck, head, chest, and hands. Her fingers went numb, and she rubbed them together to bring the feeling back. Cool sweat pricked her spine.

He's alive. That counts for something. She took a deep breath in, let a long breath out. *It wasn't you. It wasn't you. It wasn't Ireth, either. It was Kazen. It was Kazen who forced you both . . .*

Then why did she feel like her skin was trying to suck into her center? Turn her inside out?

She leapt to her feet. Paced to the window and back, window and back. Perhaps the man hadn't recognized her. Maybe it wasn't even him. She could be mistaken, and even if she wasn't, there was no knowing what he thought or remembered.

Ireth, are you there? She paused, hugging herself, trying to dig into her mind. Trying to send her thoughts into the ethereal plane, wherever it was. She closed her eyes. *Ireth?*

No impressions. No warmth. Sandis didn't entirely understand her bond with the fire horse, but she wished she could feel him more often. Send an impression of her own. Have a reminder that he was *there*.

Opening her eyes, she reached back and traced his name at the base of her neck. It had made no impression on her skin, unlike the brands, but she knew exactly where to find it. These were the sole Noscon characters she could read.

Pulling her fingers away, Sandis hurried for the window. Pressed both hands to the glass and searched high and low. *Please come back, Rone. Celestial, please protect him.*

She swallowed. Paced some more. Sat on the bed. Picked a hangnail.

Her stomach grumbled. She pulled her knees to her chest. Food could wait. Everything would be fine once Rone got back.

She stared out the window, at the glare the descending sun made against the faint scratches in the glass. The false set would happen soon—when the sun vanished behind the buildings and the wall, its rays all pointing upward, turning from yellow to orange. Then the true set, and the clouds and smog would turn pink and violet. Then violet would dull to blue and fade to black. And then the stars, somewhere Sandis couldn't see.

She let her thoughts focus on the sunset. She didn't get to see many of them anymore. Maybe it was a blessing, Rone's being late and her being alone in this room. It let her pause to appreciate the sky. She could be daring and open the window. Stick her head out and look up. Get a better view.

The yellow rays of the false set had begun to glimmer orange when someone kicked in her door, snapping the small lock right off the frame.

Sandis jumped off the bed and spun around, her hair whirling across her face and catching on her eyelashes.

Scarlet uniforms. Gold insignias of boats without sails.

The banker must have summoned them.

Sandis ran for the window.

"Grab her!" one of them yelled, and as Sandis's fingers brushed the sill, hands grabbed her right above the elbows and yanked her back. Her heel hit one of the bed feet. Another set of hands grabbed her shoulders and shoved her face down into the mattress, her mouth filling with cotton.

Someone yanked down her collar, revealing the topmost symbols of her script.

"This is her," another voice said darkly. "Disgusting. Cuffs!"

"No, please!" Sandis cried, then gasped when her shoulders jerked back and cool metal clapped around her wrists. "I didn't choose it, I swear! I didn't—"

"I'd watch what I said, if I were you." Her holders spun her around and brought her face-to-face with a man in his midfifties, short but wide. He had round gold buttons signifying rank across one shoulder. "You'll just incriminate yourself further."

Sandis shook her head, hot, wet trails running down her cheeks. "Please, you don't understand—"

The officer grabbed her by the back of the neck and steered her toward the door. Her holders easily obliged. "Take her to Gerech. These ones are dealt with swiftly."

"No!" Sandis screamed. She tried to throw her head back, to hit something, but her skull only collided with shoulders. She pushed her feet against the door frame, but the men holding her were too strong. They pushed her forward. Her ankle popped sharply, and her entire foot stung.

Two more uniformed men stood at the head of the stairs. They moved so unbelievably fast. She blinked, and she was on the second story.

"Rone!" she screamed, trying to wrench herself free. She couldn't feel her hands or forearms—the policemen gripped her so tightly they'd cut off the flow of blood. "Rone! Someone! I didn't choose it! I didn't want to do any of it!"

First floor. So many scarlet bodies. A flash of sunlight met her eyes, and then she was plunged into a wooden box. The hands released her, and a heavy door swung shut. One, two, three locks clicked into pace.

Sandis spun around. Her bound hands threw off her balance, and she fell onto her side. Wood panels surrounded her except for a narrow slit in the door. Narrow, and barred with wrought iron. Iron reinforced the panels in long strips.

A prison wagon. Celestial, she was in a *prison wagon*.

Sandis threw herself at the door, barely feeling the impact. "Rone!" She pressed her face to the slit. *"Rone!"*

The wagon jerked forward, throwing her off balance once more. She hit her head on the wagon wall. A horse whinnied, a whip cracked, and the vehicle accelerated and turned, throwing her into the other wall.

Blinking tears from her eyes, Sandis pulled against her cuffs. The chains held tight. She tried to get her hands in front of her, but the wagon jolted and she lost her balance again. Her shoulders burned. Her heartbeat sped to a high-pitched buzz.

She was going to prison. To Gerech. They were going to kill her.

"No, no, no, no, no, no." She righted herself on her knees and inched back toward the window. Leaned her head against the wood above it to keep herself upright. She couldn't go to Gerech. She couldn't die, not before she understood what Ireth wanted to tell her. Not before she stopped Kazen. Not before Rone—

Where was Rone? Was he safe? Was he still at Gerech? Maybe he hadn't yet used the amarinth . . .

The wagon turned again. Sandis's muscles strained as she leaned opposite to it, managing to stay on her knees. She had to get out. Had to.

Falling onto her back, Sandis rammed her feet into the door once, twice, three times, fighting the dull ache in her ankle. She used all the strength she had. Shimmied to the side and aimed her strikes at the locks. If she could just break them—

She pounded and pounded. The locks didn't budge. The door didn't offer so much as a splinter.

Her eyes stung—sweat? Pushing herself up again, Sandis scanned the walls around her—but of course they were secure. This was a prison wagon.

More tears blurred her vision. She crept back to the window. *Anyone, anyone . . . Celestial, please—*

She knew this street. Peering through the slit in the door, she watched the shops speed by, watched the faces of the curious people who glanced her way. They didn't know about Kazen, about Kolosos, and the Angelic had not heeded her warning. Would Rone spread the word? Would anyone protect them?

She tried to swallow, but her mouth was dry. The wagon turned, growing closer to the Innerchord. Closer to Gerech. There was nothing she could . . .

Ireth.

The thought was so loud it drained out the turning wheels, the heavy steps of the horses, the sounds of the city.

Could she summon Ireth? He was a powerful numen. He could certainly break out of this wagon.

But the last time Sandis had summoned—half summoned—him, she'd passed out. She couldn't run if she passed out. And if she ignited a prison wagon, she might as well light a beacon for any grafters, mobsmen, or policemen in the city. Kazen would find her for sure. How could he not? And what if there were innocent people crossing the street or passing the wagon? What if the flames caught them?

She squeezed her eyes shut, pushing sweat and tears from them. Opened them again. Searching the street passing under her. She tugged at her memory, making a map of Dresberg. Gerech . . . they'd turn soon, and—

The canal.

They would pass over one of the city's canals any minute now. This street bowed into a bridge to cross it. The water would put out the flames, and if the water's current was strong enough, maybe it could sweep her away. Do the running for her. She could swim, a little. Her father had taught her before he died.

But if Sandis lost consciousness . . .

Anon had drowned in a canal. Had it been this one?

She gritted her teeth. There was no other choice. Ireth, the canal . . . or Gerech. Death. She had to risk it. She had no time.

She chose.

Dropping onto her back, Sandis wrestled with her handcuffs, trying to get her feet over the chains so she could have partial use of her hands. She strained her shoulder doing so—cried out—but she got one over, then the other. Her hands were in front of her.

Now the timing. She pressed herself against the door. Stared out the window. She had to say the words fast. They had almost reached the canal—

Pressing her hand to her head, she sang, *"Vre en nestu a carnath. Ii mem entre I amar. Vre en nestu a carnath.*

"Ireth epsi gradenid!"

Flames like screams engulfed her.

They pierced like sharpened knives. She fell into the sun and kept falling, burning, wrenching apart—

The metal of her handcuffs dripped bright and molten from her wrists. The wrought iron of the wagon whined like a dying horse—and then it blew apart, blasting her into the canal.

The water hit her like acid.

It sizzled around her ears, and quicker than a gasp, the flames were doused, extinguished. There was water and cold and no air, no air—

Sandis's head burst from the surface. She gasped, even as the current tried to drag her under. The canal spun around her. Darkness edged her vision.

Stay awake. Stay awake!

She submerged. Tried to kick with the current, but her legs were leaden weights. Her body barely felt like hers. The black crept into her eyes like bleeding capillaries.

Her hand hit the concrete wall of the canal. She pushed herself up. Broke the surface again. Gasped for air.

Somehow, she managed to roll onto her back. It made it easier to stay afloat, to breathe, though the cold water continued to splash onto her face. Trash hit her shoulder and stuck for a moment before breaking away. The sky was fragmented, made of sand. Her eyes rolled back—

Water filled her nose and mouth. Sandis sputtered. Tried to swim. The current sucked at her heavy limbs. She hit the side of the canal, and the water pushed her up. Let her cough and gasp for a moment before dragging her down again.

This was how Anon died.

Her vision blinked black. She forced it to gray. *Stay awake. Celestial, let me stay awake. Help me. Help me!*

Her body slammed into metal grating.

She grasped at it, though her fingers felt fat and numb. The hands of a corpse. The canal waters surged into a tunnel and dropped into the sewers, but rusted grating barred the way, keeping out trash and bodies.

Her grip slipped—she grappled with her other hand. Her feet. It was like holding on to the surface of a mirror. Her muscles had no strength. The water pressed her against the grate, and Sandis managed to shove a hand through the crossing bars high enough to keep her head above water. To breathe.

Blackness trickled across her sight. Dark spots when she blinked. Eyelids like anvils. *No. Stay awake.* How far had she gotten? This grate . . . They'd find her if she couldn't get past this grate—

Her hand slipped from the bars. Water sucked her dead weight toward the canal bottom.

Chapter 19

Sandis's pale hand slipped under the water's surface. Two seconds later and he wouldn't have seen it. Wouldn't have known.

He was losing her.

"Sandis!" Rone shouted. He dived into the cold water, shoes and all. The grate had stopped her. Thank the Celestial, the grate had stopped her.

The canal turned black as he reached the bottom, but Sandis's pale foot beckoned to him. He grabbed her ankle and jerked her toward his chest. Got his arm under her shoulder. Kicked off the concrete and sailed for the surface.

He broke free and sucked hot air into his lungs.

He'd seen officers outside the inn. A prison wagon turn the corner. He'd nearly fallen to his death entering their room through the window instead of the door.

The room had been empty, trampled. One look and he knew.

He'd never run so fast in his life. But the cart was faster.

Right up until it burst into fire.

The flames shot three stories high, blinding and bright like a piece of sun had fallen from the heavens. They'd destroyed the carriage, its driver, and the attending scarlets, maybe the horses. Taken out part of the bridge.

Though Sandis had surely caused the fire, she hadn't been there. Ashes, glowing iron, and smoldering wood, but no Sandis.

He'd followed the canal. Thank God he'd followed the canal.

He had to stretch and leap through the water to reach the edge of the canal. Almost couldn't pull himself up with her weight added to his, but he wouldn't let her go. His heart felt twice its normal size, and he heaved, got an elbow on the lip, a knee. Dragged her with him.

She wasn't breathing. The color of her lips, the stillness of her body—it all warned of death.

"No. Sandis." He shook her. How long had she been under? Since the bridge? Then she was dead, she was—

A pulse. Her neck pulsed warm, weak.

He turned her over and beat his fist against her back. "Breathe. Breathe. Breathe." He hit her harder, between bare shoulder blades. A little water spurted from her mouth, but she didn't take in any air.

Cursing, Rone shifted her onto her back and, despite the possibility of passersby, jerked the amarinth out of his pocket and forced her cold fingers around its loops. Grabbed her limp hand and forced her to spin it.

For a second, he thought he was too late. Then water fountained out of her mouth as the magic squeezed her lungs.

The sound of her cough was wet, raw, and desperate. The sound of air entering her lungs was heavenly.

He pulled her upright, holding her against his chest, barely registering her nudity. She was dead weight. A doll. "Sandis?"

Her eyes fluttered open, dark and unfocused. "I knew . . . you'd come," she whispered. Then her brown orbs rolled back, and she was gone.

Rone stubbed his finger grappling for the hidden latch under the brick wall of the alleyway. His undershirt clung to him, both from perspiration and canal water. Sandis wore his shirt and nothing else, though he was more concerned about concealing her script than her nudity.

The hidden door swung inward, and Rone pushed his way into the dark hallway, knocking something off a shelf as he did. He kicked the door shut behind him. He was certain no one had followed him, despite the bounteous stares he had collected on the way. His arms were numb clamps around Sandis's shoulders and knees. His bad shoulder, which hadn't ached the slightest since Helderschmidt's, throbbed from carrying Sandis's weight for so long.

It didn't take long for Arnae Kurtz to come to the secret room in the back of his flat. Rone wasn't exactly being quiet, and the man kept late hours.

The door to the rest of the flat opened on soundless hinges, and the light from Kurtz's kerosene lamp spilled over them as Rone kicked a bedroll off a low shelf.

"Rone Comf." His old master's voice was stiff and low. "You cannot come back here."

"I had no other choice. Help me."

Kurtz frowned, but he set the lamp aside and knelt at the side of the bedroll, unfurling it. Rone carefully laid Sandis on the blankets. She was so still, her breaths small and deep like she lingered in the throes of a very long dream.

Kurtz looked her over, his brows tightening. "What happened?"

"She fell into the canal. The scarlets found her at the inn we were staying at and arrested her. She blew herself out." The evidence said as much.

Kurtz looked at him with wide eyes. "The numen?"

Rone nodded without explaining.

Frowning, Kurtz pressed his fingers into Sandis's neck, sides, legs. "Nothing broken. But if she's been unconscious so long, there may be brain damage."

Rone dropped to his knees by Sandis's head. "No. This happens, when she summons. She's always out for a while."

"I see."

The silence grew stiff between them.

Kurtz sat back on his heels. "You know I want to help you, Rone, but it's too dangerous for you to stay here. Other people rely on me, on that door. If the grafters, or even the scarlets, find this place, I won't be the only one in trouble."

"I don't think I was followed." He knew better than to hope they weren't being sought after by both grafters and the law, but there was a chance, however slim, the scarlets thought Sandis was dead.

"The fact still stands."

Rone nodded. He was completely drained—he could barely hold up his head. "Just tonight. I didn't know where else to take her."

Kurtz let out a long breath through his nose. Nodded. "Tonight."

"I have two places left to check for a job, then—"

"Be careful, Rone." Kurtz's dark eyes bored into his. For a moment Rone thought he would get a lecture, or a quoted verse from some book he'd never heard of, but Kurtz merely repeated, "Be careful."

Rone nodded.

Kurtz pushed himself off the floor and stood, his knees popping when he did. He rolled his head before adding, "There's wurst and potatoes on the stove."

Kurtz left the kerosene lamp in the room and closed the door behind him. He always kept it closed. One never knew what visitors he might get at the front of the house. Rone could only hope none came on account of him and Sandis.

His body was too exhausted to eat. Even the thought of standing and walking into Kurtz's kitchen filled him with dread. So he turned to the shelves and grabbed another bedroll. There were six altogether. He absently wondered who else had used these, and how recently.

A dull ache bent his elbows as he unfurled the bundle beside Sandis, then promptly collapsed atop it. They both smelled like canal water, undoubtedly. He should probably extinguish the lamp. Or he could let it burn out and refund the cost to Kurtz later. That sounded like the better option. He couldn't keep an eye on Sandis in the dark.

Rone rolled over to face her. He watched the rise and fall of her chest, waiting for it to stop, to hitch, but it continued on in a steady rhythm. The relief he felt, watching it move so steadily, coiled in his belly, warm and with an unfamiliar weight. He listened to each intake of her breath and found himself matching it.

If he had come back right after Gerech, she wouldn't have had to face this alone. He could have protected her.

God's tower, she must have been terrified.

"I knew you'd come."

Had she really?

Rone watched her face. The curve of her nose, the high set of her cheekbones. Her hair was mostly dry and fell around her face in a tangled, beautiful mess. He reached out a sore arm and smoothed some of it back. Her skin was warm, but not feverish. Soft. Smooth. Magnetic.

He rested his hand on her shoulder, then trailed it past the hem of her sleeve to her elbow. How could anyone take a brand to skin like that?

"Like every fiber of your body is being torn apart. Like it's burning up, but the fuel never runs out. Like you're twisting into something else."

He should have been there. He *wanted* to have been there.

Pressing his lips together, Rone scooted onto the line where their two bedrolls met. Moved his hand beneath Sandis's back and pulled her close. He rested his chin on top of her head. Closed his eyes.

He thought he felt Sandis's fingers clutch the fabric of his undershirt just as sleep pulled him under.

Rone woke feeling gritty and impossibly sore. His eyes and mouth were dry, and his throat begged for water. His arm was stretched out in a weird way and half-numb, reminding him of the weight that had been there when he'd fallen asleep. But she was gone, her bedroll made. There was some clinking behind the door, voices—straining to listen, Rone recognized the higher voice as Sandis's and let out a long breath.

She was fine. Still breathing. Still alive.

He groaned as he sat up, the muscles of his back, shoulders, and arms pulling in all the wrong ways. He managed to rub some kinks from his neck, at least. The fabric of his pants was stiff and rough, reminding him of his sewage days. His shirt was . . . not there.

Setting his jaw and thinking his usual string of morning obscenities, Rone got his feet under him and shuffled to the door that connected this secret space to the rest of Kurtz's flat. He opened it, and the way the sunlight hit his eyes made him feel like he had a hangover.

"Rone!"

Her voice woke him from his daze. He blinked light from his eyes and found her sitting on a stool across an island countertop from Kurtz, who looked at him with a weirdly knowing smile.

Sandis hopped off the stool, peppy and healthy and very much alive. She wore a new dress, one that fit her better than the last. Simple and dark. Her umber hair was combed out and pinned behind her ears.

She was stunning.

"I'm so glad you're awake. Here." She grabbed a bowl at the end of the counter—some sort of porridge—and set it in front of the stool closest to him. She beamed like she was presenting him with the key to Gerech. Then she returned to her seat and grabbed a piece of parchment Rone hadn't noticed before—a torn map of Dresberg, with pencil scribbles all over District Three.

Rone sat, grunting as he discovered sore muscles in his backside. The porridge smelled like cinnamon and was slightly overcooked, but two still-warm spoonfuls made it down his throat without complaint.

Sandis set the map next to his bowl. "I've been talking to Arnae about Talbur. I think we should cover the most ground in the mornings—Kazen always slept in the mornings. The others probably do, too, I think. And we'll be far from the canal."

Her words slowed for a moment. Why? Was she thinking about her close call with the scarlets? About Kazen and the numina? About nearly drowning? It was probably guilt over the scarlets.

He almost said, *They're not good people, either,* but Sandis's energy quickly returned, taking away any chance to speak. She pointed at the north border of the city. "I think we should start here. There's a mortgage broker . . ." She searched the map, then replanted her finger down and to the east. ". . . here. Arnae said that might be a good place to start. If Talbur had or has a mortgage in one of the richer neighborhoods, they might have record of him there. Trick is getting the brokers to tell us—"

"Whoa, all right, slow down." Rone let his spoon sink into his porridge. He gave his old master a pointed look. "You want her to steal brokerage records?" It wasn't a bad place to start. Maybe they'd luck out. Rone could be pleading with this man for money by the end of the day. Or, if necessary, stealing it from him in the morning.

Kurtz lifted his hands in mock innocence. "I said nothing of the sort."

"It can't hurt to ask," Sandis said.

Rone studied the map and nodded.

Sandis grinned wider than he'd ever seen her grin. "I can help with our funds, a little. Arnae said he would pay me to clean the flat—"

"She is *not* your maid." Rone stared hard at Kurtz, who merely shrugged. Rone took a deep breath and wiped his hand down his face. "Yes, we can try. I need to check two more places for work today first." *Maybe* he'd find the answer to his problems there and avoid a possible dead end with Talbur Gwenwig. "If I can get a job, we'll be set for the immediate future."

Sandis nodded. "I'll pay you back for everything, Rone. I promise—"

He raised a hand to stop her. "You don't have to pay me back. All this exercise has made me the fittest I've ever been."

Kurtz snorted. Sandis glanced at his bare chest and looked away just as quickly, the slightest flush of pink dusting her cheeks.

Rone smirked and took another bite of porridge. "I want to check my drop-off points soon, which means going in daylight." He hesitated. "It will be easier if I go alone."

Something flashed in Sandis's eyes, but it quickly vanished. She nodded and turned to Kurtz. "Do you mind if . . . ?"

The old man nodded. "You may stay here one more night, Sandis. But after that . . ." He frowned.

Sandis smiled like it was her profession. The gesture still carried her usual sincerity.

"I should go now." Rone scooped the last of the porridge into his mouth, swallowed, and slipped off the stool. "If I don't change, people will think I'm in hard times and sniffing around for coin."

"Good plan." His old master sounded more amused than anything.

Rone ignored the tone and nodded his thanks. "I won't be long." He glanced at Sandis once more before grabbing his magically laundered shirt off the edge of the counter, slipping it on, and stepping outside.

Rone didn't bother with the rooftops today—he honestly didn't think he was spry enough to safely navigate them, and the amarinth hadn't reset, though it weighed down his right pocket as usual. He took a winding route through Kurtz's neighborhood and stole a hooded jacket from a laundry basket on someone's porch. He slipped it on—it smelled like vinegar and was a couple sizes too big—and pulled up the hood. The morning hour was cool; he didn't look out of place.

Normally, with his funds nearly depleted, he wouldn't hire a cab. But he had a long ways to go for drop-off point one, and though his morning walk had loosened his muscles, he'd said he wouldn't be long. He didn't want to keep Sandis waiting, again, even though she was in good hands.

So he hired a grubby-looking *closed* carriage pulled by two under-weight horses and rode it north, into the very district Sandis had been mapping out earlier. He hopped off, wound around some tightly knit buildings and storage sheds to the checkpoint: another manhole cover. Lifted it, but there was nothing, not even a string to denote a message had been there and fallen away. He usually checked these things once a week; he was behind schedule.

Trying not to dwell on another failure, Rone walked in the wrong direction toward the nearest market, which was bustling with morning activity. He stuck to the outskirts of the booths and shops until he found a distributor heading east with a half-empty wagon. He jogged to catch up to it, then carefully hoisted himself onto the back so the drivers wouldn't feel the wagon shake. Fortunately, they didn't look back. Rone made it most of the way to his last location before a street rat tried to hitch a free ride next to him. The drivers felt that one, noticed them, and yelled at them to get off. Rone did so and hurried down the first offshoot road he found, letting himself get lost in the tangles of yet more low-income housing before winding his way back to a main street. Rone didn't feel like he was being followed, and nothing looked suspicious when he glanced over his shoulder, but one could never be too careful.

His destination was a run-down restaurant that nevertheless managed to stay in business year after year, despite its fallen shutters and obvious rat problem. The poor couldn't afford to care. Rone shook his head as he wrapped around to the back of the restaurant, toward some underway construction. What were they fitting into the tiny lot back here? More housing? More storage? Could this city really get any denser?

Chewing on the inside of his lip, Rone put his back to the restaurant, checked for watching eyes, then reached into a sagging eave. Dirt left by the rain smudged his fingers, and—

His breath hitched.

A note.

He pulled it free. Resisted the urge to read it then and there, and palmed the thing, walking too quickly to be casual through windy backroads. He passed a mother switching her whining son and turned the corner, where he sat on the porch of a tall but narrow apartment building. He unfolded the note. The paper was thick and white—someone with money to spare had left it.

> *Mr. Verlad,*
> *I have a proposition for you that I think you'll find*
> *intriguing. Meet me at your soonest possible convenience,*
> *day or night. It doesn't matter to me.*

Following the tight script was lettered nonsense, but Rone was familiar with the code. It couldn't be too obvious, else a lucky passerby might turn the note in to the scarlets for a reward.

The address wasn't close. Not as far as it could be in a city this size, but not close. Shoving the note into his pocket, next to the amarinth, Rone hunted for a decent drainpipe and climbed.

Miraculously, his body didn't feel sore anymore.

The address did not take him to a residence, but a small office space that was a single story tall. It was wedged between a much larger building and a set of lavish flats. That gave him courage. He usually didn't meet his clients in the light of day, and only sometimes did he dare to do so with his face uncovered.

He walked in. The place was simple and clean, though the architecture and style were outdated. There was actually a thriving plant in the back corner, near a narrow desk where a secretary sat, her hair pulled into a wide bun and a pair of black spectacles balanced on her nose. Her clothing was fine, and she even wore rouge and lipstick. She was paid well, then.

She looked up and studied Rone. Possibly smelled him, though she didn't make a face. "There are no appointments booked this week. Might I assume you found the note?"

Rone simply nodded.

The secretary stood and gestured to a door behind her. "Down this way, Mr. Verlad. Follow the scent of cigar smoke."

Rone opened the door and found a dark, narrow set of stairs ahead of him. Thirteen in all. He reached the basement, which was cold and smelled like mildew. He had a feeling this place was a temporary holding for this client.

The cigar smoke wasn't hard to detect; it was spicy and full, richer than what was usually smoked in taverns and bars. Rone followed its trail on silent feet, clutching the amarinth. One client who'd hired him had done so to ruin his life; he might need to fight his way out.

But he needed the money.

Two bright lamps lit the room. It had two simple chairs and a desk piled with ledgers and paperwork. An apple core sat on the corner.

The man behind the desk had thinning brown hair receding from his forehead, a large nose, and wide-set eyes. His clothes were simple but well tailored, his collar stiff. He wasn't thin, which meant he ate well. The amount of wrinkles on his face—especially his forehead—put him in his sixties.

He puffed out a cloud of smoke and looked up from his work, completely unsurprised, despite Rone's near-perfect silence. "You're quick," he said, a slight rasp to his baritone.

"Your location coincided with my schedule," he lied. His hood was still up, and his hands weighed down his pockets, one still clasping the amarinth. Rone didn't lean on the door frame, but stood tall and imposing.

The man gestured to a chair. "Do take a seat, Engel. I have something that might interest you."

"I prefer to stand, Mr. . . . ?"

"My name is not important."

Rone frowned. "And yet you know mine."

The man barked a laugh. "Do you expect me to believe that you are stupid enough to use your real name, let alone that a name such as Engel Verlad really exists? What hopeful mother would name her son after angels and truths?"

Rone didn't let his irritation show, but his fingers twitched in his pockets. He remained standing. "Tell me your proposition."

The man pushed his chair back a fraction and set his elbows on the desk, steepling his fingers. "It's a transportation job. And simple, for you, since you already have the item."

Rone stiffened, the golden ribbons of the amarinth pinching his hand.

"Her name is Sandis Gwenwig."

Rone didn't have a chance to hide the surprise on his face, but he killed it quickly. Breathed deeply to calm his pulse and voice. "I am acquainted with the vessel."

His spine itched.

The man made a knowing sound. "Then you may be acquainted with her owners."

Rone let himself glower. Who was this man? He didn't look like a grafter, yet he knew about Sandis. Had Kazen hired him? Galt? Someone else?

The man continued when Rone didn't reply. "I'm willing to offer you ten thousand kol to deliver her to these coordinates tomorrow night." He pulled a folded paper from his pocket and slid it across the desk.

Rone set his jaw, though his pulse jumped at the number. *Ten thousand?* Would that be enough to bribe his mother out of Gerech? It had to be. His mother's salvation was sitting on the other side of that desk.

His eyes dropped to the paper. *Sandis.* He couldn't. He couldn't wrap her up like some trophy and drop her off to the men she'd been running from this whole time. The men who had taken her freedom. And this *Kolosos* thing . . . If she was right about that, it wouldn't just affect her.

No, he couldn't do that to her.

Her smile from that morning burned in his thoughts. She'd been so happy to see him. So excited to start looking for her great-uncle again. So . . . hopeful.

There had to be another way. Another job. Something would come up.

The ball in his gut eddied, printing the name of his mother into his stomach lining.

He shook his head, repeated his affirmation out loud, "No," and started to turn.

"I'm not finished with you, Verlad."

He paused. Sized up the man. He could take him out easily. *Hurt* him easily. What did he know, and how could Rone use it against him? What was his connection to Kazen?

"I had a feeling you wouldn't be swayed. I'm prepared to raise the price."

Rone narrowed his eyes. "What's your motivation? You're no grafter."

The man frowned. "My reason is my own. For a man in your line of work, you certainly ask a lot of questions."

Rone's chest tightened. "No," he repeated.

He'd made it one step past the door frame when the man said, "Your mother is in Gerech, is she not?"

Rone snarled. "You keep your nose out of it unless you want me to rip—"

"Have you visited her recently? She has a date set."

Rone's skeleton turned to ice as the man's words registered. Puffing on his cigar, the man opened a drawer and pulled out a paper sitting on top of whatever else sat in there. No doubt he'd placed it there to make the moment more dramatic. He read over it. "Mm, yes, the fourteenth. That's, what, three days from now? It would be immediate, I imagine, but the line for the executioner's block gets so long at that place, you know. She has to wait her turn, just like everyone else."

Rone's fingers trembled. His underarms and hairline began to perspire. "You're lying."

The man turned the paper around and held it out so Rone could read it. His mother's name. Her prisoner number. The signature of the warden. The *fourteen*, right there in bold, blocky letters.

Three days.

They were going to kill her. The ball in his gut doubled in size. His mom was going to hang for a simple theft. For *his* simple theft.

Three days.

Rone backed away from the edict like it was fire.

"Give me Sandis, and you'll get her out." The man tucked the paper away.

Rone grabbed a handful of hair. Time was up. He couldn't wait any longer. His free hand drifted to his pocket.

The amarinth.

The time had come. He would sell it; he had to. Even so, he couldn't ignore that it wouldn't solve all his problems. The grafters . . . the grafters would still be after him. After Sandis. After *his mother*. Could he do that to her? Could he pull her into a life of squalor and crime, where Kazen, his lackeys, or his vessels could kill her at any moment?

But if he forfeited Sandis, everything would return to the way it had been. There would be no more running. No more fear.

His stomach cramped at the thought. Sandis's smile radiated behind his eyelids.

The man tapped his cigar on the side of an ashtray. "Fifteen thousand, and papers out of Kolingrad. For you *and* your mother."

Rone stopped breathing.

Papers. Out of Kolingrad.

The man likely offered the papers as a further selling point—emigration documentation sold for incredible prices in the underground. Rone could sell a single set and retire. It was *that* hard to leave this miserable place. People surrendered their entire life earnings just to see the other side of those mountains.

This man could hardly know it, but Rone wanted emigration papers more than anything else.

He turned back. Licked his teeth behind his lips. His voice was hoarse when he spoke. "And I'm to believe you have access to such things?"

"I do." He spoke with such confidence. "Believe me, Engel, I am a trustworthy man. But you won't receive any of your rewards until the vessel is delivered. I won't have you toting her to Godobia and running away from us."

Rone's stomach sank to his knees. Shivers coursed up and down his limbs. Two sets of emigration papers. Fifteen thousand . . . that would be enough to get his mother out of prison, *both* of them out of Kolingrad, and for them to start a new life in the south. A new, better life, without the crowds and the pollution and the constant reminders that they'd been abandoned by one of the country's most powerful men.

But Sandis—

"Kazen won't let you put a hole in me."

She'd said it herself. He wouldn't hurt her, right? He wanted Ireth back. Sandis was a strong vessel—God's tower, she could summon on *herself.* She was valuable. Fifteen thousand and two sets of emigration documents valuable.

She'd always have clothing and food. She wouldn't have to hide anymore. And this Kolosos she talked about . . . the Angelic hadn't been concerned about it. He of all people should know. If he wasn't concerned, then maybe there was no cause to be.

The man scratched the side of his nose. "Your dear mother will be—"

"Shut up." His finger twitched. He balled his hands into fists.

Sandis's smile. Her thank-yous, her skin—

He'd done his part, hadn't he? And his mother . . . his mother's imprisonment was *his* fault. He owed this to her! If he didn't do something, she was going to *die.* The parent who hadn't abandoned him, who had never given up on him, would die. There was no other way to get her out, to get her to safety.

Rone's mind spun for another solution, but he couldn't see one. The numbers didn't add up. The *money* didn't add up. Even if they miraculously found Talbur Gwenwig *today*, he didn't *know* the man would have the money, let alone if he'd be willing to lend it. And the amarinth—there wasn't enough time to find a good buyer, to prove the thing's usefulness, to clear the withdrawals from the bank . . . and even if he could miraculously make it all work, then what? They'd still be trapped in this horrid city, Rone without work and Ernst Renad always lurking in the shadows, seeking revenge.

Releasing the amarinth, Rone reached forward. Took the folded paper with the designated address scrawled on it. He knew the place. A few miles from where Sandis had incinerated half a dozen men.

She was dangerous . . . She couldn't ever truly be free, not with those marks permanently marring her skin. What other solution was there, logically speaking? She'd be caught eventually, whether by the grafters, the police, or the priests. Maybe it was safest for her to go back to the underground lair. Better for her.

"Engel." The man's voice was firm, impatient.

Rone crumpled the paper in his fist. Ground his teeth until they squeaked. Took in a deep breath. Met the man's eyes.

"She won't be hurt?"

The man offered a simple nod.

"I'll do it."

Chapter 20

"Whip your hand against the inside of my forearm—yes, like that—then turn your wrist over and grab me."

Sandis stood off-center in the secret room in Arnae Kurtz's sizeable flat, her back to the shelves. Arnae had his arm extended toward her, as if he meant to grab her but had stopped before reaching her neck. Sandis tried to imagine his fingers were Kazen's, long and pale, crooked like spider legs. His veins raised and half-hidden by a black sleeve.

I will be stronger than you.

She lifted her arm, too, then twisted it around to grab his.

"Yes, good. Now pull it down and do what I showed you before. Here." He pointed to the space where his neck met his shoulder.

Sandis pulled Arnae's wrist toward her hip and brought her other hand forward, flat, and aimed for his neck. She hit him, but not hard. He was not her enemy.

Arnae pulled back and smiled. "Yes, just like that. But twenty times faster and fifty times harder."

Sandis gave him a bashful smile. "I don't want to hurt you."

"Ha!" the seugrat master barked. "You couldn't if you wanted to, child."

She didn't correct him on that point, merely nodded and raised her fists. "All right, again."

Arnae reached for her, and Sandis repeated the motions, pushing his hand away and striking hers gently against his neck. She grinned. This felt like something that might work in real life. After she had cleaned the flat and helped cook dinner, Arnae had offered to teach her some self-defense, since Rone was out late again.

"One more time," Arnae said, but as he reached for her, the secret door opened and let in a burst of smoky air. Sandis's heart thumped at the same time relief fountained to her shoulders and down her arms. Rone was hale and whole. She was sure half the reason Arnae was teaching her was to distract her.

She hurried to the end of the hall at the same time Rone reached it. The sallow look on his face wasn't good. "No luck?"

He blinked, as if noticing her for the first time. "What? No. I mean, yes."

But his expression didn't match his words. His eyes were dull, his shoulders droopy. "You got work?"

"Yeah. In a couple of days. It will . . . We'll be taken care of."

There was no excitement in his voice. No hope. Sandis hugged herself, suddenly cold. "And your mother?"

His brow twitched. "Yes. I think it will help her, too."

Was there something he wasn't sharing? Had so much happened that he'd lost faith?

Sandis took his hand and squeezed his fingers; they were cool to the touch. "That's good news, Rone." She paused. "Are you all right? Did something happen?" Her heart fell. "It's not a terrible job, is it?"

"They're all terrible jobs." He pushed past her into the room, where the bedrolls still lay in the corner. An evasion, or simple weariness?

He wore a new jacket. Sandis decided not to ask where he'd gotten it.

Arnae folded his arms. "You seem dejected, boy."

Rone shook his head. "I'm just tired. I was all over the city today." He collapsed into a sitting position on his bedroll and cradled his head in his hands.

"We saved you some dinner." Sandis glanced at Arnae to make sure it was all right for them to enter his side of the flat. He nodded, and she hurried to the stove to retrieve the chicken and potatoes there. She set the plate before Rone on his bedroll.

He sighed, avoiding her gaze. "Thank you."

She hadn't done something wrong, had she? Her mind whisked back through the day. No . . . he'd been fine when he left this morning.

He's just tired, she told herself. *Like he said.*

It had been an easy day for her, but a wearying one for him. She'd repay him for all his efforts after they found Talbur. After she built herself a new foundation and discovered a way to thwart Kazen once and for all.

Let it work out. Please, she silently prayed. *I know I'm not worthy, but I'll never bother you again if you just let this work out.*

"Tomorrow, Rone," Arnae said.

Rone nodded. "We'll be gone." He took a bite, chewed, swallowed. Hesitated. "There's actually a decent place we can hide out. Found it today, but it won't be vacant until tomorrow night. It's a little ways from here."

"I don't mind," Sandis tried, wishing he would smile. Or tease her. Or curse. He seemed so beside himself. But of course he was exhausted. He'd swum the canal for her, probably carried her all the way here himself. Jumped all over Dresberg to find work to sustain *her.* Sandis hadn't done anything but clean and learn a few self-defense moves.

Her bones grew heavy. "Thank you for everything you do, Rone," she said softly. "I don't know where I'd be without you. Thank you so much."

Rone winced and touched his cheek—he must have bitten it. "It's no problem, Sandis. I'd have to do it anyway."

Arnae hummed deep in his throat. "Well, it's late. I'm retiring. Try not to ruin me before your departure, hm?"

Sandis turned around. "Thank you."

He smiled at her and left, shutting the door firmly behind him.

Sandis rubbed sleep from her eyes—it *was* late—but climbed onto her bedroll and asked, "Where did you go?"

"Lots of places. Back and forth."

"Do you want some water?"

Rone was chewing, so he couldn't answer. Sandis filled a cup from the pitcher Arnae had left in the corner and handed it to him. Briefly recounted her day.

Rone finished his plate and set it aside, then lay down, crossing his arms over his face to block out the light.

"I can turn off the lamp—"

"It's fine, Sandis."

She frowned. Watched him breathe. Let her eyes trace the breadth of his shoulders and the narrowness of his hips. "Do you want a bath . . . ?"

"Not right now."

Her chest tightened. This wasn't simply fatigue. Couldn't be. "I'm sorry, Rone."

He lifted one arm and looked at her with one eye. "For what?"

She hugged her knees to her chest. "For being such a burden. For causing all of this."

But he shook his head and dropped his arm. "You're not a burden, Sandis."

She licked her lips. "But you're so . . . stressed."

Rone dropped both his arms and propped himself on his elbow. "Not because of you. You're fine. You're wonderful, all right? I'm not angry with you. Just . . ." He shook his head. "I'm spent today."

She smiled. *Wonderful.* Nodded.

She snuffed the kerosene lantern, then felt her way back to bed. Lay down and watched the ceiling until her eyes adjusted to the darkness and she could make out the rafters. There were no windows in the room, only a sliver of light coming from beneath the door that led to Arnae's flat.

Rolling onto her side, she watched Rone, though she could barely differentiate him from the floorboards. His heat radiated through his clothes. He smelled like rivers and smoke and cigars, oddly enough. She liked the smells. They were familiar. Masculine.

He sat up and pulled off his jacket, tossing it somewhere in the darkness. Lay back down. Sighed.

Sandis reached forward and pinched the fabric of his shirt between her fingers. "It will work out, Rone. We'll find Talbur, and everything will work out. We'll help your mother, too. I'll do whatever it takes, I promise."

He grimaced. Why? "You don't owe me anything, Sandis."

"You've saved my life. Multiple times—"

"You've done the same. We're even."

She let go of his shirt. Let her hand fall on the bedroll beside him. After a moment, he reached over and took it in his. A thrill passed through her fingers and up her arm until it danced in her jaw.

He rubbed his thumb over her knuckle. "I'm sorry," he whispered.

"For what?"

Rone dropped her hand. "Just . . ."

He didn't finish the thought.

Tugging on a smidgeon of bravery, Sandis scooted herself over until Rone's heat blanketed her. Carefully, almost so he wouldn't feel it, she rested her head on his chest.

His arm circled around her, pulling her close.

Closing her eyes, Sandis smiled into the darkness and let herself sink into him. Listened to his too-quick heartbeat. Set her hand against his stomach.

This. If this peaceful, happy moment could only last forever . . . She felt sure, as Rone's pulse slowly calmed and his breathing evened, that this was what heaven had to be like. Warm and safe. A place where she belonged, with people she loved. This was bliss. This was *family*.

It was all falling into place. Soon she'd find Talbur, and the three of them would free Rone's mother and find some way to thwart Kazen, and she'd have Rone and family and belonging, and her time with Kazen would become but a memory on the wind, easily forgotten. She was so close she could feel it thrumming beneath her skin, even as she fell asleep.

The amarinth spun.

At first it made its usual whirring noise, but it got louder and louder, until it sounded like a whistle. An alarm. A scream.

Sandis stood in front of it, out of body, watching the golden ribbons spin faster and faster until she couldn't see them at all. Instcad, the center of the artifact transfixed her. It glowed white, so brilliant it hurt Sandis's eyes to look at it, but she couldn't pull herself away. Louder, faster, brighter.

She felt him there, fiery and desperate. This wasn't her dream; it was his. Ireth's.

What is it? She tried to shout, but she had no voice, no body. *What are you trying to show me?*

She remembered the sensations she'd felt at Helderschmidt's, staring at the amarinth. *But what does this have to do with anything?*

The amarinth's center flashed like the sun, leaving in its wake darkness lit by a single glowing eye.

Ireth's fear threatened to smother her.

She needed to know.

She thought about the dream and the amarinth as she stared at the floorboards, waiting for Rone to come out of his bath in Arnae's side of the flat. She didn't understand the visions. What was Ireth trying to say? The sole connection she could fathom was that the amarinth was of Noscon make and the numina were Noscon magic—at least, the astral sphere that mapped the numina was Noscon. That sphere helped summoners navigate the ethereal plane, though she didn't understand how. Could it also help her learn more about Ireth?

Was there something else?

The door opened, and Rone stepped in fully clothed, his hair still wet and his feet bare. There was something vulnerable about him like that, something that warmed Sandis deep within her core.

She considered telling him about her dream. But he had been so strained lately, and right now he looked more himself. She didn't want to ruin his mood. She owed him so much.

He grabbed his shoes from the middle of the floor, where his bed-roll had been before Sandis tucked it away. "Ready?" he asked.

Sandis nodded and stood, brushing off her skirt and stepping into the shoes Arnae had gifted her. That was another person she'd need to repay—Arnae. He'd been so kind to her. In a few years, when this part of her story was over, maybe she'd be able to visit him with her remu-nerations at his front door. Wouldn't that be something?

Please protect him, Celestial. Please don't let our errors put him in evil's path.

Her stomach growled.

Rone smiled. "Don't worry, I'll take care of that."

She pressed her hand to her belly to quiet it. "Arnae said we could open one of the jars of pickles—"

He made a face. "Pickles? For breakfast?"

"He said it'd be better to eat them before they expire—"

"Sandis." He stomped his foot into one shoe, then pulled on the other one. "Let's get something *good* to eat. Just this once."

His gaze made her stomach forget its emptiness and flutter instead. Reality tamped down the feeling. "We should be careful. The grafters—"

"Are still reeling. We'll head into the safest part of town. I'm not worried."

He didn't look at her when he said that. There was something unnatural about his nonchalance, but Sandis was likely overthinking things. So she nodded, and when he smiled at her, she smiled back. Her muscles loosened. Rone was just being Rone, and her dream was just a dream . . . for now. If only she could summon Ireth for longer, somewhere it wouldn't cause a fuss, perhaps she would learn . . . But no, she shouldn't think of that. Not now.

Arnae had left the house early that morning, so Sandis was unable to say goodbye to him. She wanted to leave a note, but her penmanship was terrible, and she figured it was safer for him if she left as little evidence as possible of her presence in this place. She wouldn't come back. She'd promised herself she wouldn't come back, not until the grafters were off her trail for good. She wouldn't do anything to hurt this kind man, or the others who had benefited from his generosity.

Rone cracked the hidden door open, surveyed the area, then took Sandis's hand and quickly pulled her through, shutting the bricked passage behind him. He held her hand as he led the way to the road, whereupon he released it suddenly. He drew into himself, hunching his shoulders. Hiding? But Sandis didn't see anything remotely suspicious around them. He buried his hands into his pockets, so Sandis placed hers on the crook of his arm. His lip twitched; then he set his jaw to hide whatever emotion had tried to show itself to her.

It hurt her more than it should have, but she pushed the pain away. He had called her wonderful last night. Whatever was bothering him wasn't something she'd done or said. His mother, most likely. He had to be worried sick about her.

They went toward the Innerchord, down a small, quaint street without any garbage in the gutters, to a tiny restaurant that smelled like sugar. They got a seat in the back. Rone told her to order whatever she wanted; she'd never ordered off a menu before. It took her longer to read it than it did Rone. Having been raised by a high priest, he must have received a good education. Did he fault her for her slowness?

But he called you wonderful, she reminded herself, and hid a smile.

She found something inexpensive and asked for that. Thanked him profusely, until it seemed to make him uncomfortable. So she stopped and enjoyed her food—something called a cream puff. It was a large sugared roll with sweet white filling. It was heavenly. Sandis smiled while she ate it.

"My cheeks hurt," she said when they left the establishment, her hand back in the crook of his arm. It *fit* there, which made her heart swell.

Rone turned toward her and rubbed his knuckle into the side of her face. She laughed and pulled away.

"Huh." He pulled her hand back.

"What?"

He shrugged. "I never noticed you have dimples."

She lifted her hand and felt the telling spots on her face. Anon had had dimples, too. They'd come from her father.

Did Talbur Gwenwig have them, too?

"Do you think we could look today?" she asked. "For Talbur? I have the map."

Rone looked away for a moment. "Yeah, sure. Can't hurt."

They bummed a ride on the back of a carriage, where the footman was supposed to go, so Rone said. He stood on the step, and she perched on his feet. When the carriage started turning the wrong way, they hopped off. It was a long walk to the closest place Arnae had circled on her map, long enough to give her blisters, but she didn't mention it. Rone was quiet most of the way.

The mortgage company was on the fifth floor of a six-floor building, tall enough that even Rone wouldn't have been able to jump from the roof to the surrounding architecture. They got a few glances, and more than once Sandis scanned the room for familiar faces or shadowy men. There weren't any. Rone must have been right, then.

There were two people in the office, an older man and a younger woman about Sandis's age. She approached the latter. "Excuse me. I'm trying to find a family member of mine. He purchased a new home in Dresberg not long ago, and I lost the address. It's very important."

She had practiced that line a lot. She thought it sounded reasonable. The woman looked at her skeptically.

"Do you have an account number?" she asked.

"I, no . . ." Sandis turned to find Rone lurking in the back of the room. Refocusing on the woman, she said, "His name is Talbur Gwenwig. I'm fairly certain this is the place with his . . . lease."

The woman looked at her a moment too long. Began opening a drawer at the bottom of the desk. "And you are?"

"Sara Gwenwig." That was her mother's name. Pins prickled her back when she said it—it'd been a long time since her mother's name last graced her tongue.

The woman pulled out a heavy binder, then another. Looked through the first, then the second, then the first again. "You're mistaken. None with that name here."

"Oh." She glanced back to Rone. "I must be. I . . . will try something else."

She turned, her face warm, and hurried to the door. Rone followed after her.

Outside, Sandis pulled out her map. Some of the charcoal writing on it had smeared—she needed to be more careful with it. Wrapping around the side of the large building, she scanned the streets. Sparsely populated at this hour, and she didn't see anyone who looked like a potential pursuer.

She let out a long breath. "All right, that's done. Which means next—"

"It's getting a little late," Rone said, looking at the sky. He'd aged ten years, and the slouch of his body denoted fatigue.

Frowning, Sandis followed his line of vision. Not terribly late, but it was a ways to the next mortgage broker, and it might very well be closed by the time they reached it. Not to mention night was the grafters' time.

He added, "That place I mentioned . . . it should be vacant now. We should head that way."

Sandis carefully folded her map and returned it to her pocket. "All right. Will it be vacant until your job is done?"

Rone started walking down the street, hands in his pockets. "I think so."

"I can look on my own, while you're gone."

"You don't have to."

She licked her lips. Watched the cobblestones pass underfoot. Her heart doubled its weight. "I'm sorry I took your amarinth."

He glanced at her. Checked his pocket.

"Before, I mean."

"I think you already apologized for that."

"It's my fault you're involved in this mess. My fault the grafters want you, too."

Rone shrugged. "We've given them a run for their money, eh? Maybe they won't bother us anymore."

But Sandis shook her head. "I know Kazen too well. He hates losing, so he makes sure he never does. Whenever I thought I'd outsmarted him, he always . . . he always knew. He watched us all so closely. If you turned your head the wrong way or said something outside your vernacular, he noticed."

But could he be getting tired of the chase? Kazen wasn't a young man, and he'd already expended so many resources chasing her and Rone—resources taken away from his work, his other vessels, and . . . Kolosos. Maybe she simply thought he never gave up because no one else had pushed him far enough.

If we can hold out a little longer and find Talbur . . . it will work out.

It had to. Sandis poured all her faith into this. If the Celestial still cared about her, even a miniscule amount, surely she could appease it with her diligence. Surely she could grasp this one blessing.

Maybe Kazen knew her finding Talbur would ultimately thwart him, and that was why he tried so hard to stop her.

"This way," Rone said quietly.

He gestured down another street, this one riddled with beggars. She followed him, searching the faces of Dresberg's poorest. She wished she could help them. So many looked diseased, thin, dirty. She pulled her eyes from one lying too still, not wanting to know if the woman still breathed or not.

"I'm sorry," she whispered as they walked past the helpless beggars. Without Rone, she would have been like these men and women, destitute and desperate, even if she'd managed to stay clear of Kazen.

"What?" Rone asked.

She shook her head. The lump forming in her throat made it hard to speak.

They walked for a long time, until Sandis took off her shoes to prevent further blisters. She was hungry and tired, but they were getting close. This part of town was full of tiny, dilapidated flats; the windows had bars instead of glass. Her gut tightened at the sight of some of them.

"We're getting close," she whispered.

"I know," Rone said, even quieter. "But not too close. See? Just this way."

He didn't look at her as he said it. He hadn't looked at her since they'd left the broker. She wanted to reach for him, but something about the way he moved made her hesitate.

The tall buildings grew closer together. Some looked abandoned, but then again, the families who lived here might be unable to afford lamps. Dusk approached too quickly, yet that might have been a trick of the shadows. It was too quiet, save for the distant wailing of a child and the barking of a dog—

The hairs on Sandis's arms stood on end.

A numen.

"Rone." She reached out and grabbed his arm with both hands. Her pulse thundered in her ears. She dropped her shoes. Cold coils of fear laced their way up her legs and knotted in her belly. "Rone, we have to go. *Now.*"

Rone didn't look at her. "What?"

"Numen. Kazen is nearby. Hurry." She pulled him back. Maybe they could hide in one of these flats. Maybe they hadn't been seen yet. The maybes flooded her mind in a twist of apprehension.

Rone resisted her.

She stared at him. Yanked. "Rone, they're *here*!" She struggled to keep her voice down.

He looked at her in a way that made the coils loosen for a moment. Instead of older, he looked younger. A boy. Wide dark eyes full of sorrow. A long face. Why was he looking at her like that?

His gaze dropped to the road.

"What a good delivery boy we have. Isn't he, Drang?"

Lightning zipped down Sandis's spine, immobilizing her. She nearly tripped over herself turning around. The wolfish numen, Drang, blocked the road behind them, but her eyes went straight to Kazen. Kazen, dressed well in a long black coat and high boots. The silver buckle on his hat glimmered with a light of its own.

Sandis didn't realize she'd been retreating until her shoulder hit Rone's chest. The clicks of cocking guns brought her attention behind him. Ace's mobsmen, a dozen of them, blocked the other way. All with firearms.

She frantically searched for windows, pipes, doors—there was nothing. She stood in a perfect cage.

The amarinth. Could it get them out of this?

"Rone," she croaked.

Rone lifted his hands as if in surrender. "We had a deal."

Sandis's stomach plummeted.

Kazen petted Drang—a giant creature that looked like a mix of wolf and lion but stood upright like a human, its gnarled hands clawed like Isepia's—and strode forward, radiating pure confidence. Sandis backed away, toward the mobsmen, sure she'd faint from her speeding heart and hypothermic limbs.

Rone, however, held his ground.

"I am a man of my word." Kazen reached into his coat and pulled out a stack of papers and a bulging envelope. He handed them to Rone.

Sandis didn't understand. Rone stood like a statue, watching Kazen's shaded eyes. Then he lifted his hand and accepted the papers.

Her body split down the middle. "Rone?" she asked, his name chopped and hoarse on her lips. He didn't fight. He didn't pull out the amarinth. He didn't run.

He hadn't reacted at all to her warning about Drang.

Sandis's knees trembled. She stumbled, barely catching herself.

This couldn't be right. There was something she didn't understand. Rone was her protector. Her friend. Her . . . *everything*.

She saw bills in the envelope he tucked into his pocket, and the truth struck her like the butt of a rifle.

She was his job.

Tears blurred her vision, then burned her skin as they trailed the sides of her nose. All the running, hiding, rescuing . . . and he was turning her in?

How much money was in that envelope?

"Rone?" She tried again, more pathetic than before. He didn't look at her. Stepped around Kazen, toward Drang. Kazen held up a hand, stilling the numen.

He was leaving her.

He was leaving her.

He was leaving her with *them*.

The mobsmen moved forward.

"No!" Sandis screamed, turning and running back the way she had come. Drang roared at her. She fell to her knees and pushed her palm on her forehead.

"None of that," Kazen snapped, and suddenly the mobsmen were on her, clawing her, holding down her limbs. She screamed and struggled, trying to get a hand free, but there were too many of them. They were too strong. A fist hit the side of her head. Her thigh threatened to break under the weight of a large man's knees.

"No! No! Rone!" she screamed, then felt a familiar piercing on the inside of her elbow. Through her blurry vision, she saw Kazen with his needle and tube. Saw her blood spiraling through it and into a syringe.

Ireth! Ireth! Help me! Celestial! "Rone!"

Kazen reached for her forehead.

Sandis screamed.

Chapter 21

Every time she cried out his name, something broke inside him. Broke, snapped, crumbled. Ash filled a cavity deep within, a pit somewhere beyond blood and bone. He'd never felt this way before, hadn't known he could, though it was similar to the ache he'd felt when he was thirteen, the day his father first refused him at the Lily Tower.

Her scream seared up his spine and popped like a firework inside his head.

He'd promised himself he'd run after the exchange. That he'd get out of there as fast as his legs could carry him and never look back. He'd gone over the plan again and again and again . . . but the pull was too strong. He'd never heard a human being make a sound like that.

He turned around.

At first he couldn't see anything other than a swarm of darkly dressed men. But within seconds they all ran away like cockroaches under the light of a lamp, and it was no wonder why.

Fire blazed from the road, bright and hot and growing, growing, *growing*. Rone shielded the heat from his face with a forearm. Burning air rushed into his nostrils and down his throat. He grabbed his amarinth and ducked behind the nearest building to shield himself as a couple of men screamed in surprise.

Go. Go now.

But he had to see her. He had to know—

Rone peeked around the side of the dilapidated building and nearly shat his pants.

Ireth.

The beast stood taller than any horse he'd ever seen—it could eat a plow horse as a snack. Its long, lithe body was the color of tarnished silver and ash, though it glowed a dark bronze where the flames burned brightest.

The flames—Rone could barely look at the thing for the blaze. A wreath of white fire encircled the numen's breast, and flames cascaded down its neck and back and formed a narrow, whiplike tail, like the appendage was made of molten steel. Its eyes were blacker than coal, and two sets of horns jutted out from the top of its head—two forking skyward, and two curving forward.

It was the most incredible monster Rone had ever seen.

And that . . . that was Sandis?

He bolted back behind the building, pressing his back to the bricks. Huffing for air like he'd swum from the bottom of the ocean. Sweat ran down the sides of his face and traced his stomach. The papers and cash under his jacket weighed like anvils.

He ran.

He'd do well to remember what Sandis was. A monster, a numen, a weapon. Kazen was a slug, but he could control her. Rone had done the right thing.

Yet no matter how fast he ran, the sound of her screams lashed back and forth within his skull, and that ball of guilt, growing heavier by the moment, churned relentlessly against his gut.

Full night was upon him when the first bullet glanced off his upper arm. Rone heard the sound of it first as it tore through fabric and skin. The sting came second.

Cursing, he ducked into the alcove of an apartment building; he was on the outskirts of the grungy neighborhood. Above his head, he heard shutters slam shut and momentarily wondered if the people here were used to grafters.

Breathing hard, Rone checked the door behind him. Locked. Of course it was locked.

He poked his head out of the alcove, then ducked down again as another gun fired. The brick behind him exploded, spraying dust in his eye. He rubbed away debris and tears.

He'd had a bad feeling something like this would happen. That Kazen and his lackeys would decide to kill him for the amarinth he carried in his pocket. Why take only Sandis when they could have both?

Nausea spiked through him. *Sandis.* No, he couldn't think about her. *Think about your mother, you sack of sludge.*

Tomorrow, they'd be reunited. They'd have passage to Ysben, Godobia, wherever she wanted to go. Money to start anew. They'd forget about Dresberg, the Angelic, the grafters.

He'd forget about Sandis.

Wouldn't he?

Pulling the amarinth from his pocket, Rone crouched and listened. He didn't know how many pursuers were tailing him, but he needed them to get closer. He only had a minute.

The night was still and stale. He heard voices within the building at his back.

Chewing on his lip, Rone calculated which appendage he'd need the least, should his quickly forming plan go awry. His left hand lost the bet.

He stuck it out, fingers splayed, hoping the shadow looked more like a head than a hand.

A shot fired. It blessedly missed both him and the brick, though he felt the wind from the bullet. As soon as he did, he pulled his hand back and cried out, *"Ah!"* followed by as many pathetic noises as he could muster. He clenched his teeth and breathed hard through them, groaning and whimpering theatrically.

The footsteps came closer. Three, maybe four men. If there was a sniper, Rone would have to be especially fast and outrun him before he could get down from his perch.

They were almost upon him.

Rone spun the amarinth and let it float to the top of the alcove.

He leapt out, surprising the closest grafter with a punch to his face. The man fell back, and the two behind him raised their guns and fired. Rone felt the pressure of two bullets travel through him—one through his shoulder, another through his heart. At least it wasn't the eye. Rone had never been shot in the eye, but he imagined it would be mightily uncomfortable, amarinth or not.

He launched at them, all his years of study with Kurtz flowing through his veins, powering his muscles. He ducked under a gun, roundhouse kicked it out of the grafter's hands even as two consecutive bullets passed through his neck and torso. He rammed the palm of his hand into the grafter's nose, crunching it before turning his attention to the third man.

The repeating rifle fired once—neck. Twice—heart. Three times—gut. Each bullet passed through him painlessly.

The clicking trigger of a gun free of ammunition was sweet music to his ears.

Rone slammed his fist into the grafter's face, and as the man dropped, Rone jerked up his knees and hit him square in the nose. Another roundhouse knocked the man over.

The length of a gun barrel pressed against his neck; Rone wasn't sure if it was from the first man or an unseen fourth. His air choked clean off, but Rone didn't feel the desperate need for oxygen. As long as that trinket spun, he wouldn't.

But his minute was almost up.

Rone slammed his head back. He didn't have a lot of leverage, so the blow was feeble, but it distracted his opponent enough for Rone to find the grafter's foot and stomp his heel into the guy's instep. The grafter's grip loosened. Dropping out of his hold, Rone swung his foot around and knocked his opponent's legs out from under him, grabbed the rifle, and smashed it against his head.

The man lay still. That might have been a killing blow, but Rone couldn't hang around to find out.

He heard the soft *clank* of the amarinth hitting the ground just as he got to the alcove. Grabbing the spent artifact, Rone shoved it into his pocket and ran deeper into the city, thinking only of his mother.

Thinking only of his mother.

Only of his mother . . .

Chapter 22

Sandis's eyes shot open, and she gasped. She stared ahead, her memories slow to return to her. Her shoulder ached fiercely from being pressed against the concrete floor for . . . she didn't know how long. Her mouth tasted like bile, and her throat burned. Even as she thought it, her stomach clenched, forcing her to dry heave. The smell of vomit burned her sinuses before she saw the puddles strewn over the floor.

A fire-laced memory surfaced. She remembered looking at Kazen, from above. From Ireth's eyes. Remembered stepping over the burned body of a teenager, walking back to—

The rest cascaded onto her like an avalanche. The grafters. The alley. Rone.

Rone.

Rone.

Tears clouded her vision. They burned her dry eyes and provoked her thirst. She remembered shadows and hands pressing her into the grimy earth. Her blood flowing out of her. Ireth had come in his full glory, erasing Sandis and doing Kazen's bidding.

Rone.

Rolling onto her back, Sandis pressed both hands to her mouth and sobbed, squeezing her eyes shut as if she could hold back all that sorrow. As if she could cage this awful, twisting feeling inside her, so much worse than a summoning.

Betrayal.

She choked and rolled back onto her side, pushing off the concrete with one hand. Her head swam, and her arm shook with the effort. Kazen must have given her something to make her retch—making her too weak to summon Ireth and break out of this cage. He needn't have bothered. She would have passed out moments after breaking down the door.

Even though she was parched from both summoning and vomiting, tears ran down her face. Her sinuses swelled shut. Her body shook and ached.

He'd been there for her, almost from the beginning. He'd helped her. He'd held her.

He'd traded her for money.

Was that it? Had he kept her around in the hopes Kazen would offer the right price? A pathetic, blunt sound ripped from her throat at the thought. Dizziness took her, and she leaned forward until her forehead met a cold concrete wall. She wept against it for several minutes before pulling back and staring at it in the cool gray light. Light that filtered in from a narrow window in a heavy door three feet from her.

Solitary confinement. She hadn't been in this room for a long, long time.

She was back, then. Ireth's memories told the story. Kazen had summoned the numen and controlled him with Sandis's blood—then he'd simply *walked* them back to their prison.

While Rone had walked away.

She bent over and cried, her breaths fragmented, her ribs sore. Had it all been a ruse? A farce? Had the man she'd begun to love really betrayed her for paper?

Her heart twisted, bent, ripped. It hurt. It hurt *so much*.

It had all been a fantasy. All of it. Her belief that she could escape. That she'd find Talbur Gwenwig and he'd take her in . . . Was he even *real*? Could her mind have played a trick on her, shown her what she wanted to see? Even if Talbur was her great-uncle, why would he care about her? If he had cared, she would know who he was. He would have been there while she grew up. He would have helped her and her brother after her parents died.

Talbur Gwenwig was nothing more than a dream, just like Rone.

Sandis huddled in the corner of the small space, away from her own mess, the cool walls spreading a chill across her skin. She was naked, her dress turned to ash from the summoning. Of course Kazen wouldn't grant her any decency. No food or water. This room was meant to break her. It had before.

She wept dry tears. Pressed her hands into her swollen eyes. She wished she'd never met him. Wished she'd never left. Wished she'd never spoken to Heath the night Kolosos ripped him apart. Wished she didn't care about any of it.

She wished Anon were here.

A hard sob shook her. Lifted her from the floor and turned her inside out. The concrete pressed against the heavy scar tissue that spilled down her back. She tried to think of something—anything—to pull her back to herself. Her heavy thoughts conjured an image of stars dotting the heavens above the Lily Tower . . . but no. Rone's silhouette was there on the edge, tainting it.

She had nothing. She had—

Taking a shaky breath, Sandis reached quivering fingers below her neck and traced Ireth's name.

"I-reth?" she whispered, choking between syllables. "I-I-reth?"

Please, she prayed. *You're all I have left.*

A warm pressure built behind her forehead and trickled down like blood, raising goose bumps in its wake. It settled warmly above her stomach.

Sandis hugged herself, trying to hold the sensation in. She balled her body around it, protecting that last semblance of love. Ireth would never leave her. Ireth was not a fancy.

Holding herself against the darkness, Sandis cried until the dregs of her energy were spent, and then she fell into a cold and fitful slumber.

Rone waited outside the front doors of Gerech Prison. He leaned against the innermost wall that separated the massive structure from the rest of Dresberg. He could tell his presence rankled the guards nearby, but they didn't make him move. The front of his shirt was stretched out and wrinkled from being wrung and knotted between his hands. His skin was cold and clammy despite the warm day. Though he had bribed the warden handsomely and had both emigration documents and travel plans inside his jacket, that ball in his gut still rolled back and forth, back and forth. An even pattern. It was smaller now, but so was his stomach. Food hadn't been particularly appetizing the last couple of days.

His whole body jerked at the sound of the left door opening, its hinges groaning against its massive weight. He stood erect, clamping his shirt in both fists. He stopped breathing, waited.

Guards came out first, and then—

Rone felt the marrow drain right out of his bones. He barely recognized her, even as his feet moved him forward of their own volition. His mother was gaunt and pale, too thin. Her dress was filthy and ragged at every seam; her hair hung in greasy strings from her scalp. She looked older, like she'd become his grandmother over the course of nine days. Her skinny arms trembled, and she winced at the sunlight.

Mom.

She startled when Rone threw his arms around her.

"Rone?" she asked. Her voice was tiny, frail.

She smelled awful, worse than the sewers. "I'm here, Mom." Her matted hair absorbed his tears. "It's all right now. You're going to be all right."

Her skeletal fingers dug into his back as she embraced him, and she wept into his shoulder, soaking through all three layers covering it. One of the guards tried to usher them along, but Rone held his ground, letting his mother mourn all Gerech had taken from her. Letting himself hold her like he was twelve years old again. Ten. Six.

Soon it wouldn't matter. They'd take their things and leave this place.

The ball in his gut rolled back and forth, back and forth.

Sandis stirred from her uncomfortable doze to the creaking of metal against concrete—the blessed sound of the door opening. Her joints groaned as she tried to push herself up. Her bones felt like overworked metal rusted over and pressed too thin. Her eyes crusted with old tears. Her stomach pressed against her spine. She wasn't sure how long Kazen had kept her in that room this time. At least three days, since the only time the slat at the base of the door had opened was to give her a glass of water so she could last her full punishment. Stale, warm water, but it had been so sweet to her. She'd licked the spilled drops off the floor.

The space smelled horrible. Sandis had been given no food, but her body had still eliminated what was left in it, and there was nowhere to go but the corner. Brushing greasy hair from her face, Sandis summoned the last dregs of her energy to sit up. Light blinded her, and a draft spread gooseflesh across her naked skin.

She tried to stand but didn't even get close before her knees buckled and she fell onto her face. A dry sob escaped her lips.

"Put those away. We won't need them," Kazen's voice crooned from the doorway as he waved away an offered set of handcuffs. "She is sufficiently broken."

The water was so hot it hurt. If Zelna wanted to drown her, she could have done so without a fight.

The old woman's hands were merciless as they scrubbed Sandis's hair and skin. Only around her script did Zelna show any care. Soapsuds burned Sandis's eyes. Every time Zelna shoved her head underwater, Sandis gulped mouthfuls of tinny water to quench her relentless thirst. Kazen stood nearby, supervising everything. His gaze felt like oil against Sandis's skin. Even if Sandis had the energy to fight back, she wouldn't. If she could just fall back into her role as the perfect slave, maybe Kazen wouldn't hurt *all* the others to punish her. Maybe he'd be lenient. She could protect them, even when no one had protected her.

Zelna dragged Sandis out of the tub and dried her with a coarse towel, then barked at her when Sandis was sluggish to get her arms into her shirt, which was open in the back to reveal her ranking as vessel. Zelna stuffed her into pants as if she were dressing a doll. Her punishing grip left its share of bruises, but never once did her long fingernails scratch Sandis's skin, not with Kazen so close.

Sandis could barely think, let alone walk, and Zelna complained of having to half carry her to the small dining room where the vessels ate. It was empty. Sandis blearily wondered what time it was.

A bowl of porridge dropped on the table in front of her. With trembling hands, Sandis gripped a spoon and began to eat. The first few bites stuck to her throat and fell leaden into her shrunken stomach. Her whole middle ached with the weight of the food and the water she received shortly thereafter. But the ache soon subsided as hunger took over. So did the fog that had encompassed her brain these last days.

Her thoughts pulled themselves into order as she assessed her situation. Remembered.

Sandis forced the last bite of porridge past the sore lump forming in her throat. She squeezed her eyes shut, but tears managed to leak from the corners of her eyelids.

She was back where she'd started. Underground. With the grafters. With Kazen.

He'd really left her.

The bowl was pulled away from her and dropped into a nearby bin for later washing. The sound of fine fabric sliding against the bench across from her encouraged Sandis to open her eyes. Kazen sat facing her, his bony hands folded underneath his pointed chin. The back of one of them was burned, and a distant thought wondered if she'd done that in the alley where she'd first half summoned Ireth. She hoped so. Galt stood in the corner, meaty forearms folded across his chest, his face twisted and sour.

"What a menace you've been, Sandis." Kazen looked her over. "You've cost me a great deal of resources."

Sandis wiped her eyes with the heel of her hand.

"We'll sort out the best way you and the others can repay me later." The words *the others* struck her like an open hand.

It took her a moment to gather her courage and croak, "How much?" She hadn't heard her own voice in days. It alarmed her how weak and hoarse it sounded. How hard it was to hold up her head.

"Do speak up, Sandis."

She straightened the best she could, though her spine was little more than an overcooked noodle. "How much did you pay him?"

Kazen's left eyebrow rose. "You mean your dear partner in crime? He took a measly thousand for you."

One thousand. In another time and place, that would have seemed like a lot of money to her. Barely a dent in Kazen's wallet. *One thousand.* Was she worth so little?

Her heart shriveled into the semblance of a raisin.

He'd held her hand. He'd called her wonderful.

She wiped away a tear.

"I don't appreciate the weepiness."

She knew Kazen hated tears. She used to be so good at holding them back. Yet even her eyes betrayed her, refusing her silent pleas to stay dry. *Do it for them. Alys, Rist, Dar, Kaili. Don't give him more reasons to hurt them.*

Take all the punishment yourself.

"I'm sorry," she whispered. Penitent. Obedient. Quiet. That was how one thrived in Kazen's clutches. So little time had passed, yet she'd nearly forgotten all the rules. His *and* hers.

An array of horrors awaited her, punishments her imagination was too small to conjure. Kazen would surprise her. He liked surprising her when she disappointed him.

Penitent. Obedient. Quiet. He wouldn't trust her for a long time, if ever. She would have to survive as best she could.

Why did he let me search the mortgage broker if he was already planning to take me back to them?

Talbur Gwenwig's name wrote itself on the back of her eyelids, then faded away.

"You may be," Kazen said, and it took Sandis a moment to realize he meant she may be sorry. "And you will be. Very sorry, my dear. It takes a lot of effort to hire decent, trustworthy men. They're expensive. You've riled the police as well, and now we'll have to kill all the scarlets that sneak too close to our little lair. That's a lot of deaths you've caused, pet."

Underneath the table, Sandis's hands balled into fists. She tucked them between her thighs to hide them from Galt.

Why did he let me love him?

She blinked rapidly, drying new tears. Stared at the table, hoping Kazen wouldn't notice, though she knew it was a false hope, just like all the others.

"They weren't all yours." The men, she meant.

"Quite the tongue we've developed, hm?" Kazen lowered his hands and sat back. "But of course not. I wouldn't bankrupt myself going after one stubborn rat."

She dared to look at his narrowed eyes. They were too intense, so she settled for the wrinkles below them. "But the mobsmen . . ."

Kazen smiled. She hated it when he smiled. "You dear, pathetic thing. The mobsmen are not on my payroll. They never have been. No, they're encouraged to prevent me from getting angry. We both know what happens when I get angry."

She dropped her gaze. Waited for him to say, *You've made me angry.* That was the next line in this mock interview. A segue into her punishment. Her stomach clenched around its meager meal.

But Kazen didn't say anything. She felt him staring at the clean, straight part Zelna had combed into her hair. He wanted her to sit, to stew, to fear. But Sandis's mind had snagged on the mobster who'd died the night Kazen forced her to march back to his lair.

The memory of a half-charred boy in black surfaced. Of her stepping over his body as she walked back to Kazen's lair. Anon had been about that age when he'd disappeared.

"You shouldn't have brought children," she whispered.

Kazen pressed his hands to the tabletop. The movement was silent, but the tension in the room tripled, causing Sandis to recoil. "If you insist on speaking," he said, a tightness to his words, "then. Speak. Up."

"You could spare the children," she said, her voice garnering strength. "If the mobsmen are your puppets to use as you please, you could at least spare children."

She waited for him to scold her for talking back. To signal for Galt to throw a fist against the side of her head. But he didn't, and she hated that he didn't. She hated his unpredictability. She feared it.

"What children?"

The edge to the question woke Sandis from her stupor. She realized her mistake. That memory—the too-young mob boy, dead at her feet—it wasn't hers. It was Ireth's.

She shook her head.

Kazen's hand whipped out and grabbed her chin, pulling it toward him. His hard eyes met hers. "*What* children?"

She swallowed. "In the neighborhood—"

His eyes narrowed. Studied hers.

She knew the moment he saw her fear. Her mistake.

"You mean the little mob boy. The lackey who got too close."

Sandis pulled free of his grip. "He held me down. He—"

"He's dead. But you shouldn't know that, dear Sandis." He leaned closer to her, his breath stale and hot. "Tell me."

She shook her head. "I didn't mean—"

"*Tell me!*"

Sandis froze. Ice. Stone. Metal. Never before had Kazen raised his voice in her presence. Never.

She stared at him, not even daring to breathe. Tension broke off him like shards of glass. The lamps in the room sweltered like suns.

He stared at her, his jaw working, for too long. Slowly he sat, never taking his gaze from her.

"Galt," he said, low and hard, "go fetch Alys."

Sandis came to herself. "No! Please."

Kazen didn't need to explain. Sandis understood. He wasn't going to summon a numen to harm her. No, what he had planned was so much worse. He was going to unleash Galt on the youngest of the vessels, right here in this room. Let her be beaten where Sandis could see. Did Kazen know Sandis had nurtured her like a sister? She'd been so careful.

And Kazen had shouted at her. He was angry. If he deemed this information worth more than Alys's well-being, he might . . .

Sandis cringed.

Galt reached the door.

"I'll tell you!" she cried. "Stop it, stop!"

Kazen lifted a hand, stalling Galt. "You've gotten loose with your tongue, Sandis, but you've also gotten soft. Now speak, or you'll be cleaning solitary with your tongue."

Tears surged into her eyes; she couldn't stop them, even under the weight of Kazen's threats. "I saw him, yes. Through Ireth. I saw him burned and lying in the alley."

Kazen's eyes widened. "You remember."

She nodded.

"Galt."

Galt reached for the door handle.

Sandis jumped from the bench, reaching across the table for him. "No, no! I remember . . . For half a year, I've remembered." And words spilled from her mouth, painting the room. She recounted every single memory she had, desperately trying to fulfill Kazen's curiosity. Desperately trying to satiate him. The only secrets she kept for herself were the messages from Ireth—the warmth, the warning, the glimpses of Kolosos. Throughout her recounting, she prayed silently in her head, *Celestial, don't let him hurt Alys. It's not her fault.*

Kazen stood when her rant was over, looking paler than she'd ever seen him. He did not summon Galt. Did not even look at him. He paced, back and forth once, then pressed his knuckles into his chin in thought.

Dense silence settled in the dining room, suffocating.

When he finally spoke, his voice hurt her ears.

"You're stronger than I realized," he said quietly, more to himself than anyone else. "I tested you. You were strong, yes, but this . . ." He eyed her, the dark gaze almost . . . hungry. "This is what I've been waiting for. First the fire summons, then this . . ."

Sandis stood and backed away from him, tripping over the bench. Her legs shook, their strength not yet fully returned. Her intestines curled around her heart before looping toward her ankles. "Kazen, no."

The hunger intensified.

She took another step in retreat, only to feel Galt's belly against her back. His hands clamped around her upper arms. His smile pressed against her hair.

"No?" Kazen asked, stepping around the table. Closer to her. "You understand my intentions. I know it is no coincidence, your leaving me the night we lost dear Heath. That my perfect"—he took a step—"little"—another—"vessel"—he stood before her and reached out, running the back of his fingers down her wet cheek—"broke my rules and spied about where she wasn't wanted."

Sandis's body went numb in Galt's grasp. He was the only thing keeping her upright. A shiver passed down her neck and spine, then curled upward and settled in her gut.

Kazen leaned forward until his nose was inches from Sandis's. Without taking his eyes from hers, he said, "I'm so sorry, Galt, but your session with Sandis will have to be cancelled. Our plans have changed. I'm going to need her ripe and healthy as quickly as possible.

"I think we've found the vessel we've been waiting for."

Chapter 23

The gold loops spun, slowly at first, but they picked up speed with every rotation.

No, Sandis thought from somewhere far away. *I don't want to see this.*

The whirring noise began, a soft, comforting whistle. The heart of the amarinth glowed a steady light. It was neither warm nor cold. It began to pulse, similar to a heartbeat.

I don't want to see this. I don't want to think about him.

The smell of copper filled her nose. Something was wrong. Very wrong.

She tried to reach for the amarinth, but she had no arms. No body.

The darkness beyond the light of the amarinth shifted. She looked up. A hot breeze whipped by her, fiery and rough. A deep, glowing red veined the blackness. Shaped it. It moved all at once, rotating—

Two narrow, stretched-diamond eyes opened and found her.

Sandis's eyes shot open. Her dry tongue formed the name "Kolosos."

She sat up, weary and heavy, weak from her time spent in solitary.

Dim light traced the outline of the door in the dark room. She was still in solitary—a room she couldn't escape—but now she had her cot and blankets, and there was a tray of food and a pitcher just inside the door, along with a bucket for elimination.

She drew away from it, hugging herself on the far side of the cot. *What does it mean, Ireth? Why the amarinth?*

Not that it mattered. The amarinth and its owner were far away from her now. A pang echoed in her chest at the thought, making her feel hollow. She pressed her knuckles into her eyes to prevent tears. She was so tired of crying.

I don't have much time. She needed to be levelheaded. To think. The food and water would help . . . but it would also prepare her for Kolosos. Was it better to be prepared and have a chance at surviving or to shrink into sickness and, *maybe*, keep Kazen from summoning his monster?

A dry, hard chuckle ripped from her throat. As if she could dissuade Kazen from doing anything.

Sandis closed her eyes. *Ireth? Help me understand.* The amarinth . . . it didn't glow like that in real life. She'd seen it enough times. What did it mean?

Did Kolosos have a connection with the amarinth? But the ethereal plane was completely separate from theirs. Kazen had said so, and he had no reason to lie about that.

A small warmth budded in her center, then faded. She pressed her palm against it, trying to savor the sensation for as long as its tendrils held. "I wish I understood," she whispered. "Give me time."

She didn't have time.

Stepping off the bed, Sandis crouched by the food, the floor cold against her bare feet. She couldn't see it well, but she detected the outline of mashed potatoes, felt lukewarm gravy with her finger. There was meat beside it—this was an especially rich meal, and for breakfast, no less. The spicy smell of apple cider wafted up from a wooden cup, and she inhaled deeply, letting the scent tickle her nose. Rone loved apple—

The thought cut off sharply. Her eyes burned. Her throat tightened and ached.

Apple cider. That's what he'd been drinking the day she met him. When he'd called her over. When he'd shared with her.

Why? She blinked away yet another frustrating tear. *Why did you ever reach out to me? Why do any of it, if I was going to end up here?*

She snatched the cup of cider without thought and hurled it to the other side of the small room. A loud, hollow sound echoed between the walls as the cup hit. Cider rained onto the floor.

All the burst of anger did was make her tremble. Make her cry even more. Her eyes were so sore from the tears and the wiping of them. From holding them back. She bit the inside of her lip and forced a deep breath into her lungs, then out again. In, out. In, out.

What was he doing now? He'd gotten his mother out of Gerech, surely. Was one thousand enough to cover that? As she pinched the bridge of her nose, her thoughts spun. *You should have let me check with the other mortgage broker. I could have found him. He might have saved us both.*

Why do you get your family, but I can't have mine?

Sandis swiped her index finger over the top of the potatoes and put it in her mouth, forcing herself to swallow. She needed to think. She needed energy. She'd work this out—

The locks on the door clicked in uneven rhythm. Sandis barely had enough time to move out of the way before the door opened. Her stomach soured when she saw Galt standing in the door frame.

He glanced at the food and scowled. "I'll shove it down your throat if you don't eat it."

She cringed. *Celestial, I'm a pig being fattened up for slaughter.* "I just woke up."

He rolled his eyes. "Eat it. *Now.*"

Sandis picked up the tray and took it back to her cot. Finding a fork on the edge of it, she worked on the potatoes. Those seemed the easiest to stomach.

Galt must have noticed the spilled cider, for he cursed and spat, "What the hell is wrong with you?"

Sandis shoveled another forkful into her mouth, staring at her tray.

Galt popped his knuckles one by one, as if trying to make her hear his frustration at not having time with her yesterday. He knew how to hurt someone without causing lasting damage. Maybe that was why Kazen liked him so much.

Maybe Kazen had been the one to teach him.

She was halfway through the meat when Galt said, "Enough. I don't have all day. Let's go."

Penitent. Obedient. Quiet. Sandis set the tray aside and followed him, though the moment she stepped out of the room, his hand grabbed her arm tight enough to hurt. She didn't let the pain show on her face.

He half walked, half dragged her through the hallways of Kazen's lair until they got to Kazen's office—a space Galt shared with the summoner so he could do Kazen's bidding without delay. Sandis chewed on the inside of her cheek while Galt unlocked the door. She rarely came to Kazen's office, even when she still sat in his good graces.

The door opened. The lamps were already burning, meaning Galt or Kazen had been in this room earlier in the day. At least, Sandis assumed it was morning. There were no windows down here. Galt shoved her in, followed, and closed the door behind them.

Kazen had a large desk with a dark stain on the rightmost portion of it, and behind that a large set of black bookshelves stood about three-quarters full. Many of the books were scholarly articles whose titles one couldn't see without looking at the front cover. Sandis had always made a habit of looking away from books and other papers, not wanting to give away that she could read them. Such covertness seemed pointless now.

In the corner near the end of the shelves stood Kazen's astral sphere—gold in color and held up on a tall wooden stand. The Noscon figures on its mobile plates were raised and nonsensical to her. There was a small bin at the foot of the sphere. It held two scrolls, one of which looked incredibly old, like it might crumble to dust if Sandis touched it. The other was white, crisp, and new. Small spots of ink bled through the paper, but not enough for Sandis to make out the words.

On the left wall was Galt's desk, much smaller and in poorer repair, littered with papers, trash, and half-eaten snacks. At least the garbage bin beside it had been recently emptied.

Against the far wall rested a simple table, about the height of Sandis's navel. Sandis remembered that table. She'd been branded while strapped facedown on its surface. And again later, to receive Ireth's name atop her spine.

"Black ashes," Galt sputtered. The curse sounded so harsh and final on his lips. When Rone said similar words, they were merely intense—

Sandis gritted her teeth, banishing the thought, though the cool, dripping sensation that filled her and made her shiver was not so easily ignored.

"One hour, he said," Galt mumbled, walking to the far end of the room as though he could find Kazen behind one of the shelves. When he came back, he kicked a chair in Sandis's direction and barked at her to sit.

She sat.

He paced back and forth, complaining under his breath. Went to a cupboard near his desk and opened it, though his body blocked the contents. Nodding to himself, Galt closed the cupboard and sat on the edge of his desk, knocking over greasy, crinkled paper, and folded his arms.

Shouting filled the hallway. It started gradually at first—a few raised voices. But within moments there was bellowing and cursing. The sound of a chair falling over.

"Black ashes," Galt swore again. He launched at Sandis and grabbed her wrist, nearly snapping it when he yanked her to his desk. Some rummaging produced a pair of steel handcuffs, and though Sandis didn't resist, Galt restrained her like she did and clapped the cuffs on her before looping the opposite side through the handle on one of the desk drawers. He shoved her onto the floor.

"Try to move and I'll make mincemeat out of you." Galt turned and hurried out of the office, leaving the door cracked open in his wake.

Normally, Sandis would have sat very still, even with her arm held up uncomfortably by handcuffs.

Instead, she yanked hard on the cuffs, intending to pull the drawer free and run for it. But the drawer held fast, locked.

If she could not escape, she'd use the time Galt had given her. Standing, Sandis looked over Galt's scattered papers.

She wished she could read faster, but she had no trouble making out the important parts. Two leases—apparently Kazen owned housing in the city—a letter in poor handwriting, blank pages with nothing on them. A small ledger, empty save for a couple of lines of Noscon writing.

She opened the drawer above the one she was cuffed to. Gagged when a half-rotted apple core rolled toward her. There were pens and some ink jars—that was it. She tried the one above that. More paper, a ruler, empty ledgers.

Sandis could barely reach the drawers on the other side of the desk. The top one was empty. Did Kazen realize how disorganized and useless Galt was?

She opened the second drawer. She couldn't see inside it but felt around. A book, another book. Something round. Something metallic—

She pulled out a key. Blinked.

The shouting in the hall intensified.

Sandis slammed the drawer shut and knelt back where Galt had left her. Glancing at the door, she tried the key in the locked drawer. It fit. Rone would roll his eyes at Galt's stupidity.

Rone doesn't matter anymore.

She yanked the drawer open, and to her relief, it came free from the desk and clattered to the floor. A menu for a local restaurant spilled from it. Sandis turned the drawer over and emptied its contents, praying with everything she had that she could use the ruckus in the hallway to escape the lair without being caught—without condemning the others to punishment on her behalf. But as she stood, the drawer dangling from her wrists, she noticed the drawer's other contents spilled at her feet.

Files. Just like the ones in the citizen-records building. And the top one bore Heath's name.

"Kolin citizens can't be sold as slaves," Rone repeated in her memory. *"I wonder if your master or whoever had it taken so you couldn't be traced."*

Shouts echoed in the hallway. Lowering herself to her knees, Sandis picked up the file. *Heath Ottobert.* She'd never known his and Rist's last name. Beneath it was Rist's file, and next, hers.

Gaping, she flipped the file open. It was all right there, with her parents and grandparents and Talbur listed above her. No mention of Anon. But this was hers. They *had* taken it.

Here was the proof that she existed. She was a legal resident.

But . . . Kazen hadn't kidnapped her. He'd purchased her from slavers.

So why did *he* have her citizen record?

Sandis's grip on the file loosened. Two papers fell out from the small stack.

A gunshot in the hallway pierced her ears. The shouting fell silent.

Galt was going to come back.

She scooped up the papers and shoved them into the file, but a name caught her eye. A name she recognized easily and without struggle: *Gwenwig.*

She froze. Pulled free the grayish paper. The top margin read, *Gold Exchange*, and beneath it, *Elvita Bank and Trust.*

This was the paper. The one that had started it all.

It shook in her hands as she found Talbur Gwenwig's name, three lines from the top. District Three, Fourteen Magdara.

An address.

The door burst open. Sandis shoved the files and the key into the drawer but didn't have time to put the drawer back into the desk.

"What are you doing?" Galt asked, red faced from whatever had happened in the hallway. He grabbed her by the collar of her shirt and heaved her upward, forgetting he'd cuffed her to the drawer. The steel cuff bit into her wrist when he tried to shove her into the wall. He spat a nasty string of words, fumbled for the cuff key, and freed her from the weight.

He shoved her into the wall. Pressed his forearm into her neck.

"Trying to be sneaky?" His voice was low, and his breath smelled like meat. "Do you think you have *any* power here?"

Galt's other hand came up and squeezed her breast. Sandis flinched; Galt smiled. "You know," he whispered, more to her mouth than to her ear, "I could have my way with you and tell Kazen that rat of yours did it."

Her breakfast boiled in her stomach. She met his eyes. "He's already summoned on me. He'd flay you from crotch to eye socket if you tried."

Galt's face darkened.

"I do hope," Kazen's voice began, and Galt instantly released Sandis and reeled back like she was a snake, "that you're treating my vessel well, Galt." Kazen strode in and removed his hat from his head. He pulled a handkerchief from his vest pocket and used it to wipe off a splatter of blood on his cheek.

Galt glued his gaze to the floor. "Just keeping her in her place."

Sandis hugged herself.

"Hmm." Kazen paused beside Galt and dropped his handkerchief, letting it fall at his assistant's feet. "Do see that I don't have to keep you in yours."

Galt nodded mutely and picked up the cloth, shoving it into his pocket.

When Sandis pulled her gaze away from the handkerchief, she saw Kazen looking at her almost . . . cheerfully. "Don't worry about that ruckus, my dear. I had to finish procuring your replacement, and his owner didn't approve of my method of bargaining. It's been dealt with."

Sandis blinked, the words churning through her head too slowly. "My replacement?"

His meaning hit her like a gunshot. Chills coursed down her cheeks, neck, arms, thighs. Her skeleton seemed to disappear from within her. Her fingers numbed; her tongue thickened.

Why hadn't she realized it before? Replacement. Kazen wanted to use her to summon Kolosos, but her body could not be used for any other numen so long as it was bound to Ireth.

A hard sob ripped up her throat. She backed away from Kazen, from Galt, until she hit the table in the back of the room. "No, please, no," she begged, but her words sounded broken and small. "Please, Kazen." She dropped to her knees. Reached behind her neck to the name inked at its base, as if she could shield it. *"Please don't do this!"*

Kazen sighed. "See what you can do, Galt. I'd like to get this done now, without reinforcements."

Galt reached for her.

"No!" she screamed, and she struck out at him with her arms and legs. She tried to reach for her forehead to summon Ireth, but Galt seized her wrist. She attempted the move Arnae had taught her, but Galt's strength far exceeded her own. He hauled her upright and grabbed her in the vise of his arms. "No!" Her throat bled with the volume of her shouts. "No! Kazen, no! *Stop!*"

Not Ireth. Not *Ireth*.

Ireth was all she had left.

Galt slammed her onto the table, belly down. She hit her chin, and her canine pierced her bottom lip.

She flailed, tried to push herself up. Galt pressed his weight into her until she couldn't breathe. Until her body threatened to snap from the pressure. She didn't feel Kazen strap down her legs until the cloth pulled tight across her calves.

Tears puddled on the tabletop. "Listen to me, please!" she begged. "Kazen, listen! You can't do this! Galt! Stop!"

Kazen pulled straps over her shoulders and, as he cinched them, said, "This is for a greater purpose, Sandis. You'll understand soon enough. I'll expose their lies to everyone." He leaned toward her ear. "I'll show them I was right."

Galt moved behind her, grabbing something from that cupboard. He handed a bottle to Kazen, who dumped the contents onto the base of Sandis's exposed neck.

She pulled at the restraints, and actually managed to move one of them.

"Galt." Kazen's bland tone reeked of disappointment.

Galt climbed onto the table and sat on her, straddling her, pinning her hands with his legs.

Sandis tried to scream, but Galt's weight pushed all the air out of her lungs. She tried to move, but she was utterly and completely trapped.

Kazen lifted some sort of scraper, maybe a razor, crafted out of obsidian. Pressed it to her skin.

Ireth? Ireth, can you hear me? Are you there? I'm so sorry, I—

The blade dragged across her skin, pinching like a fingernail. Only a small section of it; the corner of the fire horse's name. That was all it took; a simple mistake in his name, and the magic disintegrated.

Sandis's core shrunk in on itself, cold, dark, and empty.

Kazen pulled back, looking pleased. When Galt lifted himself from her, Sandis didn't move. Didn't scream. Barely breathed.

Just like that. Ireth was gone.

Gone.

Gone.

Now she was truly, purely, and absolutely *alone*.

Chapter 24

His mother looked so much better. Almost like herself.

Though her apartment had been ransacked, Rone had the money to buy her a house. He'd decided on an inn room on the south side of Dresberg, where he'd proceeded to order his mother anything she could possibly want and had four new dresses delivered to her. She was regaining her health quickly, though the cough she'd developed in Gerech still stuck with her.

She just needs good air, he told himself as their hired carriage rocked back and forth on the uneven road. Apparently not enough people came to the pass in the Fortitude Mountains for the government to put any money into keeping it up. *Some good air and sunshine and she'll heal right up.*

It was this pollution. This grime. This *place.* They were a long ways from Dresberg and its soot-spewing factories, but the sky was still gray and overcast. The land was dreary. His stomach bled with the constant rolling of that damnable ball.

His mother looked so much better. He clung to that fact.

She held a book in her hands, something she'd been eyeing in the gift shop outside the inn, so Rone had bought it for her. She was near the end now, but her gaze looked out the window at the passing landscape: jagged hills, few trees, little green. Even in the summer, everything looked gray and brown and sad.

Rone pressed his fingers into his eyes, his thoughts drifting back to Dresberg. What did *her* smile look like? God's tower, he couldn't remember her smile . . .

"Rone?"

He dropped his hand and blinked spots from his eyes. "Hm?"

His mother frowned at him. "Did you drink that tea?"

The medicinal garbage she'd gotten at the last inn? "Yeah."

Her head shook like she didn't believe him. "You look terrible."

She'd told him that more than once. How sick he looked. How pale.

Half-consciously rubbing his stomach, Rone said, "I'm fine. Just travel sick."

He saw the same question in her eyes. *How did you get the papers?* She'd wept upon first seeing them, but he'd avoided answering her every question about how he'd obtained them, how he'd freed her. Even after living her own personal horror, his mother was smart enough to recognize his evasion. She hadn't pushed it. But over the last few days, some skepticism had crept in. Maybe because Rone should have been more excited.

The ball dug in hard, making him jump. The rocking of the carriage masked the action. His mother looked back to her book.

"What's happening now?" he asked.

She offered a small smile and talked about how the Serranese duke in the novel had finally realized his mistake and was riding hard to beat a bad storm and profess his love for the duchess.

Rone pressed a thumb into his stomach to stop that ball. They had almost reached the border. It was almost over.

And his mother looked *so much better.*

Rone had thought he understood the enormity of the wall of mountains separating Kolingrad from the rest of the world.

How wrong he had been.

As the carriage pulled closer and closer to the behemoths, and Rone leaned more and more out the window, he realized he couldn't see the sky. Only the mountains, steep and relentless and reaching up until the clouds swallowed their peaks. The carriage slowed as its horses struggled to pull it up the incline. The snapping of the driver's whip echoed in his ears.

They won't hurt her, he told himself. *She said so herself.*

He clenched his teeth together to keep from throwing up.

It felt like eternity before the driver called, "Whoa!" and Rone was able to open the door to his carriage—*cage*—and stretch his legs and back. He offered a hand to his mother, who held her book under one arm. As soon as she had her feet under her, Rone went to the back of the carriage and grabbed their single trunk. Everything else they needed they could get once they were through the pass.

It wasn't much to look at. The Fortitude Mountains stood as impenetrable sentinels, free of flora of any kind. They parted for a narrow gap manned by a cluster of bored guards. A smattering of tents a ways off held more guards, one of whom roasted some sort of bird on a cooking spit over a small fire. About half a mile northeast was a single-story trading post and, beside it, a two-story inn with an attached immigration office. Directly ahead of them, to the side of the pass, was a small corral of mules and horses and a shed the size of Rone's bedroom, with a large window cut into the door.

"See there." The driver indicated two small carriages next to the corral. "Those will take you through. At least another day until you reach Godobia. Got your papers?"

Rone checked his jacket pocket, but he didn't need to. He'd felt for those papers dozens of times since receiving them. He hadn't taken the jacket off once, even to sleep.

He absently checked for the amarinth as well, then nodded.

The driver offered a close-lipped smile, an expression of well-wishing and envy at the same time. He patted Rone's back, then returned to the carriage to tend to his horses.

Fingers slipped into his, and for half a heartbeat, he was sure they were Sandis's.

"We're here," his mother said, a grin pulling up her lips. It was the happiest he'd seen her in a while. Maybe even since his father left. She squeezed his hand. "Or, we're almost *there*."

Rone offered her a smile and led her toward the corral. She was positively beaming, yet he couldn't match her mood. He cursed God in his thoughts for preventing even this simple happiness. Cursed himself.

They didn't get far up the road before two armored men wearing sail-less boats on their breastplates approached and asked them for documentation. He handed it over, looking past them to the small army guarding the pass.

The guards appeared content—impressed, even—and handed the paper back. A breath Rone had held deep in his gut rushed from his mouth. The paperwork had seemed legitimate, but until now a worry had wriggled in the back of his mind that Kazen had screwed him over.

The bastard had likely thought his goons would be successful in stealing them—and the amarinth—from Rone's corpse. At least Rone had been able to thwart him there.

Handing back the paperwork, the guard said, "It will be inspected a second time at the pass, and stamped. If you want to return, you'll have to do it in the next five weeks."

"Why is that?" asked his mother.

The guard tapped his finger on the upper-left corner of the paper. An expiration date. Because nothing in Kolingrad could be absolute, could it?

His mother shook her head. "That's all right. I don't think we'll be coming back."

The guard nodded his understanding. "If you're riding, you'll need to see the stable master." He gestured toward the corral. "Walking, come with me."

"Riding, thanks." Rone didn't think his mother could walk the entire pass, and the sooner she got to Godobia, the better.

The sooner *they* got to Godobia.

He offered his mother his arm and helped her up the growing incline. Talked to the stable master, who owned the two small cabs they'd noticed earlier. Only two were needed, the man explained, since they didn't get a lot of coming and going this way outside of exportation, and merchants always brought their own vehicles. Rone paid the rent for a cab and horses and waited impatiently as the animals were hooked up.

He glanced north, toward Dresberg.

"Here." His mother offered him some crackers from her bag. "You look terrible. Maybe you should eat something. Or there's a water pump over there."

Rone folded his arms. "I'm fine." The ball in his gut doubled in size, making him lean forward in pain.

She frowned. Tucked the crackers back into her bag. "You just need fresh air, I'll bet." She shivered at the sentiment. She hadn't even gotten stale air while caged in her prison cell. Underground, where she had no hope of escape—

Oh God, he thought. *She's never going to see the stars again.*

The ball bit into his flesh. Rone leaned forward and groaned.

"Rone?" His mother pressed a hand to the back of his head. "Rone? What's wrong? Excuse me!" she called to someone else. "Could I please get some water? For . . . yes, thank you."

Rone shook his head. "I can't do this."

"What was that?"

Rone stood, his mother's touch slowly pulling from him as he did so. "It's my fault."

Her brows pinched together. "What is?"

"You. Gerech." He pushed his hands into his hair, nearly tearing it from his scalp. He turned away, then back. "I did it, Mom. The headpiece. I'm the one who stole it."

He expected her eyes to widen or her face to pale, but she merely pressed her lips together and nodded. "I had wondered."

She might as well have punched him in the gut.

Tears stung the back of his eyes. He gripped his mother's shoulders. "Mom, I *never* blamed you. It was a setup. I didn't know they knew my real name, and—"

"Oh, Rone." She cupped his face in her hands. "I forgave you the moment the thought passed through my mind."

He hung his head. He couldn't handle this. Any of this. He might as well sink into the ground and never come up for air.

"What I don't understand is the papers, and how you got me out. They told me I had no bail—"

Rone lifted his head. "It's . . . a long story. Too long to tell you right now." The stable master led the horses and cab up to them, oblivious to their conversation. Rone sucked in a deep breath to stoke his courage. "Needless to say I did something bad to get you in there, but I did something even worse to get you out."

She finally gave him the expression he'd been waiting for. The whites of her eyes were bright against the tawny rings of her irises.

Rone pulled the documents out of his coat and counted them, twice, to make sure he hadn't missed a single page. Handed his mother's to her. "Go. Settle wherever you want." He handed her half the contents of his bulging wallet. "And write to me. If you write to me, I'll explain everything."

She gaped at the money. "What? Rone." She grabbed his shirtsleeve. "I don't understand."

He clasped her shoulders and pressed his forehead to hers. "There are sentries all along the path. No bandits. You have enough money to hire an assistant if you'd like. I have to go back. I can't stall. She's been there for too long already."

Was he already too late?

Tears brimmed his mother's eyes. "She? I don't understand."

"I know." The ball trundled, but it was smaller now, and it sat higher in his stomach. "I know. I'm so sorry. But you'll get your freedom, and you'll write to me, and I'll come to you. I am *not* leaving you, do you understand?" He pulled her into his embrace. "As long as I'm alive, I will *never* leave you. I'm so sorry. I should have . . ."

He didn't know what he should have done. All he knew was that he hadn't done it.

"Please trust me," he whispered.

After a moment, his mother pulled back, examining his face like he was a stranger. The lines between her eyebrows softened. "You've been so different lately." Yet she nodded. "I'll go. I'll write to the same address?"

"Write to yours," he said.

She placed a hand over his heart, a glint of uncertainty still in her brown eyes. "Don't hurt yourself, Rone."

Slipping his hand into his pocket, Rone tangled his fingers with the loops of the amarinth. "I won't."

His mother boarded the cab and took up the reins. Squared her shoulders. Looked back at him one more time.

"Don't make me come looking for you," she said.

He nodded.

Flicking the reins, Adalia Comf drove the cab forward, toward the passage that led to her freedom.

The stable master looked between her and Rone, confounded.

Rone marched up to him and waved a crisp bill under his nose. "You have five minutes to teach me how to ride a horse."

Horses were god-awful creatures. But a single horse was faster than a horse-pulled vehicle. Rone's method of riding came down to strapping himself into a saddle, kicking the animal into a gallop, and hoping for the best. The horses stayed on the road, for the most part. He'd run the animals thin and gotten complaints from the exchangers along the way to Dresberg. Money silenced them well enough.

But black ashes, his legs, crotch, and butt *hurt*. Walking helped ease the pain. Had he known the ride back would be so debilitating, he would have taken a cab.

Maybe.

He had a fair idea of where Sandis was being kept. Ish. He had the drop-off location from his last client. And Sandis had said they'd been close to Kazen's lair when she first summoned Ireth.

His skin pebbled and cooled at the thought. *Ireth.* He could see the horned fire horse in his vision as clearly as if the numen had branded his image there. God's tower, there were *more* of those where he was going. A one-winged witch, a crab turtle, a nightmare-spun werewolf . . . *thing*.

And the possibility of this Kolosos.

But he had to go.

He barely felt the ball in his gut when he approached a goldsmith on the southern end of Dresberg—one of the nice ones that didn't try to pawn off polished brass as twenty karat. The salesman blathered something or other to him as he looked over his wares. Rone didn't listen. The rings were too small. Chains would never be convincing. But that—that bracelet. That was perfect. Three bands of gold connected by a perpendicular band studded with pearls.

"This," he said. "But I only want the band and a pair of pliers. You don't sell gold nails, do you? I need to make some loops that sort of circle around one another."

The goldsmith looked at him like he was mad.

Rone smacked a stack of cash on the counter, and the goldsmith got to work.

He felt like a fly in a spider's nest. Not the tiny city spiders that wove their webs in the corners of windowpanes, but the nasty ones out in the dust, where no one had bothered to build in millennia. Big, craggy things with knobby joints and beady eyes. He thought he could feel one crawling up his neck. Shivering, he forced his hands to remain steady on his perch as he sat precariously on the end of a dilapidated apartment building, looking down onto the streets. For a city that craved space, you'd think someone would sign an order to have these suckers demolished. Then again, he imagined the grafters that hung around here pulled many a bloody string to have them left alone.

The area filled with shadows as the sun lowered toward the horizon. The glowing behemoth sat halfway behind the hideous city wall, stretching the old buildings long and dark. Rone stayed away from its orange light and watched. He wasn't perfect at spotting grafters, but he had developed a decent eye for them during his time with Sandis. When one was running for his life, it was a good idea to learn the look of his hunters.

Rone's back stiffened in complaint at his stillness, having had less than twelve hours to recover from its epic journey. He hadn't slept much, either, but wakefulness glued his eyelids back and sucked moisture from his mouth and sinuses. He wasn't worried about falling asleep, but he *was* concerned he was stalking the wrong place.

He crept, like a fly, along the building's edge until he reached a corner. Paused, listened. He wouldn't make the jump to the building north of him. Not because it was too far, but because he didn't think the edges of the collapsed roof would hold him. He veered east. Stood in a shadow, then leapt. He had a nearly silent landing. Not perfect, but good enough.

A few buildings later, he found another decent perch above an old outdoor stairwell. The building to the west shadowed him perfectly. The polluted sky blushed between swaths of gray as the sun sank lower and lower. Would these guys make him wait until nightfall?

Apparently not. The sound of footsteps caught his attention. Rone crept along the decking, homing in on two men coming down an alleyway. He hadn't seen where they'd come from. Had they been walking for a while, or recently emerged? Apparently he'd have to do this the hard way.

He rechecked his amarinth, then the knives in his boots. Trained his eyes on the men. Moved with them as they rounded a corner, coming closer. They strode with confidence, despite the late hour and questionable neighborhood. Wore dark clothes. Didn't talk. Definitely armed. Definitely grafters.

Maybe he was the spider after all.

Rone slinked down to the stairs, creeping with bent knees and elbows until he was one story above, and they were below—

He leapt.

His aim was true—he landed right on the shoulders of the closer grafter, slamming him into the ground like a shoe to a beetle. The man's head made a distinct, melon-like *thump* when it hit the dirt-packed road.

The other grafter pulled out a pistol. *No pistols.* Too loud.

Rone launched into the air and kicked the firearm out of the man's hand. Landed a punch to his collar, but the grafter grabbed his wrist and tried to twist it. Rone bent with the movement and came around, swinging his leg behind him. His heel met the man's temple. The grafter let go. Rone finished the rotation and smashed his elbow into the side of his opponent's neck. The grafter fell to one knee.

Rone rushed at him, pulling a knife from his boot as he did so. Whipped his arm around his neck and pressed the blade to the soft flesh beneath his chin.

"Tell me how to get to Kazen," he muttered.

But the grafter didn't say a word.

Rone tightened his grip until the man's face began to purple. "*Tell* me how to get to *Kazen*."

The man refused.

Damn loyalty. Or perhaps it was fear. Rone certainly wasn't as scary as the grafter ringleader.

Rone held on until the grafter went limp. The man fell to the ground, a stuttering breath filling his lungs. The first grafter—the one Rone had jumped on—began to wearily pick himself up.

Rone strode over and repeated the knife-and-choking routine.

"Tell me where Kazen is."

The grafter wheezed, then nodded.

This wasn't Rone's first time infiltrating a building. Granted, he'd never snuck into one *this big* with so few exits. He needed all the magical minutes he could get in a place like this, but he only had one, and he had to use it well.

The key with any infiltration was not to draw attention to yourself, either with your appearance or your approach. Rone didn't want a fight. He wanted to be invisible.

The grafter who'd held out on him had been about Rone's size, so after landing a blow that would keep him asleep for a good long while (if not kill him, but that wasn't Rone's problem right now), he stripped the guy, though kept his own dark pants. The more compliant grafter he kept close, like they were whispering to each other. Never mind that Rone's hand was under the man's swank jacket, holding the point of a knife between two vertebrae.

The entrance wasn't far, and it wasn't special. Looked like nothing more than the door to a dilapidated building. Rone could feel eyes on him, watchmen, so he leaned close to his smoke-and-whiskey-smelling friend and told him to act natural or he'd never feel his legs again.

The grafter complied. Which made him Rone's favorite grafter ever.

Unfortunately, their friendship could only go so far. They walked down a flight of stairs into a narrow corridor lit too dimly for any person who had aboveground preferences. Rone looked for a good place to dump his chap and found one in a laundry room not far from the entrance.

He didn't want to kill the man. Killing wasn't Rone's way, even if the bloke was a disgusting piece of Dresberg underbelly. But he'd kill for Sandis if he had to. He would not leave this place without her.

Closing the door to the rather large laundering space, Rone decided to give this grafter the same odds as the first—a blow that would keep him out and *maybe* kill him. Ultimately, it depended on the man's will to live. Maybe. But heels to temples tended not to work out so well.

At least the guy's body fit snugly inside the drainpipe in the corner. Rone took the crook's hat and set it on his own head, pulling it low as he'd seen Kazen do.

Walk as though deep in thought, with a purpose. Something his old friend Kas had told him some ten years ago. It was the attitude least likely to attract interest from passersby. And how many would there be? If anyone came at him and Rone couldn't quickly deal with it, he'd have to spin the amarinth and hustle out of there. Try again later. If he had a later.

The look on Sandis's face when she realized . . .

It wasn't the ball in his gut that got him this time, but a pulling from his throat to his chest. Like a taut elastic cord. Maybe he'd handled it all wrong. Maybe instead of giving her a final, pleasant day, he should have distanced himself from her. Been crueler to her. Made her grateful to be going back.

God's tower, she'd been so happy that day. So hopeful. And so concerned over *him*. Hadn't that been the first thing she'd done when she sensed that wolf numen nearby? Try to save *him*?

He shook his head and slipped back into the hallway. He couldn't dwell on that now.

As if he'd dwelled on anything else since leaving her screaming and kicking in that alleyway. Screaming *his name.*

Focus. The pain in his chest made him anxious, which would make him sloppy. He had to remember the way out. Trace his steps. Note what and whom he saw. The place appeared pretty linear—it curved, mostly one long hallway with a few branches. He wondered if this had once been a Noscon mine or if the grafters had carved it out themselves . . . or with their numina. The farther Rone walked, the more the place sloped downward. Deeper into the earth. Farther from freedom.

Just like Gerech.

It was weirdly clean, and bland. Long beige tiles covered the floor, their shine worn except for where they met the off-white walls, which met an off-white ceiling. Paint had chipped in several locations, but none had been left hanging. There were bullet holes in the wall here and there. No ornamentation of any kind. The doors were narrow and short, either wood or metal. All had locks. Some locked from the outside.

Another man came up the hall. Rone didn't look at him. Kept focused. He passed without incident, but Rone's heartbeat sped anyway. Slipping his hand into his pocket, he pinched his amarinth.

He reached a fork. Tried not to hesitate, but another man came up it, startling him. He carried a stack of folded clothes. The ones he wore were gray and drab, like any poor citizen's attire, but his hair was strawberry gold and long, his face spotted with freckles—obviously a Godobian. About Sandis's age. No weapons. Not a grafter, but who?

Rone froze when they made eye contact. Got ready to strike—

The man stepped back, frightened, but looked Rone up and down. Seconds dragged long before he settled a finger against his lips. Then he ducked his head and continued walking, as if Rone were only a ghost.

Rone glanced back at him, wondering. Just for a moment. He had to keep moving. If this guy was going to give him an in, for whatever reason, he'd take it.

It didn't *feel* like a trap.

He pushed forward instead of following the steps of the ginger. Another grafter came up, apparently in a hurry. He bumped shoulders with Rone but kept going. Rone forced air into his lungs.

A door to his left opened; he caught a glimpse of a bare room filled with cots. He recognized the girl who slipped out—small and round faced, blonde. A teenager. More so, he remembered the numen she turned into.

Their eyes met. Recognition struck her features.

Rone heard more grafters coming their way. He needed to hurry.

"Anyone else in there?" he whispered.

Alys—that was her name, wasn't it?—shook her head, her eyes wide.

"Good." He pulled out his knife in a quick, fluid motion and grabbed her shoulder. "I'm sorry, but you'll need to come with me. They won't shoot you."

The girl's eyes stared at the blade. She said nothing, but when Rone urged her forward, she complied.

"Now"—his voice was so low it was barely audible—"tell me where to find Sandis."

Chapter 25

Had this been her fate all along?

Her punishment for what she'd become?

Did the Celestial even hear her prayers anymore, or had it stopped listening the day the Noscon letters were branded into her back?

Sandis was empty. Every bit of her. Empty and cold, and yet her limbs weighed her down. She'd eaten five times a day for the last five days, rich foods that stuck to the ribs, and yet she starved for . . . something. Her mind had deteriorated into sawdust. The thoughts that kept it running were too miserable to think anymore.

She barely remembered being cleaned, but her skin was sore from scrubbing and dry from soap. She watched, as if from a distance, as Kazen's steady hand drew down her arms. Symbols similar to the ones Heath had worn. Somewhere in that ink was the name Kolosos, she knew. What gave the ink its bronze color, she didn't *want* to know. One of the letters looped around the red dot on the inside of her elbow—Kazen had drawn her blood again an hour ago. Maybe that lent to the gaping nothingness inside her.

I should fight. Her mind stirred with the sentiment. *Wouldn't it be better to die fighting than to die when Kolosos rips me apart?*

"There we are." Kazen blew gently on the last symbols to dry them. That ink would mingle with her blood once the summoning failed. And if, somehow, Kazen was successful . . . what then? What would it be like to have that monster inside her, the one she'd glimpsed in her nightmares? The one Ireth had tried so desperately to warn her about?

Sandis hadn't had a dream since her connection to Ireth had been severed. She couldn't even cry.

She was empty.

Part of her was desperate to fight. To swat the ink vial away. Smear the letters and make him start over, with Galt and whoever was left of his followers holding her down. But she didn't know seugrat beyond the trick Kurtz had taught her. She didn't have a firearm. She wasn't strong.

Without Ireth, she was nothing.

Kazen stood and crossed his office to the cupboard in the back corner, replacing his brush and vial on a shelf there. *Run.* But Galt guarded the door. Sandis had no idea what time of day it was, or who was on shift . . . yet she'd noticed there were far fewer grafters in these halls than when she'd left. So many had been hurt or killed in their endless pursuit of her and of—

No. Her mind stirred back to life. *Don't even think his name.*

She couldn't bear it. And yet, even with her looming death ahead of her, the trembling of her fingers did not stem from Kolosos.

Closing her eyes, Sandis took a deep breath. Reached for Ireth, only to remember—

Her eyes burned behind her eyelids.

"Don't sleep on me, my pet." Kazen walked around her chair, perhaps studying her. Sandis slowly opened her eyes and blinked her vision clear. Her master's spidery hand reached forward to the chain dangling from the metal collar around her neck. Had Heath been collared? She couldn't remember.

He gave it a gentle tug. Somehow Sandis found the strength to stand.

Kazen stood erect, a look of pleasure crossing his face. "It's time. Galt?"

Galt opened the door and held it while Kazen led her out like a dog. Anon had always wanted a dog. They had never possessed the means to keep even the mangiest mutt.

Kazen guided her down the hallway. The same path she had traced not long ago on silent feet, following the screams. Would it hurt more than the usual summoning? Was it possible for anything to hurt more than that?

Ireth—

No, Ireth was gone. He wouldn't hear her prayers. Nothing and no one would.

She was going to die. Or maybe, become the vessel for the most fearsome monster she'd ever known.

Her feet dragged. Her neck pulled back on the chain.

Glancing over his shoulder, Kazen's eyes narrowed. "After all our talks, Sandis, will you really resist me now?"

Talks? When had they talked? Snippets of memories danced behind her forehead. She remembered . . . yet she couldn't pinpoint a single thing he'd said. The words had merely swirled into her emptiness and passed out again just as quickly.

He was waiting for her to move.

She couldn't move.

Galt's heavy hand between her shoulder blades pushed her forward. Her pulse quickened with each step, and when the door to the summoning room at the end of the hallway came into focus, her body couldn't get enough air. She gasped for it, filled her lungs until they stretched to their brink, yet she wasn't breathing at all.

"I have the sedative," Galt murmured as Kazen reached for the door.

"No." Kazen frowned at Sandis. "It will weaken her body. I want her alert." His hand settled on Sandis's shoulder. "You know how this works, dear Sandis. The more willing you are, the better the possession will be. Less pain."

What do you know of pain? You've likely only acted as vessel once. No. Kazen knew more of how to inflict pain than how to feel it.

The door opened, and Galt shoved her through.

The light was red. Or was it? Sandis saw only red. The lamps along the wall seemed to blaze with the color. And the smell. It smelled like chloride lime and feces and blood, all mixed together into a suffocating perfume. The wide space was empty, save for an ox chained to the wall. Little steel half circles lined the wall and one strip of the floor, connectors for chains to leash sacrifices. Sacrifices were necessary when a numen wasn't bound, but usually Kazen bled a simple creature. A bird or a hare.

Not enough for Kolosos. Not enough for her.

Sandis's legs lost their strength. She fell to her knees, her collar lifting and digging into her jaw as she went.

Kazen waited patiently, his grip on the chain never easing. "Galt."

Galt grabbed her under her arms and heaved her up. She found some semblance of balance, and suddenly she was in the back of the room, near the ox. When had she walked over here? The *click* of metal from her chain locking with the link bolted to the floor echoed across the expanse.

Sweat gathered in every crevice of her skin. She couldn't breathe. Not this toxic air. *Oh Celestial, save me.*

Her god wouldn't save her. No one would. Maybe . . . just maybe, she'd be strong enough to survive this. Maybe it would be no different than Ireth . . . Kolosos would take her in a flash of light, and she'd wake up later in her room and find a way to leave. She'd have to leave somehow. The destruction Kazen could do with that monster—she shuddered to imagine it. Yes, she'd leave. Break her script. She knew where Talbur was. She could—

The outline of an old stain on the floor caught her attention. *Heath.*

He had been able to possess a seven, like her. He'd been bigger and stronger. He had died instantly.

"Oh God," she whispered.

"The only 'god' you need to concern yourself with is the one about to join us, dear Sandis," Kazen said, but there was an edge to his words. Like her oath had rankled him.

Her eyes watched his as he drew a sword from a sheath at his waist. It took her a moment to recognize it—the same blade that had slit the mare's throat before Heath died. Kazen urged the ox forward, to the end of its own chain. It had no idea that—

The sword hacked into its neck. The whites of the animal's eyes swelled. Sandis shrieked and tried to move away, but Galt's hands clamped down on her arms. Kazen swung the sword around so that it bit into the ox's jugular. This time, it sliced clean through.

The ox fell, twitching, its blood readily pooling on the floor. Sandis pushed against Galt as it crept toward her, but he was unmovable. The hot blood licked the sides of her feet, then seeped under her toes.

Kazen looked pointedly at her, then at his sword. "Let her go, Galt."

Her eyes flicked to the door.

She'd done this before she was bound to Ireth. But this time there was *so much blood*.

Galt released her. Stepped back. Choked.

Sandis shifted her gaze to him just as the ceremonial sword split open his neck, just like the ox's.

She screamed and jerked away from the gruesome, wet mouth forming under Galt's chin, only to slip and fall into the ox's blood. She screamed again, new tears streaming down her face. Kazen released Galt's hair and let him fall into the growing puddle, his blood mixing with the ox's.

"No sacrifice is greater than human sacrifice," Kazen muttered, his eyes lingering on Galt for the briefest moment. "I will make no mistakes this time."

Sandis yanked at her chain, desperate to get away from Galt's corpse, from the blood pooling ever closer to her. But the steel held, and when the hot, sticky liquid lapped at her legs, she sobbed.

"Stand up, Sandis."

She tried to, if only to limit how much of her skin touched—

"I said *stand up*." Kazen's fingers coiled in her hair and yanked her upright. Her feet slid in the crimson pool. Her scalp threatened to tear. She found her balance, but she shook so violently she was sure she'd collapse. She begged unconsciousness to claim her.

"H-He was your f-friend," she whispered.

Kazen chuckled. "My friends are far more useful." He looked over his stained sword, frowned, and tossed it onto the floor behind the corpses. Then he pinched Sandis's hand and forced her to meet his eyes. "You're my friend, aren't you, Sandis?"

Tears mottled her vision. She wrenched free of his grasp, the chain tugging on her neck as she did so. "You're a monster."

He was nonchalant. "We'll prove them wrong, Sandis. We'll finally show the world the truth."

Sandis kept her eyes on him to avoid looking at Galt, or the blood enveloping her toes. "What do you mean?"

He moved so fast his hand and sleeve blurred into gray. A silver ring on his finger bit into her cheekbone. Sandis nearly fell back into the blood.

She stared into the scarlet puddle a long moment, pain pulsating from her face.

He'd hit her. In all the years Sandis had known him, Kazen had never before struck her.

Grabbing her chin again, Kazen forced her face back to his. He inspected the damage. Sandis knew there was no blood; Kazen would never risk damaging her when he was about to fulfill his goal. He pulled a vial of water—purified water—from his coat and uncorked it. Then he dumped the stuff over her head.

Sandis tried to move away from it, but the chain held tight, and she nearly slipped. Her eyes passed over Galt, and bile rose up in her throat, burning and putrid. She tried to swallow it, but she gagged and spat it out. Shook. Fuzzy rings formed around her vision.

Kazen pressed his palm to her forehead. She shifted away, but he grabbed her hair, holding her in place.

"Vre en nestu a carnath," he murmured.

Tears trailed down her cheeks. "Please," she whispered, but the plea was swallowed up by the next words, uttered louder than the first.

"Ii mem entre I amar."

Pressure built up in the sides of her neck, her shoulders. Not like Ireth's. It felt wrong, like her spirit had solidified and was trying to escape. It pushed out, stretching her—

"Vre en nestu—"

The door to the room slammed shut. A voice called, "This is disgusting."

Sandis stopped breathing.

That voice.

That *voice*.

But . . . how?

Kazen whipped around so quickly he pulled several strands of hair from Sandis's scalp. The pressure building in her neck receded. Rage flowed from Kazen like molten iron. Sandis strained to see around him.

Rone. She blinked. It couldn't be.

Rone?

He stood just inside the door, which he'd barred with a piece of wood. Alys was wrapped up in his arms, facing them, her eyes wide with terror and focused on the blood—on Galt. Rone held a knife to her neck.

"Really," he said. "It will take *hours* to clean this up."

"You dare"—Kazen's voice was gravel and fire—"interrupt this sacred moment?" He took a step forward. "How—"

"Uh-uh." Rone wiggled the knife at Alys's throat. "Stay where you are."

Sandis's focus shifted from Kazen to Rone, Rone to Alys, Alys to Rone. He had come back? He . . . what? She strained to see better and slid, falling to her hands and knees in Galt's blood. Bile burned up her tender throat once more.

Kazen laughed. "You stupid boy. I've watched you. I've researched you. I *know* you. You won't kill my vessel. You're already dead."

Rone clenched his jaw. Shrugged. Dropped his knife and let Alys go.

Then he whipped a pistol out of his jacket pocket and fired.

Sandis's ears rang. The wall behind Kazen popped with the impact. Rone had missed.

Before a curse could leave his mouth, Kazen's hand flashed silver, and his own pistol fired. The bullet rang when it hit the metal of Rone's gun and knocked it out of his hand. Rone instinctively cradled the hand as Kazen dropped the first single-fire pistol and drew another. Aimed.

"*No!*" Sandis screamed, and she launched her blood-drenched body at his legs. She hit him a split second before he fired.

Dust exploded from the ceiling where the bullet hit. Kazen slid in the blood and fell onto his hip. Sandis tried to move away, only to reach the end of her chain.

She didn't know how many guns Kazen had. If the second pistol was a single fire or not. She grabbed his wrist, smearing Galt's blood over his hand and sleeve.

Kazen wrenched his arm free and smashed his elbow into Sandis's jaw, knocking her back into the pool. She slid in the cooling blood. Grabbed his belt and yanked him down, away from the dropped gun and the ceremonial sword.

A silver key fell from his pocket, falling just outside the blood puddle.

Then Rone was on them. He launched himself onto Kazen, and the two rolled out of Sandis's reach. Someone's fists thundered against the door. The wood holding it began to splinter.

Rone threw a hard punch into Kazen's face, and the man went limp. Sandis gawked. Was he crushed so easily?

She strained for the key. Couldn't reach it. "Rone." His name was high and choked from the collar pushing against her windpipe. *"Key."*

Rone leapt from Kazen and dropped to his knees in front of her, swiping the silver key. More fists on the door. His fingertips flew over her collar, looking for the keyhole. She bent her neck so he could find it in the back.

The collar fell into the blood, and Sandis breathed for the first time that day. She looked up into Rone's dark eyes, and for a moment they stared at each other. Confusion boiled inside her.

Why? Why *everything?*

Kazen laughed.

Sandis and Rone both jumped at the sound. Kazen stood on the far edge of the room. The sight of Alys in his grip sucked Sandis's organs together and turned them to ice. A bruise had begun to bloom on the side of Kazen's nose. "So easily distracted by a semblance of freedom, hm? You're in my domain, Rone Comf." He pushed his hand over Alys's forehead.

The key had been a distraction. The unconsciousness faked. Now Alys would be his weapon . . . They couldn't fight Alys. She would take all the injuries, not Isepia—

Rone leapt to his feet. "Wait!" he shouted, and he pulled something from his pocket. It glimmered under the light of the lamps.

The amarinth. Sandis's heart plummeted to her navel.

"Want this?" he asked. "Let's make a trade."

"Rone, you—" But Sandis stopped herself. Stared.

That wasn't the amarinth. The center was wrong—it looked like a carved piece of silver, not the sparkling, unearthly white core she knew. A fake? She struggled to get her slick feet beneath her.

Kazen grinned. "In due time." And he began chanting.

Rone bolted across the room to stop him. But Kazen was a practiced summoner. The words were out of his mouth before Rone could reach them.

A flash of light, a distant scream, as if Alys wailed from the far end of a hallway. Rone skidded to a stop mere feet away from Isepia.

"Kill him, my darling," Kazen crooned.

The gray-skinned numen stretched out a single black wing and clenched her taloned hands. Hissed at the sight of Rone.

She lunged, and the wood barring the door shut finally broke in two. Ravis and Staps ran in and froze at the sight of the numen, who would have decapitated Rone had he not dropped to the floor half a second later.

Sandis ran toward him, but Kazen shouted to Staps, "You, grab the vessel! Ravis, *get the amarinth!*"

Staps charged toward Sandis, his corded hair whipping behind him. She backpedaled, then tried to duck under his arm, but he was too fast and caught the back of her shirt. Wound her in like a snake. Struggling against him, she spied Rone wielding his knife again.

"Don't hurt her!" she cried, as Staps hauled her back to the lake of blood. "It will hurt Alys!"

"Are you kidding me right now?" Rone swiped at the numen, only to have her backhand him. He flew back and hit the wall—

Staps turned, blocking Sandis's view. She heard Isepia hiss, a gun fire.

"Hold her!" Kazen barked, and Staps's grip tightened.

Kazen, blazing with fury, reached for Sandis's head.

<hr />

Don't hurt the monster. Yeah. Good plan.

Rone's *current* plan was to, first, stay alive and, second, keep the deranged eagle woman between himself and the grafter. Who had a gun. Because this was the best day ever.

The numen launched at him again, striking out with her clawed hands. It was like fighting a giant viper. The monster could fly, but the ceiling wasn't particularly high, so she had little room to do so. Rone tried to use that to his advantage. The numen swiped; he ducked. Swiped again; he blocked—*bad idea*. The strength of her blow cracked up his arm and sent him face-first into the wooden floor, smashing his nose. He heard her wing flap behind him and rolled, barely missing her next attack. Her talons stuck into the wood floor.

Rone jumped to his feet, his nose, head, back, and arm throbbing. He flexed his fingers. Nothing broken yet, but blood from his nostrils ran down his lips.

Beyond the numen, a gun cocked.

Rone ducked. The grafter fired.

The numen screeched like a banshee and ripped her hands free from the floor in an explosion of splinters. A few drops of black blood pattered onto the ground beside her. For a moment, her hair flashed blonde, her skin peach. Alys. But the numen held on.

She also turned her attention to the grafter and, with a single beat of her wing, soared toward him and separated his throat from the rest of his body.

Rone's stomach tightened, ready to upend itself, but his thoughts kept him focused, even as the grafter's corpse fell to the floor.

The numen had killed the grafter.

Kazen hadn't *told* her to kill the grafter.

Everything Sandis had taught him about the occult zipped through his mind. Blood. Kazen needed blood to exercise full control over the numina.

Could it be that he didn't have Alys's? That in his quest for this Kolosos and for Sandis, he'd let this vessel's maintenance *slip*?

Despite the macabre scene surrounding him, a smile twitched on Rone's mouth. He could use this.

He chucked the fake amarinth at the numen.

"Hey, gorgeous," he said as she swerved toward him. "Want to play tag?"

"Vre en nestu a carnath—"

Sandis tore more hair from her scalp, trying to twist out of Kazen's grasp. His fingers touched her lips, and she bit down until blood filled her mouth.

Kazen shouted and ripped his hand back, the incantation ruined. Sandis spat. Staps squeezed her in his arms, threatening to pull her shoulders from their sockets.

Kazen's other hand flew forward and clamped around her neck, each fingernail pushing a bruise into the skin. He leaned in close, his moist forehead sticking to hers.

"You can fight all you want, but it will do nothing for you, just as it did nothing for Heath." He smiled. "But you are not Heath. He was an experiment. You are my chosen one. This has been your destiny all along, Sandis. I didn't realize it at first, but I knew. Deep in my spirit, I knew, even from the first time I saw you on the streets. You've always been special, my dear girl. Now you must live up to it, whether you want to or not."

He pulled away from her, the lingering stale smell of his breath clouding in front of Sandis's nose. She was about to spit in his face, but something from his pathetic attempt at encouragement stuck in her head.

"From the first time I saw you on the streets."

Kazen had met her in a cellar, not on the streets.

"Kolin citizens can't be sold as slaves."

Then why would slavers look for slaves in Dresberg?

It clicked then, like the cocking of a gun hammer.

"It was you." Her hands and feet were cold, her shoulders numb, her heart too big for her body. "They weren't slavers. They were grafters."

Kazen leaned back, nearly smug. "What a bright little girl you are, Sandis. An open spirit like yours is so hard to come across."

"Then why . . ." Yet she knew why. Why the "slavers" had held her for two months before taking her to Kazen. So he would be her hero. Because life with him was so much better than life in the cellar with those men.

That was why they'd been so careful whenever they beat her. Why they'd still kept her fed. Why they'd never raped her. Because she'd belonged to Kazen all along. They had merely held her until Kazen deemed fit to bring her into his fold.

Her eyes watered. Had Kazen killed Anon to get to her? Used him as bait to lure her into the darker parts of the city?

But there were no more words to be exchanged between them. Kazen pressed his hand against Sandis's still-wet hair and began the summoning spell anew, the words speeding past his lips—

Footsteps thundered toward them, closer, closer. Staps shifted to look, giving Sandis some space to turn her head.

Rone barreled their way, Isepia on his heels. He launched feetfirst into the blood, purposefully falling and sliding forward, slipping right between Sandis and Kazen. Isepia didn't even slow.

Sandis screamed, and Staps loosened his hold to avoid the numen. Sandis ducked. Isepia collided into Kazen, sending both of them hurtling onto the blood-soaked floor.

Staps grabbed Sandis's arm and hauled her upright. Remembering the move Kurtz had taught her, she turned into him and sent her hand into his neck with as much force as she could muster. It worked; Staps let go and took a step back, putting enough distance between himself and Sandis for Rone to land a hard roundhouse kick to the side of his head. His eyes rolled back, and he fell, splashing coagulating blood over their legs.

Breathing heavily, Sandis looked at Rone. Just looked, their eyes meeting for several heartbeats.

"Why?" she asked.

Rone lifted his hand to his hair, then saw the blood on it and dropped it. "That is a question I have too many answers for."

Kazen's voice cut the air behind them. *Parte Isepia en dragu bai!*

A shiver coursed through the attacking Isepia, and she shrunk and paled into Alys. Kazen easily pushed her unconscious body off him, ignoring the bleeding wound on her shoulder. It absorbed Sandis's focus completely. It needed to be wrapped, cauterized . . . something. Was the bullet still in there? Would she bleed out before she woke? Could Sandis somehow get to her before—

Kazen jumped to his feet with surprising agility. Isepia's talons had torn his coat, vest, and shirt, and his chest bled in streaks. A cut across his forehead dripped crimson into his eyebrows and down his long nose.

Rone didn't hesitate. He covered the distance between Sandis and Kazen in two leaps and threw a punch at Kazen's mouth.

The grafter's forearm thrust upward and blocked the blow, opening Rone up for retaliation. Kazen landed a fist on Rone's sternum. Rone slipped back, his shoes still wet with blood, and wheezed.

Kazen launched at him, throwing another fist, which Rone blocked just as Kazen had blocked his blow. Kazen kicked; Rone blocked with a knee. Threw a fist. Blocked. Kazen returned the gesture.

It was a dance Sandis had come to recognize. Kazen had always been so hands-off until tonight. She'd never realized he knew seugrat. She tried to find a way in, a way to slow Kazen, but the men moved too quickly. When she launched at him, a wayward kick hit her side and sent her skimming across the floor, just outside the blood pool.

Kazen deflected a blow and grabbed Rone's wrist, turning it over his head as if they were dance partners. He pinned Rone's arm behind his back, and from the way Rone's face contorted, it hurt dearly. Sandis's own hand pressed to her side, to the bruising ribs there. Each breath strained against the bones, threatening to snap them one by one.

The flicker of silver made Sandis's breath hitch. A knife. Kazen's. Its point pressed into the skin below Rone's ear. A trickle of blood traced the side of his neck.

"Kazen." Sandis's voice was oddly even. She pushed herself onto her knees. "Kazen, don't."

"You cannot thwart destiny." Kazen's voice was breathy, his eyes wild. "You're a sick dog, Sandis, crawling back to those who have already disposed of you."

Rone's jaw clenched at the words. Slowly, so slowly, his free hand moved to his trouser pocket.

"Kazen." Sandis tried to stand, but her bare feet slipped in a smear of blood, and she fell. Her toe touched something cool and metal—the ceremonial sword. She turned back to Kazen. Put one foot under her. "Kazen, listen. I'll do it."

"Oh, you will. You don't even realize what you've done. What I will do." He dug the knife in harder, sending more blood down Rone's neck. Sandis gasped.

Rone shifted from the pain—but no, he was using the movement to shove his hand into his pocket without Kazen noticing. He pulled out three familiar gold loops surrounding a sparkling center. The amarinth? Had the other she'd seen been a fake?

Sandis glanced at the sword beside her.

With a flick of his thumb, Rone spun the artifact.

Kazen peered over Rone's shoulder.

Sandis's hands flashed to the sword. Grabbed its hilt. Her sticky feet found purchase on the floor, and she ran, holding the long blade like she would a rifle, its pommel pressed under her shoulder.

She screamed as she ran.

The point drove into Rone's belly above the navel, sliding through shirt and skin like they were butter. There was the slightest resistance as it glanced off what Sandis guessed to be his backbone, then further resistance as it met a well-tailored vest, skin, muscle, organs.

Sandis crashed into Rone, the sword buried into him up to the guard, the length of the blade passing through his torso *and* Kazen's.

Sandis let go and stumbled back, the gentle whirring of the amarinth singing between her heavy breaths. Kazen looked at her, his pale eyes perfect circles, his mouth slack.

Rone pushed forward, pulling the sword out of Kazen before grabbing the hilt and yanking it out of himself. The blood that stained his shirt was from what the ox and Galt had left on the blade; otherwise, Rone was whole.

Kazen fell to his knees, then forward, onto his hands. Down onto one elbow as the life dripped out of him.

Rone leaned forward and put a hand on his shoulder. "Better luck next time."

He spun around and grabbed Sandis's hand, yanking her toward the door.

That's right. Run. They had to run.

Sandis looked back at Kazen, saw a sliver of him as they passed through the doorway. There was no one in the hallway. Had Rone disposed of them all? Had they fled? The vessels . . . were they still in their room? And Alys. They'd left Alys . . .

Around the bend. Past the doors. One man looked up from an adjoining corridor as they flew past. He didn't fight, but gaped at the blood-covered girl and the man dressed like one of them. Everything whizzed by Sandis as if in a dream. The rooms, the colors, the fight at the exit as Rone spun and jabbed, taking out men she didn't have the thought to count.

They ran, ran, ran, underneath a black, smoke-filled sky. Until her bare feet bled. Until the guns shooting behind them silenced and there was only her, Rone, their breaths, and her frantic, broken heartbeat.

Chapter 26

Sandis picked a sliver from her foot as Rone scooped water from a horse trough into his mouth. They were at a stable behind an inn about a half mile from the east city gate. Water dripped from Sandis's hair and clothes. The blood still stained them, and she thought she felt some scabbing at the roots of her hair, but she was so tired she couldn't bring herself to scrub anymore. The sky was beginning to lighten at the very edges, and a breeze brushed by. Sandis gritted her teeth to keep them from shivering.

Rone scrubbed his face, kneeling over the trough.

Ignoring her aching feet, Sandis stood and walked away, hugging herself to keep the warmth in. She limped on both legs. At least the markings on her arms were gone, though blood still painted a line under her fingernails and toenails.

She made it out to the street, lit by lamps on the outsides of buildings, before Rone's tired shuffle sounded behind her. He caught up with her, out of breath.

She kept walking.

"Sandis—"

"You can go." She didn't look at him. They passed under a lamp, and another breeze raised gooseflesh on her back, reminding her that she still wore her vessel's shirt, exposing her script to the world. She should have panicked, but she was too tired. Instead, she reached back, grabbed the loose folds of fabric, and tugged them together at the base of her neck, where Ireth's broken name tattooed her skin.

"I'm not going to leave."

"Yes, you will."

Rone sloughed off his jacket and handed it to her. She didn't want to take it. Didn't want the smell of him enfolding her, his residual warmth protecting her from the chill. But she couldn't let anyone see her script. Especially now, when she had so few defenses to call upon.

So she took the jacket and pulled it over her wet shirt. She walked. He followed.

"A thank-you would be nice," he said.

She stopped and turned toward him. "You can have it back." She began removing the jacket.

Rone held up a hand. "Not for the jacket. For the rescue."

Sandis stared at him. A single, hard cough—or was it a laugh?—ripped up her throat.

"Thank you? Thank *you*?" she asked, sour energy fueling her voice. "Why should I thank *you*? *You're* the reason I was there, Rone."

Tears burned her eyes, and she turned away from him, walking forward with new vigor if only to hide them. She brushed them away like stray embers from a fire.

"Sandis." He jogged to catch up with her. "You don't understand. My mother—"

"I hope you didn't leave her in Gerech."

He looked like she'd slapped him. "Of course I didn't! Look, I came back for *you*. It's just . . ." He groaned. "It's messed up. It's a heaping pile of crap, and I can't sort it out one way or another. But I came back for *you*. I couldn't let . . ."

He choked on the words. Silence fell between them. Sandis hugged herself and kept walking, her feet numb. Her eyes on the street. Somewhere, a block away, a horse pulled a wagon, or perhaps a carriage, judging by the sound.

311

Rone wiped his hand down his face. "We'll fix this. We'll sort it out. Kazen's dead, so you're free, and we'll figure out this stuff with Ireth—"

"Ireth is gone."

Rone stopped. Sandis didn't, forcing him to catch up once more. "What do you mean?"

She wheeled on him again. "What do you *think* I mean, Rone? Use your head. A bound vessel can only be used to summon the numen she's bound to. Kazen couldn't summon Kolosos into my body unless Ireth was gone."

"Keep your voice down."

She scowled at him. Crossed the street to put space between them. Rone caught up once more. "Gone? Like dead?"

Tears clouded her vision. God's tower, Sandis was so tired of tears. "You can't kill a numen. They're immortal." Her throat constricted. "He's been bound to someone else."

Saying the words out loud tore at her insides, like Isepia had attacked her instead of Kazen. She'd left Alys alone, again. She sucked in a deep breath to steady herself. Trudged forward.

"Oh, Sandis. I'm sorry."

"You should be."

Rone sighed. "Where are you going?"

She didn't answer. Passed two homeless people sleeping huddled together on the street corner.

"Sandi—" He stopped. Sandis kept walking until Rone uttered, "No. No . . . no, no, no."

She turned around. "What?" The word whipped from her mouth.

Rone checked his trouser pockets, then his shirt. Darted to Sandis and grabbed her—no, the jacket. He checked the pockets, inside and out.

"Take it off."

His panic pushed away her questions. She slid it off, keeping her back to a shop's wall to prevent any lurkers from seeing light glinting off the thick gold marks. Rone turned the jacket inside out. Shook it.

Squeezed the fabric in his hands. Dropped it and checked his pockets again.

Curse words spilled from his mouth the way blood had spilled from Galt.

"It's not here," he said, and Sandis's stomach sank. "It's not here."

She stepped closer. "The amarinth?"

He checked his pockets yet again, then grabbed fistfuls of his hair. "It's not here. I must have dropped it—"

His face paled. "I don't remember grabbing it." He shook his head. "You . . . Kazen fell, and I grabbed you, and I didn't take the amarinth. It must still be there. We have to go—"

"Rone."

He looked up at her.

Every inch of Sandis had turned to stone. Her eyes would fall from her head if she opened them any wider.

"You left it," she whispered.

"We can go back for it. We can—"

She lunged forward and grabbed fistfuls of his shirt. "Was it still spinning? Rone, *was it still spinning?*"

"What? I don't know, I didn't see—"

Sandis fell to her knees, her mouth dry, her heart pounding in her ears.

"Sandis? Sandis!" Rone knelt in front of her.

She shook her head. "Kazen. If Kazen took it . . . You spun it right in front of him."

He grabbed her shoulders. "Kazen is dead."

"If he took it while it was still spinning . . ."

Rone's eyes widened. She met them. "Does it work that way, Rone? Does it transfer?"

He swallowed. "I don't know."

Anvils pressed into her chest. Sandis dug her nails into the cobblestones, struggling to breathe. Kazen could have taken the amarinth.

No, knowing him, he *had* taken it. He had seen his salvation . . . if the amarinth was still spinning . . . if its powers could transfer . . .

Then Kazen was alive. He was *still alive*.

She couldn't breathe.

"Hey. Hey." Rone rubbed her back. "Inhale, Sandis. Come on. It's . . ." He hesitated. "It's so unlikely . . ."

If Kazen was alive, then more grafters could be recruited. She would be hunted. The other vessels would be used, maybe they'd be killed, one after another, as Kazen sought to find a host for Kolosos. And the amarinth . . . how would they get the amarinth back?

She had lost Ireth, and now Rone had lost his immortality.

Rone's hand stilled on her back. She looked up. Judging by the horrified look on his face, he had come to the same conclusion.

But he shook his head. "It's unlikely. I just dropped it. It's . . ." He didn't finish his sentence.

They sat like that, together, in between shops, for a long time. Until Sandis's hyperventilating made her lightheaded and she forced her breaths to lengthen, deepen. She couldn't think like this. She wouldn't.

But she had nowhere else to go. No one left to trust.

Except.

Blinking, Sandis pulled away from Rone and grabbed the jacket. The dawn was coming, and the first-shift bells would ring soon. Donning the jacket, she scanned the area, gaining her bearings.

North. She needed to go north and . . . west.

She crossed the street.

"Sandis," Rone called after her, but when she didn't stop, he peeled himself off the road and followed. "Sandis, I can get it back. I can—"

"Then go."

He drew back like her words hurt. Why? He'd already thrown her away. He didn't care about her or what she said or thought or felt. Why feign the hurt now, when he'd already gotten what he wanted?

The amarinth wasn't hers. It never had been. It was Rone's problem.

"Sandis." He grabbed her arm.

She wrenched it from his grasp. "I'm going to find Talbur."

He rolled his eyes. *Rolled his eyes!* Fury burned her hotter than any of Ireth's visions.

So she ran. Her sore feet slammed into the cobblestones. She ran past a group of factory workers dragging their tired bodies to work. Past a dog sniffing around an overflowing garbage bin.

Ran until her lungs burned and forced her to stop. She doubled over and put her hands on her knees.

She didn't know whether to cringe or cry when Rone's footsteps closed in on her. If only she could forget. If only she could pretend that it was all right now, that nothing bad had ever happened between them. If only she could throw the broken pieces of her heart into the gutter and ignorantly hold on to Rone's arm, the way she had the day he'd sold her to the evilest man in Dresberg.

But she couldn't. She couldn't.

"Sandis." He was wearing her name thin with how much he said it. "Where. Are. You. Going?"

"I have an address."

He stood straighter. "What?"

Taking a deep breath, Sandis squared her shoulders and looked Rone in the eyes, forcing herself not to feel anything.

That much, at least, she could pretend.

"I found the bank record in Kazen's office. The one with Talbur's name on it. I know where he is."

Rone planted his hands on his hips. Looked at the ground. Nodded. "All right. Where?"

"I don't need any more of your favors, Rone."

His expression darkened. "Where?"

She pressed her lips together. Held his gaze for a long moment, until the intensity of it forced her to look away. "Fourteen Magdara."

She started walking again, ignoring the waking flies on the garbage bins she passed.

"Wait, what?" Rone called behind her. He sprinted in front of her, forcing her to stop. "*What* did you say?"

"I was clear, wasn't I? Fourteen Magdara. It was a recent record. I'm going."

His jaw slackened. Sandis stepped around him.

"Stop." He grabbed her arm.

Again, she wrenched it free and kept walking.

"Sandis, for the love of the Celestial, *stop*!"

She stopped. Glared at him. "Why? Why should I?"

His eyes were wide, his face slack. He looked young, vulnerable. Sandis thought to reach out to him, but both arms remained glued to her sides.

"Because," he said, low and dark, "that's the address of the man who hired me to turn you in."

Of all the things Rone could have said, those were the last words she expected.

She retreated. "You're lying."

"I'm not."

"Then it's a shared building—"

"It's a single-story office space with a basement," he pressed. "Outdated. Barely enough room for a small shop. If he used that address on the bank record, then he either owns the place or is the sole renter."

Sandis shook her head. "You're lying."

Rone sighed, his shoulders slumping. "Why, after everything I've done, would I lie about this?"

She didn't know. She didn't know anything about him. Not anymore.

"Fourteen Magdara," Rone repeated. "It's the same. I'd show you the paper if I still had it."

"I'm going anyway."

The declaration surprised her as much as it did Rone. Silence cut the space between them for only a second before Rone threw his hands into the air. "Are you *insane*?"

They must have been close to a clock tower, for the first gong of the hour vibrated down Sandis's body and into the cobblestones.

"I'm going." Second gong.

Rone shook his head. Turned away from her. Third gong. Spun back.

"He *sold you*." Fourth gong.

Sandis glowered. "*You* sold me." Fifth.

Roan growled. "That's not fair."

Now Sandis threw out her arms. "How is that not fair?"

Sixth gong, and the clock quieted.

Rone winced. Rubbed his eyes. "Fine. *Fine.* But I'm going with you. I don't trust the guy."

Sandis scoffed.

"You're going the wrong way." He turned around and trudged back for the main street. "Unless you want to get caught in the red-light district."

Sandis opened her mouth, closed it. Balled her hands into fists.

Ignoring the splintering in her chest, she followed him.

***

The building wasn't grand in the slightest. It was an old structure in an even older part of town. Nondescript, wedged next to a set of flats with updated windows and fancy, curling eaves. An iron fence surrounded it on three sides. The sky was overcast, so even with the sun up, everything looked gray and dreary.

But appearances could be deceiving. Sandis had learned that in the hardest way possible.

"Are you sure?"

She didn't look at him. Didn't respond.

She should be the one to open the door. She half expected to find it locked, but the handle turned easily with a little pressure.

The smell of chloride lime made her sick. It was too similar to the summoning room, though the undercurrent of foul smells from Kazen's lair were lacking in this place. *It's just clean,* she told herself. Clean, and sparse. There was one chair for guests, a single desk with an immaculate woman sitting behind it, and a plant in the corner. A real plant. That was a good sign, wasn't it?

Her tamped hope dared to flicker.

The woman looked up. "Ah, Mr. Verlad. We have no appointments with you today." She glanced at Sandis and raised an eyebrow.

Something about what she said, about the look she gave, made Sandis shrink in on herself. *So this is it,* she thought. This was where Rone came while she waited for him at Kurtz's home. Or had he made the arrangement earlier, while she fretted at the inn? This was where he'd made the deal to trade her life for pocket money. Sandis couldn't help but think she was worth more than paper.

She'd thought he'd valued her more than that, at least.

She swallowed to prevent her throat from swelling. Cleared it. "I'm here to see Talbur Gwenwig."

The secretary started. Rone hadn't known Talbur was the man he'd met here, so the name must have shocked her.

She smoothed back the hair pulled into a tight bun at the back of her head. "Pardon?"

Rone strode past Sandis to the door near the desk. The secretary stood but didn't stop him from wrenching it open. "I'm guessing he's in?"

The woman frowned. Nodded.

Sandis didn't need more of an invitation than that. Keeping her gaze focused ahead of her, she passed Rone and started down a cramped set of stairs into a cold basement. It was all one short hallway with a low ceiling, the sole light coming from a room at the very end, to the right.

She marched toward it. The door was cracked open. Holding her breath, Sandis pushed against the wood and let lamplight spill over her. Rone appeared at her side.

A man about Kazen's age sat at a desk within the room. His eyes were wide set, but he had her grandfather's nose, from what she remembered of him. He was stocky, and his thinning brown hair was combed away from his forehead and oiled to stay that way.

The man looked up, his dark eyes first finding Sandis, then drifting up to Rone. He straightened. Opened a drawer and pulled out a cigar and a matchbox.

"Why, Sandis," he said, striking the match and setting it to the end of his cigar. "I was so hoping I'd get a chance to meet you."

ACKNOWLEDGMENTS

I have so much gratitude to give for the fruition of this book. *Smoke and Summons* is possibly the best book I've written to date, and I most certainly didn't do it alone.

First, I must thank my editor, Jason, and my agent, Marlene. Not just for handling all the boring businessy stuff, but for pushing me to write something bigger. The idea for this series came after a somewhat stressful phone call that encouraged me to expand my horizons (and ultimately take ideas from five other projects and mash them together into one trilogy). The end result is something I'm thrilled to share with the world, so thank you, thank you.

Being a mom, I could never get my words down without help. I want to thank my husband and my assistants, Cerena and Amanda, for making sure I got the time to plunk out my words and for being sounding boards and readers for me. And thank you to my two little ones, who still love me even when I spend the mornings hunkered down in our orange-painted basement.

Thank you so much to my alpha readers, who helped me get my hot messes in line: Caitlyn, Laura, L.T., Rebecca, and Kim. And a huge thank-you to my beta readers, who read my novel in a *week* so I could meet my deadlines: Whitney, Rachel, Tricia, and Leah. Thank you also to Joseph, who knows a lot more about guns than I do.

I must, of course, thank my developmental editor, Angela, and the 47North team who edited, proofed, and formatted this book. Though unbeknownst to some, commas, leading, and kerning are crucial aspects of every novel.

And, as always, my utmost gratitude to God, who watches over me and mine and keeps my mind sharp. He has had His hand in all my achievements, big and small.

ABOUT THE AUTHOR

Born in Salt Lake City, Charlie N. Holmberg was raised a Trekkie alongside three sisters who also have boy names. She is a proud BYU alumna, plays the ukulele, owns too many pairs of glasses, and finally adopted a dog. Her fantasy Paper Magician Series, which includes *The Paper Magician*, *The Glass Magician*, and *The Master Magician*, has been optioned by the Walt Disney Company. Her stand-alone novel, *Followed by Frost*, was nominated for a 2016 RITA Award for Best Young Adult Romance. She currently lives with her family in Utah. Visit her at www.charlienholmberg.com.